SLIPPER GIRL

Other Books by the Author

Camera Ready

For Position Only

Princess Smile

Summer's Blood

SLIPPER GIRL

adele royce

Madweek

ISBN (Paperback): 979-8-9903269-4-1
ISBN (Hardback): 979-8-9903269-5-8
ISBN (eBook): 979-8-9903269-6-5
ISBN (Audiobook): 979-8-9903269-7-2

Book Design by the Aaxel Author Group
Cover Artwork by Vincent-louis Apruzzese

Printed in the United States of America

For my beloved felines. Your sweet spirit and companionship inspired the character of *Sesame* in this novel.

PROLOGUE

Blood trickled along the cement floor like a slow-moving oil spill. A thick metallic stench hung in the room.

I froze, heart jackhammering in a relentless rhythm, pounding against the treacherous silence that enveloped the apartment. I stumbled to the window and pulled aside the threadbare curtains. The city was still there, plodding on, unbroken and ignorant of the violent maelstrom that had just rocked these walls.

Thank God they can't talk.

I had only moments to leave the scene before the police arrived. The struggle was loud and long—someone had to have heard the commotion—the neighbors—someone. I turned slowly, my eyes darting to the motionless corpse that lay sprawled unnaturally on the floor, like an oversized doll with its limbs dismantled. Only this was no doll.

The sickening reality that I'd killed a man was like ice

water gushing down my back. The blade slipped in with ease, almost effortlessly, as though it had carried its own urge to plunge in deep. The mark was clear—right in the center—the core—the heart. He was already bleeding out when a mixture of panic and rage surged in my veins, sharply mingling with an unexpected clarity. I tore the knife out and drove it back in, over and over, while blood sprayed everywhere.

The clock is ticking. I have to act now.

I scurried to the small, grimy bathroom, almost slipping on the bloody floor, and began to scrub the remnants from my body.

Someone's going to find out. I've got to get out of here now.

My mind raced, recalling the hideous display that fueled the adrenaline—the final act before that moment when sheer fury took over.

I had no other choice.

But now I'd crossed a line, and there was no going back. The blood—so much blood—embedded in the grooves of my nails—blood all over the floor—staining the walls— was like a raging wildfire, edging closer with each passing second, threatening to scorch me with an unalterable future.

I've got to get out of here now.

When I'd purged the last traces of crimson from my flesh, I staggered back to assess the scene. Sheer horror pelted my gut, and a wave of nausea washed over me. I gulped, coughing, and covering my mouth so I wouldn't vomit.

I had to kill him.

He was a violent criminal rapist who deserved to die. He forced my hand. But at some point, it became something else entirely—a sublime darkness had unleashed and consumed me.

I closed my eyes, drew in a shaky breath, and stepped around the blood-soaked mess, into the outside world that, I learned over time, would never be the same.

PART I

Chapter 1

The candles struggled to stay alive as the evening wind kicked up. Most people thought events ended when the guests left, but that was when the real work began. Skylar rushed from table to table, leaning over and blowing out the candles herself.

"Hey, boss lady, there are people who'll do that for you."

Skylar looked up and smiled before puckering her lips and extinguishing a trio of tea lights in one huge breath. "That's what I've heard. Would you happen to know where those people are?"

"I know someone who knows someone," Clay said with a grin. He pulled a two-way radio from the vest of his three-piece suit. "Where's the take-down crew?" he said loudly into the radio, eyeing Skylar, who continued to blow out candles. She moved on to the next table. "The head of marketing is doing your work as we speak.

Get them here, now." He sighed before sliding the radio back into his vest and helping Skylar with the candles.

"Are you happy?" he asked when he caught up to her.

Skylar stopped and looked Clay in the eye. "Is that a rhetorical question?" she said with a slight smirk. "Because we don't have that much time."

Clay laughed. "I mean, with the wedding."

"Ah, yes, the wedding of the century," she said, nodding. "Everything was perfect—and the happy couple seems—well, very happy." She pulled a calla lily from one of the centerpieces and handed it to Clay. "You did a fabulous job. You and your team. You should be proud."

He glanced at her anxiously before accepting the flower. "Are you sure? You aren't holding something back, are you?"

Skylar shook her head and continued to the next table while Clay followed.

"Because if anything was out of place, you can tell me. I mean, just because we're friends doesn't mean you can't be honest about my work."

Skylar slouched her shoulders as her mind went back to the email—the one she received right before the wedding. It had been gnawing at her since she saw that name. *Brit Van Ness.* The email had come as such a shock when she read it that she had almost spilled her coffee. She was just getting ready to close her computer for the day to attend her father's wedding. Donovan James Keller was marrying the love of his life, McKenna Aldrich. The wedding of DJ and Max took place on the fake beach at his own resort in Las Vegas. DJ had charged Skylar and Clay with making sure nothing was out of place.

They had started planning eight months ago. Skylar thought about how she and Clay had dreamed up the perfect wedding and reception. Neither of them had ever been married, but they'd seen enough weddings at the resort, especially Clay, who was director of catering. They brainstormed for hours on the phone at night and over business lunches at their favorite restaurant within the Donovan Resort and Casino.

She looked up at Clay, who wore a nervous expression. She patted his arm reassuringly. "You did an amazing job."

He let out a sigh of relief. "Thanks, sweetie—you know I've been down a banquet manager—makes things tough, but I think I may finally have a good candidate." He continued to help Skylar with the candles. "Want to have dinner at Suki to celebrate?"

They lunched at least three times a week at Suki, where most of the high rollers at Donovan dined in the evening. The sashimi platter was Skylar's favorite. She always ordered the six-piece special that came with miso soup and seaweed salad. Clay always ordered the Kitsune Udon with tofu. So many lunches had been spent discussing this one day. And now, it was over.

"Actually," she responded, "I still have some work to do, but let's have dinner next week."

He gave her a resigned nod before snuffing out two taper candles.

Usually, after a successful event, Skylar would have her own mini-celebration: stopping by the grocery store on her way home to pick up cooked, tail-on shrimp with cocktail sauce and a fashion magazine or two. At home, she would draw a hot bath, then curl up on the couch in her favorite pajamas with the magazines, shrimp cocktail, and her tuxedo cat, Sesame.

But today was different. She could not get the email from Brit out of her mind. *What am I supposed to do with it? Respond? How?* She drew a deep breath and let it out slowly. *Should I share it with my dad? How would he react?*

"Sky," Clay interrupted her meandering thoughts. "Are you okay?"

Skylar jolted out of her daze. "Yeah. I'm just glad today went so well." She pulled him into a wary hug. "Thank you."

Skylar strode to her office and stared up at the golden plaque with the black lettering: *Skylar Van Ness—Vice President of Marketing.* The title was prestigious enough, but it bothered her. Everyone assumed she got it because of nepotism—because she was the nepo baby of the CEO. They ignored the hours she put in, how buttoned up she was in every situation, every meeting, every event. She hit a home run all the time, mostly because she would rather die than fail. That was no joke. And no one understood that.

DJ bought the resort 10 years ago, after a long, convoluted history with its original owner, Luuk Van Ness, now deceased. The place used to be called The Regal Oasis, and DJ had renamed and branded it Donovan Resort and Casino.

Skylar entered her office, sat behind her desk, and turned on the computer. She opened emails and scrolled down to the one from Brit. She sat staring at the subject line: A note from Mom. The phone rang, causing her to lurch forward. *Who could be calling this late on a Saturday?* She glanced at the caller ID. The name MONARCH, J, was flashing. Skylar groaned aloud. *Not him. Not now.* She looked around and thought about ignoring his call. After all, it was Saturday, her father had just married, and Skylar should be home by now, soaking her feet in bathwater. She could get away with not answering the phone. But James Monarch knew her too well. He knew she would still be there. The only thing he didn't know was why.

Skylar had to make sure no one knew about the email, especially not James. He would use it against her. She pictured his snide upper lip curdling at the news. He would shame her publicly if he knew anything about her past. And although no one suspected DJ would ever fire his own daughter, Skylar knew better. One thing she knew about her father was that he was obsessed with branding and reputation. If her history were to grace the content of any news outlet, the shame itself would force his hand.

She inhaled deeply, closed her emails, and snatched up the phone. "What's up, James?"

He cleared his throat. "Oh, I'm surprised you're still here." The hard 'r' sound in *here* screamed Northern Ireland rather than typical Irish brogue. Although he allegedly grew up in Dublin and graduated from the world-famous Trinity College, which he never let anyone forget. "That was a nice wedding," he added. "But don't you think the program went on a wee bit long? I would have shut it down after the bouquet toss."

A smart-assed remark lingered on Skylar's lips. Of course, he would have to get in a dig. That was part of James's way. "What can I do for you?"

"I was just wondering what percentage of the media budget is being spent on digital advertising?"

"About eighty-five percent," Skylar answered without looking at the spreadsheets. By now, she had the media spend memorized.

"That seems excessive," he said. "How did you arrive at that number?"

James was being groomed to take DJ's position. Everyone knew that. His title was *Senior* Vice President, Casino Operations, but James acted like he was king. Or some kind of God.

"We agreed the majority of the spend should be in digital media because it translates directly into hotel room nights sold," she reported, trying not to sound too much like a know-it-all. To everyone who knew both Skylar and James, their relationship appeared adversarial. But it was more complicated than that. *Way more complicated.*

"Who agreed? Was I in those meetings?" James asked with feigned innocence.

"Yes," she returned, thinking it had been a huge mistake to pick up the phone.

"I don't recall."

The hell he doesn't recall. He was in all the marketing strategy meetings, even though he hardly belonged in them. He had been invited at DJ's insistence because he did nothing but kiss his ass.

"If it's okay with you, I'd like to be in on those decisions," James said with that false deference that tinged his voice every time he wanted something.

Skylar dipped a fake smile into the receiver. "You've been on the meeting invite for months now. It's your responsibility to attend them, not mine. Have a good evening."

Skylar put the phone down before he could say anything else.

"Asshole," she muttered. Skylar couldn't stand James, but because DJ held him in such high esteem, she had to be cool about it. He was 32, and on a mission to conquer the world. Skylar was in his way.

She slid her black blazer over her shoulders, grabbed her purse and car keys, and marched out of the office, locking the door behind her. She strolled briskly out into the smoke-filled casino and bustled her way through the aisles of shrill slot machines, screens flashing obnoxiously with vibrant graphics. Normally, the casino's energy was contagious with the triumphant shouts and laughter of lucky gamblers. Skylar would saunter through, proudly reveling in the atmospheric chaos. But today, she wanted nothing but to be alone in the serenity of her home.

With her eye on the exit sign, she navigated through throngs of players and cocktail servers balancing trays filled with multi-colored elixirs. Back-lit neon signs advertising the latest casino promotions beckoned from every corner—each promising something magnificent. Skylar glanced at the signs here and there, vaguely recalling that it was she who had signed off on them just a few days earlier. There was such a high volume of collateral grazing her desk, oftentimes her work felt like one enormous blur.

She shuffled by the buffet, packed with hungry customers, and inhaled the warm odors of food wafting from the restaurant. They nauseated her. There was no way she could muster an appetite while her mind was preoccupied with Brit's untimely email.

A note from Mom. *Mom.* The images began to pop up in her head, one by one, like ugly vignettes from a violent horror movie. The mom who turned tricks while Skylar was in the next room, trying to sleep. The mom who wore fishnet stockings and high heels with nothing else, decoying horny American men to have a gander in the peepshow window, in the heart of Amsterdam's red-light district. That's how she had seduced DJ. The mom who never bought groceries, or took her to the doctor, or gave a shit if Skylar had a warm coat. That mom took her only pair of shoes once, giving her no choice but to wear her bed slippers to school in the dead of winter. This earned her the humiliating moniker, "Slipper Girl," from that day forward. She had scars on her feet where frostbite took over, scars on her psyche from the ruthless heckling.

She still winced at the end of a long day when the four-inch pumps began to pinch the scar tissue with every step. She winced even now as she trooped to the parking garage, willing away the raw pain in her feet—the pain in her soul at the idea of having to deal with *that mom* again.

That mom had sent an email. *That mom* knew where she lived, what she did for a living, and, worst of all, she was coming to Las Vegas for a visit.

Chapter 2

At home that evening, Skylar didn't know what to do with herself. After feeding Sesame and cleaning the litter box, she paced around her four-bedroom home barefoot. The cushy carpeting soothed her aching toes. She closed her eyes and let her feet sink into the cool, double-thick under pad, which felt like memory foam. That was something Skylar mandated when her house was being built in the foothills of Summerlin. She remembered sifting through many carpet samples to find just the right color, but most importantly, the right feel. She recalled how the salespeople glared at her as she slid off her high heels and rested her bare feet directly on the samples. She settled on a luxurious buttery cream-colored plush pile, and, except for the kitchen and bathroom marble, the carpet filled the entire house.

Skylar was proud of her home. At 27, it was her first, purchased with her hard-earned income a couple of years earlier. Her dad had offered her a loan, but Skylar refused. Even her cousin, Axel, who lived only 10 minutes away, accepted a down payment from his father, Craig.

She thought about how tight-knit her family was—the family she always had but never knew about until about 10 years ago. Her childhood until early adolescence had been a mishmash of tiptoeing around her mother's parties, trying not to wake up the naked bodies passed out everywhere. The pungent stench of stale cigarettes, marijuana joints, and booze, all fused with body odor, was omnipresent. A bricolage of sordid events stacked up in her memory and refused to stop haunting her. She had turned to drugs and alcohol around age 10 and found it easier to cope with Brit's antics while under the influence. She recalled the faceless, nameless 'friends' of Brit's—the distorted sounds of laughter when Skylar got drunk. They thought she was cute and funny.

The sex came next. Skylar was becoming a woman and, by age 12, was close to reaching her full adult height of 5'10. She had the long, slender curves of a supermodel. Her naturally platinum hair hung way past her shoulders, and she had been told all her life that her shimmery aqua eyes were mesmerizing, especially when she lined them in smudgy black pencil.

Skylar never bothered with boys from school. They didn't have anything she wanted, other than an occasional half-sandwich when Brit forgot to give her lunch money, which was most days. Because Brit spent a lot of her time away from their apartment, her johns sometimes showed up looking for her. Skylar began to size them up and decided they had cash. And she was able to get it.

At first, it was scary. Skylar was dealing with men, not boys from school. She recalled the hazy cloud of faces, some clean-shaven, others not. The grownup smells of soap, toothpaste, and aftershave, the raw feeling of being opened up and violated, while her collection of stuffed animals fell to the ground like soldiers with every hip thrust. The back of her head bumping the wall of her tiny bedroom. *Thud. Thud. Thud.* Then the loud exhale of whoever was bucking on top of her. That orgasmic sigh veiling the air around her. The sticky fluid running down her thighs. Draining like grimy bathwater.

Outwardly, she pretended to be enthusiastic because that led to bigger tips. Inwardly, she pretended it was someone else's body they were invading, polluting. But the loss of Skylar's innocence—what was rightfully hers—still hung in her mind and psyche like a dark fog. With every sexual partner, a tiny piece of Skylar died inside, crushing her soul till it lay mangled at the bottom of an empty pit that the drugs and alcohol could never fill, no matter how much she consumed.

When Skylar was first united with her father, DJ, she was a tattered, defiant tween, smoking, drinking, drugging, and cursing her way around Amsterdam. She had been living alone in Brit's apartment for two weeks straight, eating canned goods out of the cupboard. While drugs and prostitution were legal in the Netherlands, Brit had been arrested for several health violations. When Skylar was discovered alone without adult supervision, Dutch authorities contacted DJ, who lived in Las Vegas under the alias Hendrick Van Ness. He immediately flew to Amsterdam, collected his estranged daughter, enrolled her in school, and did his best to be a dad. DJ was never good at being a dad, but he was a good human. He loved Skylar despite her past exasperating behavior, and, unlike Brit, he cared what happened to her.

Skylar scrolled through her phone and found the email. Her finger hovered over it. She hesitated, worried that reading the email for a second time would ruin her night. She finally gave in and tapped the email.

My dear daughter Skylar:

I'm sure it is a surprise to hear from me after so many years. You are a beautiful young woman. I've seen lots of pictures on the internet. You must be so proud.

I'm writing because I'm coming to the U.S. next week, and I want to see you. I've heard so much about Las Vegas, and I know we have a lot of catching up to do. I don't know how you feel about seeing me, but I'm a different person. I got a real job about five years ago, working at a department store here in Amsterdam. It's not great money, but I'm the manager of the children's department and can keep an apartment in the city with a couple of roommates.

I have some cash saved up for the trip, but I would like to know if you could help me with a room rate at the Donovan hotel where you work. I want to pay but was hoping for a reasonable family rate for your old mom. If not, that is OK.

I would love to be a part of your life again. Please write to let me know if you will see me while I'm there.

I'm so proud of you. I love you.

–Mom

Skylar sank into her black leather couch and let out a deep, choky sigh. Of course, she wanted a room rate, like every other sponger who called Skylar for something free. *She's a different person, my ass.* Skylar tried to imagine an older, worn-out version of Brit working in the children's department—the person Skylar remembered shouldn't be allowed anywhere near children. She did a quick internet search—images of Brit, a Facebook page—anything. Puzzlingly, she found nothing.

Skylar wondered what Brit knew about DJ's life. She chose his wedding day to reach out to Skylar. It would have been easy for Brit to stalk her daughter while researching DJ and Max. Their photos were splashed everywhere as the city's 'it' couple. DJ, with his shoulder-grazing mane of blond hair, tall and lanky, his arm casually resting on Max's shoulders, his stunning new bride and girlfriend of 10 years. Max has her glowing, olive skin, chestnut-colored hair, full red lips, and a winsome smile. This sudden appearance by DJ's ex-wife, Brit, could cause trouble. But even worse, it would unearth Skylar's unspeakable past.

She thought about James with his Irish Ivy League arrogance. She pictured him hearing about Brit and giving Skylar that smirky, all-knowing little look of his—the smile that somehow never made it to his eyes. Whenever Skylar saw that look, she just wanted to slap it off his face. He would disgrace her for sure. And it wasn't just James. Skylar had fought to become a different person, shedding the shadow of Brit and her sordid life in Amsterdam. She thought she had succeeded. Until now.

The one person who could truly understand the impact of this problem was DJ. And he was on his way to Bali right now, to bask in the sunshine with Max over tropical drinks and crashing waves. This news would ruin his honeymoon. But it was news too big to hide.

Skylar rose from her couch and began pacing again. If she were still a drinker, she'd have the vodka bottle out right this minute. She kept an emergency stash in her freezer. She'd once found edibles at her dad's home. She saw them in a cupboard and had been tempted to pocket a few gummies. *I wish I had them now.*

She scrolled through her contacts and contemplated texting her father. Then she considered forwarding the email to him. *No, that would drive him crazy, especially on that long flight.* He would want to do something. DJ was a tough Dutchman, raised by a tough Irishman. He was prone to volatile outbursts. Skylar pictured Max, with her subtle confidence, trying to tame DJ's anger and anxiety. No, that wouldn't be fair to either DJ or Max.

She walked to the French doors that led to her backyard and stepped outside, into the chilly February air, wearing her flannel pajamas. She shivered, phone in hand, and scrolled through it, wondering who might still be awake. She couldn't divulge this to Clay. Not yet. She would have to find someone within the family besides DJ—someone she could trust. She landed on one name and swallowed hard, feeling her pulse rise with each breath. *Can I trust him?*

She shakily held the phone, peering into the deep end of the swimming pool at her reflection. She saw a sad, desperate face rippling as the lights flickered every two seconds like some hideous disco decapitation … *purple, blue, green, red.* She typed a text. "I need to talk to you right away."

Skylar waited up for a while with her headphones on, blaring the latest Glass Animals album. The music reverberated through her body, soothing the anxiety like no substance ever could. She had discovered years earlier that music could drown the awful voices pounding the chorus of her past into her brain—the memories that kept her awake at night.

The music lulled her on the couch for a couple of hours, until she dragged herself to bed. But there, she couldn't sleep. She lay awake, tossing and turning, sometimes blinking her eyes open to the obnoxious glare of the bright blue digital clock numbers. *Why is that thing so big?* She made a mental note to replace it the next day with a simple clock with hands. She felt around her nightstand in the dark and found her sleep mask. She pulled it over her eyes and dropped her head back down on the pillow.

Around 2 a.m., she heard a noise and bolted upright, grasping the collar of her pajamas. Her hands shaking, she felt for the lamp switch. Before she could turn on the light, the noise continued, louder this time. Footsteps marching up the stairs and then padding along the carpet that led to her bedroom, getting closer. Her heart thumped in her rib cage. She flipped on the light and reached into the nightstand, this time for her handgun.

An elongated male shadow flashed in the hallway.

Her heart doubled. "Get the fuck out, I've got a loaded gun!"

"Sky, it's me—Axel!" The familiar voice emanated

from the hallway. Skylar's cousin stood in the doorway. His eyes were wide.

"Thank God," she said, catching her breath and lowering the pistol. "Jesus, Ax, you scared the crap out of me!"

"You scared the crap out of *me*," he said, rubbing the back of his neck in agitation. "You send me this cryptic text at, like, 11 o'clock on a Saturday night after I just saw you a few hours ago, and then you ghost me. What was I supposed to think?"

Skylar's eyes dashed around the room. "Oh shit, I must have left my phone downstairs. I'm sorry, Ax."

"I texted like three times and then called." He relaxed his broad shoulders. "Good thing I have a key and the code to your alarm system, which I noticed you didn't even set." He paused to look her in the eye. "What's going on? Are you okay?"

She hugged her arms around her body. "Yeah."

Axel studied her gun. "Is that thing really loaded?"

She nodded and replaced the gun in her nightstand, watching his mouth bunch together, a judgy expression shading his handsome features. When he made this face, he looked exactly like his father, Craig, Skylar's uncle, the one older man on whom she had always crushed.

Axel was her age and the closest thing to a brother. *But I didn't grow up with him.* She peered into his light jade eyes, fingers trembling.

His eyes tapered slightly in the corners. "What did you want to talk to me about?"

She hesitated. "You want to talk now?" *Is it a bad move to pull Axel into my drama?* She trusted him enough to give him the key to her house, plus the password to her security system. But she wasn't sure about trusting him with the key to her past, which Brit would soon reveal.

"Well, I'm here, and I'm guessing it was urgent for you to send that text." He glanced around Skylar's bedroom and then shrugged off his black hoodie before placing it neatly on a chair near her bed. In the faint lamp light, Skylar could see the tiny threads of blond speckling his dark hair.

Axel lowered himself into the chair, and Skylar sat on the edge of her bed, thinking about what she would tell him.

"My mother sent me an email today," she started, recalling the panic she felt upon seeing that name. "She's coming to visit this week. From Amsterdam." Skylar glanced up at Axel. His expression had an *I have no idea what you're talking about* quality.

"Your *mother*?" he repeated. "I didn't think she existed."

"I haven't seen or heard from her since I was 12. That's when I went to live with my dad."

Axel narrowed his eyes. "Do your dad and Max know?"

She shook her head. "I don't want to interrupt their honeymoon. I'm not sure what to do."

Axel frowned. "Sky, you don't have to do anything. You can ignore her if you want. She can't do anything to you." His face clouded over with concern. "Unless there's some reason you're afraid of her."

It was at that moment Skylar realized Axel was clueless about the depth and enormity of her past. He knew she was troubled when the two cousins met as teenagers. But he didn't know the hellish reality of her history in Amsterdam. The familiar shame crawled up her spine.

Axel cocked his head. "Hey—are you okay? You seem—I don't know—spooked."

Skylar cast her eyes to her lap.

"What does the email say? Can I see it?"

She looked up at Axel, with his indisputably Keller features. The chiseled face with the long eyelashes, defined cheekbones and jaw, perfect nose, and set of blinding white teeth. There was no way she could explain to him now how frightened she was to have her past laid out in front of her by her biological mother. But there could be a way to research Brit without revealing too much. "Let's go get my phone," she urged. "I'll show you the email."

Skylar led the way downstairs, still perplexed as to how much she wanted to involve her cousin. Axel was a lawyer—Donovan's general counsel. He had always been a good judge of character. But he was still a Keller.

When they reached her kitchen, Skylar saw her phone lying crooked on the floor. She picked it up, located Brit's email, and handed the phone to Axel.

She watched his eyes scan it, scrolling down as he read. When finished, he handed the phone back and shrugged. "There's nothing there. I mean, she actually sounds nice. I don't know what you're so worried about."

Skylar went cold inside. Of course, Axel wouldn't get it. He grew up in a Bel Air mansion with his Italian model mother and rich, dashing father. Axel went to Stanford and excelled. He was a gentleman with old money, good manners, and a strong character. He had a polished grace and confidence only bred by wealth and class. That's why he would never understand the hell Skylar came from— how she had lived the life of an impoverished, unloved toy, raised by Eurotrash in Amsterdam. She barely earned her marketing degree from UNLV. He would be repulsed if he saw where Skylar grew up, in that tiny, stinky apartment while her mother turned tricks.

"You know what?" Skylar blurted, tossing her phone on the counter. "You're right. I never should have bothered you." She forced out a small, fake laugh.

Axel drew himself to his full height of 6'3. "What? Are you sure?"

"I'm sorry I sent that text. It's just … well, I blocked her from my life so long ago. I was emotional. But you're right. I don't have to do anything. She's dead to me." Skylar felt a sharp pain knot in her chest as she gave Axel a wry smile.

He just stood staring at her, like he was trying to work out a math problem in his head. "Tell you what. Let me do a background check on her tomorrow. Okay?"

A chill cleaved through her. A background check would reveal everything about Brit and Skylar. "No," she protested. "That's not necessary. Just like you said, her email is pleasant enough. There's no need for it."

He frowned. "Well, if she's trying to stay at the hotel, why don't I do a credit check? That will at least show you whether she's telling the truth about her financial situation."

Skylar considered that. A credit check would limit the amount of information revealed. "I guess that would be okay."

"What's her name again?" he inquired, pulling his phone from his pocket.

"Brit Van Ness." Skylar hated saying the name out loud. She no longer wanted to be associated with Brit or her younger self. In fact, she tried to destroy that girl inside her—make her disappear forever. When it came down to it, Axel was right. There was nothing Brit could do to hurt her. She had already been trampled on and crushed.

Axel typed a note for himself and then pocketed his phone. "I'll have something for you Monday."

"Thanks," she answered, giving him a quick hug. His hair smelled freshly washed.

"Don't worry about it," Axel said in a soothing tone.

"I won't," Skylar lied as she followed Axel to the front door. She ushered him out, closing and locking the door behind him. She paused at her security panel to make sure it was set, then headed back to her bedroom.

CHAPTER 3

Skylar raced to work Monday morning, preoccupied with the day ahead. She had spent all of Sunday obsessing over Brit's email. Finally, after many attempts to respond, she deleted the email. Then, she emptied her deleted folder, feeling, in some fabricated way, freed.

But as the new week dawned, the same anxiety returned at the thought that Brit would be in Las Vegas—*would it be today? Tomorrow? When?* She berated herself for not finding out, but that would have required a response to the email—an acknowledgement that she had read it. The fact that she didn't respond would send a clear message to Brit. Axel's words hung in her mind. *"You can ignore her if you want. She can't do anything to you."* Sure, when you were someone like Axel Keller, that made sense.

Her phone rang, and KELLER, A. flashed on the screen. "Hey, Ax," she greeted him, doing her best to sound relaxed and confident despite the heaviness that flooded her chest.

"Did you hear from her again?"

Skylar sighed. "No. Did you find anything on her?"

"Well, it's sort of odd. I tried Brit Van Ness, and there's nothing. Not one entry. It's like she doesn't exist. Are you sure that's still her legal name?"

Skylar had to think about that one. The original email came from Brit Van Ness. *Or I thought*. She half-wished she hadn't triple-deleted everything. "It's possible," she said. "She and my dad divorced when I was a baby. She could have remarried."

"That's strange, there's no record. I checked the hotel, and there's no registration under that name. But that doesn't mean she's not staying here. She could be staying under someone else's name."

Skylar drummed her fingers on her desk. "Well, then I guess there's nothing more to do for now," she said, thinking she needed to watch her back from then on.

"Sorry, Sky. Let me know if there's anything else I can help with."

"Thanks." She hung up.

～

Every other Monday, Skylar led the marketing strategy meeting in the big conference room near her dad's office. She had over-prepared, knowing James would be breathing down her neck, especially with DJ temporarily out of the picture.

She took a quick look in the full-length mirror behind her office door, smoothed her pale blue wool pencil skirt, and adjusted her black turtleneck. Her outfit was an afterthought this morning; she was so jittery. She touched up her lipstick and tucked in the strands that held her updo in place. Then she dashed toward the conference room.

When she got there, it was empty, so she sat and double-checked her reports. Her marketing manager, Sebrina Bonds, shuffled in with her usual harried gait, like she was trying to keep up with life. She carried a stack of papers in one hand and a heavy stapler in the other.

"Hey, Sebrina," Skylar greeted her. "How was your weekend?" She watched as Sebrina pushed her tortoise-rimmed glasses toward her nose and began straightening the papers.

"Oh, fine," she responded, barely looking up, her short brown hair slightly ruffled on one side. Sebrina always wore all black clothing—swore it made her look thinner. "How's yours?"

"It was good," Skylar said, rising to help Sebrina, who had just dropped half her stack on the floor. "The wedding was beautiful," she added, kneeling to gather the papers, then handing them to Sebrina.

"Oh gosh, I'm sorry, Skylar. I totally forgot about the wedding." She began manically stapling her media reports together and placing them in a stack. When finished, she turned to face Skylar with a worried look on her slightly rounded face. "We have another issue with the Craic billboard." *Craic* was a name her father chose because it was Irish slang for 'good time'. It was also very close to *Craig*, his brother's first name. From a marketing standpoint, Skylar didn't love it.

"What now?" Skylar asked. She was intimately familiar

with the billboard in question. *Craic Fun Drinkery* was the most popular club in Las Vegas, and its new advertising campaign featured a topless model wearing a green bowler hat. Her long, wavy dark hair covered her breasts, but the Nevada Gaming Control Board wouldn't approve it. Only a certain amount of exposed flesh was allowed on a billboard, so Skylar kept having the ad agency use digital image manipulation to cover the breasts with more hair.

"Same issue."

Skylar instinctively crossed her arms over her chest. "I thought they approved the last round of ads."

"They did. I have the approval in writing," she said. "But someone drove by and said it was still too revealing. They don't want children to see it while traveling by car through Nevada—said parents are complaining, mostly from Utah."

Skylar rolled her eyes. "Bring me the billboard printout and the written approval," she said, feeling an excruciating pinch in her toes. "I'll run it by legal."

Before Sebrina could respond, Mila Schappert burst in, taking a seat at the far side of the table. Mila was a casino host who had been at the Donovan for 15 years. She started as a host and never earned a higher position. She didn't have to. It was not-so-secret that Mila had affairs with some of Donovan's biggest customers.

Mila was beautiful but had long ago lost the blush of youth. She was petite and slender, with long, brown hair worn in loose, frizzy curls. Mila reported to James, but DJ made it clear that Mila was never to be fired, no matter how useless she was. Everyone knew she had no business sitting in such a high-level meeting; however, at DJ's insistence, she'd become a fixture.

Today, Mila wore tall over-the-knee high-heeled boots, clicking down the marble hallway as her mini-skirt swished from side to side. Her face looked puffy, and she wore huge dark glasses, as though she'd had a late night.

As soon as Mila sat in the chair to Skylar's left, James sauntered in looking humorless in a dark grey suit, white shirt, and no tie. Sometimes, when Skylar saw James enter a room or from afar, somewhere in the casino, she would momentarily forget who he was and check him out.

James was taller than Skylar; six feet, she guessed, with midnight blue eyes, and dark blond hair that was always a bit too long. His overall look was scruffy, yet slick and stylish. To Skylar, he had the devilish countenance of a casino scoundrel. She must have been curling her upper lip while she studied James, because he gave her a stern look and nodded without saying anything.

James slid into the seat to Skylar's right, at the head of the table, like he always did, even though it wasn't his meeting. He did it to show superiority and dominance. Skylar never insisted on taking that seat. In her mind, she rationalized that she was in the trenches, working while James delegated all his work, like a king with his subjects. Everyone chose the same seats they had claimed when the meetings first began years ago. Skylar thought it funny how they were such creatures of habit, her included. James was close enough for Skylar to detect a waft of his subtle woodsy scent. He crossed his legs and began scrolling on his phone, a bored look on his face, while the usual suspects filed into the conference room and settled.

Mila gave Skylar a sarcastic smile. "Did you hear about last night?"

Skylar shook her head. "What did I miss now?"

"Another insane request from a blackjack player." She leaned in. "He insisted on chocolate-covered eggrolls." She laughed with a snort. "I took that request to the chef, and he went ballistic—started yapping about his culinary integrity."

Skylar chuckled. Outrageous food requests from players were a daily occurrence. "Did the chef end up making them?"

"Hell, yeah! A whole bucket of them." She paused to snicker. "The player'll probably send me to retail this morning after he splits his pants." She broke into a fit of laughter.

James glanced at his smart watch and then pulled a face. "Can we dispense with the small talk? I have a hard stop at 11."

"This isn't small talk," Mila retorted, tossing her dark frizzy hair. "This is serious gossip."

James rolled his eyes, then glared at Skylar. "This is *your* meeting, yeah? Is it happening or not?"

Skylar pursed her lips. *Such an asshole.* His accent made him sound even more flippant. She fantasized about clocking him in the jaw with Sebrina's stapler. "No, James. I invited everyone so we could all hold hands and discuss our plans for the weekend." She ended the statement with a mocking grin.

***

By the end of the day, Skylar was sufficiently exhausted, her feet swollen in black pumps. She kicked them off under her desk and let out a low groan. It felt so good.

She spread out her toes and felt them tingling. She started clearing things for the day, and her office phone rang. The phone screen read, LIMERICK. Limerick was an elegant cocktail lounge near the hotel tower. *Must be the bar manager wanting something from marketing.* Skylar picked up the phone. "Skylar Van Ness."

"Skylar," a woman's voice said. "It's Mom."

Skylar nearly dropped the receiver. She caught her breath and tried to calm herself. *She's in the hotel.* "Who did you say it is?" Skylar asked, racking her brain for a way to brush this woman off.

"It's your mother, Brit. Did you get my email?" she asked in a voice tinged with the familiar Dutch accent Skylar had long since shed.

Skylar paused, trying to remember Axel's advice. *You can ignore her if you want.* It was hard to ignore someone when they were calling from the very building you were in. She shuddered. "I, um, didn't get an email," Skylar lied. "Sometimes outside emails go to my spam. Did you say you're my … mother?"

She heard a cigarette lighter flickering, then a loud exhalation. She pictured her mother, as she was when Skylar was 12, taking a drag of her cigarette before sniping at her over some perceived infraction. Hairs rose on the nape of her neck.

"Oh, that's a shame," Brit said, this time with a hint of regret. "I wrote to tell you I was coming to Las Vegas. I'm here now, and I really want to see you, Skylar. I look around this beautiful hotel and think, my daughter is the vice president."

"Of marketing," Skylar corrected her.

"Pardon me?"

"I'm vice president of marketing. Listen, I'm going to be crazy busy over the next week. I don't think I'll have time." She tried to keep the panic out of her voice, but her breathing had become shallow, and she was having a tough time even formulating words.

"Skylar, look, I understand you may have mixed feelings, but I've changed. I want to show you I've become a good person. Even if we just meet for coffee, I'd be happy. I'm staying here in the hotel."

Skylar took a deep breath. *She can't do anything to you. She can't do anything to you.* "I'm sorry. I really am." She hung up the phone, feeling her stomach flip-flop. She picked it up again and dialed Clay's cell phone.

"This is Cl …"

"How far are you from the hotel?" Skylar interrupted breathlessly. She could hear Clay's turn signal.

"Um, I just left. I'm at the light out front. Are you okay?"

"I need you to pick me up at the back entrance. I'll explain later. I'm walking there now." She shoved her feet back into the unbearable pumps, grabbed her bag, and limped out, her feet now throbbing.

She emerged from the building and realized the sky had darkened and the temperature had conspicuously dropped. She'd not left the casino all day and had no idea of the time. When she saw Clay's white Lexus enter the back entrance valet, her nerves calmed at once. He stopped, got out, and opened the door for her. She quickly climbed into the car.

"Skylar, what's going on?" he asked, glancing at her before driving out of the valet and taking a right onto Las

Vegas Boulevard. His sunroof was open, and Skylar could feel the chilly air filtering in and blowing directly onto her. She crossed her arms around herself with a shiver, thinking she had forgotten her jacket at the office, she was so upset.

"Can you close that?" she asked. "I'm sorry. I'm freezing."

"Of course, sweetie," he said, reaching up and fiddling with a button on the car ceiling. "Where are we going?"

Skylar thought about the best place to dodge Brit. By sneaking out the back entrance, she had avoided passing the Limerick Bar and the hotel tower entrance. Now she needed a place where no one would see her. "Let's have dinner somewhere," she said. "Somewhere dark."

Clay stole a look at her like he thought she'd lost it. "How about the Peppermill. Is that dark enough for you?"

The Peppermill had been around since the 1970s and sat right on Las Vegas Boulevard, north of Donovan. Skylar thought about the tacky, neon fuchsia and blue-violet interior, just light enough to glimpse the servers in their long black dresses, with a slit up one thigh.

"That's perfect," she said. "I probably won't eat much."

"You have to eat something."

⸻

The Peppermill was active with the usual noise from the barflies huddled around video poker machines. The place had always been touted as a celebrity hangout and backdrop for movies and TV shows. Plush booths made of magenta and royal blue velvet stood out in the muddy glaze of pinkish Tiffany chandeliers that screamed garish

Vegas ardor. Although the restaurant was not cheap, there was something gritty about it, a shabby afterthought that matched Skylar's mood.

The host led Skylar and Clay to one of the corner booths. The place reeked of must and grease from years past. Clay wore a navy three-piece suit with a skinny tie, his dark hair swept neatly with a dab of hair gel. He took long strides, as though he was late for something. Skylar would never tell Clay this, but she was always proud to be seen with him. He made her feel important and, in some odd way she could never explain, normal.

Once ensconced in a velvet booth, Clay ordered a vodka martini, straight up with olives. He dipped an eager grin at Skylar.

She cocked an eyebrow. "You know I can't."

He shrugged. "Suit yourself."

Skylar glanced at her watch. It was almost 8 p.m. She wondered what Brit was doing. She also wondered what Brit looked like now. *Would I even recognize her?* Her memories of her mother were dull and murky at this point, but her long blonde ponytail and tall, slim figure were hard to forget. The memory conjured her smell—always of cigarettes and strong perfume—a cloyingly sweet variety mimicking honeysuckle. Skylar's stomach lurched.

The server delivered Clay's martini and Skylar's mineral water, and she immediately picked up her glass and took a large swig.

Clay sipped his martini and then slid it toward Skylar. "I'm not trying to be an enabler, but you look like you need a drink."

Skylar eyed the martini, thinking it had been a long

time since she'd had even a drop of alcohol. It had been such a problem when she was a teenager. It wasn't just the booze, though. It was what the booze represented and what it accompanied—the coke, the pills, the pot, and, of course, the rampant sex. *But how bad would it be for me to have a small taste?* She licked her lips and lifted the drink while Clay eyed her—a look of curiosity on his face.

He waited until Skylar had taken a few sips of vodka before leaning toward her and saying in a serious tone, "So, what's up with the emergency meeting? I felt like I was driving the getaway car."

"You were." Skylar swallowed hard. *Okay, here goes.* "I got an email from my mother on Saturday," she said, the vodka warming her stomach. She had forgotten how fabulous that feeling was. "I deleted it, and then she called me just before I called you … from the Limerick."

Clay shrugged. "I didn't know you had a mother."

She leaned in conspiratorially. "Exactly. I haven't seen her since I was 12. She … she's a horrible person … or at least she was." Skylar paused for a reaction from Clay.

A server appeared through the din of clattering trays and dishes, asking for their order.

"We'll both have the porterhouse steak, medium, Caesar salad, and baked potatoes," Clay said, handing the menus back.

Skylar put up her hand to protest, but Clay cut her off.

"Honey, I'm making you eat. That's all there is to it." He then smiled at the brassy-haired, gum-chewing server, who stifled a yawn and headed off to the kitchen. "You get anorexic when you go through emotional crap."

"Fine," Skylar said. "Did you hear me? My mother is

here visiting. She came all the way from Amsterdam. She wants to see me."

The server came by with a breadbasket, which Clay accepted and placed on the table. "Bread?" he asked her.

"No," she said, looking around.

"What did you tell her?"

"I told her I was too busy. I hung up on her." Skylar took another sip of Clay's drink, plucked a vodka-soaked olive, and popped it into her mouth. She realized it was the first thing she had eaten since breakfast, which was a protein bar.

"Okay, you're going to have to give me some context, Sky," Clay said, spreading butter onto a piece of bread. "So, this is DJ's ex-wife? Does he know she's here?"

"No," Skylar said. "I don't want to involve him."

"He deserves to know his ex-wife is prowling around his casino," Clay said matter-of-factly. "You think Max might have a problem with that?" Clay crunched into his bread. "The timing's a little suspicious, too, don't you think?"

"Yes, I know." She sighed. "But that's not the worst part."

He frowned, still chewing.

Skylar looked around the restaurant again. "She's a reminder of my awful childhood. My past …" Skylar paused, thinking this could either bring her and Clay closer or drive them apart forever. She was taking a massive risk that Clay would still love her, knowing who she really was. "I was a bad kid," she confessed. "A … a bad *girl*."

Clay suddenly let out a cackle. "Honey, you were always a bad girl. You still are. And I love it." Then he saw the look on Skylar's face. "Sorry, that wasn't meant to sound the way it did."

"Clay, this is serious. She could ruin me," Skylar said with pain in her voice. "I was on all kinds of drugs." She stared down at the martini and suddenly felt lightheaded. She had already polished off half. "I lived in a shithole. My mother screwed strangers in front of me. I'm not using it as an excuse, but I … fell right into it. I … I was …" she looked up at Clay, tears threatening to surface. "I was a *sex worker*." *There, she had said it.* She waited for a chandelier to come crashing onto their table, tearing them to shreds with brass and light bulb fragments. Either that or a lightning bolt.

Skylar watched his eyes widen, but he didn't look shocked. As a gay Italian man with a rough East Coast background, he had never been a judgmental person. Still, telling your friend that you once screwed people for money was no small thing. *Especially when I'm the CEO's daughter.*

"Um …" he began. "How long ago?"

Her mouth tightened. "I was 12 … so fifteen years."

His look turned to pure shock. "Oh my god, where were your parents?"

She shook her head, feeling tears threatening to surface. "They divorced when I was a baby. My dad wanted nothing to do with my mother. I was stuck living with her, and … well, she was never there."

Clay's look melted into one of compassion. He scooted over in the booth and put his arm around her. That was it; she was crying, tears spilling down her cheeks. She fanned her face to stop them, but they kept coming. Clay grabbed a cocktail napkin and handed it to her. She dabbed at her eyes, now mortified. She inhaled deeply and turned her gaze to meet Clay's.

"Do you hate me?" she asked, in a tiny voice, one that didn't even sound like her.

Clay squeezed his eyes shut and pulled her closer. "*God*, no. You were a little girl. That mother of yours was supposed to protect you. How on earth could that be *your* fault?"

Skylar nodded, sniffling and dabbing again at her eyes. "You'll never know how hard that was for me to tell you. No one knows that now except for you and my mother. I mean, I'm sure DJ knows on some level, but he would never bring it up."

"Skylar, listen to me. The past is not you. It's what happened to you. We all have things that happened to us, but it doesn't make us bad people." Clay paused. "And I'll be damned if this bitch is going to hurt my friend. She'll have to answer to me."

The server was back and placed their salads in front of them. "Would either of you care for pepper?" she asked, smiling.

Clay shook his head and waved her away. "No, thanks."

Skylar watched as Clay moved back to his original place in the booth. She pushed the martini toward him.

"You can have your own," he whispered. "I won't tell anyone."

"I don't care about the martini, but you can't, I repeat, *can't* tell anyone what I just told you." Skylar brushed her forehead with her hand. "I mean it, Clay. That story will ruin me."

Clay put his fork and knife down, looking wounded. "Skylar Van Ness, how could you even say that?"

"I'm serious, Clay."

"I know you're serious. I won't breathe a word. But she

may not give up, you know. Especially since she flew all the way from Amsterdam to see you."

"I know," she said. "That's what has me worried."

"Let's change the subject," Clay said between bites of his salad. "How's that handsome devil you work with?" He took a sip of his martini, which was almost empty. He signaled the server for another round.

Skylar picked at her food and made a face. "I have no idea who you're talking about."

"You know exactly who I'm talking about. I can tell because you're blushing."

"That's the vodka," Skylar said with a wry smile.

"How's the Monarch?" Clay teased. "I saw him today in the casino. Hot, hot, hot." He uttered those last three words in a sing-song manner.

Skylar rolled her eyes. *Here it comes.* Clay had a huge crush on James ever since they first met, and made it clear that if James were gay, Clay would go after him. At 33, Clay had been mostly single except for one long-term relationship that had ended badly.

"And that accent—talk about a catch," Clay went on. "Why don't you just give in to the temptation and sleep with that gorgeous man … if only to report back to me." He gave her a wink.

Skylar frowned. "Now you're really ruining my appetite."

"He's the only one who could keep up with you, sweetie. And it's so clear he's crushing on you." He let out a wistful sigh. "I can't believe he's still single."

"James *hates* me almost as much as I hate him," Skylar protested. "He's an egomaniac. I mean, you should have seen him in today's marketing meeting, badgering me about every detail."

"Well, he *is* smart—maybe he's just detail-oriented. He graduated from Trinity College Business School, you know."

"Right, and don't think I haven't heard that story a million times. He acts like it's so exclusive, but no one here cares. It's not like he went to Stanford like Axel did. But do you ever hear *him* bragging about his education?"

"Axel Keller," he said with a low whistle. "He's another one." Clay cocked his eyebrow at her. "But if I had to choose, it would be the Monarch. He just looks … more fun." He gave her a devilish grin before finishing the martini.

"Trade places with me for a day and you'll find out just how much fun he is," Skylar retorted. "Anyway, can we please stop talking about James? I really need a plan of action with my mother staying in the hotel."

"Okay, okay," he said, flipping his palms toward Skylar. "I was just trying to give you a distraction. Now let's talk about your dear old mom."

Skylar nodded as the server set down martini number two. Clay took a sip and slid it toward her. "Help yourself," he said.

As Skylar took a giant slug, she decided to leave her car at Donovan, and have Clay drive her home. She could have a car service drop her at the back entrance again. *No chance of running into Brit.*

Chapter 4

When Skylar's alarm went off at 6 a.m., she lurched awake and turned it off, mouth like cotton and heart pounding. *Damn. Why did I break down and drink last night?* She sprang out of bed, wincing as her swollen feet hit the carpet. She leaned over, examining each foot for blisters, and wondered how she would stuff them into high heels for another full day at Donovan.

After feeding Sesame and cleaning the litter boxes, she took extra time to do her hair and makeup, so no one would suspect she had been drinking the night before. She derided herself for being so weak as she stared into the mirror at her hungover face. *Whitening eye drops and dark eyeliner will help.* Instead of curling her long blonde hair, she used a flat iron, which always made her face look sharper and her eyes larger.

She had chosen the most forgiving heels she could find in her closet—chocolate-brown suede boots, which she paired with a cream wool skirt and a camel cashmere sweater. She had thrown a chocolate trench coat over her shoulders and oversized black sunglasses to cover her eyes. She walked to the garage and was reminded that she'd left her car at work. *Oh crap, I'll have to call an Uber.*

Somehow, Skylar managed to make it to work. Her headache was so intense that she had taken two pain relievers with her morning coffee. They didn't seem to be taking effect.

On her walk to the office, she caught sight of herself in a retail store window reflection. Her body swayed forward because her feet were killing her. She straightened up and did her best to break into a rhythmic saunter, even though the pain was immeasurable.

Just as she rounded the corner to her office, she stopped short. James was seated in a chair, waiting right outside. He was reading the *Wall Street Journal*, legs crossed, like he belonged there.

"Oh, it's you," Skylar said, thinking he was the last person she wanted to see.

He looked up from his paper. "Good afternoon."

Skylar dashed a glance at her watch. She never arrived at the office later than 8 a.m. It was now past nine. She shoved her key in the lock and pushed open her office door.

James folded his newspaper and stood, trailing Skylar into her office. She hated it when anyone did this. It was such an intrusion. She just wanted to close her door, drink a Red Bull, and avoid people.

Skylar's thoughts went back to her dinner with Clay. He had recommended she simply lie low until Brit left. He thought she had given a sufficient hint for Brit to stay away. He also felt Brit didn't have the money to afford more than a couple of days at Donovan. *I hope he's right.*

She hung her trench coat on the back of the door, stashed her handbag in her desk drawer, and locked it. James stood opposite her desk, hands resting on the chairs facing it. He leaned forward casually, eyes following Skylar's every move.

She pulled the black sunglasses from her face. "Do we have a meeting?"

He folded his lips and then smiled. "No, but I was walking through the casino checking out signage. I have ideas—so many missed opportunities."

Skylar had to stop herself from groaning aloud. "Does it have to be now?" she asked, unable to muster a fake smile. "I have things that can't wait."

This time, he laughed. "You see, I'd believe that if you were already here when I came in." He checked his watch. "Almost an hour ago."

She could feel her face heating up. "You waited here for an hour? To talk to me about signage? Don't you have anything to do?"

His features softened. "Come on, Skylar. I'll buy you a coffee." He grinned that lopsided grin. When James smiled, his upper lip curled higher on the left side, revealing even teeth and a bit of gumline. He had a square jaw and thick, well-defined eyebrows. His quietly disheveled, blond-streaked brown hair gave off a whisper of cool.

"I've already had coffee," she said wearily. *Why won't this guy just leave me alone?* The thought of taking a stroll through the casino to hear James's unwelcome opinions about marketing signage made Skylar's stomach tumble.

Plus, her feet had not yet recovered from yesterday's excruciating black pumps, and her toes pinched. She shifted from side to side to find a comfortable stance, dying to just sit at her desk for a few minutes.

"Well, then you can watch *me* drink coffee," he said, giving her a mock-stubborn look with amusement in his eyes.

"Fine," she said, grabbing her phone and keys. "Lead the way."

As James and Skylar paraded through the casino, heads turned. And it wasn't just because they both had high-profile jobs and were recognizable by almost every employee. They cut a striking pair.

They stopped every now and then so James could pontificate. He turned to Skylar. "Are you getting all this?"

Skylar nodded and spoke into her phone to record the signs in question. Her design team would not be happy with a fresh hit list from James about what needed improvement. Although Skylar could hardly argue with what he was saying. As much as she hated to admit it, his suggestions all made sense.

When the impromptu walk-through was over, they were passing the Black Clover Bistro, and James turned to Skylar. "I promised you coffee."

She shifted in her boots and clenched her teeth at the raw pain in her feet. *I just need to sit for a few minutes.* She eventually nodded and followed James into the Black Clover Bistro.

Once the host found them a table, Skylar dropped into the chair and felt immediate relief. James ordered an espresso, and Skylar ordered hot peppermint tea. When the server delivered the drinks, Skylar fantasized about soaking her feet in the tea.

"Now, that wasn't so bad, was it?" James asked.

She sipped her tea. She had no idea how to talk to James on any level beyond defending herself from his critiques. But since she wanted to stay off her feet for at least the next 20 minutes, she decided to play nice.

"I guess not," she finally answered.

"Have you heard from your dad since Saturday?" he asked.

Skylar shook her head. "No. And I'm glad. I want him to enjoy his honeymoon without worrying about this place." She picked up her tea and took another sip, feeling the sublime warmth and cool peppermint soothe her throat.

"How thoughtful," he remarked.

"And somewhat selfish," she added, noting the sarcastic glint in his eyes. "The less he hears from us, the better we look."

He nodded. "I'm curious if he'll be able to stay away. The guy practically lives here."

Skylar grinned. "Did you see Max in that dress?" The wedding was an all-black affair, and Max wore a breathtaking floor-length silk sheath with spaghetti straps.

James gave her a breathy laugh. "More importantly, did you see *DJ's face* when he saw Max in that dress?"

They both laughed, and for a second, Skylar forgot how much she hated James.

"Speaking of Max and DJ, I got some good photos of the wedding. Would you like to see?" He waggled his phone.

She shrugged. "Sure."

James began scrolling through his photos and leaned

toward Skylar. She got a waft of his attractive scent—a breezy, musky wood. She was never sure whether he was wearing a fragrance or if he just smelled that way. Or perhaps it was some kind of soap. She examined his fingers as he scrolled through photo after photo. They were long and slender, like those of a pianist. His fingernails were short, but his nail beds elegantly long. A strong current shot through her, causing a shiver.

"Are you cold?" James asked. "Because we can move to another table."

"Not at all," Skylar said, cheeks flaming. She quickly erased the thought of James's fingers and continued viewing the photos on his phone.

He stopped on one. "Here's my favorite." It was a photo of DJ and Skylar on the dance floor, talking and laughing. James looked up, and their eyes met.

A woman's voice came from behind them. "Skylar? Skylar Van Ness?"

Skylar peered upward and gasped. *It was Brit!* She looked like a much older, scraggly version of the Brit she remembered. She wore her platinum hair in a chin-length bob with loose waves. She had it tucked behind her ear on one side. Her fair skin creased around her light-colored eyes, and her full, yet slightly crinkled lips were shining with pale pink gloss. She resembled a phantom who had once been a beautiful woman—one scarred and tainted by tough times and reckless living.

She smiled brightly. "You're Skylar, yes?"

Skylar jumped up, ignoring her aching feet. "Yes. What can I do for you?"

"It's me, Skylar. It's your ..."

"Of course," Skylar interrupted. "I'm so glad we ran into each other. Maybe we can arrange a time to discuss those cardstock samples you dropped off at my office."

Brit's smile disappeared, and she stared at Skylar. "Skylar, don't you recognize me? It's M ..."

"I know who you are," Skylar interrupted again. "We can meet this afternoon, okay?"

She tore her eyes from Brit's astonished face to James. His mouth had cupped open, as though he was perplexed by Skylar's abrupt behavior. She felt faint with panic, picturing all the disastrous outcomes.

She turned back to Brit. "In fact, as long as you're here, let's go to my office now."

"But I didn't pay my check," Brit said, hitching her thumb toward the opposite end of the restaurant.

"I've got it," Skylar responded, grabbing Brit's arm. "James, please forgive me, but this is the project that couldn't wait. Thanks for understanding!"

And she tugged Brit toward the exit. Once they were out in the casino, Skylar dropped Brit's arm and stopped to face her. "Here's what's going to happen. We're going to walk to my office, and you're going to pretend to be selling me cardstock for an invitation. You are *not* to interact with my employees. Got it?"

Brit's face clouded over. "You seem so angry. I just want to see you. Look at you!" She broke into a huge smile and gave Skylar the once over, taking the ends of Skylar's long, loose blonde hair and twirling them in her fingers.

Skylar swatted Brit's hands away in disgust. "Don't touch me. And when I say it's time for you to go, you're going to leave quietly, okay?"

Her face fell in dismay. "Okay," she said, hiking her large black tote bag higher on her shoulder.

Skylar managed to sneak Brit into her office without anyone noticing. Her employees were milling about and chatting at the copy machine or in their offices. Once she had the door closed, Skylar moved behind her desk and studied Brit from head to toe.

Her faded navy-and-white striped t-shirt peeked out from under a stiff-looking jean jacket. Black fake leather pants hung loosely on her slender frame. She had always been tall—she wore clogs, which only added to her height and shabby appearance.

Up close, she possessed the leathery look of someone who never wore sunscreen. Still, Brit wouldn't stop smiling. Her teeth were straight but yellowed from years of cigarettes.

"Skylar, thank you for seeing me," she said, eyes darting around the office.

"You didn't leave me a choice. Do you want to sit?" Skylar gestured to one of the chairs opposite her desk.

"Yes," she said, dumping her tote on the floor and plopping down. "Thank you."

"Good, now what are you doing here?" Skylar asked.

Brit blinked back tears and pursed her lips. "I wanted to see you. You're my daughter." She cast her eyes to her lap and drew her hair behind one ear. "I know I wasn't good to you, and, believe me, I regret everything. But I'm better now." She looked around for something to wipe her tears with.

Skylar handed her a box of tissues and leaned back in her chair. "I'm glad you're better. But I'm 27 years old, and I haven't seen you for 15 of them. Dad took me in when you wanted nothing to do with being a mother. He made me go to school like a normal kid. And I worked my ass off to get where I am now. You can't just breeze in here and tell me you've changed, and that I should suddenly want to see you, Brit."

Her face froze. "Brit?" she asked, sniffling as another spate of tears leaked down her cheeks. She dabbed at her eyes with a tissue. "You can't even call me *Mom*?" Her voice quavered dramatically.

Skylar felt a stab in the gut. "Are you serious?"

Brit rose to her feet and walked, shakily, to Skylar's tall bookshelf. She picked up a framed photo of DJ and Max, taken at a gala event, and examined it closely. Then she replaced the picture and turned to face Skylar. "How was the wedding?"

Skylar bit her lower lip. "Why do you ask?"

She dropped her gaze to the floor. "I don't know. I just think about him a lot. I saw his engagement announcement in one of the Amsterdam newspapers. Saw your picture with him. I never thought he'd remarry."

"Well, he did," Skylar said sharply. "He's a different person, too."

"I know," Brit responded, looking Skylar in the eye. "He even changed his name."

"That's right. He goes by his *real* name."

"And why didn't you change *your* name?" Brit asked, eyebrows raised.

Skylar shrugged but didn't respond. The truth was,

Skylar liked her name. She didn't feel the need to change it as DJ had. It just felt right to leave it as is. *Skylar Van Ness* was a good name, and it was the only name she had ever known. It wasn't her fault that it was attached to her grandfather, the evil, murderous Luuk Van Ness.

"I never knew Hendrik Van Ness was really DJ Keller," she said, now with a defiant look in her eye. "In fact, as far as I know, we never really got divorced. He just sent me away. I'm still *technically* married to Hendrik."

Skylar felt her stomach knot. *That was it.* She had emailed Skylar on DJ's wedding day because she caught wind that he had remarried, *as DJ Keller.* "I'm sure that's not true," she said, rising to her feet and ignoring the pain from her boots. "Technically, Hendrik Van Ness never existed. It was a made-up name to hide my dad's identity—a fantasy that Luuk fabricated a paper trail for—*my father*—DJ was born in San Francisco, as Donovan James Keller."

"I know all about his story," Brit said without emotion. "And I don't care. He married me as Hendrik, and I want what's rightfully mine." She twisted a lock of her hair and then glared at Skylar. "When does *your father* return from his honeymoon?"

Skylar caught her breath. "I don't know."

"You *do* know," Brit said, baring her lower teeth. She resembled a towering scarecrow—a brittle, pale-faced apparition in fake leather.

"It's time for you to leave," Skylar said, pointing to the door.

"Fine," Brit said, pulling her tote from the floor and once again hoisting it up over one shoulder. Her hands shook like she was trying to contain her emotions. "But I'll be here watching and waiting for my *husband* to return. You can pretend all you want that you're some high-end casino vice president, but everyone at home ..." She took a threatening step towards Skylar. "We all know *the truth*."

Skylar felt her throat closing and the hairs on the back of her neck standing at attention.

"You live here in this bubble with your expensive clothes," Brit continued, sizing Skylar up with a once-over. "You have no idea how the rest of the world lives."

"I have a pretty good idea of how *you* live," she retorted, "which is why I want nothing to do with you."

She gave Skylar a wicked smile. "How would you like the fancy Irishman to know the truth?"

Skylar grasped the edge of her desk to steady herself— as though it were anchoring her to the malicious inversion of reality. She had been right all along. Brit didn't care about seeing her. She wanted to extort DJ. And to ruin her. That was clear. She steeled herself. "Get out," Skylar commanded, taking an aggressive step toward Brit.

She glared at Skylar with the corners of her mouth turned downward, like a fish that had just gotten hooked.

Skylar took another step toward her until she was so close, she could smell Brit's cigarette breath. "I said, get out. Now!"

Brit stood seething, but she eventually turned toward the door. Skylar shouldered her way in front of Brit and opened the door.

Brit exited, looking around, confused. Skylar didn't care if she got lost. Brit had already played her cards. Now Skylar knew what she was in for. *The question is, what am I going to do about it?*

CHAPTER 5

*I*f she called DJ now, he would be on the next plane back to Vegas. Skylar slumped in her chair. He had instructed his staff to call him only in emergencies. They all knew what an emergency was—shootings in the casino, a major robbery, or fire. *Was this an actual emergency?* She thought back to Brit's threats. *She thinks she's still married to DJ.* Then she had a horrendous thought. *What if they are?* Her hands shook as the words *"We all know the truth"* trembled through her.

The phone disrupted Skylar's chaotic thoughts. BONDS, S. was flashing. Skylar briefly wondered whether Brit was coming back for an encore. "Sebrina," she answered.

"Mila's here to see you."

Skylar exhaled in relief. "Tell her to please come in, thanks."

Mila was a welcome distraction—dressed, as always, in

eye-searing flash. Today, she looked as though she had just waltzed out of a fashion shoot advertising Scottish tourism. She dropped into one of Skylar's chairs dramatically and launched into a monologue about a customer. "I'm the highest-paid babysitter in the building," she moaned, tossing her long frizzy hair, which poked out from underneath a red cashmere beret.

Skylar withheld a giggle. She'd been an audience to Mila's tirades about babysitting more than a few times—*Mila's routine*, as Skylar referred to them.

"Christ," she continued, smoothing her tartan plaid kilt and crossing her legs. "One of them actually asked me to take him to his fucking colonoscopy appointment!"

"I didn't realize James was old enough to be getting those," Skylar quipped, and the two women burst into laughter.

Mila, who now had tears in her eyes, added, "Speaking of old, who was that fossil leaving your office?"

Skylar's smile disappeared. "Not sure who you're talking about."

"She asked me how to get to the service elevator," Mila said, "Was wearing fucking clogs. Reeked of smoke."

"Oh, yes, right. She's a vendor. Selling cardstock. I was trying to get rid of her."

"Tell her if she really wants to make a sale, she should try taking a shower," Mila said with a cutting sneer, pulling a vaping pen from the inner pocket of her blazer. Mila loved to hide out in Skylar's office and vape because employees weren't allowed to smoke anywhere while working in the casino. She drew in a deep drag and blew it out, then returned the pen to her blazer pocket.

Skylar leaned forward, sniffing the familiar watermelon vaping scent. "Hey, Mila, if you see that woman hanging around in the casino anywhere, will you please let me know?"

"Sounds like you're doing a little babysitting yourself," she said, rising to her feet. She swung around behind Skylar's office door to look herself over in the full-length mirror. After adjusting her kilt, she blew Skylar a kiss and flounced out.

～

Skylar spent the rest of the day in her office, with the door closed, consumed by the conversation with Brit. So many veiled threats wrapped up in one vitriolic bundle. She tried to imagine what DJ would do in this situation. Only DJ didn't have all the information. Sure, he knew Skylar had a rough past. And she was pretty sure he suspected the prostitution. He had married Brit, so he had to know whether he had, in fact, divorced her. But there was a big thing he didn't know. No one knew except Skylar. *"We all know the truth."* That was the most troubling of Brit's comments. *How much of the truth did she know?* Skylar swore she would take that secret to her grave, but what if Brit somehow found out? She was only 12 when it happened. *Could it be that there is a statute of limitations?* She had no idea about the laws in the Netherlands. She would have to do some research.

She swallowed hard and thought back to DJ. The first thing he would do is consult a lawyer—one who understood international law. If he was technically still married to Brit under his former name, Hendrick Van Ness, his marriage to Max as DJ Keller might not be valid.

And he might owe Brit money. *Maybe a lot of money.* And that could affect his business, gaming license, and stock. It would affect everyone.

Skylar's fingernails dug into her palms as her thoughts ran amok. There had been a whole crisis with DJ's identity, back when Skylar was just 17. DJ had to live as Hendrik since he was 22 because his father, Luuk Van Ness, made up a lie that DJ's life was in danger. As Hendrik, DJ flew under the radar. He never even had a steady girlfriend beyond the strippers he brought home in the wee morning hours. Most of the time, they were gone by the time Skylar got home from school. Then, DJ's brother Craig just showed up one day, and everything changed.

She recalled the moment she first saw Craig. She thought he was some random guy from the casino and winced at the memory of having tried to seduce him. That was the old Skylar—the one who threw herself at any attractive, older man. When she found out he was her uncle, she was both surprised and humiliated. She now had a cousin, Anabel, a grandmother, Julia, and an aunt, Jane. Shortly thereafter, she met three more cousins, Axel, Jackson, and Des.

Even so, Skylar always felt like an alien who had fallen from the sky, landed in Las Vegas, but had never taken root. She spent many evenings lost inside herself, bewildered as to where she stood.

After freeing himself from the elaborate web of lies Luuk had spun, DJ had no trouble assuming his real identity and returning to being a Keller. But as much as DJ wanted Skylar to have a family, she felt even more strongly that she was just a random name on the family tree. *Who am I? And who am I supposed to be?*

She had cleaned up her act when Max and the Kellers became part of her life. Gone were the drugs, alcohol, and random sex. She had literally taken out the trash—changed her phone number so those dregs from her former life could no longer contact her, and transferred to a different high school. She focused on her grades and strengthened her resolve to graduate from UNLV. She had always been massively talented with online apps and had a keen understanding of digital marketing, which was why she had quickly soared to the top of the ladder at Donovan. Even though she was the CEO's daughter, she never took her job for granted. It hurt Skylar when people like James dismissed her or didn't take her seriously. She knew that, with or without DJ, she was talented and worthy of the position she was in.

Love was a whole different story. Skylar had shut off her love life like a water faucet. She rarely flirted. But something was missing. She was still a woman who needed to be loved. *By someone.*

She dreaded the thought of going backward, and men were part of that. Skylar knew what people said behind her back. The hypothesis that she was an asexual misfit made its rounds through the management team at Donovan. The gossipy casino grapevine dished out labels like 'frigid,' 'frosty,' and 'aloof.' Skylar had heard them all. And, although they hurt her deeply, she was in no position to change. Not now.

Clay was the only one who understood her—especially now that she had shared pieces of her torrid past. Clay knew it was not that Skylar didn't want to be in love. He knew it scared her to death.

Skylar could tell DJ was in love with Max the first time he brought her to the house—the way he looked at her—the gentle way his fingers grazed her shoulders. It was a magic love affair without fights, cheating, or games. Skylar dreamed that someday, she would find that kind of love. But until she found it, love had to take a backseat to survival.

A loud knock at the door interrupted her musings. "Come in," she called, straightening in her chair, and collecting herself.

Sebrina walked in holding a file folder. "I came to drop off the printouts we discussed for legal."

~

Axel happened to be there when Skylar slid into his office lobby, which was in another area of the hotel, closer to DJ. She stopped by his open door and peered into his office. He was busy studying a document.

"Have a minute?" she asked, hovering in the doorway.

"Of course." Axel motioned for her to enter.

She approached her cousin, who wore a studious dark navy sweater vest over a white button-down. *So lawyerly.* "We're still having issues with that Craic billboard." She laid Sebrina's printouts on his desk.

Axel read the approval letter and then studied the ad. "Where is it?" He asked with a subtle swivel of his chair to one side.

"On the I-15, where everyone driving north can see it," Skylar replied.

He pulled a face. "Isn't that the whole point?"

"Um, yeah. The more eyeballs, the better." She let out a small laugh. "Marketing 101."

"Don't these people have anything better to do?" He shook his head. "How do you want me to handle it?"

"I think you should just call and talk to them. They seem to respond better when legal gets involved."

"That *never* happens," Axel returned with a wry grin. "Is that all?"

"That's it for now. Thanks, Ax." She started toward the doorway.

"Hey, Sky—did that woman, Brit Van Ness, well, did she ever show up?"

She felt her pulse spike. *I'm glad you asked because she came by my office to tell me she thinks she's still married to DJ.* If she told Axel the truth, it would unearth a lot of other shocking things about herself and her past life, and she just wasn't ready to go through that. It was painful enough sharing what little she had with Clay. Lying was her best option. She gave him the most casual smile she could muster. "Haven't heard a word."

Axel sprang upright, discomfort altering his striking features. "Oh, that's good. I guess I was expecting a different answer. I tried a few angles to get some intel on her, but ran into roadblocks. Makes me think there's more to the story."

Dear cousin, you don't know the half of it. She nodded, wondering how Brit had managed to erase herself from society. The whole thing was baffling.

"I was thinking about it," Axel continued. "And if she does show up, we need to call DJ. I don't care if he's *in bed* with Max when he answers his phone. He needs to know."

She sighed. Axel was so strait-laced all the time when it came to work. She knew, as general counsel, he had to be. She occasionally saw the real person behind the stoic face after he'd had a drink or two. She smiled. "I'll keep you posted."

Before he could say anything else, she backed her way out of the office and hurried to the elevator. *That was close.*

When Skylar got home that night, the first thing she did was drop to the floor and unzip her suede boots. She yanked each one off and lay on the carpet, her trench coat still clinging to her body. She stretched her aching feet and took a deep breath, pressing the balls of her feet and toes into the cushy carpeting. She closed her eyes and let her head sink as though she was anesthetized on a gurney, while fragments of her day scattered like crumbs through her mind. She saw James' smug face. *That wasn't so bad, was it?* Brit's yellow teeth breaking into an evil grin. *I'll be here watching and waiting.* Goosebumps covered her body, and she grasped her trench coat, pulling it tighter. She felt herself drawn into the slurry of her childhood, to one particular day. *We all know the truth.* She tried to stop the pictures from streaming in, like she always did when the memory came back to haunt her.

The gray, dingy apartment with that man. The one who called her 'sugar,' and wrapped her hair in his fist before yanking it backward and tearing half of it off her scalp. The fist cracked down hard on her left cheekbone.

Something rubbed against Skylar's head, and she let out a frightful shriek. "Oh my God, no!" Her eyes shot open and came into focus. Sesame's furry body huddled up against her. She must have pawed her hair because she worried Skylar was sick. Or dead. *Who knows what cats think?*

Skylar raised herself to a sitting position and picked up Sesame, cuddling her close. She felt warm and soft against Skylar's pounding heart. "It's okay, baby," she whispered. "Mommy's okay." Sesame meowed and then purred in Skylar's arms. "At least I think I am. What should I do, Sesame?" She breathed deeply. "Do you think she'll leave me alone?" Sesame let out a big yawn and struggled to get free. She gently set the cat down and rose to her feet. "You must be hungry. Mommy will feed you, sweet Sesame."

Later that night, Skylar put her headphones on and lay on her bed, listening to the entire length of an old Pixies album. The winding chord progression of "Where is My Mind?" had her entranced. Afterwards, she washed her face, brushed her teeth, and slipped under the covers. The wind had kicked up. It was blowing so hard against the bedroom windows that she worried they might explode in a fury of shards. She shivered and pulled the covers tighter. A loud growl sprang from her stomach. It was then she realized she hadn't eaten today. It was too late to eat now.

Great, she thought. *It's going to be another one of those nights.* Skylar had always suffered from insomnia, but in times of stress, it was much worse, especially when she stopped eating. After about two hours of tossing and turning, Skylar broke down and fumbled in her nightstand for her bottle of sleeping pills. She washed a pill down with a bit of water, put on her eye mask, and drifted off to sleep.

CHAPTER 6

Three full days had passed, and there was no sign of Brit. Skylar started to wonder if she had scared her off. If she had, Skylar would have no reason to call DJ, no reason to involve Axel, and no reason to worry. But something deep inside told her it was not the last of Brit's visits. Ever since Brit showed up, Skylar had this nervous habit of glancing around every corner when she was in the casino or anywhere outside her office. Even while she was at home lately, she had a creepy feeling of being watched.

Skylar had scheduled a meeting in one of the ballrooms to debut potential cocktail server uniforms for a new restaurant. While she waited for the group at the ballroom entrance, her eyes darted around. Clay had set the room perfectly. Even so, Skylar had the jitters. The meeting would be brimming with Kellers—Craig, Jane, and Anabel.

Technically, her family, but they always made her nervous. She hoped the meeting would be a success, especially while DJ was out.

"Skylar." It was her uncle, Craig, in an olive suit with a cream shirt.

He kissed her on the cheek, and she caught a whiff of his clean scent, which always gave her goosebumps.

"Great job on the wedding." Craig was the managing partner of Keller Vance, the company's advertising agency. "How are you?"

"I'm well," she told Craig, looking up into his light jade eyes. At 6'5, he was the only man taller than her when she wore heels.

Trailing behind Craig was Marco Ricci, a celebrity chef with his own show on Cooking Network Television. He was opening his new Italian restaurant, 'Marco,' at Donovan. Skylar had met him briefly when DJ was negotiating the contract. She eyed his distressed motorcycle jacket, black T-shirt covering his large pot belly, and ripped, faded jeans. His dark curly hair formed an unruly halo that girdled his rotund face.

Skylar unbuttoned the top button of her boxy navy pinstripe jacket to look a little more casual. Her tall, chunky-heeled pumps were just starting to ache, despite having wrapped sports tape around her individual toes like a ballet dancer to prevent blisters and bleeding from getting worse.

"Skylar, you know Marco Ricci," Craig said. He turned to Marco, "Marco, you remember Skylar Van Ness, VP of marketing?"

Marco took Skylar's hand and shook it brusquely. "Ah,

Skylar, of course I remember you." He spoke with a slight Italian accent.

Skylar already knew of his reputation as an egotist. "It's a pleasure to see you again, Marco," she said, forcing a smile. "Are you as excited as we are to see the new uniforms?"

"Very excited," he answered, eyes peering beyond Skylar in the event someone more important had entered the room.

"Where would you like us to sit?" Craig asked her.

Skylar always felt butterflies when Craig was around. *How could anyone not admire him?* She could never tell what Craig was thinking because he was an iceberg in public, with his mostly austere demeanor.

She led them to the front of the room to sit in the theater-style reserved seats. "Here is great," Skylar said. "We have coffee and refreshments." She waved her hand toward a skirted table with coffee, tea, fruit, and bagels. Marco beelined for the buffet and grabbed a bagel.

"Thanks, Sky," Craig said with his familiar stiffness. *That's where Axel gets it.*

"Hello Skylar." Craig's wife, Jane, had just entered the room. "I never see you, and now it's been twice in one month." She approached Skylar and gave her a hug. "What a beautiful wedding! You should be proud."

"Thank you," Skylar responded, admiring Jane's smart burgundy shift dress with three-quarter sleeves. The dress reminded her of Joan from *Mad Men*, fitted in all the right places on Jane's petite frame. Her hair color was a little like Joan's, too—long, shiny, and auburn. Her tall black Louboutin pumps had pointed toes. Skylar wondered whether Jane's feet killed her, too. She somehow suspected they did not, as Jane gracefully glided to Craig's side.

"You should come visit us sometime," Craig suggested, taking Jane's hand. "Take a break from all this work and spend some time at the beach."

Skylar shrugged. The concept of a vacation was alien to her. She tried to remember the last time she had been anywhere outside Las Vegas. It seemed as though she had worn a path from her house to work and back. She even used the hotel's fitness center whenever she had time. She and Clay always fantasized about going on a cruise together. But they were such workaholics, nothing ever materialized.

"That sounds wonderful. Though I suppose I should stick around here at least until my dad returns," she said. "Have you heard from him?"

Craig smiled that self-assured Keller smile—one that never actually reached the upper part of his face. "Sort of. He sent pictures of the beach house they're renting in Bali. I think just to make me jealous."

Skylar felt a rush of deprivation. She longed to have DJ back. She needed him to take her in his arms and hold her like a dad—tell her everything was going to be okay and that no one could harm her. DJ would never do that, however, even if he was standing next to her now.

"Seriously," Jane interjected. "We'd love to have you stay with us—anytime you want."

I'm sure you're just dying for me to stay with you, Auntie Jane. Skylar never knew where she stood with Jane. She figured Craig must have told Jane what had happened when they first met—about Skylar trying to seduce him. Skylar was still mortified about that incident. Beyond mortified. She hated herself for it. She also envied Jane.

Jane had Craig, and he worshipped her. Skylar wondered what it would be like to be worshipped by someone like Craig. Or anyone, for that matter.

"I'd better say hi to our client," Jane said with a glance toward Marco. "Have you two met?" she asked Skylar.

She nodded.

Jane leaned toward her and whispered, "He's going to be work."

"Great," Skylar said. "He'll fit in perfectly." She glanced at her watch. "Is Anabel here?"

Before anyone could answer. Anabel soared in leading a bellman who was rolling a cart with numerous hanging garment bags labeled Keller & Co. Atelier. Jane had become a fashion designer some years ago when her boys became teenagers. After she got the company off the ground, she hired Anabel as her marketing manager. She started with women's dresses and then branched out to separates. Her business had a strong Instagram following but had not necessarily caught on. Jane had never designed uniforms, but she knew if she acquired Marco as a client, her business would take off.

"Cuz!" Anabel cried when she saw Skylar. The two women embraced. Anabel looked a lot like DJ, with her long, straw-colored mane. Axel was Craig's doppelgänger. The fact that Skylar didn't look like any of them exacerbated her feelings of being an outsider. She had minor similarities to DJ, such as the shape of her hands and feet, and the way she walked, but that was all. She prayed she didn't look like Brit, especially after seeing the older version. *What if I end up like that?!*

"It's good to see you, Anabel," she said, wincing at her

own forced tone. Anabel had everything easy; although Skylar had a decent rapport with her cousin, she considered Anabel a spoiled, demanding princess. Anabel grew up in the luxurious Brentwood neighborhood, graduated from Pepperdine, and was given a job in the fashion industry by her stepmother. Plus, her father was Craig Keller. She could get anything she wanted, whenever she wanted it.

"Are the models going to be here soon?" Anabel asked, twisting the shiny gold buttons of her black coatdress.

"They should be here any moment. There's a dressing room right over there." Skylar pointed toward an area Clay's team had set up with pipe and drape so the models could change on the spot in privacy. Anabel had asked for a tall woman who could wear a tiny size and a 'younger version of Axel.' Skylar recalled commenting to Anabel with sarcasm: "That'll be easy."

Several of Skylar's colleagues filed into the ballroom and started taking seats. The room was filling up with executives, but the models were nowhere to be seen. Skylar spotted James sauntering in. She ignored him.

She anxiously dialed her contact from the modeling agency. "Arnie," she said into the phone. "Where are the two models I requested?"

"I left you a voicemail," Arnie responded.

In the corner of her eye, Skylar caught James eavesdropping. She turned her back on him.

"Their flights from LA were delayed and then canceled," Arnie continued. "I'm so sorry, Skylar. I'm trying to find local alternatives, but just not having luck. Any chance you can reschedule the meeting for later this afternoon? I can get the original models on another flight."

Skylar scanned the room in panic. "No, Arnie. We have a full house. You need to find alternates now."

"No models, huh?" James inquired while sidling next to her with a snickering smile.

Skylar shot him a scowl. "It's not funny, James. The Kellers brought Marco Ricci from LA, so we'd better get someone in here to try on the damned uniforms." She turned again to scout the room, which was almost full, and saw Jane approaching.

"Is everything okay with the models?" Jane asked, a cloud of concern swathing her pretty face.

Skylar sighed and shook her head. "They can't make it. Our agency is looking for local models to fill in, but I doubt they'll have anyone on such short notice."

Jane folded her lips and gave Skylar the once-over. "Wait right here," she said. As Jane hurried toward the rolling cart, Skylar instinctively watched James to see whether he was checking Jane out as she walked. To her surprise, he was studying Skylar. She looked away.

Jane returned with a garment bag, which she unzipped. She pulled out a long, sparkly, royal-blue velvet dress with a bustier top and thigh slit. She held it next to Skylar. "You could fit into this dress, and you're the perfect height."

Skylar felt her face overheat. There was no way she was going to parade her body half-naked in a room full of her colleagues. She couldn't believe, as a fellow professional, Jane would even ask. She smiled, seething underneath. "I'd love to help you out, but ... no."

Naturally, James felt the need to chime in. "Problem solved." He gave Skylar a triumphant grin.

She wanted to slap it off his face. She turned to Jane. "Let me see if I can find a sub."

"Come on, Skylar," James said, now visibly amused. "Take one for the team."

"Why don't *you* take one for the team?" she snapped back.

"Actually, you're *both* perfect," Jane said, hope brewing in her eyes.

James broke into a huge smile. "It would be my pleasure."

Jane looked from James to Skylar, then took Skylar by the hand and moved her a few feet away. "I really need your help, Sky," she pleaded.

"I'm sorry. But I'm here to do marketing, not model server uniforms."

"I know. I'd do it myself, but I'm too short. And Anabel is a size six." Jane bit her lower lip. "I know this is not ideal, but I designed the uniforms to be classy."

"You designed them to be sexy," Skylar corrected. "That's the direction *I gave you*." She now felt nauseous. Number one from not eating and number two from the thought of exchanging her smart pantsuit for a skimpy costume. But she had no choice, and her crowd was getting restless. Plus, she knew enough about Marco. The media and his own staff portrayed him as a tyrant who threw exaggerated tantrums if he didn't get what he wanted. And they needed his buy-in. If the deal fell through, it would be Skylar's fault.

"Fine," she said. "But I'm not undressing in there." She pointed at the pipe-and-drape dressing room. "I'll go to the nearest Ladies' room. Have Anabel come with me."

Jane let out a huge sigh. "Thank you, Sky. I owe you on this one."

<hr>

"Do you have it on yet?" Anabel called from outside the roomy bathroom stall.

"Not yet." Skylar had carefully removed her suit and hung it. She eyed the sparkly strapless blue dress and realized she couldn't wear a bra with it. She unhooked her bra, and an immediate chill climbed up her spine. She was standing in her chunky heels, wearing nothing but her underwear.

"Let me know if you need me to help zip you up," Anabel said.

Skylar snatched the dress and dragged the long side zipper down. She pulled the dress over her head and adjusted it, then zipped it up with ease. "Okay, I'm ready," Skylar said, unlatching the stall door and opening it a crack.

When she came out, Anabel's mouth dropped open. "Oh my God. You're … you're so beautiful. That color with your eyes." She grabbed Skylar by the arm and tugged her to the mirror. "Look at yourself."

Skylar peered into the mirror, and the first thing she noticed was her own exasperated facial expression. She eyed the plunging neckline and how her perfectly rounded breasts peeked out. She took a step forward, and the thigh slit revealed one of her long, slender legs. She shook her head in disdain, then turned to face Anabel, who was still marveling.

"I can't go out there like this."

"But … why not? Every woman would kill to look like you in that dress."

"Well, in case you didn't notice, most of the people in that room are men—men I have to sit in meetings with and convince that I'm smart."

Anabel's face clouded over, and a frown rested above her large honey-brown eyes. She cocked her head to the side. It was that same earnest look DJ gave her when he was trying to talk her into something. "You *are* smart. You're one of the smartest people I know."

"How would *you* feel if someone asked you to do this?"

"If I looked half as gorgeous as you, I'd be thrilled." Anabel was attractive, but her body was more athletic. She didn't have Skylar's dangerous curves. Anabel looked around frantically and grabbed Skylar's boxy blazer. "You can wear this until you have to take it off."

Skylar grabbed the blazer and threw it around her shoulders. "Let's get it over with then."

"I'll be by your side the whole time. It'll be over in a few minutes, and then you can put the blazer back on."

Skylar took a few steps toward the door.

"Wait," Anabel said, eyeing her face. She pulled the pins holding Skylar's hair in an updo, and her long platinum locks fell past her shoulders. Anabel pulled a brush, lipstick, and a makeup compact from her bag. She brushed Skylar's hair and rearranged it. Then she touched up her lipstick and makeup. "There," she said finally. "Now you're ready."

When Anabel and Skylar reached the ballroom entrance, they spotted James standing near the side of the stage.

His uniform was a black tuxedo with royal blue lapels and a bow tie, the same glittery velvet as Skylar's dress. When he turned to Skylar, he gave her a little nod but didn't say anything.

Anabel grinned at him. "Wait 'til she takes off the jacket!"

Skylar gave her a scolding look. "Don't make this worse."

Jane stood facing the executive team. Skylar spotted Marco sitting front row, center, with Craig to his left.

"Thank you for being here today," Jane began. "My apologies for the wait. But I think it'll be well worth it. We had a last-minute shortage on models, but Skylar and James graciously volunteered to show off what I hope will be Marco's beautiful new uniforms." There was a false ring to her voice.

Jane turned and caught Skylar's eye. "Ladies, first."

Anabel grabbed Skylar by the arm and whispered, "Let's go."

The two women walked arm in arm until Skylar reached the stage steps. Her heart pounded, and she felt lightheaded.

"You okay to walk up the stairs by yourself?" Anabel asked, eyeing her chunky heels doubtfully.

Skylar felt the shooting pain in her feet but nodded. "I think so."

Anabel let go of Skylar's hand and, without warning, yanked the blazer off her shoulders, which felt like someone pulled the towel off after a shower, her nakedness exposed to the world. She somehow managed to climb the stairs to the stage and turned to face the audience.

An audible gasp hushed the room. The lights were

so bright that Skylar could barely see the front row. She glimpsed James standing to the right of the stage, an awe-struck look on his face. She was not sure whether to cross her arms over her breasts or just run off the stage. A long shiver worked its way up her spine. She looked to Jane for help, but she was too busy describing the dress's details.

"… the fitted bodice with sweetheart neckline and cinched waist will flatter most every figure, while the slight sparkle on the vibrant blue velvet creates a dramatic mood." Jane's fingers gripped Skylar's waist, like she was a prize pig up for auction. Jane leaned in and whispered, "Walk towards the front of the stage so we can see how the dress moves, then turn, and come back to me." Then she gave her a little push.

Blood boiling inside, Skylar did as she was told.

"The slit goes to the thigh," Jane continued, "lending it that classic glamour reminiscent of 1950s Hollywood."

By the time Skylar reached the front of the stage and returned, Jane was chattering about accessories and how to pair the dress with strappy sandals. When she was again within earshot, Skylar took the opportunity to hiss, "Am I done?"

Jane looked her in the eye, slightly surprised. "Oh, sure, of course."

Skylar tromped to the stage steps where Anabel stood holding the blazer, which Skylar seized to cover herself. Over the sound of her own panicky mind racing, the room rang loudly with applause.

Skylar finished changing back into her suit while Anabel waited outside the bathroom stall.

"You were amazing!" she announced in her shrill, achingly enthusiastic voice.

Skylar refused to respond. She traipsed out of the stall and thrust the hated dress into Anabel's arms. "Here you go."

Then she stormed past. She longed to get her keys and go directly to her car, drive straight home. But she had to follow up with Jane, Marco, and the rest of the predators. She took a long, deep breath and marched toward the ballroom, thinking that the day would soon be over, and she would be cuddling with Sesame in her flannel pajamas.

She entered the room and ran smack into Craig.

"Hey," he said with a grin, pulling her aside. "Congratulations. You sold the uniform. Marco loves it."

"I'm glad I could be of use." She felt the anger lingering in her throat and prayed she wouldn't say anything offensive.

Confusion veiled his normally placid expression. "You know you just saved the day, right?" he asked, hand now grazing Skylar's arm.

Her skin tingled underneath the warmth of Craig's fingers.

"Marco's a tough client to please," he continued, leaning closer—so close she smelled him again. "And he's ecstatic right now."

"I'm sure he is," she answered, yanking her arm from his grasp and taking a step back. "I have that effect on people. *You* know from personal experience."

They locked eyes, and the indelible memory of him fumbling in the darkness for a light switch while Skylar felt his crotch flooded her mind. It was 10 years ago, but she recalled how warm and hard he was in her hands, as if it were yesterday.

She caught her breath and gulped back tears.

It was humiliatingly clear that Craig was remembering the exact moment. "Um, that was a long time ago. You're a different person now."

"Am I?" Skylar fumed that her own family used her to get a contract with an egotistical asshole. Of course, they did because they were Kellers, and she was not. She would never be. "How different am I? Explain that to me."

Craig now looked hurt and embarrassed. He scanned the room to see if anyone was paying attention. "Let's talk somewhere else. May I buy you lunch?"

"For services rendered?" Skylar felt the tears coming again. "You'll have to do better than lunch, *Uncle Craig*."

"Come on, Sky. It wasn't as bad as you think. At the very worst, your colleagues know you're a team player. At the very best, they think you're stunning."

He abruptly cleared his throat and drew himself to his full height. James was lingering nearby. "Oh, hello, James. I was just telling Skylar how great you guys were, pitching in to help. Thank you."

He eyed Craig with an air of suspicion and turned to Skylar. "You're a hard act to follow," he said with that playful Irish lilt. "You want to get lunch?"

Skylar swallowed back the tears that were hiding beneath her lashes, just waiting to spill onto her cheeks. She couldn't let James see her cry. *I can't let anyone see me cry!* She drew her shoulders back and observed James, with his wayward hair and those dark, mischievous blue eyes. In a way, he had also been used. He had given up his senior vice president status to allow a room full of his colleagues gawk at him in a flashy tux. Her eyes moved to Craig, who stood like a flawless stone sentinel in a dark olive suit. There was no way she would have lunch with him. *To talk about what?* The fact that she was no longer a drug-addled, jaded nymphomaniac who showed up naked in his bed 10 years ago pretending to be Jane? She was in no mood for Craig's forthcoming lecture about how she'd become a different person and give her that empathetic look that reduced her to emotional wreckage. She would much rather spend an hour listening to James brag about his education and criticize her signage.

A wave of real hunger passed through her stomach, and she gave James a genuine smile. "I'd love to get lunch."

Chapter 7

By the time Skylar and James found a booth at Suki, it was well past lunchtime. Even so, Skylar was not hungry. She was still stewing over the cocktail server uniform indignity. And the confrontation with Craig didn't help. The familiar old, sad feelings of unworthiness surged within her. She hated that part the most. The only good thing about the incident was that she had momentarily forgotten Brit.

"What's good here?" James asked, thumbing through the menu.

She looked up at him and shrugged. "You should know the menu by heart with so many customers to schmooze."

"Unlike you, I don't eat here all the time," he snapped.

"Because you're so busy." *I should have known we'd spend lunch bickering.* Regardless, it was better than having another awkward conversation with Craig. "I usually get the sashimi platter."

He twisted his lips sideways. "That sounds a little too healthy. I need carbs." Again, the hard *r*. He studied the menu. "You think I'd like Mongolian beef ramen noodles?"

"How could I possibly know what you like to eat?" she snorted. As soon as she heard her own tone, she softened it. "It's super spicy."

"The spicier, the better." He set the menu down and focused on Skylar. "Look, I know you're still nettled over how that meeting went down. But it's over, and you won. So, stop whinging."

"Easy for you to say." Skylar sulked, staring down at her phone.

"Hey, Skylar."

She placed her phone on the table and looked James in the eye.

"You think I fancied dressing up like a '70s disco club bouncer?" he asked. "This is a casino, and sometimes our work is … I don't know, daft. You can go home bulling, but you've got to come back with a smile on your face, right?"

Before Skylar could argue with him, the server stopped by to get their order.

"The lady will have the sashimi platter," James asserted. "I'll have the Mongolian beef ramen noodles." He handed their menus to the server and turned to Skylar. "Anything to drink?"

"Water for me," she answered.

"One water and one Coke," he said to the server.

Skylar giggled. "If you keep eating stuff like that, you'll never be asked to model anything again, except for maybe a toga costume at the New Year's Eve party."

That made James laugh. "If that's the case, I'll eat here

every day like you." He gave his disheveled hair a little pat. "I have to ask … what went on between you and Keller just now?

He had to go there. Skylar wished she had been able to control herself around Craig. Now, everyone in the room knew there was something between them. James must have read their body language. She forced a confused expression. "I'm not sure what you mean."

James shrugged. "It just looked like you two … I don't know, had words or something."

Skylar sucked in a deep breath and shook her head. "No, nothing like that."

James made a face. "Guy seems a little full of himself, don't you think?"

"That's your boss's *brother,* and my uncle, in case you forgot." Skylar didn't disagree with James. Craig *was* full of himself, but Skylar chalked it up to having grown up a spoiled, rich kid and then fathering four more spoiled rich kids. His was the seed that perpetuated the whole spoiled, rich solar system.

He shook his head. "Oh, come on, Skylar, lighten up. I was just kidding."

She sighed. "It's hard to lighten up—especially with so many family members breathing down my neck." She didn't know why she was opening up to James, but it felt good to just say it. "Sometimes, it's downright stifling."

"Sorry," James said with a contrite look. "Sometimes I forget he's your uncle." He cleared his throat.

I wish I could forget he's my uncle. She fidgeted in her seat.

The server placed their lunches on the table, and

they ate in silence. At least James ate. Skylar gingerly maneuvered her chopsticks around her plate, picking at a small bite of seaweed salad here and there.

James's eyes followed Skylar's chopsticks with curiosity. "Did you know Sal Vincenzo's back?"

Sal Vincenzo was one of Donovan's most prominent players. He lived in Scottsdale and visited the casino several times a month. He only played blackjack and the occasional craps. Though Sal was married, he had a roving eye and liked hot young blondes. Both DJ and James kissed his ass, comped him suites, dinners, anything he wanted. Sal had the power to take his business elsewhere, along with a lengthy list of other top players. He was the whale of all whales.

"I didn't know," Skylar responded. "What does he want this time? A flying Pegasus to take him to the Sphere?"

"I wouldn't put it past him," James said with a smirk. "But he does have a new lady friend." He floated air quotes over *lady friend*. "Mila told me she's asking for everything straight away."

Skylar groaned aloud. "Another one already? How long do you think this one's going to last?"

"Who knows with Sal? But Mila said he must really fancy her, because he's been using his comps on her all over the place—spa, retail—you name it. I see this woman's name on everything. Maud Jansen. Must be pretty special for Sal to be going this crazy, yeah?"

"Have you met her yet?" Skylar asked, wrinkling her nose. She was relieved that Maud was James's problem and not hers. Although many of Sal's whims ended up falling into her lap in the form of a marketing request.

"Nope. Just signed off on his marker—he's been going to town on the craps table—says his new girl's good luck." He inserted a forkful of noodles into his mouth.

Skylar stared at her sashimi. She hadn't eaten a proper meal since Brit made her presence known. She picked up her chopsticks and plucked a piece of salmon, dipped it in wasabi-laced soy sauce, and popped it into her mouth. The salmon tasted fresh and clean, but she had no interest in another bite.

Skylar had a pleasantly uneventful weekend. She only worked a half-day on Saturday and spent the rest of the day lounging by her pool. She finally felt like she could relax. Brit had not called, shown up, or communicated in any way. Skylar slept a whole night without sleeping pills and awoke Sunday morning feeling refreshed and contented. She even made herself breakfast—an omelet with wheat toast and fruit—fed Sesame and showered.

After scooping Sesame's litter box and reloading her automatic feeder for the day, she and Clay went hiking in Red Rock Canyon, a place where Skylar often turned to center herself. Clay was in a talkative mood, chattering on about his work week.

"Did you hear about Sal's new love interest?" he asked, as they began the six-mile Calico Hills trail.

"Sort of," Skylar answered, picking up the pace. The mid-day sun glared down through a cave-like canopy of rocks, and she adjusted her baseball cap. "Maud somebody, right?"

"Yeah," he responded. "Maud Jansen. I had to cater a

last-minute brunch up in Sal's suite so he could impress her. He wanted caviar and chilled vodka, crab benedict, you know—the works."

Winded, Skylar slowed her pace. It struck her with a disquieting revelation that Maud Jansen was a Dutch name. "Did you see her?"

"No, but there was evidence of a woman everywhere. You know, empty champagne glasses with lipstick on the rims, signature hotel robe lying on the floor. Couple pieces of lingerie scattered on the bed."

"Gross," Skylar commented, her pulse increasing with every step. They were going uphill. "James was telling me about her at lunch yesterday. Where do you think she came from?"

"Stop," Clay said with awe in his voice. "You went to *lunch* with the Monarch?"

Skylar rolled her eyes. "Oh, Clay, it was cringey. I had the worst day. The models didn't show to the Marco Ricci meeting, so I had to wear the skimpiest uniform on stage in front of everyone."

"I heard," he responded, with an apologetic grin. "My new banquet manager has the hots for you. I only hired him a few days ago, but sweetie, he sure noticed you right away. You two should hook up."

She grimaced. "I don't think so." *The last thing I need is attention from some banquet manager who works for Clay.*

"What did the Monarch say when he saw you dressed like that?" he asked, a lascivious wink to his tone.

"Nothing. They made him wear the men's uniform—flashy sequined tux." Skylar shuddered, thinking back to the shameful experience.

"I'll bet he looked hot!" Clay exclaimed, rubbing his palms together. "Wish I could have been there to see that."

"Never mind," Skylar said. "The whole thing sucked. But James and I had lunch afterward at Suki."

Clay gasped and gave her arm a playful swat. "You mean you cheated on me at *our* restaurant with the Monarch?"

"I would have much rather had you as my lunch date, trust me." She paused to catch her breath. "Anyway, James told me Sal's dropping loads of cash to keep his new girl happy."

Clay stopped to adjust his polo shirt. "At least you didn't have to have lunch with *her*."

"Tell me about it." Skylar's feet skidded in the dirt as she walked. They were on the downhill part of the trail, sandwiched between blankets of dense foliage. She worried that her favorite running shoes, with their extra width and cushioning, might get dirty. They were the only comfortable shoes she owned. "But I'm so curious as to how Sal met this woman." She was having terrible difficulty controlling her paranoia that Brit was in some way involved.

"You know how he works," Clay replied. "He goes for young, blonde, and hot—the younger and hotter the better."

Clay was right, and that was the only fact comforting her. Brit was *anything* but young and hot. She was haggard and unkempt. "Let's talk about something other than work."

"What else *is* there?" he asked, laughing.

"Let's go on vacation," she suggested, smiling wistfully. "Somewhere fun—a place where we can forget about work."

"Sure," he said. "Why not?"

Skylar stopped walking and grabbed Clay's hand. "I'm serious. We never do anything but work and go out to eat.

And when we eat, it's mostly at work, and all we talk about is work. *Work, work, work.*"

"That's not true," Clay protested. "We eat off-campus all the time."

"Yeah, but it's still *here*. It's still in *Vegas.* I want to go to a place where no one knows or cares who I am."

Clay suddenly stopped. "Sky, is your mother still around? I mean, did she ever try to contact you again?"

Skylar thought back to her last meeting with Brit and realized she hadn't even filled Clay in since they had dinner at the Peppermill. She wondered if it was worth bringing up now. Brit had somehow disappeared, and that was a good thing. Skylar was superstitious. She couldn't shake the fear that the moment she mentioned Brit's name, the bitch would suddenly appear with escalated harassment—a jinx of sorts. "Not really," she answered.

"What's that supposed to mean?"

"It means I'd rather enjoy my walk with you and not let that woman's bad Karma enter our serenity." She paused and turned to Clay. "Promise you'll go on vacation with me."

He laughed. "Okay. I promise."

Skylar smiled and felt a surge of euphoria as they walked side-by-side, picturing herself free to roam a city where she could be completely anonymous—totally herself—free from the Kellers, free from work shenanigans and, most of all, free from Brit. She imagined waking up in a cruise ship cabin with nothing but the vast blue ocean surrounding her. She would bask in the fresh, clean sheets of the cabin's bed, wearing a white cotton nightgown instead of baggy flannel pajamas, feeling the warm, moist embrace of the Caribbean air envelop her. She would sleep as late as she wanted. She envisioned a breakfast tray delivered, with hot coffee and freshly squeezed orange juice. She smiled at the image of a private butler peeling the oranges with a sharp knife. That's when the image came to mind, and she tried to block it: *The knife. Waking in that apartment, naked and alone on a cold, hard stone floor. Her head was throbbing as she tried to sit up in a pool of warm, slippery blood that had just started to coagulate into sticky patches. A bloody knife lying next to her along with that man's naked corpse.* She felt a knot in her stomach and tried in vain to paint an imaginary black X over his face. But it kept coming back.

Chapter 3

onday came quickly, and Skylar got to work a little earlier. The truncated Saturday made her feel as though she had somehow fallen behind. She sifted through hundreds of emails and stopped on one. It was from Maud Jansen, a name that had already reached infamy, even though most of the senior staff had not yet met her in person.

She clicked on it and read, *"Hi Skylar. I'm Sal's new girl. He said you were the one I should share my marketing ideas with. Please give me a call when you get this email. I'd love to set up some time with you. Best, Maud Jansen."*

Skylar sat up in her chair. *Great.* She was on this idiot's radar already. *Everyone's a closet marketing expert.* She grabbed the phone and keyed in James's extension.

"Good morning," he answered.

"I *thought* it was."

"What happened now?"

"Sal's girlfriend sent an email to meet and share her marketing ideas. Naturally, at the request of Sal."

"Then why are you calling me?" he quipped. "You know how to handle it, yeah?"

"I thought that woman was *your* responsibility," Skylar complained.

"As long as Sal's our customer, she's everyone's responsibility. Come on, Skylar, you know how this works. She's going to be an utter pain in the arse until he moves on to the next one."

He was, of course, right. She would have to suck it up and meet with Maud. "Will you at least be at the meeting?"

James chuckled. "Why would I do that? So far, she has no bloody clue who I am. I'd like to keep it that way."

Skylar ignored his comment and clicked into her calendar. "What are you doing today at four?"

"Having my casino staff meeting, like I always do on Mondays."

"Let's make it 5:30 then. I'll have her meet us at Cork Wine Bar."

"Are you buying me a cocktail?" He sounded amused.

"I'll buy you anything you want to get this woman off my back."

"Fine," he said before hanging up.

Skylar turned to her emails and began typing.

"Hello, Maud. Thank you for your email. I'm happy to meet with you. How about 5:30 p.m. at the Cork Wine Bar located in the center of the casino? I'll be with my senior vice president of casino operations. He's technically the point person for all of Sal's requests."

She read the email and then removed the last two

sentences. *She doesn't need to know I'm bringing James.* She signed it, *Skylar Van Ness*, and hit send.

Skylar gathered her things around 5:15, intending to go straight home as soon as she finished meeting with Maud Jansen. She ran into Sebrina in the ladies' room, brushing her teeth. Sebrina wore hard plastic retainers and was always brushing her teeth and flossing.

"How's it going?" Skylar greeted, rummaging through her handbag for lipstick. "I haven't seen you all day."

Sebrina was now spitting the toothpaste, hands grasping for paper towels. When she had wiped her mouth sufficiently, she turned to Skylar. "I've been busy revising the media plan for Marco."

"What does he want to change?" Skylar softly tapped her full lips with the slanted edge of the lipstick.

"He wants a billboard near the airport."

"I hope he knows how expensive they are," Skylar replied, pressing her lips together to blend the rose-colored lacquer.

Sebrina let out a chuckle. "He acts like he has more money than God."

"But we pay for the marketing," Skylar reminded. Then she had a thought. "Will you do me a favor and call me at 5:45?"

Sebrina gave her a puzzled look.

"I have a meeting I'd like to keep short, if you know what I mean."

Sebrina glanced at her watch and then nodded. "Sure."

"Thanks." Skylar dropped her lipstick into her handbag, gave Sebrina a little wave, and exited.

She found James in a light gray suit and red tie, leaning against one of the backlit columns near the casino entrance. James always seemed a little uncomfortable in a suit. He was what Skylar would describe as lean, but not skinny. He didn't work out in the gym like most men she knew. He talked about playing soccer on the weekends. He was typing on his phone with a slight smile curling the edges of his lips. Skylar knew that look. It had to be a love interest. He didn't look up as she approached. He didn't notice her presence at all until she said loudly, "Hello, James."

He jumped a little and then pocketed his phone. "Sorry."

"I'm guessing that wasn't a doom scroll," she commented, recalling Clay's remark about how he couldn't believe James was still single.

He didn't respond.

Skylar never considered that James might be embroiled in a steamy love affair. She tried to picture him at home, wherever he lived. She realized then she knew little about James, even though she saw him and talked to him almost every day. James could live right on her street, and she wouldn't know. She imagined him parking a fancy BMW in his garage, entering his house, shrugging off his jacket, and his girlfriend there to greet him. Skylar tried to imagine what kind of woman James would be into. She pictured a young woman giving all-American vibes—perky with dark hair and green eyes. Probably highly educated with a solid career and money—someone who grew up in a beautiful neighborhood, went to expensive schools, and was surrounded by loving friends and family. That was the kind of woman James would date, she decided. She wondered whether he had been texting her to plan a romantic evening.

Everyone in Skylar's world had a romantic partner. Even this Maud character.

"How's your day?" she asked James.

"Better now," he answered. "Looking forward to a fine glass of Cabernet courtesy of your comp code."

Skylar smiled and studied his profile. He always walked with his chin up a bit, which added to his cocky gait. "You can have as many as you want, as long as you stay for the whole meeting."

When they reached the Cork Wine Bar, James held the glass door open for Skylar. They entered the softly lit bar, which resembled a wine cellar.

"Do you know what this woman looks like?" James asked.

That had not occurred to Skylar. Neither of them had met Maud.

Skylar approached the host with James in tow. "We're looking for Maud Jansen. Is she here?"

The host pointed toward the bar. "The one with the hat."

Skylar's eyes ping-ponged around until they settled on a woman's back. She wore a black, wide-brimmed hat with long blonde hair spilling over her shoulders. She had what looked like a martini sitting in front of her.

Skylar pointed toward the woman and whispered to James, "I think that's her."

James and Skylar approached, and Skylar tried to catch a glimpse of her face in the bar mirror, but the woman had the hat pulled low over her eyes and was looking down at her phone. Skylar stood next to her at the bar. "Excuse me, are you Ms. Jansen?" she asked.

She almost fell to the floor when the woman turned

to face her. *It's Brit!* Brit with a dramatic makeover. Her face was taut as a drum; her lips plumped with filler. Her blue eyes shimmered under expertly applied eyeshadow, liner, and mascara. Her lashes were obvious extensions, as was the long platinum hair. She smiled, and her teeth were bright white.

"You must be Skylar," she said, tipping her hat and beaming with pleasure. She stood, and Skylar observed an expensive-looking, snug black dress. She thought she had seen it hanging in the window of one of the designer shops within Donovan. The midi-length dress with long, elegant sleeves and a ballet neckline revealed Brit's collar bones and elongated neck.

Skylar was speechless, standing, staring at the new, much-improved Brit Van Ness. She tried to piece together how this happened. Brit had obviously discovered Sal Vincenzo in the casino, hit on him, dazzled him in bed with her peep show maneuvers and whatever other kink of the moment Sal was into, and used him to reinvent herself as Maud Jansen. Then she connived her way into a meeting with Skylar. *Thank God I didn't come alone.*

She felt James tap her shoulder. "Are you going to introduce us?"

She snapped out of her daze and remembered why they were there, giving her mother a fake smile. "Of course. Ms. Jansen, I'm Skylar Van Ness, and this is my colleague, James Monarch."

"It's a pleasure to meet you, Ms. Jansen," James said, thrusting his hand forward.

Brit shifted her attention to James and took his hand. "The pleasure's all mine. Call me Maud."

Skylar's heart raced, and her breathing became difficult and uneven. *What is this about?* She rifled through her thoughts, trying to find the right way to deal with Brit. Of course, this was not surprising. She even saw it coming—knew Brit was involved—she just didn't know how. Brit had spectacularly one-upped her. She had entrapped Sal, and Sal held all the cards. Sal had enough power to get them all fired. And Brit had to have known that. *Damn!*

James was seeking a table for their meeting. While he circled the room and was temporarily out of earshot, Skylar's eyes deadlocked on Brit's. It was like a game of chicken, and the two were barreling toward each other at breakneck speed. If one of them didn't swerve, they would collide head-on. Skylar decided she would not swerve.

"Just what do you think you're doing?" she demanded.

Brit gave a mock surprised look. "Well, Skylar, you didn't give me any choice. What was I supposed to do? Wait around for my husband to show up? I'm out of money, and as I'm sure you know, this hotel isn't cheap."

"So, you thought you'd use Sal until my dad comes back from his honeymoon, and you can blackmail him?"

She laughed, revealing her freshly polished whites again. "You'd do the same thing, and you know it. You've always been a crafty girl." She picked up her martini and took a sip. "Tell me, lovely daughter, why aren't you drinking vodka? I know how much you enjoy it." She leaned toward Skylar. "Come on, have a little drink with your old mom."

Skylar's stomach pitched uneasily. *How would Brit know how much I like vodka? Was she spying on Clay and me at the restaurant the other night?* "You're not going to get away with this," she intoned, anger simmering.

Brit shrugged. "Watch me."

James reappeared. "Ladies, I have a table for us."

Skylar followed James, and Brit carried her half-empty martini close behind.

When they reached the table, James turned to Brit with a smile. "Maud, I see you already have a cocktail. Skylar, what would you like?"

"Mineral water for me," she replied, not taking her eyes off Brit.

James waved his hand for a server and ordered a Cabernet for himself and water for Skylar.

Once seated, Skylar gave Brit a serene smile. "We've heard so much about you. You must be very important to Sal. Tell me, how long have you two been dating?"

Brit's smug grin disappeared. "Long enough."

Skylar continued to twist the knife. "Well, it sure seems serious. Maybe you'll be shopping for diamond rings soon. I know a jeweler in town who'll make you whatever you want. We've known Sal a long time, Maud. He's never satisfied with anything but the very best."

Brit adjusted her chair so that she was closer to the table, all the while glaring at Skylar. She picked up her martini and took a large sip.

Skylar glanced at James, whose eyes fixated on her. His expression had darkened into perplexity.

"In fact," Skylar continued, "my father's the chairman and CEO of this hotel. He just married the love of his life, and you wouldn't believe the diamond he bought for her. And, you know the saying, 'a diamond is forever.'"

Brit cleared her throat loudly. "I doubt Sal and I are that far down the road," she said through clenched white veneers.

James let out an uncomfortable laugh and turned to Brit. "I hope you're enjoying our hotel. Sal has nothing but glowing things to say about you," he said, stealing a sideways glance at Skylar.

"Speaking of glowing," Skylar interjected, "you and Sal just missed the wedding of the century. I wish you both could have seen my new mom in her wedding dress."

"New mom?" Brit repeated. Her generous Botox injections staved off a scowl.

"Yes," Skylar beamed. "I mean, technically, Max is my stepmom, but since I've never had a *real* mom, I made her mine. I loved Max the minute I met her—10 years ago." She smiled and turned to James. "Can you believe they've been together that long?"

James was now frowning, mouth jutted open. He ran his fingers through his untamed hair and leaned in. "Maud, you look familiar. Have we met before?"

Brit sipped her martini and shrugged. "Maybe."

James gave her one of his stylish grins. "Well, we heard you're interested in some of our marketing efforts."

Skylar's phone chimed loudly from inside her purse, and she whipped it out and read the screen. "I'm so sorry, but I have to take this." She stood and said to James, "It's my dad, would you mind finishing up with Maud?" Then she dipped a smug grin at Brit. "Such a pleasure meeting you." And she was off.

Skylar flounced out of the Cork Wine Bar and made her way through the casino straight to the executive parking garage, ignoring her poor, screaming toes. She quickly found her car and sped away, toward home.

She had barely reached her driveway when her phone rang again. This time it was James.

"What the hell happened to you?" He sounded furious.

"I hadn't talked to my dad since he left for Bali." That was the truth, but Skylar was contemplating whether to concoct a lie to satisfy James. She had to remember James would be jealous that DJ called her and not him, even though she was his daughter. She sighed at the absurdity of the whole situation.

"What did he say?"

"Just family stuff, James. Nothing about work." DJ had not communicated with anyone that she knew of, except for texting Craig beach photos.

"Are you still in your office?" he asked.

"I'm not." She entered her house from the garage and saw Sesame sleeping on the living room floor. She stretched and yawned at the sight of Skylar, who suddenly wished she were a cat. "Why?"

"I was going to stop by and talk to you about Maud."

"You mean to pass along her expert marketing advice?" Skylar kicked off her heels and felt the plush delight of her feet sinking into the carpet. "No, thank you."

"You can't avoid her forever," James said. "And what the hell was up with all that marriage crap? You know bloody well that relationship is new. And *quite* temporary."

"Oh, I thought they were a serious couple. Weren't you the one telling me how Sal's using his comps on her everywhere?"

She heard him inhale deeply and then exhale into the receiver. "Skylar, I don't know what you're trying to pull, but she's important right now because Sal's important to our business every day."

She felt her face burning. "I'm aware of Sal's importance."

"Then do your job." James sounded like he was about to burst into flames.

"What's that supposed to mean?"

"It means take your spoonful of shit from this woman until Sal moves on."

The line went dead.

That was it. Skylar had pissed off the almighty Monarch. She pictured his exasperated face. She'd seen it many times. James had a hot Irish temper. And she hated to admit this, but when James got angry, he was gorgeous. His eyes became opaque, pools of dark navy, almost black, and his cheeks barely flushed. His mouth closed into a tight, crooked line, and his square jaw clamped shut.

Later that night, Skylar circled her kitchen, mulling over the events of the day. Maud was really Brit. Brit was out to destroy her. And DJ had no idea.

Sesame cozied up to her legs and rubbed against her. She knelt to pet the cat. "Sesame, what am I going to do about this crazy woman?" Sesame looked up at her with loving eyes. Skylar began massaging behind her ears. "You know better than anyone how to play these cat and mouse games, right?" Sesame just purred.

Skylar stood and turned on her Sonos system. She cranked up "Supersonic" by Oasis and paced back and forth, trying to piece together a new plan of action. James was right. Maud would not go away as long as Sal kept her around. Skylar couldn't avoid her. She absentmindedly opened her freezer and spied the unopened bottle of vodka—her emergency stash. She hadn't touched it in years. But it somehow comforted her that the bottle was there. She stared at the silver letters on the elegant lavender label. *Why is it that booze is so lovely in theory, and the advertising makes it look so glamorous?* The images were always of beautiful people, in beautiful clothing, in some exotic place—all smiles—all romantic. No one ever showed the ugly reality involving impaired judgment, regrettable decisions, and the inevitable hangover the next morning.

She remembered how she felt when Clay shared his martinis. She reached in and stroked the bottle at its neck. It was frosty and moist to her touch—alluring. Just as she was about to yank it out of the freezer, her doorbell rang.

She slammed the freezer and grabbed her phone to see who was on her home camera. A picture of her front porch came up. A car was speeding away.

Skylar hastened toward the door and flung it open. There sat a large bouquet of red roses. She snatched up the bouquet and carried it into the house.

She had no idea who would send her flowers. It was such a rarity. *What month is it?* She cringed at having to look at her phone. *Still February.* Maybe it was a late Valentine's gift. *But from who?* She took a deep breath, grabbed the card tethered to the roses, and tore it open.

> *"Roses are red,*
> *Violets are blue*
> *A man is dead*
> *All because of you*
> *Love, Your Real Mom."*

Chapter 9

The next morning, Skylar slid into her white Mercedes Roadster. She rarely drove with the top down on the way to work because she didn't want to mess up her hair. But today was different. She needed as much fresh air as possible.

Last night had been vicious. After Brit's dramatic overture, Skylar checked her door camera to see who had placed the flowers. Whoever delivered them had shone a light directly at the camera to obscure the view.

She was so exasperated that she went directly for the emergency vodka. It stung her throat as she quaffed shot after shot. She had finished half of the bottle before passing out on the couch. She awoke to the glaring kitchen lights and Sesame licking her hair. She couldn't figure out whether to be ashamed or angry. This morning, she just felt hungover.

She intentionally chose a fiery red long-sleeved shift

dress with tall black Louboutin pumps. The red soles matched the dress. Red gave her the confidence to deal with reality. She knew it was false confidence, but she didn't care.

The wind whipped her hair as she sped down Desert Inn Drive, dark glasses shielding her eyes from the ruthless sun. She thought about the sly little poem with the red roses. Brit had now played her cards—she knew Skylar was a murderer. That night with that man—her pimp—who was now dead—was Skylar's deepest, darkest secret. The memory of him holding her down, tying her hands, feet, and torso, reducing her to a helpless, cross-legged ball, pounding her face with his fist while he brutally raped her—it was permanently engraved in her mind. *I had to kill him.*

She braked for a red light and then whipped her head toward the passenger's side. A burly man with shaggy hair and sideburns was leering down at her from a big truck. She gritted her teeth and, as soon as the light turned green, she growled, "Fuck off, asshole!" then gunned the engine at full force, cut off his rig, and weaved in and out of traffic to lose him.

She pulled into the executive garage and began the trek to her office. She couldn't imagine what was in store for her today. She had gotten so drunk the night before that her brain was foggy. She didn't even formulate a response plan for Brit. *That was so stupid, Skylar!* She berated herself repeatedly for drinking. She needed her wits about her to deal with the conflict.

As she entered the casino and inhaled nauseating cigarette smoke, Skylar considered diverting her path to visit Axel. She needed legal advice, now, more than ever. She glanced at her watch. Still early. She debated whether to go directly to his office. If she did, she would have to tell him the truth—show him the real Skylar. She would have to divulge her twisted past, which included prostitution and murder. *Murder!* She had always thought of it as murder, even though he would have killed her first. The knife had been meant for her. *I had to kill him.*

What started as a sick bondage game turned into a fight for her life. After pinning her arms behind her and securing armbinder straps over her chest, he went ahead with the sexual abuse and torture. When finished, he slashed the armbinder straps to toy with her before attempting to extinguish her life forever.

What happened in those fleeting moments after grappling with him was a blur. She had always thought the momentary blackout was her psyche's way of protecting her. She only remembered seeing him dead. She sneaked out of his unit unseen and found her way back to Brit's place. Later that evening, she saw him on the news. She stared, dazed at the television, seeing her dead pimp's photo, along with the story of him found stabbed to death in his apartment.

Three weeks later, holed up in her mother's empty dwelling, her dad found her. The Dutch authorities finally caught up with her because she hadn't been to school for so long. She had been eating old cans of sardines for sustenance because she didn't want to be seen on the streets—at least until after the murder had blown over a bit—buying food.

Then DJ entered her life and changed it forever. He

never asked about the bruises and cuts. He just took her home with him—took her to a kind doctor, who examined her, dressed her wounds, and recommended counseling, which Skylar refused.

Life with Dad was safe, but Skylar never felt like she had his full attention. He was constantly embroiled in his own drama. Living as Hendrik Van Ness for so long had locked him out of life and detached him from his emotions like some kind of sensory deficit chamber. Skylar was his daughter, born into an irreconcilable mess. He knew he had an obligation to raise her but had no clue how to do so. She ignored all the boundaries he tried to set, constantly getting into trouble, skipping school, sleeping with strange men; her father treated her as if she were too fragile to discipline. She knew he feared she would attempt suicide if he tried. He was probably right. She had certainly considered it. More than once. Even so, Skylar always saw DJ more as an older roommate than a father. That is, until Uncle Craig came into the picture and forced DJ's hand.

She recalled how her uncle regarded her—the awful, awkward, pitying looks that whispered, *"You're beneath me."* She was nothing like his wife, Jane, who sat enshrined in admiration, in a custom beach home in Malibu with her two towheaded sons. Their looks were a combination of Craig and Jane, which could go in only one direction: stunning. While Skylar considered herself attractive, she was the antithesis of Jane. She felt like she was playing the part of a tragic anti-heroine in a play that had no ending. She trudged in every day, feet throbbing in high heels that never fit. The painful heels were part of the façade—part of the act of being someone else.

That was what her life amounted to now. She tried in vain to wipe out who she was to become someone else. *Why?* To shed the fucked-up memories of her miserable childhood. She steeled herself and blinked back tears. She was still wearing black glasses, so no one could see her anguish. If she told Axel, he would tell Craig, Craig would tell Jane, Jane would tell Anabel—the story would round every corner of the Keller tribe. She made a mad dash for her office. *No. Axel will not be the one to help me now, or ever.*

By her second cup of coffee, Skylar started to feel more like herself. She had closed her door earlier to focus on returning emails. In the back of her mind, her next move with Brit percolated. She tapped away at the keyboard, slamming responses. Her mind was fine. She hadn't thoroughly polluted it with vodka. Not yet.

She thought about her conversation with James and realized she should make things right with him. It would be stupid of her to alienate James at this point. He was her only hope of diverting Brit while she figured out what to do.

She snatched up her phone and dialed his number, only to get voicemail. "James, it's Skylar." She paused to collect herself. "I … um … just wanted to touch base on some things. If you get a minute, please call me."

She hung up and stared at her computer screen, suddenly feeling weary about her life. Her eyes snagged on a framed photo of herself with DJ, one she kept on her desk but largely ignored. She was 22 and graduating from UNLV. She picked it up and examined it closely— DJ's earnest smile—his arm carelessly slung around her shoulders—his fingers grasping the sleeve of her scarlet gown. Her cap was cockeyed on her head. She studied her face in the picture, trying to remember what she was thinking—whether she was proud or happy, but her memory failed her.

There was a knock at her door.

"Come in," she called tentatively, halfway expecting it to be Brit with a fresh threat.

The door creaked open, and James poked his head in. "You called me?" He had a contemplative look in his clear, dark blue eyes, like he had spent the evening calculating his work options rather than pounding vodka.

"Oh, yes," she said, waving him in. She recalled his comments before he hung up on her—before she received Brit's evil bouquet—and before she turned to alcohol for comfort. It seemed like a world ago.

He stepped in and shut the door behind him. Skylar was surprised by his casual look: a black sweater over a white button-down and jeans. She had never seen him in jeans. She vaguely wondered what he was working on to make him dress so un-James-like. He caught her eyeing his clothing. "We started casual Tuesdays for the casino management team," he said, glancing down to observe his own outfit.

"Ah, that makes sense," she said. "Tuesdays instead of Fridays when all the weekend players arrive." The high-end casino guests appreciated the formality of suits and ties/dresses, and high heels among the staff when they visited—it made them feel important.

He took one of the chairs opposite Skylar. "What's up?"

She swallowed hard. "I'm sorry about yesterday."

He leaned back and pursed his lips, as though suppressing a grin.

"I'm serious, James. I shouldn't have left you there like that."

He cleared his throat. "I don't really know what to say—I got an apology from Skylar Van Ness." His voice had a smile in it. "I never thought I'd see the day. Apology accepted." He tilted his head and lowered his eyes to his lap, and Skylar got an up-close look at the natural blond highlights in his purposely disheveled hair.

"So ... what does our new best friend Maud want from marketing?" she asked just to slice through the awkward moment.

He shut his eyes and shook his head. "You won't believe it. She had an idea—has to be the worst idea I've ever heard."

Skylar sat upright in her chair, her blue eyes glued to James. "Go on."

"She thinks we should rebrand the Limerick Bar to be a Dutch theme. Wants it to be called 'Red Light District' with authentic peep show girls serving drinks and dancing on the bar."

"What?" Skylar rolled her eyes. Then her mind churned. *What the hell is Brit up to now?*

"Did you know she's from the Netherlands?" he asked. "I did a background check. She has an Amsterdam address, a Dutch passport, and a work visa."

Naturally, Brit has a legitimate alias. Maud Jansen was likely one she used regularly. And maybe that's why Axel failed to find a digital footprint of Brit Van Ness. Maybe she did what DJ had done—shed the Van Ness name for good. "Did you ask her why we would do such a thing?"

"Of course. She said she ran it by Sal, and they both seem to think authentic peep show girls will attract gaming customers." He leaned toward Skylar as though sharing a secret. "I don't get Sal's attraction to this woman. I mean, she's *slightly* older than his usual demographic, don't you think?"

Skylar was reeling. She imagined a troupe of Brit's cronies from Amsterdam giving lurid performances in the lounge. Then, when she realized they would all be about Brit's age, she was puzzled. "Did Maud say she was bringing the girls here herself?"

"That's the impression I got."

"Is Sal really in on this?"

James suddenly straightened in his chair. "In on it? For fuck's sake, Skylar, he's the one who sent her our way. Why do you think I was giving out last night?" He brushed his hand over his forehead.

Skylar bit her lower lip. "Did Maud give details? Like how many girls there are? Set list? Opening date?"

"Are you seriously considering this?" James glared at her, mouth open and eyebrows knitted.

"Hell, no! But since Sal's involved, we'd better give our best attempt at faking it." She leaned toward him, elbows on her desk. "How did you leave it last night?"

James crossed his legs. "I told her it was a branding issue. I politely asked her to look around—we're an Irish-themed casino, not a Dutch one. That's why I needed you there to back me up."

Skylar shook her head. "I know. I'm sorry. But a branding issue won't be enough to deter her. The only way to stop her will be bugging her with the details."

"What details?"

She leaned back and swiveled her chair from side to side. "Think about it, James. We're a Las Vegas casino. We'll put her through the typical Nevada Gaming Control red tape—permits, visas, *drug tests*. It'll be so overwhelming, she'll give up."

James suddenly grinned. "Or it'll take so bloody long, her shelf life with Sal will run out full stop. Brilliant."

She smiled and got to her feet. "Where do you want to start?"

James rolled his eyes. "Let's start with what'll take the longest: a contract."

Axel listened carefully while James explained their predicament. He twisted his pen around in his fingers, studying James' face while he spoke. James and Axel were hardly best buddies, but they put the business before their natural aversion to each other. The feud began when DJ brought James in during the rebrand of the Regal Oasis to Donovan. He gave James a long leash and high status because of his education and especially his Irishness. He had so many ideas—ideas that Axel often nixed or at least restrained because of adverse legal ramifications. James hated restraint.

When James said the word, *Amsterdam*, Axel shot an alarmed look at Skylar.

Shit, she thought. He's connecting the dots. *Axel is too smart to be outsmarted.* She glanced at James, who apparently hadn't noticed the change in mood.

Axel stood and walked around his desk to where Skylar

and James were standing. "Let me get this straight," he began, now avoiding Skylar's eyes. "You want me to draw up a contract with this Maud Jansen, for a lounge concept that will never materialize?"

"Yes," Skylar answered before James could. "It'll be a shell to delay the process. We don't want to offend Sal."

"If we draft a contract, DJ will have to sign it," Axel said in an even tone tinged ever-so-slightly with sternness.

"The contract will never be executed," James replied. "DJ shouldn't be involved. It's just to appease Sal until he moves to his next *session mot*."

Skylar had to muffle a giggle at James's use of Irish slang. She had by now learned the meanings of most of his phrases. And she knew 'session mot' meant *party girl*.

Axel blinked and shook his head. "I don't like it. If we're drafting a contract to be signed by both parties that we have no intention of honoring, we'll be acting in bad faith."

Exasperation stabbed Skylar in the stomach. "Look, Axel, this will never go further than a review of the shell. We won't let it."

Axel's eyes locked on Skylar's. "James, will you please give us a moment?"

James hesitated, then glanced at Skylar. "Since we're talking about Sal, I'd like to remain here for the conversation."

Skylar considered where the conversation was heading and felt her pulse race. The last thing Skylar wanted was to face Axel's scrutiny alone. But having James present meant the potential for an embarrassing revelation about her mother. She breathed deeply, praying Axel would respect her privacy. "It's okay," she told Axel finally. "James can stay."

James crossed his arms over his chest.

"Fine." Axel turned to Skylar. "How do you think Sal hooked up with Maud Jansen from Amsterdam? I mean, was he in Amsterdam lately? Did they arrive at the hotel together?"

Skylar studied Axel's demeanor. "I don't know. I heard about her through James …like I always hear about Sal's *acquaintances*. Most of them want to have a say about marketing. And they usually last two or three months, tops."

James nodded in agreement.

Axel shifted his focus to his office window, which overlooked one of Donovan's five pools. He sauntered toward the window and just stared out. Skylar softened her eyes and imagined Axel was Craig. He turned to the side and squeezed the space between his eyes with his thumb and forefinger. Both he and Craig did this when they were either staving off anger or thinking something through.

After a long, uncomfortable silence, he finally set his penetrating gaze on Skylar. "You were born in Amsterdam, and DJ ran casinos there for years."

Skylar knew exactly where he was going, and she couldn't believe he would betray her in front of James. But she chose to let him go further without a reaction.

"I mean, that's pretty coincidental. Could it be that either you or DJ knew this woman in the past?" His eyebrows furrowed.

Skylar drew herself to her full height and smoothed the skirt of her red shift. "Amsterdam is a big city. We don't all know each other."

"So, you're saying you *don't* know her?"

Skylar felt her cheeks burning. "Jesus, Ax, why are you cross-examining me?"

He shrugged. "I'm just trying to get to the bottom of this story. There's something off about it." He took a few steps closer to Skylar, so he was facing her. "Don't you think it's time we called DJ?"

"No, I don't," said Skylar. *I should have known he would balk at our plan.* "Sal is imperative to our business. We can all agree on that. James is in charge of Donovan in DJ's absence. James possesses a Nevada gaming license. His approval is enough to move forward."

"I understand," Axel said, light jade eyes darkening to a deep olive. "But DJ would want to know about any business decision that involves Sal Vincenzo."

"DJ knows all about Sal and his girls," Skylar argued. "He'd totally be on board with how we're managing this problem."

"Let's not speak for DJ," Axel answered, briskly tugging at the collar of his shirt—another Craig-like move.

Skylar and James exchanged glances, and Skylar noticed a slight flush inching up James's cheekbones.

"You're right, Axel, let's not speak for DJ," said James. "But with all due respect, Skylar's right. I *am* in charge of this casino and its players while DJ's out. He gave explicit instructions not to bother him unless it was an emergency. Now, write the bloody contract already."

James stormed out, leaving the door open behind him.

Skylar and Axel were left together, and silence filled the room again. Skylar started toward the open door.

"Wait," Axel called after her. "We're not done yet."

But she was already halfway out the door and bounding toward the elevator. She felt his eyes follow her as she fled.

Skylar spent the rest of the day in her office with the door closed. Her vulnerability, augmented by the hangover, had dissolved into a dull headache. She picked up her calendar and counted the days until DJ's return. He had already been gone for 10 of them. His scheduled return to the office was on a Monday—*11 days from now.*

She thought through her options. With Brit safely ensconced in Sal's orbit, there was nothing Skylar could do to control the situation. She was there to stay. The only way Brit was going anywhere was if Sal turned her out. She thought about Sal and his capricious behavior over the years. James was correct. Brit was way older than the prototypical mistress Sal picked up. She was also not a US citizen. Skylar again wondered what the legal ramifications were for a murder committed 15 years ago. Her mind went back to Axel. While she secretly enjoyed seeing James call him out earlier, she knew it wasn't smart to alienate Axel when she needed his help.

And James didn't know about anything Skylar was hiding. Axel only knew a part of it. She mentally berated herself for confiding in Axel. If she hadn't done that, he wouldn't be so suspicious—watchdogging her now. The only other person she had brought into the situation was Clay, but there was only so much he could do. And she certainly wasn't ready to share her criminal past. She kept going back to the murder and how Brit would use that against her.

She pictured herself getting handcuffed and dragged

out of the casino. She could be extradited back to the Netherlands to stand trial. *Then what? Prison?* She put both hands on her abdomen, which was now groaning with anguish.

The ruse to rebrand the Limerick bar as a Red Light district, with peep show performers, was bizarre on its own. But coupled with the idea that Brit might unearth that small population of insiders who were familiar with Skylar's background and, potentially, the murder, shook Skylar to her core. And she knew that's precisely what Brit wanted.

Skylar recalled the run-in with Brit in her office. *I want what's rightfully mine.* Obviously, she wanted DJ's money. She wanted to blackmail him into paying her off in some kind of settlement. Hooking Sal into her lair was her way of cementing her position.

But what if Sal could be lured away from Brit?

CHAPTER 10

The bath water ran hot against Skylar's wrist. She unhooked her smartwatch, placed it on the sink basin, and climbed into her wide-rimmed jacuzzi tub. She had stopped at the food store on the way home and bought tail-on shrimp with cocktail sauce and three fashion magazines. She placed the shrimp platter and a goblet of sparkling water on one side of the tub, and a fashion magazine on the other. She set her phone on the edge of the sink basin where she could reach it in an emergency. Then she turned up Beach House's *Bloom* album, an old favorite that filled her with relaxing, dreamy vibes.

She sank into the hot bubbles until she was neck-deep and took a few long, controlled breaths. If she could bottle this feeling—the feeling of a warm, blanketing cuddle of bathwater—and take it with her everywhere, she would. She inhaled the enticing scent of her favorite bubble bath—it was called "Sugarplum," but smelled like a combination of fresh vanilla and peaches. She badly needed a vacation, with or without Clay.

She pictured her dad and Max in Bali, toasting their nuptials as they overlooked the remnants of a searing sunset. Dad loved his cocktails, and it suddenly dawned on Skylar that maybe his love of alcohol was the one thing she had inherited. *Naturally, it's something bad for me.* But at that moment, she felt a tiny bit more connected to him. Maybe she *was* part of his family—of *a* family—some sort of continuum. She wished he had sent her even one picture, but he only sent it to Craig. *Why couldn't he have just added my name to the text?* Maybe he was trying to let her run the marketing department without tempting her to call or text him for advice. He did that from time to time. He stepped out of the loop when he wanted her to learn something. "The only way to grow is to do things yourself," was his mantra. She didn't want to let him down. She was a highly paid executive with significant responsibility.

She reached over and picked up a shrimp by its tail, dipped it in cocktail sauce, and bit off half of it, chewing slowly, as her favorite song, *Lazuli,* played. She forced herself to swallow and take another bite, even though she wasn't hungry. She dropped the tail back on the platter.

James popped into her mind. She found herself wondering what he was doing. She pictured him with that playful little smile he had while texting. Again, she pondered who he was with. He had to be with someone. Men like James didn't sit around alone. Waiting. And most men needed constant sex. She tried to remember the last time she had had sex. It was so long ago—several years. She had almost forgotten what it was like.

She closed her eyes and tried to block the stubborn image of James having sex with his fictitious girlfriend—the one she'd made up earlier. It wouldn't go away. In her mind, he slipped his hands around her waist, smiling his uneven smile. She had always imagined James to be intensely sexual, but not aggressive. She pictured him French kissing his girlfriend, hands wandering over her curves. Skylar fancied what it might feel like to comb her fingers through his stunningly messy hair. Her whole body sank deeper into the hot water, her mouth salivating in the mesmerizing trance of James on top of his girlfriend while she undulated beneath him. Skylar was now in so deep that she accidentally swallowed a massive gulp of bathwater and began coughing and spitting.

She sprang up quickly, water splashing in her face, just in time to hear her cell phone blast obnoxiously from the sink basin. She grabbed the phone and viewed the screen. It was Axel. He never called this late. She knew what he wanted, but she was in no mood to talk to him. She let it go to voicemail and climbed out of the bathtub, suds dripping down her body. She caught sight of her reflection in the mirror, noting the pallor of shame covering her cheeks—a shame that stemmed from her secret, forbidden thoughts about James.

***

Skylar padded down the stairs to her kitchen in a robe, carrying the barely eaten platter of shrimp in one hand, holding the banister with the other.

When she reached the kitchen, she set the platter on the counter and looked around, feeling a draft of icy wind whistle through her robe. The window above her sink was open. She tried to remember why she would have opened a window. She was in the kitchen earlier, prepping the shrimp platter and feeding Sesame. There was no way she would have opened a window. She slammed it shut and tugged the edges of her robe tighter. That's when she noticed the freezer door open a crack. She hadn't noticed that either. *What is going on?*

She opened the freezer and peeked in. A vodka bottle stared her in the face. But it wasn't the one she had guzzled from the night before. It was a new, unopened bottle. Much larger. The bottle's neck sported a lavender ribbon fastened to the top. The nape of her neck tingled as she grasped hold of the heavy bottle, wrenching it out.

She unfolded the card and read its message:

"Drink me. You'll feel much better. Love, Mom."

After double-checking every door and window in her house, making sure her front and back doors had been bolted, Skylar closed all the shutters and drew the curtains. She felt like a prisoner already, sequestered in her house like a sitting duck, waiting for Brit's next move.

Brit must have done an internet search to find the address. Skylar shuddered to think how easy it was to do a simple search and find out where anyone lived. Brit had somehow entered her home, violated her sanctuary, and planted a nasty barb—one intended to make Skylar question herself and eventually melt down. She imagined

Brit breaking in through the kitchen window and Sesame scurrying away to hide. *Sesame! What if she hurt Sesame?* The thought that someone could break into her house without getting caught and arrested made Skylar's stomach roil. The idea that Brit had sneaked in when Skylar was naked in the bathtub, fantasizing about James, gave her a shiver of humiliation and outrage. *I have to do something.*

She stared at her phone. She couldn't even call 911, because breaking and entering was a much lighter offense than murder. Even more perplexing was that Skylar couldn't get her mind off the huge bottle of vodka in the freezer. Any normal person would have thrown away the vodka simply because of what it represented, the card it came with, the person associated with it. But she didn't. She put it right back into the freezer. She headed upstairs to her bedroom to remove herself from the temptation.

Later in bed, alone with her thoughts, Skylar couldn't sleep. She tossed and turned and awakened to the sound of her alarm at 6 a.m. sharp. The start of yet another workday filled with Brit's psychological warfare made her head throb. Skylar hated to admit it, but Brit was wearing her down. She had her cornered. *There's no escape.*

She showered and dressed in a black wool pantsuit with tall, uncomfortable heels. Turning to examine herself from head to toe in the full-length mirror, she noticed the pantsuit hung a little too loosely. She was dropping weight, and not in a good way. *I have to eat lunch today, no matter what.*

The casino was humming with the usual chaos when Skylar arrived. She passed the Limerick bar and caught a glimpse of Brit, holding court with a group of young women she didn't recognize. Skylar almost jumped when Mila tapped her on the shoulder, materializing out of nowhere.

"Hi, Mila," Skylar said, putting her hand on her throat. "You scared me."

"You don't know what scary is until you've spent time with that woman," Mila retorted, pointing toward Brit. "Is this your doing? James said there's a contract in development for a lounge act."

Skylar caught a mouthful of cigar smoke as a man strode by. She coughed. "How much did he share?" She tried to remember what she and James had talked about since yesterday in Axel's office, and she realized they didn't get a chance to regroup. Axel must have come through with a contract, and James must have already given it to Maud for review.

Mila shook her head. "Nothing. But Sal insisted I give Maud whatever she wants. Did you know anything about this?"

Skylar sighed. "Yes, but we're certain …" She looked around and pulled Mila by the sleeve of her black leather jacket to an area where no one could overhear. "We're certain this will all go away. We just need to play along with it until Sal … you know, dumps her."

Mila drew in her chin and pursed her dark red lips. "I don't know how much time you've spent with Maud and Sal, but she's not going *anywhere*. She's a total skank, but I've never seen Sal so infatuated with one woman. Especially one that old."

"How do you know?" Skylar asked. "I mean that he's so infatuated."

Mila pulled Skylar by the arm so they could peer inside the Limerick again. "You see all those girls?"

Skylar took a closer look at the women surrounding Brit—all young, blonde, and top-heavy. "Who are they?"

"Sal flew them in from Amsterdam on his private jet last night. He had me comp the rooms. There are seven of them. All Maud's *friends*." Mila paused to check her phone. "We didn't have enough suites available for non-players, so I had to go to James for approval."

Skylar brushed her cheek with the back of her hand, and it felt warm. Brit was determined to move her ludicrous vision forward at lightning speed. "What are they doing in there?"

Mila shrugged. "Who knows? But those girls look underage if you ask me." She turned to leave, but Skylar stopped her.

"Wait. Didn't you check their IDs?"

"No, I just led them to a craps table and walked away," Mila said with a caustic grin. "Of course, I checked their IDs. Their passports say they're all at least 21." She glanced at her watch. "I've got to go," she said before storming off into the casino.

Skylar turned to take another gander at what was going on inside the Limerick. Brit lifted her chin and caught her eye. Skylar pretended not to notice and scurried toward her office. She had almost rounded the corner to the elevator.

"Skylar, wait!" Brit shouted from behind her. She was heaving and breathless.

Skylar stopped and turned to face her mother. "Hello, Maud." Her jaw clenched.

"Why hello!" She was smiling brightly and adjusting her black sparkly tunic. "You're a hard one to catch."

Skylar did not return her smile. "So are you. You're so busy rebranding our lounge. And yet you still have time to break into people's homes. I don't know how you do it."

The edges of Brit's lips tugged downward. "I don't know what you're talking about."

Skylar looked around to make sure no one was lurking close to them. "You're telling me you didn't send me two dozen red roses? Wasn't it you last night who broke into my house through a window and left a bottle of vodka in my freezer? The notes are all signed by you." She took a step forward. "Brit, why are you doing this?"

She frowned and shook her head. "I don't even know where you live. I didn't send any roses. Now, if you'll excuse me, I need to get back to my friends. They came all the way from Europe, you know."

Skylar gawked at her. "Who are those girls and why are they here?"

"Why, they're for Sal, of course." She winked at Skylar. "You know I can't hold his attention forever, which is why I needed backups. At least until your father returns."

So that was it. Brit promised Sal his pick of the young, Dutch litter. Her stomach lurched in disgust. The girls were imported for Sal's pleasure only, while Brit waited for the opportunity to extort DJ. She pictured a frenzy of breasts and buttocks tangled together in a fleshy heap.

"You know what we call that here?" Skylar asked, eyebrows raised.

"Oh, come on, honey," Brit said, waving her hand in dismissal. "You of all people shouldn't be surprised. And what do you think goes on every day in this casino? You think these are the first working girls to come around?"

Skylar leaned toward Brit, so their faces were almost touching. She stared into Brit's icy, blue orbs. "I may not be able to control what you're doing here, but you need to stay the fuck away from my home, do you understand?"

She took a small step back. "I told you I've never been to your home."

Skylar glowered at Brit, nails digging into her palms. *This is a losing game.*

"Skylar, this may surprise you, but I'd never do anything to hurt *you*." Her eyes watered beneath her heavily mascaraed lash extensions. "In fact, I'm the only one who's trying to help you."

"Help me … how?" Skylar watched in disgust as crocodile tears spilled over her mother's high cheekbones. "You think coming here to embarrass me and blackmail my father is *helping?* In what twisted cosmos?"

Brit sniffled and then wiped her face with the back of her hand. "Someday you'll understand." She looked around. "I'd better get the girls upstairs for breakfast. Sal's waiting." She turned on her heel and zoomed off. The back of her sparkly black tunic read "Director," in gold lettering.

Skylar shook her head and turned toward the elevator.

She muddled through meetings all day, vexed about the circumstances. Sebrina even brought up that she'd already heard a rumor about the Limerick rebrand. Skylar quickly quelled the rumor but was worried that word was already out. She would have to act fast before it hit the media.

She thought back to what Mila had said—how Sal was devoted to Maud. But he didn't know she was really Brit and that Brit had once been married to DJ. He didn't know she was conning him, like she was conning everyone else. But that could open a can of worms with Sal's loyalty to the casino, and Skylar couldn't afford to take any chances. With seven young Dutch prostitutes, Brit wasn't going anywhere. Her shelf life with Sal had just increased infinitely. Skylar knew she should call DJ. She knew Axel was right about everything. But now things had gone too far. DJ would be furious that she'd allowed Brit to stay, intertwine herself with their most valuable customer, and commit crimes at the same time. Skylar was DJ's daughter, but he would have to fire her anyway. And if he found out about the murder, he might even send her back to Amsterdam to face her criminal past. Sentimentality was not one of DJ's traits. *You're either in, or you're out.*

After work, Skylar sat alone at a bakery in Summerlin. She ordered green tea and a scone, even though she hadn't eaten all day and should be at a proper restaurant, having a balanced dinner. She sat scrolling through her phone, seeing several missed calls from Axel. He had left a voicemail, but she didn't listen to it. She just couldn't talk to him. Not yet. She wanted something concrete—to be able to tell him, with confidence, that Brit was leaving—that Sal had moved on. But that was wishful thinking.

"Come here often?"

Skylar looked up and saw Clay, who sat down across from her. He was a refreshing change of scenery with his big smile and neatly gelled hair. She grinned. "What are you doing here?"

"My new banquet manager suggested this place for a bite to eat. He's in the little boys' room, but do you mind if we join you?"

Skylar looked around. "I guess not." She needed Clay more than ever, even though he had no idea what she was going through now. "Is this the banquet manager we spoke about?" she asked, recalling Clay saying he had a crush on her. "Because if it is, I'm not interested."

Clay let out a huge guffaw. "Well, why don't you meet him first and then decide?"

Before she could reply, a man appeared at the table. He was around her own age and wore a simple white button-down shirt with black pants. Shaggy brown hair framed his thin, angular face with fair skin and a sharp, lightly freckled nose. He had large brown eyes. He was not at all Clay's type. Clay admired men like James and Axel—movie-star good looks with a blend of academia and ruggedness. This guy was what Skylar would call a semi-cute nerd.

"Sky, meet Evan Meyer." Clay moved over in his seat to make room.

The man smiled and held out his hand. "It's a pleasure to meet you, Skylar."

Skylar felt awkward. "Sorry, I don't shake hands while I'm eating." She looked at her untouched scone and felt her cheeks redden.

"That's okay," Evan said, lowering himself into the booth seat next to Clay. "How's your day?"

Skylar forced a smile. "Just great."

Clay rolled his eyes. "We don't have time to do our normal jobs with Maud Jansen in town. Did you know Sal flew in a bunch of her young women friends, and they're partying non-stop? He wanted his pool cabana stocked with something called *genever*, and a bunch of weird things like herring and pumpernickel bread. Lots of cheese, pate, and boiled potatoes."

"I think *genever* is Dutch gin," said Evan. "It's super strong," he added with a twinkle in his eye. "You ever had it, Skylar?"

Skylar thought back to the horrible sting of *genever* in her throat as a teenager. She had it the night she murdered that man. He forced her to take shots, and she obeyed him, just to make the liaison less repugnant. She did credit *genever* for giving her liquid courage in struggling with the man and ultimately knifing him to death. "I don't think so," she said finally. She looked around for the server. "I really need to get home. Got to feed my cat."

Clay's expression clouded. "Are you okay, Sky? You haven't touched your scone."

She examined her plate. "I'm not really hungry—Clay, you take it." She pushed her scone toward Clay and began gathering her things.

"I'll call you later," Clay said to Skylar, while Evan sat quietly watching her.

"Maybe we can hang out some time," he called as Skylar fled out the door.

When Skylar reached her neighborhood, she scanned the street with anxiety. In the back of her mind were the two incidents, one of which involved a break-in. The street appeared bleak and deserted as she sped up her driveway and into her garage. She hit the garage door opener to close the door while she was still in the car. *What if Brit is waiting in the house?* She no longer felt safe at home.

She emerged from the car and removed her spike-heeled pumps—they could serve as weapons. Her heart pounded as she opened the door and heard her security alarm go off. She quickly advanced to the alarm panel, punched in her code, and then tiptoed around the house, turning on the lights.

She unlocked and opened the front door. There was nothing on her doorstep. Relieved, she closed the door and locked it.

"Sesame," she called, cautiously approaching her kitchen, still clutching the heels. She found the cat curled up on the kitchen counter. "Hi, baby girl!" Skylar gathered the cat in her arms and held her close to her heart. "I've missed you." She kissed behind Sesame's head and inhaled her warm, heavenly scent.

She gave Sesame her wet food, then sat on the hardwood floor, crossed-legged, just watching. Sesame ate hungrily while Skylar massaged her aching bare feet, mind ablaze with thoughts of the quagmire she had plunged into. Her phone vibrated in her jacket pocket. She jumped. It was Clay.

"So? Do you think he's cute?"

She let out a nervous laugh. "Clay, if you like him, go for it. I'm not interested."

"He's straight, my dear. He was just nervous. Trying to impress you."

"He really shouldn't bother." She glided her hand down Sesame's soft back while the cat gobbled her wet food.

"Well, I thought you two hit it off."

She bit her lower lip. "Clay, you know I love you, but the last thing I need right now is a hookup. Especially from work."

"Sweetie, you should be dating someone—anyone. Listen, I know that guy's not the Monarch. Not even close. But he's cute, and he's all about you. You don't have to sleep with him but let him buy you dinner."

She sighed. "Listen, I need to tell you some stuff— serious stuff." She rose to her feet.

"Does it have to do with why you ran off earlier? I ate your scone, by the way. It was yummy."

Skylar cast an uneasy glance around her home, wondering whether someone was watching, listening. The eerie silence sent chills through her. She began turning on every light and checking windows and doors.

"Well?" Clay said. "Are you going to tell me what's going on?"

"Yes," she answered. "Hold on a minute." She wandered through the house frantically looking around for a safe place to have this conversation. She ended up in her walk- in closet, where there were no windows. Once inside, she shut and locked the door, then switched off the light.

"Are you still there?" she asked in a low whisper.

"Yes."

"Good. Clay, my mother is out to get me. She's been stalking me. She won't leave me alone until DJ comes back. She wants his money—says they're still technically married. She even broke into my house yesterday."

"Sky, what are you saying? And why are you whispering?"

"Because, for all I know, she's here now."

"What? You need to call the police."

She rubbed her temple. "Clay, it's much deeper than that. She's posing as Maud Jansen. She's living in Sal Vincenzo's suite as we speak."

"Oh, shit." He paused. "You mean *that* woman is *your* mother?"

"Yes, that's correct." Goosebumps covered Skylar's body as she spoke those words.

"Poor you! But you're right. It *is* much deeper. What are you going to do? I mean, have you told anyone else?"

"Sort of. James knows about her. But he doesn't know her true identity." She thought of all the missed calls from her cousin. "And Axel knows my mother was here trying to see me. He suspects something's up with Maud, but I've not shared the connection. He's hounding me to call my dad and tell him everything."

"Isn't that what you *should* do?" Clay said, fear in his voice. "I mean, I've seen your dad in action. He's going to go ape shit crazy if he finds out from someone else."

"Listen to me," Skylar said, feeling her heart bounce in her chest. "I know all about my dad's temper. The real problem is …" she stopped short, unwilling to let the words come out of her mouth.

"What? The real problem is what?" Clay sounded

flabbergasted, like his best friend was going off the edge and there was nothing he could do to stop it.

Skylar hesitated. "The real problem is, well, there was a crime. I … committed a serious crime when I was in Amsterdam. It was while I was a sex worker. I was never caught. But Brit somehow knows about it. She's the only one. She's taunting me—hoping it will get DJ back sooner, so she can collect the money she thinks he owes her."

Now it was Clay's turn to stay silent.

"Clay? Are you still there?"

"I'm here," he said slowly. "Whatever you did, don't you think DJ should know about it?"

Skylar gasped a big, shuddery breath. "Honestly, I don't think he could do anything, other than send me back to Amsterdam to deal with it."

"But you don't know that, do you?"

"I don't for sure. But I don't want to take that chance. Clay, what I did comes with a heavy prison sentence—there's no statute of limitations. And if *anyone* knew I was holding the title of vice president in Nevada, it could kill Donovan's business. The press alone would crush us. This is serious."

He remained silent for another full minute, but Skylar could hear him breathing.

"What do you want me to do with this information?" he finally asked.

"Just be my friend," Skylar said. "I just need you to be … my friend." Her voice faltered as tears welled in her eyes.

"I'm worried about you." He paused. "And no matter what you've done, I'll always be your friend."

Skylar smiled into the phone, a deep welter of sadness brewing in her throat. "Thank you."

CHAPTER 11

When Skylar entered the Donovan resort the next morning, she knew something had changed. The place was fraught with nervous energy—casino hosts shuffling around—pit bosses hovering over their stations—security officers at attention.

Skylar spotted Mila huddled with two of her male hosts. She approached, and Mila turned to her, visibly concerned about something.

"What's going on?" Skylar asked.

"You tell me." Her mouth tightened.

Skylar glanced around. "I don't know."

Mila cocked her head. "DJ's back in town. He's on his way from the airport now. Rumor has it, he's in a foul mood."

"My father?" Skylar tried to remember how many days were left of DJ's honeymoon in Bali.

"Yes, Skylar. Tall guy, long hair, hot head?" Mila looked at Skylar like she was an imbecile.

"Mila, I had no idea. Do you know why he came back early?"

"Obviously, someone fucked up royally. Just hope it's not you." She snapped her date book closed and stomped off in the direction of the host office.

Skylar made her way to her own office as though she hadn't just heard the news of DJ's surprise reappearance. *Why would he be back early?* The familiar nausea mixed with inadequacy gnawed at her gut. Her own father returned from his honeymoon and didn't even call or text.

Everything was silent when she unlocked and opened her main office door. She was always the first one there, but the place felt spooky. She wished that at least Sebrina or one of the others were there for moral support.

She opened her emails, and there was nothing from DJ or anyone else who might know what was going on. She picked up the phone to dial Axel, then hung up. She recalled the voice mail he left yesterday—the one she hadn't bothered listening to, and dialed in.

His already uptight tone was wound even tighter. "Skylar. I called DJ. He's on his way back. I didn't want either of you to be blindsided. Call me."

She sank into her chair and swallowed hard. *Axel is a narc.* DJ returned from his honeymoon to call her on the carpet. She didn't know what to do, so she sat returning emails, all the while glancing nervously at the clock.

Finally, her office phone rang. It was DJ's secretary.

Her pulse quickened as she picked up the receiver. "Hi Sonia."

"Mr. Keller is here, and he wants to see you right away," she said before hanging up.

Skylar grabbed her pen and notepad and gave a quick glance in the full-length mirror. She wouldn't have chosen a sweater dress if she knew DJ would be back. She would have worn a suit. He responded to her better in suits—it made him forget, for a moment, that she was his daughter and treat her with the same respect he gave every other professional. She adjusted the soft navy wool to smooth it out. She pushed the long sleeves to three-quarter length and started for DJ's office, toes pinching in tall Mary Janes.

DJ's office lobby was empty, and his door was closed. Sonia looked up when Skylar entered, and she just nodded toward the door. "You can go in."

Skylar slowly approached the door with a plaque that read, "Donovan J. Keller, Chairman and CEO." She twisted the doorknob and poked her head in.

DJ was facing the floor-to-ceiling windows in his mammoth office overlooking the Strip. Skylar could tell he had come straight from the airport by his dress: black jeans, moto boots, and a dark green pullover sweater. A herringbone tweed jacket hung asymmetrically from his desk chair, like he had angrily flung it.

Axel sat in one of the chairs opposite DJ's desk. The other chair that faced his desk held a two-foot stack of files. Sonia always piled his work on one of those chairs when he was out of the office. Axel-the-narc barely acknowledged Skylar as she entered.

"You wanted to see me?" she asked DJ. She knew better than to be familiar with him or even comment on his premature return. Even though his back was to her, she could feel his ire.

He slowly turned. His shoulder-length, blond mane fell

to one side of his face, as though he had just raked it with his fingers in frustration. His shadow of a beard was gray, and he had the beginnings of a mustache. The one thing DJ never did when he was off work for any length of time was shave. His gold-rimmed aviators had pink-tinted lenses. His face and neck were golden tanned from the Bali sun.

He sauntered to where Skylar stood. DJ was 6'3, but today he seemed even taller. He pressed his full lips tightly together. "I heard you've been busy these days," he said in his trademark rasp.

Skylar just stood there, robbed of words. She felt his eyes behind those pink lenses piercing through her.

His phone rang, and he swung around behind his desk and hit the speaker. Sonia's voice boomed, "James is here."

"Send him in," he rasped, with an icy glance toward Skylar. "Perfect timing."

A wary curl grazed James's lips as he approached where she was standing. The two stayed awkwardly in front of DJ's desk. DJ had a long, comfortable black leather couch on one side of his office, along with a matching easy chair with an ottoman. Skylar wouldn't dare sit.

DJ pulled a cigarette out of a pack on his desk and set it between his lips. Skylar knew he was trying to quit smoking. He had been trying to stop as far back as she could remember. Max couldn't stand his smoking, but he never quite got a handle on it—especially in times of stress. He lit his cigarette with a shiny gold lighter and began to pace his office. He stopped at his window, again with his back to everyone.

The cigarette smoke made Skylar even more queasy than she already was from not eating. She coughed and stole a glance at Axel, who was stone-faced, and then at James, who wore a neutral expression.

DJ turned to examine his well-heeled staff, took a long drag of his cigarette, and blew out a plume of smoke directly at them. "When I leave this place," he began, "I expect you to run it." He started pacing again, walking directly in front of Skylar and James, then turned and passed them, smoke swirling as he swaggered back and forth. "Running the place means you make every decision the way I would." He stopped in front of James. "Making every decision the way I would means you take care of this property, the customers, and our brand."

He puffed his cigarette, and another cloud of smoke gusted toward them. Nausea pelted Skylar's stomach in the form of a loud growl. *Glad I didn't eat breakfast.*

He paced by them again. "So, when I'm 9,000 miles away, and I get a call that my highly compensated executives went off half-cocked with our biggest player, well, you can imagine what went through my mind."

There it was. *Axel had blown the whistle on Skylar and James about Sal.* Axel had tried to warn Skylar, but she didn't answer or return his calls. She doubted it would have changed anything.

DJ crumpled his cigarette butt in a desk ashtray, removed his sunglasses, and tossed them on his desk. They clattered all the way across and stopped just short of falling over the side onto the floor. He approached Skylar and James again, arms folded across his chest. "Now, you want to tell me what the fuck's going on?"

James cleared his throat. "I'll assume you're referring to Sal?"

DJ's lips broke into a smile. "You're a damned genius, James. It's a good thing you went to Trinity. They sure taught you how to use your noggin."

Skylar glanced at Axel, whose eyes lowered to the floor. She knew he would enjoy watching James get the ultimate dress down. She felt the need to intervene on his behalf. "Look, DJ, in all fairness, James had little to do with this."

"The hell he didn't!" DJ shouted. "His name's on a contract to open a fucking lounge act in the Limerick."

Before Skylar could say anything, DJ interrupted. "And in what universe are you defending James?" he thundered. "The Skylar I know would rather see him eat shit."

Skylar winced before pulling her shoulders back. "Sal has a new girlfriend—she's from Amsterdam—Maud Jansen—and she convinced Sal that hiring authentic peep show performers in Limerick is a good idea."

DJ just glared, blinking, chin drawn in.

Skylar glimpsed James's expression quickly before continuing. "We've been going along with it because Sal is smitten with this woman. We had Axel create a dummy contract, so Sal would think we were moving forward. But we never had the intention of seeing it through."

"And what did you think was going to happen?" DJ asked, eyebrows raised.

Skylar took a deep breath. "I thought we could stall long enough for Sal to move on to the next bimbo in his lineup."

DJ pressed his eyes shut and shook his head. "For fuck's sake, Skylar. Do you realize the fire you're playing with here? Do you understand that Sal Vincenzo has the power to close our doors?" He was pacing again. This time, when he passed his desk, he slammed his fist on it.

Skylar jumped at the noise.

He focused on James. "You remember how we stole him, right? He has huge fucking influence over our entire VIP base."

"DJ, we get it," James answered calmly. "That's why we're handling it this way."

"You're *handling* it?" DJ looked incredulous. "You're not fucking *handling* anything, James. Why the fuck do you think *I'm* here? If you were handling it, I'd still be on the beach with my wife."

"You don't have the whole story," Skylar interjected, heart pulsing. "There's something else you should know."

He blinked his eyes at her. "Oh, I can't wait for the rest."

"Maud Jansen …" she hesitated. "Maud Jansen is really Brit."

"Brit, who?"

"My mother, Brit. Your ex-wife, Brit." *There.* Skylar had finally said it.

Axel cleared his throat, and James let out a barely audible gasp.

"The fuck?" DJ sputtered. "Brit is fucking *here*—in my hotel?"

Skylar drew in another deep breath. "Yes. She sent me an email on your wedding day. I ignored it, but she showed up the week after, in the hotel."

DJ's large, honey-brown eyes were incredulous, but his shoulders relaxed slightly. "Continue," he said in his rasp.

"She wanted to see me. I told her I was too busy, but she found me, anyway, having coffee in the Black Clover with James."

"Wait, what?" James interrupted, giving Skylar a befuddled look.

"The woman I said was selling cardstock—remember? When we did a signage walk through the casino?"

"I remember a woman who looked homeless. That was *your mother*?" He scratched his head. "That was Maud?"

Skylar nodded, shame searing her. It was only a matter of time before the entire sordid story of Skylar's life would be cracked open for everyone to see. A quick scan of the room told her she had dropped a bomb. James, Axel, and all her colleagues would soon know of her past as a sex worker. The only thing she would hold on to as long as she could was the murder. *Skylar Van Ness murdered her pimp in an apartment when she was 12.* Skylar could already see the clickbait headline, hear the quote echoing in her mind, as though it were on everyone's tongue and on social media. Mila, James, Sebrina—her whole gang would be eager to spread the gossip. When it came down to it, no one there was a real friend. Clay was the only human she could trust.

She turned back to DJ. "I got her out of there fast and took her to my office, where she explained that she's technically still married to you—that you never divorced her and that you owe her money." She paused to catch her breath.

DJ lit another cigarette, took a drag, and gently let the smoke stream out. "What did you tell her?"

"I told her she was lying. And I made her leave. I didn't hear a thing from her for several days—I thought maybe she left of her own accord—until we all found out she was dating Sal, under the alias, Maud Jansen."

DJ shook his head. "Un. Fucking. Believable." Then the question Skylar was dreading. "Why didn't you call me?"

Skylar felt her knees buckle. "Because I didn't want to ruin your honeymoon." *I sound like an idiotic child. Why did I just say that?*

"Well, congratulations! You did anyway."

Skylar let out a deep, heavy sigh. "I hadn't seen her since I was 12. You know that better than anyone. I had no idea she'd go this far, and certainly no idea she'd become entangled with Sal. She's so …"

Skylar looked around the room for help.

DJ frowned. "You can just say it, Skylar. She's too fucking old."

"She brought friends with her," Skylar admitted, now just wanting to free herself from the awful secrets. "Young Dutch girls—there are seven of them. They're staying in suites. Sal had Mila comp them."

"You've got to be kidding me," DJ grated. He turned away from Skylar and stomped to his desk, where he put out his cigarette. Then he sat in his chair and swiveled it from side to side, thinking.

Skylar stole a glance at Axel, who still wouldn't make eye contact. James's face had become fraught, but he didn't say anything or turn his attention to Skylar.

DJ's voice cut through the tension. "All right, everyone, sit. Sky, James." He gestured toward the black leather couch. "Time for a little family powwow."

The fact that he called her 'Sky' meant his tantrum was over. Skylar sat on the end of the couch, feeling lightheaded.

James's face tightened. "You want me to excuse myself?"

"No. You're a part of this family, whether you want to

be or not." DJ sank into the easy chair and hiked his feet over the ottoman.

Skylar and James sat side-by-side on the couch. Axel dragged his chair into the circle DJ referred to as his "living room." This is where they gathered on big casino nights, like New Year's Eve, for a joyful champagne toast. Today, however, there was no champagne toast and certainly no joy.

Skylar thought about the big bottle of vodka in her freezer. If there were ever an occasion to drink, today was the day. She tried to shake the thought out of her mind so she could focus.

"How many people know about this?" DJ asked Skylar.

"You mean that Maud is really Brit? Just the people in this room," she answered, purposely excluding Clay. No one else needed to know he was involved.

"You sure about that?" DJ asked.

Skylar nodded. "I haven't told anyone. And I don't think Brit has either."

"Good," he said. "Let's keep it that way."

"What about Max?" James had the balls to ask.

DJ released a deep, wheezing sigh. "One painful issue at a time."

Axel cleared his throat. "I think the first thing we need to establish is whether you ever legally divorced Brit."

Skylar's eyes tapped Axel's briefly. His expression was tinged with genuine concern.

DJ drew his fingers along his temples and closed his eyes. "Do you really fucking have to ask that question?"

He opened his eyes and turned to Axel. "I was once a lawyer, as you may have heard."

"But you never practiced, and you didn't study family law. How long were you married?" He didn't even flinch at DJ's impatience.

"Look, Axel, this isn't a deposition. I divorced the bitch, okay? I have proof, but that's irrelevant." He stood and began to pace his office again. "The real priority is getting her away from Sal."

Axel straightened in his chair. "No disrespect intended, DJ. I just want to make sure there's no company liability."

"The only liability here is losing Sal to another casino. So, save your interrogation."

James finally spoke. "If there's no legal issue, can't you just pay her to go away?"

DJ shot him a look. "Thank God someone came in today with a working brain. Yes, James. That would be the desired outcome."

DJ turned to Skylar. "You mentioned she brought women from Amsterdam?"

"Mila told me Sal flew them here on his private jet, and insisted they have suites. I saw them with her in the Limerick. They travel around in a pack—hard to miss. She knows that without them, her days with Sal are numbered."

"Nice. Snow White and the Seven Hoes," DJ muttered, scratching his chin. "So, she needs them to remain here. That's helpful." He stood and paced the floor again, stopping here and there to gaze out his window.

After a few silent minutes, he finally whirled around and addressed the group. "Folks, we need to divide and conquer. James, you arrange a dinner with Sal alone in the steakhouse. Tell him you want his input on a new high-roller suite we're building just for him. Get a couple of drinks in him and gauge his loyalty to," he hesitated, "*Maud.*"

James nodded. "What if he wants his posse with him?"

"Have Mila invite the seven hoes to the spa for free services—hair, nails, you know—girl stuff. Keep the cheap champagne flowing."

He glanced at Skylar. "Sky, you and I are taking the mother of the year to dinner … somewhere off campus. Position it as a friendly outing. Make it sound like you really want to see her. Don't tell her I'm here. Not yet."

He stood and examined his watch. "Let's synchronize everything to begin around 8 p.m." He scanned the room. "That's it."

The trio began to file out the door, but DJ stopped Skylar. He shut the door after Axel and James exited.

"Hey, you okay?"

Skylar pursed her lips. "Yeah." That was all she could muster. The truth was, she was reeling from the sheer humiliation of it all. Axel tattled on her. James now knew what a degenerate her mother was. Her fingers tightened, and her nails dug into her palms.

"Don't say you're okay when you're not even close." He ambled to his desk and lit another cigarette. "That had to have been weird. Seeing her."

"It was," Skylar said, recalling Brit showing her face for the first time in the Black Clover Bistro. "I'm sorry I didn't tell you. I'm sorry you had to come back early from your honeymoon."

"It's okay. I mean, it was stupid, but it's okay. That was a hard call, I know."

Skylar bit her lower lip. "What are you going to tell Max?"

DJ shrugged. "The truth. But I'd prefer to tell her after it's been taken care of. Or at least after we have a solid plan." He went to his wet bar and pulled out a bottle of scotch. "Want one?" he asked her.

"No, thanks." DJ knew Skylar didn't drink. *Why would he even ask me?* He had to be so preoccupied, he forgot.

"Look," he said. "We need to be on the same page tonight. Just follow my lead." He turned to her, scotch in hand, and drew a drag from his cigarette. "How much do you think it'll take to get rid of her?" He sipped his drink and leaned casually against his desk.

She thought about it. "I don't know, Dad. Probably a lot less than if she could credibly accuse you of bigamy. She's desperate. That's all I know."

He shook his head. "She doesn't have jack shit on me, Sky. I'm wondering what else she thinks she has, though."

Tingles of fear and anxiety flooded up her spine, but she said nothing.

"Okay. Let me find some hole in the wall for us to meet with Brit, so if there's a scene, no one will know us." He nodded his head in dismissal.

Skylar wanted him to hug her. She wanted so badly for him to tell her he missed her—that he loved her—that everything was going to be okay. But that was just not him. She obediently turned and exited his office.

CHAPTER 12

Skylar climbed into the company's long black limousine alone. The strategy was for her to meet Brit at the Crown and Anchor Pub on Tropicana. DJ would take a separate car and arrive shortly after Brit. Skylar objected to DJ's choice of the Crown and Anchor because it was too loud, but he insisted.

On the drive over, Skylar pulled out her phone. There was a text from James to both Skylar and DJ:

Sal's in a mood. Going to suggest a double martini.

Skylar thought about James and how much she had dreaded him knowing about Brit. She wondered what he would say—what he would ask when they were finally able to have a conversation. *Alone.* Her thoughts went back to the 'gifts' from Brit—roses and vodka. And her vehement denial of sending them. She prayed Brit would not say anything to DJ about the murder. She decided, although it made her stomach roil, that her best approach with Brit was to play nice. She had done the opposite, and it had only made Brit more aggressive.

When the car arrived at the pub, Skylar stopped at the entryway to the bar she had frequented many times during her youth—especially when she attended classes at UNLV. She slowly entered, eyes adjusting to the dim interior. The Crown and Anchor still smelled the same as she remembered—stale beer, vomit, and pine-scented cleaning solution. British flag pennants dangled in an endless stream along the ceiling of a backlit bar, and soccer memorabilia were plastered everywhere. The décor was a riot of chaotic trinkets donated by customers over the past 30 years.

Skylar was struck with a memory from when she was there with a college boy who had a major crush on her. A large chalkboard hung on the all-gender bathroom wall, and she recalled the boy sneaking in to write on it. She remembered being pleasantly surprised when she entered the bathroom and saw, "I LOVE SKYLAR" scrawled on the board. He used a heart instead of spelling out "LOVE." She smiled, realizing he was the last man she had briefly dated. Then he moved away. She caught herself wondering where he was now.

Skylar searched the bar but didn't see anyone—it was entirely empty, except for the service staff. She glanced at her watch. *This drunk tank for local college kids is never empty on a Friday night.* She found a four-top table, set her purse on the chair next to her, and sat facing the front entrance. She placed her hands lightly on the table, then recoiled when she realized it was sticky. *Gross!* She grimaced and searched her purse for hand sanitizer.

A cute female server in a short red plaid skirt and tight black tank sauntered up and handed her a menu. "You with the private party, hon?"

Skylar cleared her throat and examined the butterfly tattoos winding up the server's neck. Her name tag read, 'Sophie.' "Private party? That explains why this place is empty. I should let the rest of my group know." She fished her cell phone out of her purse.

Sophie smiled. "Is your name Skylar or Maud?"

Of course. DJ had bought out the place for the night, so no one could spy on their rendezvous. She nodded. "Skylar."

"Can I get you something to drink?" Sophie asked.

Skylar paused, recalling evenings at the large central pool table, quaffing Guinness on draught between shots of Jameson's. Skylar was glad the staff had turned over so many times; no one would recognize her from those days. "Just water for me. Thanks."

She perused the menu, which aptly consisted of bar food—chicken fingers, mozzarella sticks, fish and chips, and onion rings. *Better to soak up the booze.*

She glanced at her watch. It was already 8:15. Her eyes darted to the front entrance again. *Where the hell is Dad?* Her thoughts went rogue, and she imagined being stuck with Brit for an hour because DJ got distracted. She took a deep breath to try to tame her irrational feelings. *This is a priority. He has to show.*

"Yoo-hoo!" Brit chirped in Skylar's ear from behind, which caused her to jump out of her chair.

"Oh, hello, Brit." Skylar touched her chest. "I didn't see you." *How did she sneak up on me?* She'd been watching the front entrance the whole time.

Skylar watched as Brit took the seat opposite her. She had obviously been taking advantage of the VIP pool, because her face was crisply sunburned to a deep fuchsia beneath a white straw hat.

"Hi, lovely daughter," she greeted Skylar. "I was excited when I got your message. I don't know what happened to change your mind but thank you for inviting me." She scanned her surroundings. "This is an interesting choice of venue. You get tired of the high-end resort you work in?" She chuckled, then murmured, "This place is so dead."

Skylar glanced at the bar entrance, hoping DJ would get there soon. Before she could respond, Sophie interrupted with a glass of ice water, which she set in front of Skylar.

"Can I get you something to drink, ma'am?" she asked Brit.

Brit's lips cracked into a big grin. Her white linen suit jacket and pants matched her teeth. "I'd love a vodka on the rocks," she croaked in that cigarette voice. She added, "Make it the best vodka you have." She gave Skylar an expectant look. "You going to drink with me?"

Skylar forced a smile, thinking that Brit sure had acquired fine taste since she took up with Sal. "I'm good for now."

When Sophie the server left, Skylar leaned forward and asked, "How are you finding Las Vegas so far?"

"I just love it ... thinking of moving here for good." She picked up the menu and scanned it.

"Sorry, there's no caviar," Skylar muttered with a fake smile, considering what it would be like to have Brit as a neighbor. *How in the hell did this happen?* She again glanced at the entrance to see if DJ was there.

Sophie came back with Brit's vodka and set it in front of her.

She picked up her drink and did a mock 'cheers' to Skylar. "Skol!" she exclaimed before taking an extra-large slug.

Skylar saw the front door swing open aggressively. It was her dad. She watched, feeling sudden relief, as DJ sauntered to where they were.

"I heard there was a little family reunion," he rasped. "Didn't want to miss it."

Brit looked up and almost dropped her glass. "Hendrik!"

DJ ran his hand through his hair and pulled off his sunglasses. "Not anymore. I'm DJ now. DJ Keller. But you already know that."

Brit's eyes were glued to DJ's body as he tugged off his tweed jacket and tossed it on the open chair next to Brit.

"I heard you changed *your* name, too." DJ took the chair next to Skylar, turned it around, and sat with his arms draped over the back. "What was it, Sky? Mandy or something?"

"It's Maud," Brit said, a note of sarcasm in her voice. "Skylar didn't tell me you were joining. But I must say, I'm happy you're here."

"Knew you would be." DJ's eyes skimmed the room. "I'm getting a drink. Meet me over there," he said, nodding toward the opposite side of the restaurant. He sprang up and headed for the bar.

Brit's gaze followed him, and she licked her lips, tilting her head to one side. "He still looks good," she said under her breath, then turned to Skylar. "Why didn't you say he was coming?"

"Because I wasn't sure he'd show up." Skylar saw DJ leaving the bar area with a scotch in one hand. She shot up from her chair and trailed him to avoid being alone with Brit.

Brit slowly and reluctantly rose from her chair and followed, her tote bag in one hand, her vodka in the other.

DJ placed his drink on a small table. Sophie approached DJ and handed him a canister. "You wanted this?" she said to him.

He nodded, then winked at Skylar. "Talking's no fun without activities, right?" he asked Brit as she sauntered toward them cautiously. He opened the canister and plucked out three darts.

"It's been years since I've played," said Brit, eyeing the front-weighted, sharp, pointed little weapons.

DJ grinned. "Don't be so modest. Remember all the nights we spent in pubs just like this? You were always on fire." He raised his eyebrows when he said *fire*.

Brit twisted her lips to one side.

He held up the darts and dangled them. "Don't you feel a little nostalgic tonight, Mandy? It's been thirty years—just like riding a bike—comes right back to you." He gently pulled Brit by the arm to the line separating them, about eight feet from the dartboard.

She wrenched her arm from his grasp. "I said my name is Maud."

"Whatever," DJ said with a dismissive wave. "Let's play Cricket. If you lose, you get the fuck out of Vegas by morning. Take your seven hoes with you. Don't say a fucking word to Sal. Don't talk to Skylar. You just fucking move on. *Capisce?*"

She narrowed her eyes. "And if I win?" she asked with a vindictive smile.

DJ shrugged. "What do you want?"

"Are we negotiating?" she asked, unbuttoning her suit jacket and removing it. She wore a skintight white spandex shell with no bra. Skylar grimaced at the sight of her large breasts, squished into the top, dark nipples showing through the white fabric. Brit tossed her jacket on the table that held DJ's drink.

"You can try," DJ said, eyes not straying from hers. "What do you want?"

She put her hands on her hips and glared at him. "I want what I'm entitled to as your ex-wife of nearly 30 years and the mother of your only daughter."

"For fuck's sake, Brit. You can't be serious. You fucking abandoned your only daughter—left her in that shitty apartment while you screwed your way around Amsterdam."

"I *had* to screw my way around Amsterdam," she yelled. "You left me no choice—no alimony, no child support—no nothing!" Her voice echoed with false drama.

"The fuck I didn't—I paid you through the moment I took Skylar home with me," he snarled. "It's not my fault that money went up your nose and in your veins."

Brit's eyes bulged, and her mouth jutted open.

"But at least you finally admitted in front of our daughter that we were legally divorced." He picked up his drink and took a long swig.

Skylar felt lightheaded and grasped for a nearby chair to brace herself. This had turned ugly fast. She could barely fathom watching her two *parents*—the two who slept together to conceive her—go at it in such a brutal exchange. Nausea crept up in her gut.

"Look, I haven't got all night." DJ pressed. He inched toward her, his face reddening with each step. "Just tell me what the fuck you want."

Brit gritted her teeth. "I'm sure you don't have *all* night. You could barely get it up—as drunk as you always were. Does your new bride know you can't last five minutes?"

"I don't need booze with her." He gave her the once over in disgust. "In fact, seeing you now makes me wonder how the fuck I *ever* got it up with you."

With that comment, Brit picked up her drink and jerked her arm to throw it in DJ's face, but he ducked just in time, and it splattered all over the wall behind him.

Skylar jumped aside so she wouldn't get a shower of vodka.

"If that's any indication of how well you'll do at Cricket, you may as well book your flight. Now, you going to tell me what the fuck you want?"

"Two million should do it," she finally said.

Skylar did a double take. *Holy shit! Brit wants $2 million.* She turned her attention to DJ, whose face remained expressionless.

"Just curious. How did you get to that number?" he asked.

"One million for me to leave *and* one million to keep my mouth shut." She turned to look Skylar in the eye, again with the vindictive smile. "You know how important *that* is."

DJ's eyes strayed to Skylar and then back to Brit. "Keep your mouth shut about what?"

"Ask your daughter," she snarled, pointing at Skylar, who knew better than to say a word.

DJ handed the darts to Brit. "I would say 'ladies first' but …"

She set her drink and tote on the table and stepped up to the line.

Skylar stood slightly to the side and behind them, just watching, praying their tête-à-tête would end soon. She thought about Sesame and just wanted to cuddle her right then—to shut the world out—the ugliness of her childhood, the mess caused by these two people who didn't give a shit about what they were doing, creating, putting out into the universe. She wished she could disappear in some magical puff of smoke, like a Las Vegas magician.

Brit steadied herself and smoothed her white linen pants before throwing her first dart. It landed on the floor near the board. She made a face and braced for the next dart. It also hit the wall and fell to the floor. Her final dart did the same thing. "Shit!" she shouted.

DJ shrugged. "We're just getting started." He retrieved the darts and stepped up to the line. He eyed the dartboard and then his left hand, which held the dart. He lifted his chin and threw the dart in one skillful swoop, hitting the bullseye directly. He threw two more, and the darts landed on the small ring outside the bullseye. He turned to smile at Skylar. "Your old man's still got it."

Skylar could not return the smile. This was in no way pleasant or fun. She was seeing her parents duke it out, while she sat on the sidelines, freaking out about murdering that pimp. She had no idea how this was going to turn out. She wondered if she should take DJ aside and tell him once and for all what Brit had on her—on them. But her two aching feet were frozen and glued to the floor like a tree with deeply implanted, immobile roots.

Brit grew more aggravated by the minute. She pulled her phone out of her pants pocket and fumed while DJ retrieved his darts.

DJ frowned. "Oh, I'm sorry, Marilyn, Mandy, or whatever the fuck your name is. Are we keeping you from something? Your boyfriend, perhaps? Don't worry about Sal. He's fine."

She scowled and took a step back. "I don't want to play this game."

"Fuck's sake, Maud," DJ said, breaking into a grin. "You stole my line." He threw a dart, again hitting the bullseye. "Looks like you forfeited the game. So, you lose. I'll have Sonia arrange your flight home first thing tomorrow."

She struggled into her suit jacket, face purplish. She grabbed her tote and turned to DJ. "You can't make me go," she growled. "Sal won't let you. You forget *I* have the power here. All I have to do is say the word, and he's out the door. I know you can't afford that."

She took a step toward DJ and gave him a white-toothed sneer. "Your piddly two million means nothing to me. Sal drops that in the casino on a Tuesday."

"And what do you think Sal's going to say when he finds out you're just an old, washed-up junkie hag who's been conning him from day one?"

She smiled with defiance. "Who's going to tell him?" She snatched the remaining darts out of DJ's hand and turned to Skylar. "Here," she said, thrusting them toward her. "I've heard you're good with sharp objects."

She turned and waltzed out of the Crown and Anchor.

DJ threw his head back as he watched her leave.

Skylar's breath became shallow, as sweat trickled down her forehead. The nausea came next. Before DJ could say anything, she grabbed her purse and fled to the bathroom, locking the door behind her and dropping to her knees. She held her hair in one hand and vomited. Pure bile poured out of Skylar's mouth. When she finally purged her guts, she grasped the toilet paper roll, tore off a batch of sheets, and dabbed at her mouth and face. Slowly, she rose to her feet and peered into the mirror.

Her face was pale, and her mascara ran down her chin, creating two black streaks that smothered her face as though she had taken a face plant into a muddy gutter. She wet a paper towel and began swiping at her cheeks to remove the mess. *Time to buy waterproof mascara.* She dug out her lipstick and applied it, the sour taste of vomit lingering in her mouth. That's when she saw it ... the chalkboard behind her. At first, Skylar froze. Because she was looking in the mirror, the letters were backwards.

Her hands shook, and she slowly turned to examine the words, crudely etched in pink chalk:

Skylar is a murderer.

Chapter 13

Someone was banging on the door, but Skylar just stood staring at those four words, frozen in shock. "Sky, you okay in there?" DJ yelled. *Boom, boom, boom!*

She realized she'd been in the bathroom more than 15 minutes and grabbed the chalk eraser. She frantically swiped at the board. Chalk dust sifted through the air, small particles triggering a swirling pink cloud around her. She inspected the board for any remnants of her name and criminal act. Nothing was there.

DJ banged on the door once again. "Skylar?"

She took one last look in the mirror and tried her best to minimize her horrified expression. "I'm okay, Dad."

She took a deep breath and unlocked the door, opening it to DJ's troubled face. His long blond mane looked ruffled, as if he had jerked his fingers through it.

"You had me worried."

"I … um," she faltered, the powdery pink words still boldly sketched in her psyche. "I wasn't feeling well."

DJ patted Skylar's back, then rubbed it in his clumsy, roughshod manner.

Skylar relaxed slightly at the warmth of his touch.

He shook his head, lips pressed together. "I don't blame you. That woman's enough to make anyone sick."

Skylar stared past DJ into the dark bar. "Is she gone?"

DJ nodded. "Yeah, let's get out of here. I'll give you a ride to your car."

<hr>

The roar of DJ's Jaguar engine throbbed underneath Skylar's legs. She had not ridden in his car for months. She watched him shift gears, her body swaying with each turn. DJ was an aggressive driver who rarely paid attention to speed limits.

When they stopped at a light, DJ glanced in the rearview mirror, then at Skylar. "This is not your fault. You know that, right?"

Skylar's thoughts jumbled together like a collage of colored paints, swirling around on a palette. She could not stop thinking about the chalkboard, once a source of exhilaration—how she had discovered a boy's innocent crush—and what it stood for now. Brit was torturing her— bludgeoning her with the truth. *I have to do something.* She chewed her lower lip, tasting blood from a loose sliver of chapped skin. "Things would be so much easier if I weren't here," she blurted.

"What?" DJ tore his eyes from the road and glared at her.

Skylar met his gaze. "I just meant that … you know, if I

hadn't gotten involved with Brit and kept the information from you, we wouldn't be in this situation."

"Sky, listen to me," he said calmly, shifting gears to slow the car down. "Brit's a crazy lunatic, and she was coming after me anyway. I'm sorry you had to watch what happened just now, but it's not your fault. You can't help that she's your biological mother, just like I couldn't help that Luuk was *my* biological father. I mean, the guy committed murder for fuck's sake. We've got that bloodline running through us." He shook his head like he was freeing it of dirt.

Skylar's stomach lurched again. DJ was, and always would be, clueless about her feelings. She wondered how Max put up with him. His blunt, irreverent, and often vulgar style didn't bother her. In fact, she seemed more amused by his antics than anything else.

She pictured Max, beautiful in an understated way. Her oval, olive-toned face, with full red lips and large, clear dark eyes—always a stunning sight. Her thick chestnut hair hung neat and shiny, in a long bob. Skylar contrasted her with Brit—the new, improved version of Brit. At 40, Max was nearly 20 years younger than DJ and 15 years younger than Brit, but Max took care of herself; she ate a healthy diet and practiced yoga. It was clear Brit did no self-care, other than what Sal's money could buy. Even with the long hair extensions and facial injections, Brit still looked cheap, old, and decrepit.

"Dad, why did you ever marry her?" she asked.

DJ was pulling into the executive parking garage. He stole a glance at her but didn't answer. He was deep in thought.

"I mean, you knew she was a working girl, right?" she

pressed, thinking this may be the best time to have a conversation about her own past.

DJ pulled into his reserved space but didn't shut off the car. He sighed and turned to look her in the eye. "You want to get dinner? Sounds like you have a few things on your mind."

Skylar nodded. "Is Max coming, too?"

DJ shook his head. "She's at home. Just you and me tonight." He cut the ignition, got out of the car, and walked around to open the door for Skylar. She carefully stepped out of the vehicle, smoothing her navy sweater dress. The day had lasted forever, she thought as she followed DJ into the casino, feet throbbing to the point of numbness.

The casino was hopping with the usual commotion when they entered. Heads turned as DJ sauntered next to Skylar. He moved an occasional free-standing sign here and there and stooped to pick up stray cocktail napkins from the floor. DJ treated Donovan like it was his own home and urged his management team to do the same.

He led the way to Waterford, the fanciest restaurant within Donovan. They sat in a quiet booth near the back, and the waiter handed them menus. Skylar's hunger was so intense, she attacked the breadbasket, tearing off pieces of the crust and slathering them with butter before popping them into her mouth. She just stared ahead, blindly chewing, forgetting her dad was sitting across from her.

He watched her thoughtfully before leaning forward and gently laying his hand on her arm. "Hey, take it easy on the bread, Sky. You act like you haven't eaten in weeks. You want an appetizer?" He summoned the server. "Let's get some crab cakes, a couple of green salads, and …" he scanned the menu again. "And how about jumbo shrimp cocktail? I know my girl loves her shrimp." His expression was deadly earnest as he set the menu down. "Oh, and a bottle of Silver Oak. Two glasses."

"Dad," Skylar protested. "I don't want wine."

DJ shrugged. "You don't have to drink any." He leaned toward her. "Now let's have a chat. You were asking about Brit."

Skylar was so exhausted—she was having trouble remembering her questions. She took a long sip of her ice water. "I just wanted to know why you married her." Her mind was still swimming after the scene in the Crown and Anchor, and the subsequent chalkboard messaging horror. "She's not exactly marriage material."

DJ looked her in the eye. "It wasn't love. I can tell you that." He snatched a piece of bread from the basket. "I was in a weird place, Sky. You know the story."

Skylar thought back to the time when she only knew DJ to be Hendrik, and her grandfather, Luuk, was the only family she had outside of Brit. It felt so long ago. "Yeah, I know that story," she replied, recalling the murder of Luuk at the hands of her uncle Craig, after Luuk had kidnapped Jane and held her hostage in one of the suites within Donovan. Skylar could never imagine Craig, with his posh suits and glossy dark hair, a tiny sprinkling of gray dusting his temples, pointing a gun, and killing someone. The thought occurred to her that DJ was right. Murder was in her genetic makeup. She shuddered.

"At the time, I had nothing to lose," DJ said while he waited for the sommelier to pour the wine.

Skylar placed her hand over the mouth of her glass to show she didn't want it filled.

"But it was more complicated than that," DJ said, swirling the blood-red liquid in his glass, holding it up to the available light, and inspecting it. He took a sip and swallowed before continuing. "Way more complicated."

The server placed the appetizers. Skylar felt her mouth water. DJ must have read her hunger because he moved the shrimp dish right in front of her.

Skylar snatched a prawn at once and put it on her plate. She spooned some cocktail sauce onto her shrimp and squeezed a lemon wedge over them before diving in. The shrimp was cold and fresh tasting as she chewed.

"You've got to start eating more," DJ commented. "You don't want to get any thinner."

Skylar stopped chewing and glanced at her lap, self-consciously, but didn't respond. "Was she in love with *you*?" she asked.

DJ helped himself to a crab cake and doused it with remoulade. "Brit? I don't think she's capable of love. *I* never was until I met Max." DJ reached for Skylar's plate and scooped the remaining crab cake onto it, spooning a dollop of remoulade on top. He placed her plate back in front of her. "Eat up."

Skylar eyed the crab cake. She was getting full, but DJ's comment was on her mind. She *was* too thin, and if *he* noticed, others were noticing, too.

"We were together only a few months before she got pregnant with you," he said.

Skylar's eyes widened as a horrible thought ran through her mind. "How did you even know I was yours?"

His look became somber. "Fuck's sake, Sky—don't let that wild imagination of yours go nuts."

"Okay, sorry, Dad. I had to ask." Skylar drew back her shoulders, the tension beginning to unwind. The food was satisfying. She picked up her fork and attacked the crab cake, one big bite at a time.

"When she got pregnant with you, I married her straight away. I didn't even think about it. I just did. It seemed like the right thing." He took a sip of his wine, a meditative softness in his eyes.

Skylar pictured Brit being pregnant and DJ urging her to keep the baby. He had been raised a devout Irish Catholic up until his early twenties—before the yacht accident. *If Dad hadn't stayed vigilant, I wouldn't be here.* "What did Luuk say?" She recalled her late grandfather's snobbish greed and lack of empathy.

DJ laughed out loud. "He went crazy. I don't think I'd ever seen him that pissed."

"What did you do?"

DJ shrugged. "I fought him at first. But things fell apart so fast with Brit, I just let her go."

Skylar tried to picture her dad and Brit together as lovers—as married people. And she just couldn't. It was too absurd and disgusting to imagine. Her thoughts went back to the chalkboard. *'Skylar is a murderer'* echoed in her mind like a wicked chorus of jeering, middle school mean girls. She had to do something. *But what?* She turned to DJ, who was gazing off in a different direction, a brooding look on his face.

"How are you going to get rid of her?" Skylar asked, thinking DJ was her only hope of removing this heinous albatross from around her neck.

He sighed and sipped his wine. "Not sure. Still thinking." Then he looked past Skylar, eyes wide and eyebrows raised. He nodded at someone.

Out of the corner of her eye, Skylar saw James approaching. An uncontrollable shiver ran through her—a shiver so powerful, it reminded her of an intense orgasm. She swallowed hard, watching his familiar overconfident gait with his chin slightly lifted. He brushed his fingers through his glamorously disheveled hair, and she had the urgent desire to touch it herself— to feel him in some way.

James nodded at Skylar when he reached the table. She felt her face flush at her own embarrassing thoughts—thoughts about the man who had always been her nemesis. *Thank God, he can't read them.* She caught her dad observing her reaction.

"James," DJ greeted. "You have news?" He gestured for Skylar to scoot over and make room.

Skylar got up and moved, feeling the miserable pinch in her toes from the pumps. James slid into the booth next to her. His leg rubbed up against hers, and she fantasized about him putting his arm around her—the warmth of his hand rubbing her shoulder. She envisioned herself going home with him and tried to imagine what it would feel like to sleep next to him, to have him touch her—kiss her. She imagined feeling his weight on top of her, his woodsy fragrance enveloping her senses as he ran his long fingers up and down her naked body. Another tremor ran through her. *Stop it, Skylar! Everyone knows the imagination is much more potent than reality.*

"Well?" DJ asked, as chipper as he always was.

Skylar, roused out of her lingering James fantasy, glanced at her watch. It was getting late, and she had begun to feel worn down.

"Sal's ecstatic about the suite buildout," James volunteered.

His accent was more obvious than usual. Skylar guessed he must also be exhausted by this endless workday. Somehow, DJ never acted tired. Even after 22 hours of travel and a vicious scene with his ex-wife. At 60 years of age, he had boundless energy that no one could match, not even his 27-year-old daughter. *Especially not me.* Skylar often wondered whether he was on something stronger than Red Bull.

"So, we're on the hook to actually do it," James continued, eyeing what was left of the bread.

DJ pursed his lips. "That's easy. What else?"

"He had a bunch of other requests." James paused to look around and then leaned in. "To be perfectly honest, he wasn't excited about spending time away from … Maud." He threw a sideways glance at Skylar. "He likes the arrangement with the seven *friends*, too."

"Exactly what did he say?" DJ asked, drumming his fingers on the tablecloth.

"His *exact* words were 'I don't remember having a better time,' and—you'll love this one— 'they make me feel young.'"

DJ ran his hand across his face. "Fuck's sake. We're screwed."

Skylar had never heard her dad sound defeated. She looked to James for help, but he looked defeated, too. She tried to conceive of the situation as if she were not part of it. If Skylar had not committed murder, Brit would have nothing to blackmail her with—no scandal to hold over their heads that could potentially damage the business. *If I disappear, the biggest obstacle would be gone.*

She suddenly turned to James. "I'm sorry, I have to get home and feed my cat." He immediately rose and stood aside so Skylar could exit the booth. As she passed him, she almost tripped on her own aching feet and instinctively grasped James's arm.

"Are you okay?" he asked, lightly grazing her shoulder with his free hand.

His touch sent an electric shock wave through her body.

She peered up at him and felt her face flush. He was never more attractive than in this moment—his deep-set blue eyes tapered slightly in the corners—his features decorated with a kind of warmth and familiarity she had never noticed before. His eyes lowered to her right hand, still clutched onto his arm.

She steadied herself and gently removed her hand. "Yes, I'm okay."

She moved past James, then leaned over and planted a swift kiss on DJ's cheek—something she rarely did in public, or ever. "Good night, Dad. I'll see you tomorrow."

DJ's brows crinkled, then his eyes followed her. "See you in the morning."

Skylar turned and limped out of the restaurant as fast as she could. When she reached the parking garage, her feet were so inflamed that she stopped, pulled off her shoes, and sprinted to her car, barefoot, not caring whether she hit nails or glass on the way.

She flew into the house and searched for Sesame, who was waiting by her bowl, meowing loudly.

"I'm sorry, honey," she said, throwing her things aside and pulling Sesame's canned food from the fridge. She shoveled wet food into Sesame's bowl, then watched as the cat voraciously went after the food. Skylar looked at her watch. 10:30 p.m. She was wiped out.

She shuffled up the stairwell and, upon reaching the top, tugged at her sweater dress and yanked it up over her head on the way to her bedroom. She stood in front of her mirror in her underwear, assessing her figure. Her ribs and hip bones shone prominently, and there was a sizable space between her thighs. *Have I always looked like this?* She tried to remember the last time she sunbathed at her pool. It was not too long after Brit's first email. She took a deep breath and let it out, slowly tracing her fingers along her ribcage, feeling the bones of her skeleton. Her dad was right about her weight loss. She stared at her reflection and vowed to eat a balanced diet. The few bites she'd had at Waterford were her first step in the right direction.

After she had changed into her pajamas, washed her face, and brushed her teeth, she shuffled to her bedroom. *Such a long day.* Though she was thoroughly exhausted, she was still keyed up about the meeting at the Crown and Anchor. She needed a sleeping pill, but decided it was too late to take one.

Skylar climbed into bed and turned off the light; when

she shifted her pillow and lay on her stomach, she heard a noise. It sounded like paper crackling. She rolled over on her back and turned on the light once again to inspect the pillow. Nothing was there. She pressed it and heard the crackle again.

This time, she sat up and slid her hand inside the pillowcase, feeling something. She pulled out a thick envelope, then looked around wildly. *Someone's been in my bedroom!*

She caught her breath as she opened the envelope and removed a stack of photos. Her pulse raced as she sifted through them—at least 20 shots, each causing her head to pound harder. They were of her and that pimp before she killed him. Sweat beads formed on her temples and forehead, and her stomach churned at the photos commemorating that horrific day when she had been tied up, raped, and beaten. *Who took them?* She never knew they existed. She looked around again, hands shaking violently.

Skylar tossed the photos on her bed and grabbed her handgun from the nightstand. She slipped out of bed, taking shallow, shuddering breaths, treading cautiously to the hallway that led downstairs. She listened but didn't hear a thing. She stole toward the stairs and skittered down, flipping on lights as she went until she reached her kitchen, her heart pulsing through her body. Sesame was resting contentedly on the area rug—she rolled over and stretched her paws in front of her, mouth stretching into a big yawn.

Skylar went through the house, checking every door and window. She passed by the security keypad and noticed she had not set it before she went upstairs. She tried to recall if she had set it that morning before she left for work and berated herself for not being more careful, knowing she was being stalked. Brit must have broken in again and, this time, planted photos that would frighten Skylar into a confession. *But how is she getting in and out of my house without the key?*

Skylar rifled through her thoughts. Only DJ and Axel had the key, and Axel was the only one with her security code. *None of this makes sense.* She couldn't fathom how Brit was getting away with it, but she'd always had a cunning, criminal mind. She resolved that she could no longer sit still and let Brit taunt and threaten her. She had two options: One was going directly to her dad and sharing what happened when she was 12. The second was removing herself from the situation. It didn't take Skylar long to figure out in which direction she must go.

She marched upstairs and brought out the backpack she used for long hikes—her version of a 'go-bag.' It was packed with survival kit items, like a small flashlight, a Swiss Army knife, a lighter, a backup power source for her phone, and batteries. She went through her closet, selecting jeans, a gray hoodie, underwear, socks, and her running shoes. She quickly changed out of her pajamas, then folded them into the backpack. They still felt warm from her skin. She added a clothing change and packed her toiletries. Once finished, she returned to her bedroom, made the bed neatly, then returned to her closet to deposit the unspeakable photos in her safe. While there, she removed an envelope holding $10,000 in cash. She turned her cell phone over in her hands, thinking she had to abandon it. It was company-issued, and anyone could easily trace it. She opened the app she used to program texts and wrote one to DJ. He would receive it the next morning at precisely 7 a.m. She locked the phone in her safe, grabbed the backpack, and lugged it down the stairs.

She found and filled her thermos with water, then rifled through her pantry for protein bars, a few of which she shoved into the backpack. She grabbed a pen and notepad, her smart tablet, and a charger.

"Sesame!" she called, racing over and scooping up the little cat. She held her near her pounding heart. "We're leaving, baby. I promise you'll be okay. You're going to stay for a little while with Clay. He knows what you need." Sesame meowed loudly and struggled in her arms.

Skylar felt her eyes water with fear and sadness. "But we can't stay here any longer. Mommy's in big trouble." She held Sesame so they were looking into each other's eyes. She studied Sesame's bright amber orbs and kissed her softly on the back of her head. Sesame's fur got into Skylar's mouth as the tears began to fall. "Listen," the word came out muddled and breathless. "I'm going to come back for you. I promise, baby."

She deposited the cat in her carrier, put the carrier in the car, along with her backpack and a bag of cat food, a litterbox, and several toys. She placed the handgun in the glove compartment and drove toward Clay's home.

PART II

Chapter 14

DJ strode to his car, his thoughts consumed by his daughter's appearance. She was wispier than he'd ever seen her. He tried to picture her looking that way in the past. Skylar now resembled Brit. And he couldn't stand to even think about Brit. The most troubling part of the day's events was seeing Brit after almost three decades. *She's a hot mess! Not surprising.* He thought about Skylar's questions. *Why did I marry her in the first place?* He could barely figure that out himself—all he knew was that he needed her to go away. She was a nightmarish reminder of his previous self—a reckless human frantically searching for a new identity—the opposite of who he had been as the elder son of the late Donovan C. Keller, attending law school at Stanford, with promise—*so much promise.*

DJ opened the door to his Jaguar and slid into the seat. James, who was usually the smartest person in the room, had been of little use. *I'll have to get rid of Brit on my own.* He lit a cigarette and rolled down his window.

He sailed west down the 215, barely noticing the street signs until he realized he was going faster than 100 miles per hour. He took his foot off the accelerator, shifted to a lower gear, and slowed to 70. He glanced in his rearview mirror to see if he'd caught the attention of a cop. There were no cars behind him as he exited onto Town Center Drive.

DJ entered his Summit Club mansion through the garage. The lights were out except for the glow of a few candles and the chandelier that hung over the entryway from 30-foot vaulted ceilings. He tossed his car keys on the credenza by the front door and blew out the candles, then bounded upstairs. Max was probably sound asleep, given it was well past midnight.

As DJ rounded the corner toward the master bedroom, he saw a dim skewer of light seeping through a crack in the bathroom door. He gently pushed the door open. The sunken marble tub brimmed with a deep layer of bubbles. Soft candles glowed around the bathtub rim.

"Max?" DJ called, looking around.

"Where've you been?" she asked. He watched her in the mirror reflection as she entered in a soft cream-colored bathrobe.

She sauntered up to him and put her arms around his neck.

DJ inhaled her citrusy scent.

"I missed you," she said, drawing her fingers through his blond mane.

He glanced at the bathtub. "This looks pretty romantic. Sure you were expecting *me*?"

"Are you saying the honeymoon's over?" She turned her dark eyes up to him. They sparkled in the candlelight.

How can I explain that I'm in no mood for anything other than plotting Brit's demise?

Max leaned in and lifted her chin, so her lips were close to his. DJ turned his head, resisting her mouth.

"Someone's been smoking," Max remarked, wrinkling her eyebrows.

"Someone's had a shitty day," he responded. He gave her a peck on the cheek before adding, "Sorry, but I just want to go to bed—and sleep."

Max sighed. "I should have stayed in Bali. At least there, I'd have the ocean to keep me company."

DJ ignored the jab and began undressing, peeling off one garment at a time as he walked to his closet.

Max followed without taking her eyes off him. "May I ask what went on today to put you in such a mood?"

He pulled a pair of pajamas from a drawer and put them on, thinking about what to tell her. Max used to have James's job, so she understood why they had to abruptly cut off the honeymoon vacation. She personally tended to Sal at one time. The whole Brit issue was another story altogether. They had never dialogued about Brit, other than to dismiss her as the reason for Skylar's dysfunction.

DJ silently returned to the bathroom while Max trailed. He wet his toothbrush before squeezing toothpaste onto the end. "Let's talk about it tomorrow," he finally said before inserting it into his mouth.

Early the next morning, DJ badly needed a cigarette. He and Max had a rule—he could smoke in his car as long as she wasn't in it, but he was not allowed to light up in or around the house. He had been up all night, mind running in endless circles. He finally got up and started pacing the hardwood floors of his living room, calculating his next move. He sipped his coffee and gazed out the panoramic floor-to-ceiling windows toward the Las Vegas Strip, the neon lights still glittering as day began to break.

Max had carefully chosen the floor plan of their 10-thousand-square-foot home in the heart of Las Vegas' most luxurious neighborhood. DJ thought back to his previous mid-century modern home in the Scotch Eighties, where Rat Pack kitsch took center stage, in contrast to the kind of luxe glamour of his new home with Max.

He was comfortable, yet uncomfortable with the new, improved lifestyle. On the one hand, he wanted to shed his bad habits; on the other, the bad habits had made him who he was for most of his life.

His brother, Craig, was the opposite. And although Craig spent years cheating on his first wife, his second marriage caused an about-face. Annoyingly, he had turned into the one who always said the right thing—always did the right thing. He was a little taller than DJ and much better looking. Craig had inherited his father's genes, and he and his son Axel were doppelgängers. He had to have everything in order, everything perfectly planned, every hair in place, which rankled DJ most of the time. Craig didn't like to get his hands dirty, although 10 years ago, he took down Luuk Van Ness with one gunshot to the head. That was something to behold.

DJ liked to play dirty, which was how he had ended up with Brit in the first place. Brit—the Dutch hooker he had impregnated and then married. Brit—someone Craig would have thumbed his nose at upon first sight. DJ thought back to Skylar's interrogation—her implication that DJ was not her father. He had deliberately spared her the whole paternity story.

Sunlight twinkled through the comic strip that was the Las Vegas skyline as DJ recalled the time right after Skylar's birth. Luuk, who was crazy pissed at DJ, insisted Brit go through a battery of tests, including one for paternity, sexually transmitted diseases, and drugs. Brit had miraculously stayed calm and dedicated to DJ during her pregnancy. And the paternity test checked out. DJ was Skylar's father by blood. But up until now, DJ had avoided the topic of why he would have left Skylar until she was 12 to be raised by Brit. Initially, it wasn't his decision. It was Luuk's mandate. And while DJ had argued against leaving Brit, Luuk threatened to cut DJ off and force him to live a life of poverty. In the end, DJ was relieved by Luuk's decision, but Skylar didn't need to know any of that.

"You're up early." Max had entered the room, interrupting his thoughts. She was in her workout clothes with her chestnut hair pulled into a ponytail.

"Going to the gym?"

She nodded and grabbed an apple from a bowl on the kitchen counter. "Want to come with me?"

The last thing DJ wanted was to huff and puff at the gym. He hated the gym, but Max pushed him to exercise regularly. All he really wanted was to finish his coffee with a smoke. Maybe two. "Think I'll hold off for now—have some things to take care of."

Max gave him a wry smile and bit into the apple.

Just then, DJ's phone bleeped with a text. He glanced at his watch—7 a.m. He reached into his pocket and pulled out the phone. "It's Skylar. She never texts this early." He opened the text and read:

Dad, I'm taking a leave of absence from work. Sebrina has all my files and James knows the status of every project. Don't worry about me. Be back soon. Love, Sky

He reread the lines again, then tore his eyes from the phone, bewildered at Skylar's message.

Max cocked her head. "What's it about?"

DJ reread the message, then dialed Skylar's number. It went straight to voicemail. "Sky, I just got your text. Call me."

He opened the text again and handed the phone to Max. "You'd better sit down."

⸺

Max dashed her apple into the wastebasket, then sat on the couch in their living room. DJ paced in front of her, still dying for a smoke.

"Sal's taken up with a new girlfriend," DJ began, eyeing Max while he paced. She started to say something, but he cut her off. "I know, that's nothing new. But there's a twist." He stopped in front of her and folded his arms across his chest. "His new girlfriend is my ex-wife, Brit. Skylar's mother."

Max's face fell, and her hand spidered across her chest. "What? How would she even *know* Sal?"

DJ took a deep, wheezy breath. "She contacted Skylar

the day of our wedding. Skylar thought it best to keep that to herself. But Brit came to visit her in Las Vegas."

Max folded her lips and gave DJ the once over, as though trying to figure out what really happened. "Go on."

DJ started pacing again. "Brit told Skylar she's still married to me under my old alias, Hendrik Van Ness—that we never got a divorce."

Max's mouth dropped open. "Are you serious?" She began to slowly rise to her feet, eyes wide.

"Calm down, Max. It's not true." He gestured for her to remain seated on the couch. "Brit has an alias. Maud Jansen. When Skylar told her to take a hike, she started dating Sal. He's all wrapped up in the relationship now." He paused. "You remember how Sal used be—it's worse now that he's older."

Max's face tightened as though she were doing everything to restrain her exasperation. "Wait, that makes no sense. How old is that woman? Skylar's mother, that is."

Before DJ could answer, she added, "Skylar's 27, so Brit must be somewhere in her fifties, correct? From what I know of Sal, he'd never be interested in anyone older than 22."

He nodded and sighed. "Yes. But that's the tricky part. Brit brought her young Dutch hooker friends here under the guise of rebranding the Limerick to be a Peep Show Paradise."

Max knitted her brows and drew in her chin. "Are you kidding me?"

"I wish. The girls are all young, and Sal's loving his newfound harem." DJ gave Max a sarcastic smile.

This time, she got to her feet and marched over to

where DJ stood, putting her face close to his. "What are we going to do about this?"

DJ shrugged. "I don't know yet. She obviously came out here for some kind of shakedown—says she wants $2 million to go back to Amsterdam."

Max gave DJ a stern look. "Are you telling me you've *seen* this woman? That you were *with* her? When were you planning to tell me?"

DJ took another wheezing breath and blew it out slowly. "Jesus, Max. Mellow out. Yes, I saw her yesterday. Skylar went with me. It was a short meeting, but she made it clear she's not going anywhere, and Sal is her calling card."

"How does Skylar feel? I mean, that's her mother, right?"

Max had that reproachful look DJ knew all too well. It was disappointment fused with disgust—a familiar expression that made him feel like a child—a child who was not good enough for her. And he hated that. *If there's one thing I could change about Max, it would be to wipe that look off her face forever.* But he knew full well people don't change. Only suckers held onto the foolish hope that others might change for them.

"Look, don't blame Skylar. She and James were trying to keep this whole thing on the down-low so they wouldn't ruin our honeymoon. Axel was the one who blew the whistle on them—the whole Limerick peep show thing with Sal's involvement."

"I'm not blaming anyone. Why did Skylar take a leave of absence? Is she afraid of her mother?"

"I don't know," DJ said wearily. "She watched me tear into Brit last night. Then she got sick. I think she made herself throw up in the bathroom. She looks like a bag of bones since the wedding."

"Well, she's always been slim," Max commented. "Being that tall makes her look even more so."

DJ pictured Skylar's face the night before, how sunken her cheeks had become. "No, I'm telling you, she has a problem. I took her to dinner last night to fatten her up."

Max pursed her lips, worry creases lining her forehead. "Did she say anything at dinner about leaving?"

"Not a word."

Max put her hand to her face and shook her head. "So, why don't you just give Brit the $2 million and send her on her way? Sal could shut our lights off."

He shrugged wearily. "She decided Sal has more to give. And with Sal in her pocket, she's got me by the balls." He moved closer to Max. "Look, I need your help with a solution. I have no problem throwing money at her, but she's made it clear she's not leaving Sal anytime soon."

"You know I'll help." Max looked DJ in the eye, face softening slightly. "You think I want her crawling around? You're *my* husband."

"Damned right," DJ said, putting his arms around her waist.

Max nodded and put her mouth on DJ's. He pulled her close for a lingering kiss, and his shoulders unwound for the first time since they had been back from Bali. *This is what marriage should be.* He slowly withdrew from the embrace.

She smiled. "Don't worry, honey. We'll figure it out." She glanced at her watch. "I'm going to the gym now—it'll help clear my mind. Let's regroup at the hotel later."

DJ nodded and watched her walk away, out the door to the garage. When he heard the garage door close, he hurried to his car and pulled out his pack of cigarettes. If he smoked outside and disposed of the evidence, Max would never know.

Chapter 15

"Craig," DJ rasped. "You have a minute?" He eyed his wall clock and couldn't believe it was only 10 a.m. He felt like he'd been at work for hours.

"Sure," Craig returned. "Let me go to my office." DJ heard phones ringing in the background, slowly fading, then the sound of Craig's office door closing. "Everything okay? Are you back already?"

He lit a cigarette and inhaled deeply before blowing out smoke. "I've got a major problem. My ex-fucking-wife decided to resurface, and she's screwing Sal Vincenzo."

He heard nothing but silence until Craig cleared his throat. "What?"

"She came out trying to get Skylar's attention so she could soak me for a couple million. Says I'm still married to her. Total bullshit, of course, but the real problem is she's fucking Sal. I've got to get rid of her."

"Should we be having this conversation on the phone?"

DJ took another drag of his cigarette and scanned his office. "Maybe not. Skylar disappeared. Sent some cryptic note about taking a leave of absence. It's all pretty fucked up. Can you get out here?"

There was another long pause. "Do you think this can wait until the weekend?"

"Does it *sound* like it can wait until the weekend?" DJ brushed the hair out of his face with a jerking motion. *So typical.*

"No, DJ, but this is sudden … I can't just up and leave for Las Vegas. I have clients to take care of."

"Yeah, I know, Craig. I'm one of them." He took a long drag of his cigarette. "Sal's in the middle of rebranding the Limerick Bar into a Dutch peep show paradise with authentic hookers straight from the Amsterdam Red Light district. They're already on site, and contracts were signed while I was in Bali!" DJ needed Craig—the only one he could trust with this mess, other than Skylar.

"All right. Calm down. I'll figure something out."

"Good," he said before slamming the phone down. He got to his feet and paced by his window, squinting at the bright sunlight glaring down on the Strip. He recalled his wedding day and how everything seemed peaceful and even harmonious when he walked out the door and got into a limo for the airport. He shook his head and stubbed out his cigarette.

He picked up the phone to call Axel, then hesitated. If Axel knew anything about Skylar's whereabouts, he'd be a tight-ass over attorney-client privilege. *He won't tell me anything.* Then he dialed Sonia. "I need James in here, please. Tell him to bring Mila."

James arrived promptly with Mila in tow. DJ swiveled around in his chair and gestured for them to take the seats opposite his desk. He lit another cigarette and watched them settle. Mila was never attractive to him, although she had many admirers. She wore the worst getups. Today was another classic: a tight-fitting, bright blue sweater and a matching plaid cheerleader skirt, with white knee-high socks and high heels. She was barely distinguishable from the hookers they regularly eighty-sixed from the casino. All she was missing was a huge tote bag and a devious expression. But DJ valued her opinion.

"It goes without saying this is highly confidential," he began. "But I need some information." He studied both James and Mila. "It's about Skylar." While Mila's expression remained neutral, James's eyebrows crinkled slightly. DJ leaned in. "She's taking a *leave of absence*."

James and Mila tapped eyes.

James cleared his throat. "Is she okay?"

DJ blew out a cloud of smoke and shrugged. "Your guess is as good as mine. All I have is a text from seven this morning. I've been calling for the past few hours, and it just rings, then goes to voicemail. I'm about to put a trace on her cell phone, but I thought I'd talk to you two first."

James drew in his chin, glancing Mila's way again.

She stretched her lower lip against her teeth and crossed her sock-covered legs, knees peeking out from underneath the cheerleader skirt.

"Did either of you get an indication that she might be leaving town?" DJ asked.

Mila spoke first. "She freaked when she found out you were coming back. The whole thing with Maud and Sal had her on edge. Think she's blaming herself. Not sure why, though. Sal's going to do whatever he wants."

DJ felt his impatience rise into a headache. "But did she say *anything* about leaving?"

Mila shook her head and turned to James. "Not to me. You?"

James cocked his head. "I can tell she's been stressed lately, but we don't … she and I don't share personal information." He broke eye contact briefly before continuing. "So, no. She didn't tell me anything."

DJ nodded and rose to his feet, grinding his cigarette in the ashtray. "Then, do you know anyone she *does* talk to?"

James shrugged. "No clue. Axel, maybe?"

"There's one person," Mila interjected. "He works here—gentleman named Clay—Clay Moresco."

"Oh, right. The catering guy," James said with a nod. "They often have lunch together."

DJ's eyes widened with hope for a split second. "I know who that is. Is she dating him or something?"

Mila couldn't resist a snicker. "Skylar's not his type." When she saw DJ's stern expression, she quickly added, "They're strictly friends. But good friends, I know."

DJ hit the speaker on his office phone and dialed some numbers. "Sonia, get a hold of Clay Moresco from catering. Tell him I need to see him in my office as soon as possible."

He looked up at James and Mila. "That'll be all for now."

Mila stood and exited, cheerleader skirt opening and twirling like a chrysanthemum in bloom.

James lingered before shutting the door behind her.

He turned to DJ. "I have some information, but I didn't want to share it in front of Mila."

"What's that?" DJ sat and leaned forward on his desk.

"It's something I saw. While you were gone, Skylar and I had to jump in as last-minute models for the new Marco uniforms."

"Really?" DJ asked, stifling a sneer.

James gave him a tight-lipped smile. "Yeah, I know. The models didn't turn up. Skylar was a wee bit miffed."

DJ frowned. "So, what does that have to do with her disappearance?"

"Well, I saw her with Craig afterwards. She was upset. I—it's hard to describe, but they looked like they were having a bit of a row."

DJ rolled his eyes. "Would you just speak English?"

"Sorry. It looked like an argument. I interrupted to ask Skylar for lunch, and, well, the whole thing was awkward as arse."

DJ gave James a dismissive wave. "I'm sure it was nothing. He's my brother and her uncle. You just told me she was complaining about having to model the uniform. Skylar can be stubborn, you know."

James let out a small chuckle. "I never noticed."

"And Craig," DJ said, rolling his eyes. "Craig can be an arrogant asshole."

"I never noticed that, either." James looked as though he were now suppressing a grin.

"It's a bad combination." DJ grabbed his pack of cigarettes and shook out another. He paused to light it. "But I'm sure there was nothing to it."

DJ understood that James and Craig didn't mix. But

neither realized it was because they were the exact same type: Both had Ivy League educations, powerful positions, and a charming gift for Irish blarney. Both attracted women everywhere they went. Craig did it with his movie-star good looks and elegant manners; James with his quick wit and Irish cool factor. Whatever James saw Skylar and Craig arguing about was bound to be informed by his unfiltered distaste for Craig.

James straightened up and nodded. "Well, I thought it was worth mentioning."

There was a knock on the door.

"Come in," DJ called.

Sonia popped her head in. "I have Clay Moresco here for you."

DJ nodded. "Send him in."

DJ had no real contact with Clay, other than seeing him work his ass off at events. He was a classy guy. Spackled the hell out of his hair with gel. Still, he seemed affable enough, if not a bit nervous, as he sat across from DJ and adjacent to James.

"How can I help you, Mr. Keller?" he asked with deference.

DJ took a deep, wheezing breath and glanced at his almost-empty cigarette pack. He decided against lighting another. A bluish haze had already blanketed his entire office from all the smoke. "It's about my daughter. Rumor has it you two know each other quite well."

Clay blinked and fidgeted in his chair but said nothing.

"Am I correct to assume you see her frequently?"

DJ asked with a slight smile. He already knew he was scaring the guy.

"I … um, yes, I … we're friends. Just friends, Mr. Keller."

"But you talk to her all the time, right?" DJ asked, feeling his lawyer interrogation roots cropping up. *If this guy's lying, he's going to fall into my trap.*

Clay looked down at his lap. "Yes, we have lunch together a lot, but I … we haven't talked for several days. I know Skylar's been busy while you were out of the office."

DJ watched closely as Clay's eyelids peeled upward to glimpse James. He seemed to shiver in his light gray suit. *This guy is nervous as hell—a telltale sign he's lying.*

DJ cracked his knuckles and leaned in. "Clay, your good friend sent a text this morning saying she was taking a leave of absence from work. I can't get a hold of her. I don't know if she's in trouble yet, but I need to know if she told you anything about going away."

Clay bit his lower lip and shifted in his chair. "I'm sorry to hear that, Mr. Keller."

"Okay, you can cut the *Mr. Keller* shit," he blurted. "Just call me DJ."

"DJ," Clay repeated. "I really don't know anything."

"Nothing?" he pressed. "Has she ever talked to you about, I don't know, taking a vacation?"

His eyes lit up a bit, like he was recalling something. "Well, she's been talking lately about going on a cruise," Clay said, chewing his lip again. "Maybe she finally did it."

DJ glanced at James, who was giving Clay the once-over with suspicion.

"Okay. You'll let me know if you hear from her?" DJ asked, nodding.

"Yes." He rose to his feet, backing toward the office door to make an escape. "Of course, Mr. Ke … DJ."

As soon as the door closed, DJ addressed James. "Have you ever heard Skylar talk about going on a cruise?"

James shook his head. "I told you we don't talk about personal things."

DJ took a step closer to James, studying his dark blue eyes to decide whether he was holding something back. He almost wished James *did* have a personal relationship with Skylar. The animosity between them boggled his mind. Everyone had a match out there, somewhere. And to DJ, Skylar and James were a perfect fit. James was strong and confident—secure enough in his own masculinity to handle someone as fiery as Skylar. And that combination was not easy to find. *If Skylar dated James, at least I wouldn't have to worry about her so much.* "Fine," he finally said. "Have surveillance keep an eye on her friend, Clay. He seemed a little squirrely in here."

"Right," James said. "Door open or closed?"

"Open."

It took DJ less than 30 minutes to trace Skylar's cell phone to her home in Summerlin. DJ was sure he had a key somewhere. He stormed out of his office and almost ran right into Max.

"You're here," she said. "I've been trying to call."

"You know where we keep the key to Skylar's house?" he asked. "That's where her phone is."

Max's eyes widened, and she fanned her hand over her throat. "That's a relief."

"Not really. Why would she leave it there?"

Max shrugged. "You're assuming she's not there. I've been thinking … is it possible she just needed some downtime at home?"

DJ pictured Skylar with her Type A personality, sitting around flipping TV channels. "The girl doesn't know what to do with downtime, Max. I know her." He scratched his head. "There's something strange going on."

"Well, I'm sure the key's at home. But what I really want to discuss is our situation with Sal." She looked around. "Let's go in your office to talk."

When Max crossed the threshold into DJ's office, she wrinkled her nose and waved her hands around. "Jesus, DJ. Smoke much?"

He wheezed a deep sigh. "Sorry, but you know what stress does to me."

She shook her head. "Maybe you should find a healthier outlet."

"Never mind. What's your idea about Sal?"

"I think it would be prudent for you to have a meeting with both of them—meaning together." She shrugged off her long khaki trench and hung it behind his door before closing it. Her plain white silk blouse fell loosely on her slender frame, tucked into dark crimson pants. "I think you should start treating them like a real couple, you know, give them some credibility."

"You mean grin-fuck them," DJ said, noticing Max had curled her hair. She usually wore it straight. "I'm not sure I can do that."

"Here's my strategy," she said. "We invite them to lunch as *couples*, you know, a foursome. For all Brit knows,

I have no clue who she really is. I'll play dumb and, to Sal, it shows we're legitimizing his new girlfriend."

"What are we supposed to talk about at this wholesome gathering?" DJ patted down his pants pockets with his hands, in dire need of another cigarette.

"Talk about the peep show paradise, you know, schmooze them like nothing's amiss," Max answered.

"And what's the end run, darlin'?" he asked, taking a step toward Max and running his fingers through her loosely curled locks. *I like this softer look.* The straight bob made her look unapproachable at times.

Max gave him a sarcastic smile. "The end run is that you get your ex-wife to lower her guard."

He sighed and drew in his chin. *She has no idea of the monster she's dealing with.* "Max, I know you want to help, but that's not going to work. She's already refused the money I offered—thinks she can do better with Sal's unlimited cash."

"Oh, I know." She blinked her eyes thoughtfully. "But I think we need to go a little further than a lump sum." She leaned her face toward him. "Think about it. If we let her believe we're serious about her peep show idea, it might turn her head. We can let her know we ran numbers and think it could be a real revenue generator."

DJ thrust his chin upward. "Look, I don't want anyone thinking we'd do business with her, let alone *that* business. What if it gets out to the press? It has nothing to do with the Donovan brand and could damage the hell out of what we've built."

Max shook her head quickly. "I'm not suggesting we actually *do* anything. We just make her think she has a shot at a legitimate business—with autonomy, meaning she'd be responsible for her own marketing, revenue—you know, a four-wall. Then, when Sal moves on, the coast will be clear to call metro police to raid her suite and get both her and her Dutch hookers the hell out of here."

That caught DJ's attention. He smiled at the thought of Brit being hauled out in handcuffs. He nodded. "Damn, Max. That's it. A *colossal* grin-fuck."

Chapter 16

After searching his office and home, DJ could not find the key to Skylar's house. He wondered if anyone else had it. The only good news was that he reached Sal to set up lunch for the following day.

He got into the shower and spun the faucet handle to the hottest setting, contemplating how he'd handle dealing with Brit and Sal together—in the same room. *I'd better control my urge to tell her to fuck off.* As he rubbed soap suds all over his body, he realized that was going to take some doing. But that was not all. *I'll have to kiss Sal's ass in the process—make him feel like the whale he is.* The only thing that bothered him about Max's plan was for Max to be there at all. It wasn't that he worried Max was insecure or jealous. DJ was more concerned about how her presence would affect him. He squeezed shampoo onto his scalp and began lathering up, picturing Max in the meeting. She would try to control the flow of the conversation. Make him feel confined.

When DJ was out of the shower, he examined his body in the mirror. His long blond hair hung to his shoulders like a wet mop. He had always been tall and lean, but his fitness had declined over the years. He pinched his belly fat with one hand, recalling that he had once competed in intercollegiate boxing and swimming on the Stanford team. But the stress of surviving the yacht accident and living most of his adult life under an alias had driven him underground to the point where he slipped into a reckless, unhealthy lifestyle. He knew he should quit smoking and work out more. *Max would like that.* He pulled on his pajama bottoms, and his thoughts centered on Craig. He was DJ's opposite. Sometimes, DJ watched how women reacted to Craig's presence when he merely entered a room. The green bedroom eyes and dazzling, white-toothed smile knocked women out. The drooling would start within seconds. That's when he got the idea. *Craig should be in the meeting, not Max.* He visualized Brit laying her acquisitive eyes on DJ's only brother—the gorgeous one, and he felt his lips crack into a smile. He dialed Craig right away.

"Hey," Craig answered. "Sorry, I didn't get back to you ... I just got out of my last meeting."

"No worries. Listen, I have a plan to deal with Sal, and it involves you."

Craig sighed into the receiver. "How did *that* come up?"

"I have a late lunch scheduled for tomorrow with both Sal and my ex. I need you to be there, bro." *More than you'll ever know.*

"I'm meeting your ex?" he asked. "Don't you think that's a bit odd?"

"I know, but I have a solid plan. Can you get out here

tomorrow morning? We'll go over the details then." *Come on, Craig. Don't be a tight ass. Just this once.*

There was a long pause.

"Well?" DJ asked.

He sighed again. "Well … as you said before, you *are* one of my bigger clients. And you're my brother. I suppose I can get on an early flight. What's going on with Skylar?"

DJ was so wrapped up in the issues with Sal, he had temporarily forgotten about Skylar. He still needed her key. "She's MIA. Hey, would you happen to have a key to her house in Summerlin?"

"Why would *I* have a key to her house? If anyone has a key, it's Axel. Aren't they neighbors?"

"You're right." DJ had forgotten about that. "I'll ask him first thing in the morning. See you soon." DJ was about to hang up. "One more thing—make sure you *look* the part, if you know what I mean."

"Pardon me?"

"Break out one of those Italian suits that gets women all hot and bothered," he said with a snicker.

Craig chuckled. "Yeah, right. See you tomorrow."

Max didn't take the news that Craig was replacing her well. In fact, she wouldn't stop arguing up until the point when they were in bed, and DJ made love to her with all the passion he could muster. At first, he did it to calm her down, but he needed a release, too. It felt good to be with her again, like when they were in Bali. Afterwards, he fell asleep.

DJ got up early the next morning and called Axel to inform him of Skylar's disappearance. He sounded deeply concerned, which told DJ he knew nothing about it. Axel then confirmed he had Skylar's key, and DJ asked him to meet at her house as soon as possible.

When DJ pulled up in his Jaguar, Axel's Range Rover was already parked in her driveway. DJ saw Axel standing on Skylar's porch. From a distance, he could barely distinguish Axel from Craig. The main difference was in how they dressed. Axel shunned fancy suits for a more business-casual style, mainly because he had to wear suits in court. Today, he wore an olive-flecked navy wool jacket over a white button-down shirt tucked into black pants. His serious demeanor belied his softer style. Axel meant business, and he rarely backed down unless DJ flat out told him *no*. Even then, he argued like a trial lawyer. Seeing Axel in action always reminded DJ that his circumstances blocked him from ever practicing law. DJ was originally slated to succeed his father as managing partner of the law firm. The yacht accident had changed all that. He often imagined what life would have been like had things gone as planned. *I wouldn't be in Vegas. I wouldn't be doing this job. Would I be happier?* He raked his fingers through his hair and got out of the car.

"Hey, Ax," he said, approaching his nephew.

"Good morning," Axel replied with a smile.

DJ wasn't sure why, but he gave Axel a hug. "Thanks for meeting me on such short notice."

"Of course. I'm worried about Sky—can't believe she'd

just disappear like that. It's not like her." Axel handed DJ the key.

"Yeah, I know. You have the code for her alarm system?"

Axel nodded and glanced around for the doorbell. "That's funny. Usually, she's got a door cam. But it looks like someone removed it."

"That *is* weird." DJ glanced around them. "We'll have to knock loudly then."

Axel banged on the door several times. Nothing happened. They waited, and he tried again. Still nothing.

DJ took a deep breath and shoved the key in the lock, pushing the heavy wooden door open while Axel advanced swiftly to the security panel. He punched in a few numbers to disarm the system.

DJ cautiously led the way into Skylar's living room. It smelled faintly of her scent—vanilla with a hint of musk. He looked around at her modern décor. He had only been to her place a couple of times—once when the sale closed during the inspection, and once when she had invited him for dinner. He recalled her making a pasta dish that was quite tasty. He felt a sudden twinge of guilt over not being more involved in his only daughter's life, other than at work.

"Skylar," DJ called loudly. "Are you here? It's Dad and Axel." His voice echoed against the vaulted ceilings. He yelled it again when they got to her kitchen. Then he turned to Axel. "Let's find where her phone's hiding."

DJ called Skylar's cell in the event she left the ringer on, but they heard nothing. DJ looked around her kitchen and then opened the refrigerator. Other than a half-empty carton of eggs and a wedge of Swiss cheese, it was mostly condiments like ketchup and salad dressing. "No wonder she's so skinny," he mused while opening her freezer, spotting the massive bottle of unopened vodka. He pulled it out and examined the label. "Good stuff."

"That's odd," Axel commented. "To my knowledge, she doesn't drink."

DJ placed the bottle back in the freezer and shut the door. "She didn't open it. Maybe it was a gift."

He moved to the pantry and began going through her dry ingredients and supplies, again marveling at how little was there. He pulled out a box of coffee pods, then replaced it on the shelf. He saw a few cans of cat food and turned to Axel. "Does she still have that cat? What was its name?"

"Sesame," he answered. "She was here when Skylar called me the night of your wedding. She's a small cat—black and white. I've taken care of her here and there when Skylar works late or goes hiking."

DJ frowned and drew in his chin. "Wherever she went, she took the cat with her. Who does that?"

Axel scanned the room. "I know where the litter boxes are. She has two. If there aren't any, she took Sesame, which means she planned a long leave of absence."

"Good idea."

DJ followed Axel to where the litter boxes were kept, and they found nothing. Finally, they bounded up the stairs, two at a time, to Skylar's master bedroom, bath, and closet area. They examined the bathroom first, finding two fashion magazines, a razor, and shaving cream on the edge of her bathtub. DJ looked through her medicine cabinet and sink drawers but found only beauty products and everyday bathroom supplies.

DJ summoned Axel to follow him into Skylar's

bedroom. The bed had been neatly made, and pillows placed as though untouched.

"Wait, did she even sleep here last night?" Axel asked. "How long has she been missing?"

DJ didn't answer. He recalled getting the text at precisely 7 a.m. He spotted the nightstand and glanced at Axel. "I know I shouldn't do this, but I have to look in there."

Axel nodded. "Go ahead." Then he added, "I know she keeps a loaded handgun there, so I'd be careful."

"How do you know that?"

"Because that night I had to use my key to get in, she pulled it on me," he answered. "She thought I was an intruder."

DJ shook his head with a wry smile. "That's my girl." He pulled open the top drawer and began rummaging. He found an empty prescription bottle of sleeping pills, which he examined closely. *Skylar doesn't sleep*. He dug through and found nothing more than fashion magazines.

They moved to the final destination: her closet. DJ began sifting through her hanging clothes. "These look like all her work clothes," he commented, pulling out a pinstriped jacket, then hanging it up again. There was a granite-colored island in the center of her closet with drawers underneath. He opened them one at a time, finding gym clothes, hosiery, and socks. He happened upon her lingerie drawer, opened it, and peeked inside. He saw small, folded piles of colored underwear and bras. But one side had been cleared out. "Looks like she took some stuff with her," he remarked, closing the drawer.

He glanced at Axel. "If Sky were to hide her cell phone, where do you think it would be?"

"Maybe it's near an electrical outlet. You'd think she wouldn't want to drain the battery. You were able to trace it, so maybe it's sitting somewhere charging."

DJ nodded and looked around the closet. He swept a row of blouses to one side and found a safe, which was not bolted to the shelf. *This ought to be interesting.*

He pulled out his cell phone and dialed Skylar's number. A barely perceptible ring sounded from within the safe. "Bingo," he said to Axel, and carefully lifted the safe from the shelf. He set it down quickly. He estimated it weighed about 50 pounds. "I'll have security crack this open when we get to the hotel. You want to help me with this?"

The two men slowly descended the stairs, lugging the safe. Axel helped him carry it to DJ's car, and they carefully placed it on the passenger's seat.

They returned to Skylar's front entrance and, as Axel punched in the security code, DJ's thoughts were a jumble. *What the hell is going on?*

When they were outside again, DJ turned to him. "Okay, so Skylar locked her cell phone in her safe, took her handgun, cat, purse, ID, and a few clothes—then left."

Axel shook his head. "Yeah, but why?"

DJ sighed. "It's like she's running away from danger and didn't want anyone to track her. So where did she go?"

Axel shrugged and pursed his lips. "I don't know. But whatever her reason, she's afraid. She's got to be really scared."

DJ pulled his car keys from his pocket. "See you back at the hotel."

When Craig showed up at DJ's office, he didn't disappoint. DJ found him at Sonia's desk, being his usual flirtatious self. Sonia was giggling and blushing. DJ stood back and watched his brother in action. He had charisma—a presence he'd inherited from his father. DJ popped a breath mint into his mouth and approached.

"I knew I'd find you harassing my secretary," he said in his gravely rasp, clapping his hand on Craig's back. He wanted to hug him badly, but he resisted because it was in front of Sonia. DJ had a strict rule about showing family affection in front of his employees. Nepotism was always his biggest concern, even more so than when Luuk owned the casino. Back in the day, Luuk was mercilessly criticized for having his son run the marketing. DJ putting most of his blood relatives in high-level positions took nepotism to a new level.

Craig gave him that million-dollar smile. "You look tan. How was Bali?"

"Magnificent," he answered. "Too short."

"Well, you can always go back."

DJ ushered Craig into his office and shut the door. "Thanks for coming out so fast," DJ said, scanning him from head to toe. He went all out this trip, with a dark—almost black—navy suit and white button-down shirt open at the collar. His skin, evenly tanned from the Southern California sun, was smooth and mostly wrinkle-free. And his dark hair was not too long and not too short. *How does he do it?* Craig was only five years younger. DJ whistled. "Damn, bro. As Don used to say, *you're one good-looking son-of-a-bitch.*"

Now that they were alone, DJ gave Craig a hug. "It's good to see you," he murmured.

He let go of Craig and stood back.

Craig gave him a wry smile before sauntering to DJ's window to gaze upon the Strip. After a minute, he turned to DJ. "Other than the obvious, how's Las Vegas?"

"Same. Gaming revenue's up, hotel's full, and restaurants are making money."

Craig listened intently. "Maybe I can pump up your retail sales, too. Jane and I have an anniversary coming. Fifteen years. I'd like to buy her a piece of jewelry."

"By all means, drop some cash. But do me a favor and don't mention Jane in this meeting." DJ settled into the easy chair and propped his feet on the ottoman. He felt a cigarette craving coming on but resisted it.

"Why not mention Jane?" Craig parked himself on the leather couch and crossed his long legs.

"Because I want Brit to think she has a chance with you." He ran his hand over his face. He hoped Craig wouldn't be his usual tight-assed self. *He's way too serious about his relationship with Jane.*

Craig cocked his head and then shook it. "DJ, everyone knows I'm married. All anyone would have to do is search my name online—there are dozens of photos and news stories."

"Doesn't matter," DJ argued. "No one gives a crap about your marriage—especially Brit. She makes her living off of bored, married men."

Craig's look became indignant. "I'm hardly in that category."

DJ shrugged. "Maybe you're having problems.

Whatever the reason, I need you to turn on the charm, so my ex gets hot pants for you and forgets about Sal."

"Wait a minute, DJ." Craig's face was a jumble of anger and disgust. "I said I would come out to help, not be your ex-wife's gigolo."

"Craig, there's no other way. We have to do this right. If she stays here with Sal, I'll be ruined. And so will you." DJ patted his pants pocket and grabbed his pack of cigarettes. *Craig's pussy routine is ratcheting up my anxiety.*

"What are you talking about? How does this affect me?"

DJ pulled out a cigarette, lit it, and inhaled deeply. To his surprise, Craig didn't stop him. "I'm your client. A big one at that. We just hired Jane to create uniforms, and your son is our legal counsel. If Sal's business goes away, it puts our whole family in jeopardy. We may all lose our shirts."

Craig frowned and uncrossed his legs. "DJ, I have other clients besides you. And Jane's doing just fine. Axel can get a job outside your company, so stop manipulating me."

DJ took another drag and leaned forward. "Brit potentially has dirt on me—on this casino."

Craig pulled in his chin. "What does *she* have?"

DJ lowered his voice. "Craig, I violated Anti-Money Laundering standards with Sal. Don't you remember? I could have the FinCEN Network all over my ass if anyone finds out what I did for one player. The Gaming Commission could shut us down."

Craig's frown deepened. "DJ, how would Brit know about that?"

"Think about it. Sal's loose-lipped about stuff like that—especially when he's whacked out on alcohol with some floozy in bed. He's also a loud-mouthed asshole who loves to brag. And don't forget that she asked for $1 million to leave town and another million to '*keep her mouth shut.*'"

Craig's eyes widened.

"We didn't file all the SARs we should have," DJ continued. "As a favor to Sal, for some of his buddies. I mean, with Sal, how can you really tell what's *suspicious activity* and what's just Sal being Sal."

Suddenly, Craig's expression softened. He finally got it. And he knew his participation was crucial. He lowered his eyes to his lap, took a long breath, and blew it out slowly. "Okay. What exactly do you want me to do?"

"It's simple. I'll introduce you as head of our agency of record. You're going to be art-directing the plans to convert the Limerick into something from the Red Light District.

"Wait, are you really going through with it?" His jaw muscles tightened.

"Hell, no! We're just making them think we are." DJ took a deep drag of his cigarette and let the smoke stream out of his mouth. "It needs specific branding to turn it into a peep show paradise." He let out a chuckle. "Come to think of it, that's a good working title for this piece of shit production." He tapped his finger on his cigarette to dash the ash. "Then you roll into your brilliant ad-speak. Make a lot of eye contact with Brit—she goes by Maud Jansen now. I want her to walk away thinking you're sexy, rich, and, most importantly, interested in making her dream successful."

"And you don't think she'll be suspicious? I mean, she knows I'm your brother. Don't you think she knows you've told me everything? She can't be that stupid." A cynical look clouded his face.

DJ tapped his lit cigarette against the ashtray. "Not stupid, just greedy as hell. If she thinks there's an opportunity, she'll take it. Trust me, I know her working-girl maneuvers. She can't help herself."

"You asked me to flirt. Don't you think she'll wonder why I'd have anything to do with her?" Craig asked.

"She'll dangle the carrot of her young Dutch whores—just like she's doing with Sal. Do you think he'd stay with her past five minutes if she didn't have them?"

Craig grimaced. "You realize this could backfire on all of us, right?"

"We have to take the chance, Craig. I'm desperate."

His phone buzzed. Sonia announced Tony, his security director.

"Send him in," DJ said, smashing out his cigarette butt and standing.

Tony, a large, burly man, entered, carrying Skylar's safe. "I got it open, sir," he said. "Where do you want it?"

DJ patted his desk. "Here's fine. Thanks, Tony."

As soon as Tony left, DJ turned to Craig. "Axel and I went through Skylar's house this morning. Her cell phone is inside." DJ opened the safe's door and began rifling through its contents.

"She left without her phone?"

DJ nodded. "All we know is she took her handgun, her cat, wallet, credit cards, and some clothes with her."

Craig knitted his brows. "She knows you can track her."

"So? If she's in trouble, why isn't she coming to me? What kind of trouble can she be in that she's afraid to come to *me* about it?" He paused to close his eyes for a brief moment. "When she was growing up, she drank, smoked weed, had sex—everything was out in the open. She's never had to hide anything from me."

"That you know of," Craig interjected. "What if something happened back in Amsterdam? All of this started when Brit showed up."

DJ nodded and returned his attention to the safe. He peered in and pulled the phone out. "Here it is." He connected it to a nearby charger, then resumed rummaging through. He pulled out a stack of small jewelry boxes and tossed them on his desk. There was an envelope containing cash—Euros—at least a few hundred. He peered into the safe and saw one remaining item. A larger envelope. DJ grabbed it and tore it open. He stifled a gasp at what was inside.

Photos. Hardcore porn photos of Skylar—as an adolescent. Bound, gagged, naked, looking at the camera. She was having sex with a grown man—an unsightly, degenerate one at that. DJ winced as he examined each photo, one by one. He grew more nauseous as poses of his daughter in various stages of sex with a greasy-haired pervert flashed before him. He finally got to a close-up of Skylar giving the man a blow job, her darkly painted eyes closed, child-like red lips suctioned around the protrusion coming out of his pants. "Jesus!" he exclaimed, flipping the photo to check the date. He did the math. *Skylar was only 12.*

"What is that?" Craig asked, advancing to where DJ was standing—holding the stack of evidence that his daughter had been violated as a young minor.

"Photos … the worst fucking photos," DJ said, faltering. He felt his face getting hot. "I had no idea … she was 12 years old." *And where the fuck was Brit?*

"May I see them?" Craig asked.

DJ glared up at him while flipping the stack over and pressing it against his chest. "No. You may not." His breathing became shallow. "Unless you want to see your only niece bound up like a piece of meat, getting it from every angle."

Craig's eyes widened, and his mouth dropped open. "DJ—what the hell?"

He didn't answer. He lowered himself shakily into his office chair and just stared straight ahead. "I can't fucking believe it. My own daughter." DJ slapped the photos face down on his desk. "I mean, I knew things were bad, but … not like that."

Craig stepped behind DJ's desk and put his arm around his shoulders. "Why do you think she has them, anyway?"

DJ shrugged. "No clue. But that was right before I went to Amsterdam to take her home with me." The memory came flooding back of him getting a call from the Dutch police because Brit was in jail and Skylar had been left unsupervised. He recalled finding Skylar in Brit's apartment, alone and hungry, bruised and cut up all over. He shuddered at the thought that the man in the photos, who looked around 35, had sexually assaulted Skylar and forced her to do the depraved things depicted in the images. "*Why didn't she tell me?*" The coffee and toast he had that morning were threatening to come back up.

"Maybe she was embarrassed," Craig suggested. "I mean, that's not the kind of thing a 12-year-old tells her dad."

"You think?" DJ was shocked at the vitriol in his own tone.

"When I met her, she was … well, I don't need to remind you." Craig lowered his eyes to the floor.

"Right, she was fast and loose. Is that what you were going to say?" DJ scrambled up from his chair and squared his shoulders at Craig. "You think she *wanted* that?"

Craig bit his lower lip and looked uncomfortable. "All I'm saying is that she had some major issues when I met her. What you're describing—isn't it called BDSM? That could've been her particular kink at the time."

"So, you think it's *her* fault? Craig, she was 12. And she doesn't look like she's into anything in those photos except for drugs and alcohol."

"I'm sorry." Craig put his hand on DJ's shoulder and rubbed it. "Are you okay?"

"No, I'm not." He looked up at his brother and saw compassion in his eyes. "We have to find her."

Craig nodded. "Wasn't your ex-wife responsible for her then? Could it be she was pimping her own child out?"

"I don't know." DJ got to his feet and put the photos back in their envelope, then slid them into his desk drawer. "But I'm going to find out." He glanced at his watch. "You ready to go meet her?"

"I suppose." Craig finger-combed his dark-brown hair. "How do I look?"

DJ gave him the once over. "Take off your wedding ring."

"Are you serious?" Craig was about to argue, but he must have changed his mind. He pulled the ring from his left finger and dropped it in his pants pocket. "Now, how do I look?"

"Just ravishing, darling," DJ said with a sarcastic smile. "Let's go."

Chapter 17

As DJ and Craig made their way through the hotel, DJ couldn't wipe the disturbing images from his mind. His daughter trussed up and photographed in graphic, compromising poses that rivaled the most vulgar porn he'd seen. *Why would she keep those photos? Was there a relationship between her and that man?* Skylar had always lusted after older men. He recalled her trying to seduce Craig before she found out he was her uncle. But she seemed to have kicked that nasty habit in her '20s. Come to think of it, he never knew her to date anyone after the age of 22. It's like she just stopped caring. *I have no idea what to think.*

And now he had to sit through what was sure to be the worst lunch of his life with the worst mother on the planet. His only consolation was that Max was not there to see the photos and subsequently confront Brit. She would not be able to check her revulsion. He eyed Craig, walking coolly beside him, looking every inch the LA advertising executive. Women all over the casino craned their necks to get a good look at him. Just having Craig there made him feel stronger. Their plan had to work in getting Brit away from Sal. But even more important was that DJ get time alone with Brit to find out where their daughter might have gone.

DJ had arranged a private lunch in the Polo Room at One Pico, which was modeled on the original in Dublin. James had brokered a deal several years earlier with the owner of One Pico in Ireland to create a replica in Donovan, serving a blend of contemporary French and Irish cuisine. DJ thought a private lunch would make Sal feel special, and hopefully loosen up Brit.

When they arrived, no one else was there, except Clay the caterer with some geeky-looking guy in tow. Clay was giving the geek instructions. When DJ and Craig approached, Clay stood at attention, like he was in the presence of royalty. The geek clumsily dropped his pen and bent to pick it up.

DJ nodded in Clay's direction. "How's it going?"

"It's fine, Mr. Keller." He gave Craig an approving smile and held out his hand. "And you are?"

Craig shook his hand. "Craig Keller."

Clay appeared to be uncovering a mystery. "Oh, you must be Axel's father. I'm Clay Moresco, catering director."

"Is everything ready for our guests?" DJ interrupted.

"Yes, sir," Clay answered. "The chef has the menu you requested. He gestured to the geek. "This is Evan, our banquet manager, and he'll be supervising your lunch to ensure everything is to your liking."

Evan went to shake DJ's hand, but DJ didn't offer

his. He merely nodded. "Make sure the servers get in and get out, meaning they don't linger at the table. We have high-level business to discuss. *Capicsci?*

Evan's face flushed, and he nodded. "Of course, sir. I'll make sure they know."

Clay led the way to their booth with Evan trailing behind. DJ gestured for Craig to sit. His wish was to have Brit across from Craig and Sal next to her.

"Is there anything else you need?" Clay asked.

"Yes, there is," DJ said, turning to Craig. "You want a drink?"

Craig glanced at his watch. "Don't you think it's a little early?"

DJ snickered. "Not with this crowd." He turned to Clay. "I'll have a scotch. Bruichladdich Black Art 1992."

Craig shook his head as if to say, 'Here we go.' "Make that two," he said to Clay.

Evan piped up, "Right away, sir." And he scurried toward the bar.

⸺

As soon as a server brought the scotches, DJ picked up his glass and raised it in a toast. "To one fucked-up situation."

He clinked glasses with Craig, and they both took a sip. DJ sucked in a breath after he swallowed the liquor, inhaling its smooth-as-silk flavor. This was Don's favorite scotch, and while Luuk was DJ's biological father, DJ hated to acknowledge it. As far as he or Craig was concerned, Don was DJ's father. And he and Craig were full brothers—not half. DJ refused to see his life and family any other way. They had found out 10 years ago that their mom,

Julia, had had an affair with Luuk and produced DJ. Julia hid that fact for most of their adult life until she had no choice but to confess. DJ recalled his unbridled fury upon finding out. It took him months to forgive his mother for the lie. He detested the thought of being Luuk's son and now wondered whether that was part of Skylar's issue. *Her grandfather was Luuk, her mother is Brit, and her father is me.* His shoulders sagged.

"Do you think these two are going to show up or what?" Craig's impatient voice broke into DJ's musings.

Before he could respond, Sal entered the room first and held the door for Brit, who sashayed in wearing what looked to be a shiny black catsuit with long sleeves. She wore lace-up boots that had outrageously high silver platform heels. A wide black leather belt cinched her waist, adorned with a large, round silver belt buckle. A pair of large black sunglasses covered her eyes. DJ stole a quick glance at Craig, who looked aghast at the approaching spectacle. DJ kicked Craig's knee under the table and mouthed the words, "Be cool," to which Craig mouthed back, "You owe me."

When Sal and Brit got to the table, both Craig and DJ stood, and DJ was the first to speak.

"My man," he greeted Sal. "Good to see you."

Sal shook DJ's hand with vigor. "How's the big boss?"

Sal was a middle-aged Italian wearing a fitted black leather jacket and sporting a slightly unkempt appearance. He wore his dark hair slicked back, revealing a receding hairline. He hadn't shaved in a few days, based on the shadow of dark stubble swathing his face. Sal's coal-like, piercing black eyes made him appear both cunning and slimy. In the muted lighting of the Polo Room, Sal seemed to blend into the shadows, like a rat hovering in the gutters of New York City. DJ knew a bit about Sal. He grew up in a rough New Jersey neighborhood and, although DJ had never tested Sal's temper, he knew his hot buttons well. Sal was both resourceful and dangerous.

"I don't believe you've met my gal, Maud," he said to DJ. "Maud, meet DJ. He's the one supplying us with all the good booze and grub."

Brit gave DJ a nod. "Pleased to meet you," she intoned. "I've heard a lot about you."

DJ held back a sarcastic dig. "Nice to meet you, Maud." He tore his eyes from Brit's heavily made-up face and turned to Craig. "This is my brother, Craig. He's the managing partner of our agency of record."

He wished Brit would uncover her eyes so he could see her expression, but she did not.

Craig took a reluctant step forward and shook her hand. "Craig Keller," he said. She just pinched her lips together and wrinkled her nose like she smelled something foul. Craig then turned to Sal. "Nice to see you again. It's been a few years."

"Likewise, Keller," Sal said congenially.

Once everyone had taken a seat, the server came out to take drink orders. Both Sal and Brit ordered vodka martinis.

"So, what's this meeting about?" Sal said to DJ.

"I know you've been talking to James about our themed suite buildout. Sorry, I didn't get to join you the other night for dinner." He glanced quickly at Brit, who was clutching Sal's arm, long red nails digging into his leather jacket. "I was busy with a few things at the time."

"Not a problem," Sal replied. "That James is a good man, he is." The server placed the two martinis in front of Sal and Brit. Brit, of course, pounced on hers at once, raising the glass to her lips for a generous sip.

"Today, I wanted to meet the lovely Maud," DJ said with a grin. *Grin fuck.* That's the mantra he repeated over and over in his mind. "And discuss her tremendous idea to rebrand the Limerick as a Peepshow Paradise."

He watched Brit's lips split into a big smile. *Great. So far, so good.*

"And where's your beautiful new bride?" Sal asked. "No offense, Craig, but I was hoping Max would be here today. She's a little *easier* on the eyes if you know what I mean."

DJ stole a glance at Craig, who sat with a placid expression.

"Well, that all depends on who's at the table," DJ remarked. "Most women find my brother to be the *easiest* on the eyes." He winked at Brit, who shifted in her chair but didn't say a word. Her nails still burrowed into Sal's arm. *What the hell is Brit doing?* She definitely was not playing into DJ's plan. Not in the slightest.

DJ decided to shift gears. "Max sends her regrets; she had a lot to catch up on after our honeymoon in Bali. I invited Craig so he could get your collective vision on how the showroom should look—you know, how it should be branded."

Sal looked to Craig with feigned interest.

Craig cleared his throat. "Of course, since we're looking for something more in line with what we've all seen in Amsterdam, I have a few ideas. But if there are colors you like—or want to stay away from, textures, furniture styles, etc." He turned to look Sal in the eye. "I'm thrilled you brought Maud because women always know what their men want." Craig finished the sentence with that knee-melting Keller smile.

Damn, he's good! DJ had almost forgotten Craig's own grin-fucking prowess. He wasn't only good at it; he wrote the book on it.

The server interrupted to place baskets of bread on the table. "This is our specialty brown bread with salted farmhouse butter." He looked expectantly at DJ. "May I bring you some starters?"

Sal glanced at his watch, then studied the one-page lunch menu. "Let's go straight for the mains. The lady will have the wild mushroom ravioli." He paused, then announced to the table, "My girl's a vegetarian."

Since when? The woman's not only a carnivore, but she's also a man-eater! DJ tried to rein in his disgust.

"I'll have the scallops." Sal declared. "I'm in a bit of a hurry."

After Craig ordered the grilled mackerel and DJ ordered the glazed veal, Craig continued.

"I'm picturing something warm, yet sultry, with rich colors and dark woods. I also like the idea of velvet furnishings and lavish sweeping drapes." He gave Brit another dashing smile. "I'm thinking the centerpiece of the Limerick stage could be a king-sized bed with an intricate, hand-carved wooden headboard. That way, the girls would have a place to rest and relax between sets. And the patrons will have a sexy visual even when the girls aren't dancing on the bar."

DJ was deeply impressed with Craig's impromptu

brilliance in painting this lurid scene. *Where does he come up with this stuff?*

"We could decorate the bed with luxurious satin sheets and pillowcases." He turned to focus his light green eyes on Brit. "Tell me, Maud. Do you like satin sheets?" He lowered his voice.

She pulled the black sunglasses down her nose and examined Craig with her pale blue eyes, rimmed with black eyeliner, and caked with mascara.

Finally! DJ felt his heart surge with triumph. *She's going to fall right into my trap.*

"That's really none of your business," Brit shot back, a harsh edge to her voice.

Sal gave her a surprised look, then patted her hand. "It's okay, doll. You can trust these guys. They're family if you know what I mean."

"I meant no offense," Craig said, face tightening. "If we focus on what you both like, we'll be able to put together a mockup and get you samples."

Brit stood. "I've got to visit the ladies." She sauntered toward the exit. DJ watched Sal turn his head to check out Brit's shiny vinyl-swathed ass. *It's a good thing Max isn't here.*

As soon as she was gone, Sal leaned toward Craig. "I like where you're going with this, Keller. Don't worry about her. She gets a little cranky when it's that time of the month, if you know what I mean."

DJ did an inward eye roll. Brit had to have been in menopause for years. "It's okay. We just want you both to be happy with the revamped lounge."

The server placed the starters just as Brit reentered the

room and seated herself. Her vinyl pants squeaked against the leather chair.

They ate in awkward silence until Sal pulled out his phone to read a text message. "I've got to take a call up in the room," he said to Brit. "Listen, sugar, why don't you finish lunch and meet me in the casino later?"

Brit's face fell a little. "Oh, Sal, can't the call wait?"

"Sorry, doll, but it can't. You tell Keller here what you want in the bar, and make sure you keep in mind the needs of our *guests*." He gave Brit a little peck on the cheek and got to his feet. "Guys, thank you for the spread. I'm sure I'll see you in the casino."

DJ winced at the reference to the seven hoes. But with Sal out of the way, and Craig's help, perhaps he could reason with Brit. That was DJ's only hope in getting her to disappear.

As soon as Sal left the room, DJ turned to Brit. "Now that we no longer have an audience, can we dispense with the bullshit and have a real conversation?"

Brit removed her dark glasses, revealing a cat-like gleam. "Whatever could be on your mind?"

Craig nudged his chair forward, looking uncomfortable.

Just then, Evan appeared at the table. "How is everything?"

"Fine," DJ snapped without looking his way.

"Are you ready to order dessert?" Evan queried.

"I'm good on food," Craig answered.

Brit started to chime in, but DJ cut her off. "We need a little privacy, so tell the chef we'll wait before we order anything else."

Evan nodded and disappeared through the kitchen doors.

"What if I'm still hungry?" Brit protested, giving DJ a sour look. "Sal won't like to hear that you made me wait."

"I don't give a shit, *Maud*." He looked around the restaurant to ensure they were alone. "Let's talk about Skylar."

Brit eyed him but didn't respond.

"She texted me that she was on a leave of absence with no indication of when she would return."

Brit grabbed the breadbasket and snatched a piece. "What do you want me to do about it?" She began buttering the bread.

"Do you have an idea of where she went?" DJ pulled a cigarette out of his pocket.

"She's a grown woman. She doesn't check in with me."

"She can barely stand to look at you. But that's not the point." DJ lit his cigarette and blew a huge cloud of smoke in Brit's direction. "Why would she leave?"

Brit shrugged. "Maybe her father's an asshole."

"Maybe her mother's a piece of shit!" DJ shot back, getting to his feet.

"Hold on," Craig interrupted, rising from his chair. "Like it or not, you two have a daughter. And she's missing. Don't you think you should focus your efforts on resolving your differences?"

Brit stood and put her hands on her hips. "Who the hell are *you*, anyway?"

"He's my brother, and he's Skylar's uncle." DJ took another drag of his cigarette and let it stream out of his nostrils. *Why did I think Brit would be attracted to Craig? She only likes ratty gangsters, like me.* He took a step toward her. "Skylar was fine until you showed up."

Brit's face hardened. "You're going to blame this on me? There's quite a bit you don't know about Skylar."

"I know plenty." DJ stabbed his cigarette out on his empty bread plate, recalling the graphic images. "She left because of you. She'll return when you leave."

Brit scowled. "I'm not leaving until I'm good and ready."

"You selfish bitch!" DJ thundered.

Just then, Evan appeared again with a sickly smile. "Are you ready to order dessert and coffee now?"

"Didn't I tell you to stay the fuck out of here?" DJ shouted at him.

Evan scampered away with his head down.

DJ took a minute and tried to soften his demeanor. "This is getting us nowhere. You gave me a number, and I told you I'd pay it. If you get the hell out of here, you'll have everything you need to go back to Amsterdam and live like a queen. Isn't that better than prowling around here, hurting your own daughter?"

"I've done nothing but fall in love with Sal. He'll be miserable if I leave. And angry with you. He might even pull his business. He's shown an interest in the Paramour, you know."

"That dump? There's no way in hell." The Paramour was a seedy casino-hotel on the other side of the Strip, with cheap wall art and lousy restaurants. Sal's fine taste would never be satiated there.

Craig finally interjected. "Look, you may be in love with Sal. But we've known him for a long time. He always wants something new. If you take DJ's cash and leave now, you'll spare yourself the humiliation of him leaving you."

Brit threw her head back and let out a guffaw, long

blonde hair whipping around her face. "That's why I have my girls. They take turns sitting on his face, and then mine. Someone's always coming in our suite. Does your *wife* do that for you?"

Craig glared at her coldly, his green eyes turning dark and glassy. "Don't talk about my wife."

She smiled. "Since you're designing us a new club, I'd suggest you pay attention to a little of what goes on in our suite. Satin sheets are the last thing you'll want. In fact, I'd suggest a nice, slippery rubber set for easier cleanup."

Craig turned to DJ. "I've heard enough. Call me when you're done with this … person." He strode out of the room, leaving only a whisper of his serious scent.

Brit watched him leave and then turned to DJ with a roguish sneer. "You thought you'd tote in your pretty boy brother and get me to lay down. I have to admit, he's awfully fuckable. But neither of you has any idea who you're dealing with."

"So that's it," DJ drew himself to his full height. "You don't care if your daughter's in trouble."

Her features softened slightly. "Of course, I care about her." She paused to look around. "But she's a big girl. She's lived a lot of life. If she needed to leave town, I'm sure there was a good reason." With that, she turned and strutted out, vinyl squealing when her thighs touched.

Chapter 13

After she had dropped Sesame with Clay, Skylar headed south toward downtown Las Vegas, stopping at a drugstore for a burner phone and a few other supplies. Once she had them loaded into her car, she cruised the garishly lit blocks in search of a hotel. She had learned the game of hiding in plain sight from her dad, who paraded around Las Vegas under an alias for years before his cover was blown. She just needed a place to hide out until the mess with Brit and Sal blew over.

The usual touristy crowd meandered on Fremont Street. She was looking for a smaller, more obscure hotel, and hopefully so cheap and dumpy that no one would suspect it to be a place where Skylar Van Ness might dwell.

She settled on the Rocket Palace, a relic of a hotel casino from the '50s, with its protruding red and white rocket that lit up the sky. The top floor housed an ancient steak house touted as one of the 'best views in Las Vegas.' She parked her car on the penultimate level of the garage and entered the casino, which reeked of cigarette smoke and musk. Once she was at the front desk, she realized she needed to check in under an alias. She put on dark sunglasses and tossed her long blonde hair.

"May I help you?" The front desk attendant was an older man with a scruffy gray beard.

Skylar gave him a sweet smile. "Yes, I'm checking in." She prayed he hadn't already recognized her. She and her dad were often pictured in the Las Vegas media. But maybe the people who worked in this hovel didn't pay attention.

"What name is the reservation under?" he asked.

"I don't have one. Assuming you have rooms available?" She located her Amex Black card, but then realized her credit card could be tracked. And it had her name on it. "I'd like to pay cash, if that's okay."

He eyed her with suspicion. "May I see your ID?"

"Unfortunately, I don't have one at the moment," she said, going through her wallet. "But as you can see, I have plenty of cash. She pulled a couple of hundred from her wallet and flashed them."

He rubbed his chin. "I'm not sure what you want me to do."

She pulled her black glasses halfway down her nose. "Listen. I'm hiding from an abusive ex-boyfriend. He took my ID and credit cards."

He sighed and rolled his eyes, as though this level of sleaze had crossed his desk numerous times. "Look, lady, I'm still going to need some kind of credit card for incidentals."

She slid four hundred-dollar bills toward him. "This should cover me for a few days. Plus, a little something for you." She threw him a flirtatious smile.

He looked up and studied her face, then stared at the cash. "I don't know."

She felt beads of sweat forming around her face and forehead. *This guy's not making it easy.*

He reluctantly picked up the stack of bills, counted them out, and asked her to spell the name she wanted on the room.

"Jordana Tinley, please." *How in the hell did I come up with that name?*

He gave her a slip of paper and a pen. "Write it out."

He looked at the name and typed away on his computer. Then he handed her the keys to room 501. There were only 550 rooms in the hotel, microscopic compared to Donovan or any of the major Strip hotels.

She prayed the rooms were bed-bug free. Based on what she'd already seen, it was a total dump. If Skylar worked there, she would recommend a deep cleaning. Either that or an implosion.

She imagined what DJ must have done when he saw her text. She pictured him shrugging it off and then going about his business. She had scheduled the text to send at exactly 7 a.m., and then she locked the phone in her safe with a dying battery—only 10 percent left. By the time anyone might become concerned about her whereabouts, the phone's battery would run out, leaving her untraceable.

Skylar entered the hotel bathroom, where the badly peeling wallpaper and the scent of mildew made her nose crinkle. *This is going to be fun.* She leaned into the mirror and studied her face. The chipped glass made it appear blemished. She finger-combed her long platinum locks. She needed to go incognito to hide in plain sight. She washed her makeup off and wet her hair, then began slicking it back. She had never once worn her hair that way. The style accentuated her narrow face, making her look skeletal. Once she had it all pulled back, she examined herself. *This isn't going to work.* After several attempts to make her hair look different, she gave up. *I need a wig.*

Her eyes were a different story. They were a unique color blue—almost aqua. Skylar's employees joked around the office that it was a specific Pantone color blue, and when they used that blue in graphic design, they all referred to it as *Skylar blue.*

It was a good thing she had grabbed her pair of non-prescription colored lenses before she left her house. The gray lenses were part of a Halloween costume she wore years ago. Dark, black sunglasses would also help.

She put in the lenses and set out on foot to explore the kitschy neon odyssey that was The Fremont Street Experience. That area of downtown Las Vegas had been rebranded years ago and turned into a snaking brocade of bright lights, gaming, and endless zeal.

Skylar inhaled the chilly marijuana-permeated air as she passed through the cacophony of humanity wandering the streets. She felt both hunted and freed at the same time, blending in with the horde of wanderers. She gazed up into the night sky, blinded by the flashing lights and marquee signs. *This is my home for now.* And for the first time in weeks, Skylar felt safe in a bed of anonymity within the city's transient population. She idled by a corner novelty store selling all manner of Las Vegas memorabilia. There, she bought a cheap pair of dark black sunglasses. She found a taxi and directed the driver to Serge's Wigs. She'd heard the store had the most realistic human hair wigs.

An older, heavyset woman approached Skylar as soon as she entered the shop.

"Hello, gorgeous! Boy, do you have a head of hair on you." Her accent reeked of Brooklyn. "My name's Marge," she said. "May I?" Without waiting for an answer, she boldly ran her fingers through Skylar's locks, murmuring in appreciation. Marge backed up and gave her the once-over. "You must be a dancer—or a showgirl."

Skylar recoiled from the audacious sales associate and began sorting through the mélange of Styrofoam heads with more hairstyles and colors than she could ever dream up. One caught her eye because it was so different from her own hair. The style was long and straight, parted in the middle, and dark auburn-black, with a smattering of cherry highlights. She turned to Marge. "I'll try this one."

Marge helped pull her hair back, covered it with a wig cap, then fitted the wig on her head, the long, dark hair draping down the middle of her back and shoulders. "Ooh, this one's gorgeous on you," she cooed, arranging the hair in pieces to frame Skylar's face. She pulled her to the closest mirror.

Skylar gasped. *I look like a different person.* Her gray lenses took on a unique hue against the dark hair, which framed her face, making her appear much younger than her years. She smiled and tried to imagine herself as someone else. *Jordana Tinley.* "I'll take it."

Skylar had one more stop on the way back to the Rocket Palace: a tattoo parlor.

She had one small tattoo on the lower part of her tummy, directly underneath her bikini line—left over from when she graduated from UNLV. The tattoo was of a snake slithering downward. It was about the time Skylar swore off men and dating. She had selected the spot on her body where no one would see it unless they were being intimate with her, which she vowed would never again happen. She interpreted the snake as a symbol of her own evolution—someone who had grown and shed a pernicious skin.

This time, Skylar wanted to mark her body in a prominent place to throw off anyone who could potentially be looking for her—identifying her. She entered Downtown Tattoos and met the female artist who would be inking her skin permanently. After sifting through several designs, Skylar selected one featuring a large treble clef with musical notes and foliage growing from it. It was perfect for her left wrist and extended up her forearm about four inches. The artist told her it would take at least four hours. The studio was open around the clock, so she sat and endured the painful pricks to her wrist and arm, looking away to avoid seeing blood. She remained there until late in the night.

When the ink artist had finished, Skylar paid for the tattoo in cash and drifted back to the Rocket Palace. Her room felt dark and dreary, except for the rocket's flashing red and white lights stabbing through threadbare drapes. A wake of leftover cigarettes tainted the bed linens. She had forgotten entirely to buy an air freshener, but she could get some in the morning. She washed her face, brushed her teeth, and put a bag of ice from the hall machine on her wrist. As soon as the lights were off, she drifted into a deep sleep.

CHAPTER 19

DJ entered his office and found Craig settled on the couch, reading the *Las Vegas Review-Journal.* "That went well," DJ remarked, sighing, and plopping down across from Craig. "What now?"

Craig noisily folded the newspaper and tossed it on the coffee table. "Tell me you never *married* that woman."

DJ wiped his forehead with his hand. "Look, I don't need a lecture. You know my taste in women was horrible before I met Max."

"Horrible doesn't even begin to cover it. How about disgusting and vile?" Craig had a familiar look on his face, like he'd smelled a foul odor and was ready to throw up.

DJ rose from his chair, jaw clenched. "Do you have amnesia? If I remember correctly, you weren't exactly a saint. What about all that trash you collected before you met Jane? You went through rubbers faster than I go through toilet paper."

Craig knitted his eyebrows, mouth now a straight line. "At least I didn't marry any of them. And the condoms were to prevent an unwanted pregnancy. Maybe you should have considered using them."

"What are you saying, Craig?" DJ countered. "That Skylar is a mistake?" He shook his head, disgusted. *Craig thinks he's better than me. Always has. And that attitude clearly rubbed off on poor Skylar.* "No wonder she took off alone. And no matter what you think about Brit, she's still with Sal and staying in my hotel."

Craig's face softened, and he leaned back. "I'm sorry, DJ. That's not at all what I meant. Skylar's my niece, and I love her. As far as Sal goes, you may have to just ride it out until he gets bored with the whole scene."

"Craig, you just heard what she said. The guy's got a sexual goldmine up there. You think he's going anywhere anytime soon?"

Craig sat up straight. "Wait, what about his wife? Isn't Sal married?"

DJ nodded. "Of course, he is. We can't divulge Sal's dirty habits to her. Then we shoot ourselves in the foot."

"No, I'm not talking about that. When does he usually go back home?"

DJ shrugged. "It depends. The longest he's ever stayed here is a few weeks—occasionally a month."

Craig looked thoughtfully at DJ. "Then it's possible he'll be leaving soon. If that's the case, you can put surveillance on Brit—catch her in a compromising situation—even if it's of your own creation."

DJ's mental wheels were spinning. *All we need is proof she's using Sal.* "Right, like we send a hot guy upstairs to give her a massage and catch the horny bitch doing something illegal."

"Exactly," Craig responded. "With her, it's just a matter of time. Once you have extortion material to show Sal, you can use it to get rid of her before he ever returns."

"What about the seven hoes?" DJ asked, suddenly feeling lighter.

Craig leaned forward. "Once their main hustle is gone, pay them off—somewhere in the neighborhood of $40,000 each—that's much cheaper than paying Brit. When Sal returns, he'll be free to start up with a new batch."

DJ rested his hand against his cheek. "I suppose that could work."

"Do you have a better idea?" Craig then let out a smirk. "By the way, where do you think she picked up that outfit?"

DJ shrugged, recalling the skintight catsuit with the ridiculously high platform heels. "Maybe she dug it out of the dumpster at a tire factory?"

"It looked more to me like she fell into the La Brea tarpits with the other extinct artifacts," Craig shot back.

They both burst into laughter. For DJ, it felt good to laugh for the first time since he was called back from Bali—especially picturing Brit unearthed, covered in tar, and on display with LA's ancient dinosaurs. *I'd enjoy seeing that.*

Then his missing daughter came to mind, and the photos he found in her safe. "Now I just need to find Skylar," DJ said, gnawing on his thumbnail.

Craig nodded. "Has she ever done something like this?"

"Never." He regretted not prying more into the conversation they'd had right before she disappeared.

I've never paid attention to her feelings—never paid attention to her. He ran his fingers through his hair.

"I know you don't want to show me the pictures," Craig said, "but is there any clue as to who she was with? Or even who snapped them in the first place?"

I hadn't considered who took the photos. The guy's face was sort of clear in a few of the shots. Overall, they were murky, which told DJ that whoever photographed them was either spying or a kinky voyeur. Brit suddenly floated through his mind. *What if it was her?* It certainly wouldn't surprise him. He wondered whether Brit brought the photos to Las Vegas to blackmail Skylar and extract money from DJ. If that were the case, he needed to get to Skylar and let her know that no one, including Brit, could harm her.

He looked up at Craig. "As much as it pains me, I'll have to take a closer look."

Craig rose to his feet. "If I were you, I'd have a private investigator run a facial identity check on the man—you have nothing to lose at this point."

I hadn't thought of that either. This is why I need Craig—he's much more logical than I could ever be in this situation. DJ rose from his chair. "I will. But not today." He glanced at his watch and then at Craig. "Since that wasn't much of a lunch, you up for an early dinner somewhere off campus?"

Chapter 20

Gusty wind nearly blew Skylar over as she fought her way down Main Street in search of food. She flipped up the hood of her sweatshirt and walked a little faster, hunting for shelter. She ran inside the first restaurant she could find. From the size of the crowd, Skylar realized everyone else had the same idea. She found a high, four-top table in the back of the restaurant and took the booth on the side so she could face the restaurant and people-watch. She pulled off her black glasses, glanced over the menu, and shivered. Las Vegas was cold in the winter months, and she wished she had brought a warm coat. She would have to buy something. She dialed Clay while waiting for the server.

She had texted Clay her burner phone number the night before signing it, with the message "Love, Sesame."

He answered on the second ring. "Hey," he began. "Hold on a second. Going to my office."

Skylar heard some scuffling and his office door closing. "You there?" he asked. "I can talk now."

"Hi, yes. I'm sitting in a café downtown trying to get lunch. "How's my Sesame?"

"She's okay. I can tell she misses her mommy, though."

"Why? What is she doing?"

"She just seems a little disoriented, you know. It's a strange house, and you're not there."

Skylar swallowed hard and tried to remember why she had to leave in the first place. Brit was out to get her and hold her accountable for murder. "Yeah, I know. It's strange for me, too."

"I've been trying to call, but you don't have voicemail set up."

"That's on purpose," Skylar responded, examining her tattoo, which was still pink and swollen. "Did something happen at work?"

"Oh, nothing much. Just the entire executive team questioning me about you."

"What?" Skylar felt a shiver. "How would they even know to question *you*?"

Clay breathed a deep sigh. "They know we're friends. Someone told DJ, and I was called on the carpet. You know, it's not easy for me to lie to that man. He's only the CEO *and* your father."

"What did he say?" she asked, trying to picture DJ badgering her best friend about her whereabouts.

"He called me into his office. The Monarch was there, too. Your dad was asking all kinds of questions about where you might be."

"What did you tell him?" Pringles of fear shot up her neck.

"Nothing. Not even that I have Sesame. But he didn't give up easily. I swear I felt like I was lying under oath."

The server showed up, and Skylar cupped her hand over the phone and ordered a vegetable omelet. "Oh, and can I get some coffee, please?"

The server nodded.

"How did you leave it?" Skylar asked as soon as the server was out of earshot.

"I said something about you always wanting to go on a cruise. It was all I could think of. The next day, we had to cater lunch at One Pico for your dad, Maud, and Sal. Oh, and your uncle Craig was there. Total stunner. You never mentioned that."

Of course, Clay was taken with Craig. *What else is new?* "That's an interesting group. Do you know why they were meeting?" She imagined Brit sitting at a table sharing airspace with Craig Keller, the rock star, and she had a sudden urge to laugh out loud. He had to have hated that.

"No clue. They kept it under wraps and told Evan to steer clear because they wanted privacy. I asked him later, and he said the vibe in there was tense—said DJ yelled at him."

"I can only imagine," she commented, recalling the scene at the Crown and Anchor over a bogus dart game. DJ and Brit were like fire and gunpowder with sparks flying—it was only a matter of time before an explosion blew everyone away.

"Sweetie, how long are you going to keep this up?"

She inhaled deeply. "I don't know yet. I'm just laying low until Brit gives up and goes away. I have no idea how long that'll be. You've got to keep covering for me for now."

"You know I will," he said, sounding weary. "What are you going to do today?"

"You mean besides wander the streets like some kind of fugitive? I don't know. It feels weird not to be slave to my calendar."

Clay let out a nervous laugh. "Well, enjoy it while you can. I'll send you pics of Sesame tonight."

"And give her lots of kisses for me." She imagined Sesame padding around Clay's home, looking for her. She caught her breath.

"You got it. Take care."

The server came back with a large cup of coffee. Skylar accepted it gratefully and took a long sip. It was good and hot. She set the cup in front of her and rubbed her hands together. She stared down at her reflection in the mirrored tabletop. She was surprised at the long, dark wig. *I'll have to get used to seeing myself like this.* She almost lost herself in the thought until a familiar voice came out of nowhere.

"I'm sorry to bother you, but would you mind sharing your table?"

Startled, she looked up in horror to see none other than James Monarch. She shuddered as though someone poured ice water down her back, and she almost knocked over her coffee.

"Sorry, but this place is totally packed and …" he glanced around the restaurant. "Well, I'm in a bit of a hurry."

She could do nothing but nod. Then she watched, panic mounting, as he peeled off his navy peacoat and hung it on the back of his chair. *How did he find me so fast? This can't be a coincidence!*

He adjusted his tweed jacket and settled into the chair facing her. She instinctively covered her eyes with the black glasses. *Why didn't I just leave the city?* Las Vegas had always been an overgrown small town. *I never know who I might run into.*

"Thank you," he said. "This place is popular."

Skylar gave him a tight-lipped smile but didn't say a word. She didn't dare. James knew her voice, and she hadn't considered disguising it. *Why is he downtown in the first place?* It was well past noon. Unless he had a meeting with someone in the near vicinity, and decided to eat before returning to the Strip. She scoured her thoughts and tried to remain calm.

"What's good here?" he asked in his charming Irish accent, giving her a quick glance before returning to the menu.

Skylar shrugged with another slight smile. Her hands shook so violently that she put them under the table. Although petrified James would recognize her, she felt warm and safe having him this close again. In a very real sense, she longed to have a conversation with him. She thought about how she might disguise her own voice, but it was distinctly hers. She had a throaty sound that would surely be recognizable, especially to James, who had talked to her multiple times a day for several years.

"Your first time, too?" he asked, eyeing her hair.

Skylar nodded. *I need to get out of here as soon as possible.* She looked around frantically and spotted the server. She held up her index finger to James, signaling that she would be back, and slid out of her seat.

She cornered the server. "I have to leave now. Could

you please box up my lunch and bring the check? Or I can wait up front."

"No problem," she responded. "Just have a seat, and I'll be by with everything."

Skylar took the opportunity to visit the restroom. She stood staring into the mirror, considering how she might change her voice. She couldn't do English accents. James would be able to sniff out a fake anyway. But she was good at a Southern drawl from watching Dolly Parton in *9 to 5* more times than she could count as a child. "Ha, ma name's Jordana. Ahm from South Carolina," she said into the mirror. "If ah had mo tahm, ah'd stick around, ya know?" She repeated a few more lines. *God, I sound idiotic.* She racked her brain for another idea. *What if I had laryngitis?* Then she could do nothing but whisper. She didn't have makeup on, which was different from her usual work look. The black glasses and gray contacts obscured her unique blue eyes, and her casual clothing was something James had never seen. Without the high heels, she was several inches shorter than James. *I just need to fool him until I get my check.* She took a deep breath and exited the bathroom.

Back at the table, James was scrolling through his phone and drinking coffee. Her to-go box and check were sitting there. She slid back into her seat, and James looked up as she grabbed her backpack.

"I hope I didn't scare you away," he said pleasantly.

Skylar rummaged through her backpack and pulled out cash. "No, I'm fine," she said in a whisper. "I have laryngitis. Lost my voice last night at the craps table."

He gave her that insanely attractive crooked smile, eyes on the cash in her hand. "You must have been a big winner."

Oh my god, does he really think I'm someone else?

He examined her face with knitted brows. "You remind me of someone. Are you a local?"

Oh shit. He recognizes me. Time to go!

Skylar shook her head, feeling the long, cherry-black hair cascade down her shoulders. She picked up her check. "No. From Minneapolis."

James didn't release his penetrating gaze. "My name's James, by the way."

Skylar lowered her eyes to her check and then slapped some cash on the table. "Nice to meet you. I'm Jordana."

"Nice name," he said. "Sure you don't want to stay and eat your lunch? I promise to stop talking, full stop."

Is he flirting? Skylar looked up quickly. *This is a James I don't know.* He was never anything but annoyingly professional and condescending. But this James was the opposite. She eyed the exit before their eyes met again. He was still smiling at her.

"Maybe I'll stay and finish my coffee," she whispered. "You don't sound like you're from here either."

He laughed. "I'm from Ireland, actually."

Here comes the part where he brags about Trinity College. She felt the corners of her mouth tug into a grin, thinking that she was about to find out how James hit on women. *This might be fun as long as he doesn't catch on to who I really am.* She tossed her dark hair over her shoulders. "What part of Ireland?"

"Originally from Belfast. Northern Ireland," he said. "Have you ever been?"

She was surprised to hear he was from somewhere other than Dublin, which was the story he told at the office. "I've only been to Dublin," she answered, thinking she would goad him into talking about his education. "I like the Temple Bar District," she added.

The server showed up and asked James for his order. "I'll have the scrambled eggs and bacon," he said. "White toast and jam."

Skylar recalled him ordering beef noodles at Suki during lunch. She respected his openly scrappy food orders and felt a sudden kinship. *I've worked with this man for years but know nothing about him.*

"You doing okay?" The server asked Skylar with a mischievous smile. "I see you're going to enjoy your lunch *here*," she said, angling her head toward James.

Skylar just nodded.

The server left, and James began studying her again. His eyes lowered to her left wrist and forearm. "That tattoo looks fresh. Did you just get it?" he asked innocently enough.

"Yesterday," she whispered, opening the box where her vegetable omelet sat getting cold.

He laughed. "You're really living a Vegas stereotype. Looks like a treble clef. May I see it?"

She nodded, thrusting her wrist forward. He touched it, and a prickle shot up her forearm under the warmth of James's fingers.

"Does it hurt?"

She shook her head. "Not really."

He let go of her hand. "So, what's up with the treble clef? You into music?"

She nodded and pushed her black glasses up her nose.

"So am I. What kind of tunes do you fancy?"

"Indie Rock," she responded. "And you?"

"I can listen to anything but country," he answered with a smile. "There's a lot of live music around here. It's not like the Temple Bar District or anything, but it's still fun. Where are you staying?"

She panicked. *I can't tell him where I am.* "With friends."

The server returned with his food and placed it in front of him.

Skylar realized that she hadn't yet touched her omelet in its to-go box. She grabbed her utensils and picked at the omelet.

James ate hungrily. He paused to drink his coffee and wipe his mouth with a napkin. "Sorry to scarf this, but I didn't eat breakfast. Had an early meeting at the convention center."

That's why he's downtown. "You must be important," Skylar commented.

"Not at all," he answered between bites. "Just work for a casino."

"You have a girlfriend?" She wasn't sure what answer she wanted to hear. She just wanted an answer. *I'm in the perfect position to get it.*

He shook his head. "Not today."

What does that mean? She decided not to comment.

He crunched into his white toast and chewed it thoroughly. "You have a boyfriend?"

She shook her head and smiled. "Not today."

He pulled out his card and handed it to her. "This is me. If you get bored with winning on the craps table or getting tattoos, give me a call. I'll take you to see some live music."

She glanced at the card. "So, you *are* important," she said, admiring his blue eyes and streaked hair.

He shrugged and finished the last bite of his toast. He waved down the server, and she brought his check. As soon as he had signed off, he got to his feet and drew the peacoat over his shoulders. Skylar watched his long fingers fasten the double-breasted buttons and realized he was leaving her. She may not see him until she was Skylar again. *And who knows when that will be?*

"James."

He looked up.

"It's nice to meet you," she whispered. "I might call you."

He gave her a lopsided grin. "I'm counting on it." And he disappeared through the exit.

Chapter 21

*C*raig was in the mood for a 'fat guy steakhouse,' as he called it, so DJ suggested the Golden Steer, an old Vegas favorite. On the way, he dialed Max.

"Well?" she asked upon answering the phone, which was on Bluetooth so Craig could hear every word. "Where are you?"

DJ grimaced. "I was just calling to let you know Craig and I are headed to the Golden Steer."

Craig closed his eyes and shook his head as if to say, *"Don't do it.*

"First you bump me from lunch, and now you're blowing me off for dinner?"

Before DJ could defend his decision, Max interrupted.

"I didn't spend all day cooking beef bourguignon only to have you stand me up."

DJ felt a pang of guilt. "I'm sorry, Max. I had no idea you cooked. We'll be there in a bit."

"Fine."

And the line went dead.

DJ tore his eyes away from the road to look at Craig. "What time's your flight?"

Craig glanced at his watch. "10 p.m."

DJ let out a sigh of relief. "Plenty of time for a home-cooked meal."

When they entered the house through the garage, the smell of red wine and garlic invaded DJ's senses.

Max was flitting around the kitchen, wearing potholders. He thought she was a little overdressed for a casual evening at home—in a sleeveless black jumpsuit with a collar that reminded him of a tuxedo.

"We're home," DJ called, giving Craig a sideways glance.

Max turned and approached the two brothers, and DJ watched her face as Craig kissed her on the cheek. She smiled widely, and DJ caught a glimpse of her cleavage as she leaned in. Max rarely wore low-cut blouses.

A shot of pure insecurity pelted DJ in the stomach. *What is she doing?* Whenever women were around Craig, DJ sought out the usual signs—the flushed cheeks, hopeful gleam, and general giddiness. Although DJ knew he was not the most perceptive person on the planet, he had never sensed a spark between his handsome brother and Max. *She must be playing a little game of revenge.* He sighed.

"May I get you two something to drink?" she asked. "I have a beautiful Pinot Noir."

"It smells incredible in here," Craig remarked with that smile. "Sorry I showed up empty-handed."

"You were on a last-minute mission," she commented. "DJ, would you like Pinot Noir, too?"

He nodded. "I'll open the bottle."

Craig and Max trailed DJ into the kitchen and stood around the marble-top island.

Craig shrugged off his suit jacket. "You've done a lot with this place already," he said as DJ pulled a bottle of Pinot Noir from a pantry-sized wine cellar located right off the kitchen. "It looks great."

Regardless of the pleasantries, awkward tension blanketed the room. *This is going to be a long night.*

"Thank you," Max responded. "Let me hang up your jacket." She leaned forward to retrieve it from Craig, and DJ caught sight of her cleavage again. "You're staying with us tonight, right?"

DJ popped the cork on the wine bottle and frowned. *She never invites anyone to stay the night without advance notice.* Again, he wondered what she was up to.

"I hadn't planned to," Craig said with a mildly apologetic smile. "I didn't bring an overnight bag."

Her face became shrouded in disappointment, and then she perked up. "You left some clothes here on your last business trip. They're hanging in one of the guest rooms."

Before Craig could respond, Max continued.

"You can borrow some of DJ's pajamas—the bottoms might be a little big on you." She let out a sarcastic laugh as she side-eyed DJ. "Say yes!"

Now she's just being mean. Fuming, DJ poured a glass of wine for each of them, then handed one glass to Max and one to Craig.

"Salut," they said in unison before clinking glasses. DJ took a large gulp.

"I'm dying to hear how your lunch went." Max said directly to Craig.

He pressed his lips together and gestured toward DJ. "I think your husband should lead on that one."

Max raised one eyebrow and turned to DJ. "Well? I'm all ears."

DJ took another extra-large swig of his wine, swallowed, and suppressed a belch. "Not much to tell. Other than my ex-wife's not leaving until I throw her out."

Her face tightened, and the corners of her lips curled downward. "Really? What about the grin fuck? I thought you were going to lie about moving forward with her absurd peep show idea."

DJ sighed and nodded. "She and Sal already assumed that. The meeting … um … got a bit derailed."

Max's eyes bulged. "Derailed?" How?"

DJ and Craig exchanged uncomfortable glances.

"Let's just say she threw us a bit of a curve ball," DJ said.

Max drew back her shoulders and lifted her chin. "Brit didn't throw a curveball at all, DJ, *you* did. You insisted on Craig being there when they were expecting me." She tossed her shoulder-length bob and turned her back to stir the gurgling crock of beef bourguignon.

DJ watched her back twitch as she held the pan lid with one pot-holder-covered hand and jerked the spoon with her other arm in a circular motion. He took a deep breath and blew it out slowly, noting the uneasy expression clouding Craig's face.

DJ moved closer to her. "Max, she knows how to push my buttons. What was I supposed to do?"

She noisily threw the spoon on the counter, slammed the crock lid back on, and spun around to face her husband. "You fucked up, DJ! Pushing your buttons is way too easy. Especially for a sex-worker like Brit who does it for a living."

She took a step toward DJ, so she was looking straight up into his eyes.

Shit, she's seriously pissed. DJ stepped back.

"I should have been there, and you know it. *I* wouldn't have fucked it up so badly." She threw her potholder on the counter.

"Jesus, Max. Calm down. Craig came up with an alternative plan to get rid of her." He turned to his brother. "Tell Max your idea."

Craig took a small sip of his wine and then cleared his throat. "It seems to me that all we need is a reason for Sal to go home to Arizona to see his wife. Once he's away, it'll be easier for DJ to take care of the problem."

Max moved her gaze to Craig. "Really? Have either of you thought that through?" She turned to DJ. "I know Elena Vincenzo. And she prefers Sal stay in Vegas as long as he wants. They get along better when they're apart."

"Sounds familiar," DJ muttered under his breath. But she gave him an idea. "You're right, Max. You've known Elena for years. I wonder if you can help speed up Sal's departure."

She shot him a cold look. "Sure. *Now* you want my help."

Later that night, in bed with Max, DJ felt restless.

Over dinner, they'd laid out a plan for Max to visit Elena in Scottsdale the next day and "run into her" at Neiman Marcus's Mariposa Café. She hung out every afternoon for drinks after shopping in the Fashion Square Mall. Once Max returned to Vegas, she would drop a hint to Sal that Elena didn't look well and that she's concerned. Sal, highly respected Max, so he might go home in a hurry to check on his wife. At least that's what they hoped.

They risked that Sal would do the opposite, but they had to take the chance.

DJ reached over and touched her arm. "Hey."

She looked up from her book. "Hey."

At least she's no longer frowning. "How are you doing?" he asked, caressing her arm tenderly. Her muscles felt stiff as he kneaded her skin.

She shrugged. "I guess, I'm okay."

"I'm sorry for all this." He studied her face. She wore no makeup, but her olive skin glowed in the soft lighting.

"We'll figure it out." She set her book down on the nightstand and then shifted in bed to face her husband. "Did you loan Craig some pajamas?"

He nodded. "Yeah, the pants fit okay, but the top was a little tight. His shoulders are broad."

"I never noticed." She gave him a coy grin, leaned back, and lay her head on the pillow with a wistful sigh. "Must be nice."

"What must be nice?"

"Oh, I don't know. I guess it must be nice to be *that* good-looking *and* fit."

It struck DJ who Max was referring to. He groaned aloud.

"What?" she said, now with a playful smile. "Don't be jealous. He's your brother. You have to admit he looks great." She rested the back of her hand on her forehead. "I don't envy Jane, though. She must have a tough time fighting off all the admirers."

He sat upright in bed and glared at Max. "Well, in case you haven't noticed, Jane's not exactly hard on the eyes, either." He felt a tension headache coming on. *Why the hell is Max suddenly falling into the Craig Keller crush club?* It was not at all what he wanted to hear coming off an apocalyptic day featuring Brit and the discovery of Skylar's hidden photos.

"What are you getting so upset about?" Max was now sitting up, returning DJ's glare. "The man takes care of himself. He works at it. You could do the exact same thing if you wanted to."

DJ threw her a fuming scowl. "Look, Max. I've been watching you flirt with my brother all night. If you want to fuck him, he's in the next room. Just don't come back to my bed without a shower." He flopped down and pulled the covers over his head, his back facing Max.

Max threw the covers aside and jumped out of bed so fast, she almost fell. "Don't you talk to me like that!" She grabbed her robe and threw it over her shoulders, snatched the book and her reading glasses off the nightstand. "And, by the way, *no one's* as impressed by Craig's looks as *you* are—not even your ex-wife."

DJ's face was so overheated, sweat droplets formed at his brow. He got out of bed and turned on the light. "Don't leave. I'll go." He began to make his way out of the room. "Sweet dreams," he grated through his teeth as he stomped past her.

"Fine," she shouted after him.

DJ barreled into the kitchen and yanked his bottle of Bruichladdich Black Art 1992 scotch out of the cupboard. He poured a stiff one and sat at the kitchen table, mind tumbling with thoughts. *Max is trying to press my buttons. All these women want to push my buttons.* She was angry about the situation with Brit, and the only way she knew how to hurt him was to focus on Craig. *And my weaknesses.* He guzzled the rest of the scotch and poured another. *She wants me to take better care of myself. I get that. Always nagging. Stop smoking. Drink less. Exercise more.* But that was his vulnerability. *If you can't trust your own wife to be kind about your vulnerabilities, who can you trust?* He took an extra-large slug of his second scotch. The alcohol burned his throat and went to his head. He didn't care. He wanted to numb his emotions after the day he'd had.

After polishing off his third drink, he had one singular thought. He was dying for a cigarette. He rose to his feet and found the alarm keypad, punched in the code to turn it off, and stole out to his car to retrieve his pack.

He re-entered the house and did the unthinkable. *The forbidden.* He lit up. He puffed away and watched the smoke clouds billow and curl towards their 30-foot vaulted ceiling. He found a perverse satisfaction in flouting

Max's omnipresent rules and regulations. He loved that the smoke would soon seep into their bedroom and drive her mad with rage. He wanted to see her lose her cool. "I want fucking fireworks!" he shouted out loud.

"What's going on?" It was Craig's voice behind him. "What fireworks?"

He looked up at Craig and tried to see him through Max's eyes. He was shirtless, wearing DJ's pajama bottoms that hung low on his waist, barely held up by the drawstring. DJ examined the sheen of his tanned abdominal muscles, the round, hard biceps, and lean waist. Then he lifted his eyes to Craig's chiseled face, now wearing a concerned look, his dark glossy hair mussed from sleep. *He* was who Max should have. He was everyone's ideal husband, lover, boyfriend. He was so perfect in the moment that DJ wanted to throw up.

But the awful truth stood staring him in the face. Craig was, and always would be, his half-brother. He inherited his masculine good looks from Don, while DJ inherited whatever looks he had from Luuk Van Ness, a fact that shamed him every day when he gazed back at his own reflection.

"It's not fair," he blurted.

"What's not fair?" Craig's forehead wrinkled, and his eyebrows knitted. His green eyes were aglow.

"That you look the way you do. Who has eyes like yours? They look like hard fucking candies. It's always so damned easy for you." He took another drag of his cigarette.

"DJ, what happened? What's all this?"

Just then, Max appeared in the doorway, robe on halfway, like she didn't waste time marching down the stairs. She waved her hand in disgust to dispel the smoke. "I can't believe you! I can't believe you'd pollute our home."

DJ quaffed more scotch and rose from his chair, staggering, pointing at Craig with his smoldering cigarette, lurching into a stumble towards him, scotch sloshing out of his glass. "Here he is, Max. Here's your perfect man. He doesn't smoke, and he looks like a god. Go ahead. Have him if you want." DJ knew he was slurring his words, but he was beyond caring.

"I don't know what happened tonight," Craig said calmly. "But DJ, you're out of line."

"He's worse than out of line," Max fumed. "DJ, put that cigarette out this minute."

DJ let out a loud snicker. "Right away, honey."

Craig moved toward DJ. "Hey, let me get you to bed." He gently touched his arm. "Come with me. It's been a tough day." Craig removed the cigarette from DJ's hand and disposed of it in the kitchen sink.

He returned and addressed Max. "Look, this is obviously a stressful time. I should have gone home to LA tonight. Don't listen to DJ right now. He's going through a lot. I don't know if he told you, but ..." he looked around and took a step closer to Max, leaning in. He said in a loud whisper, "He found some disturbing photos of Skylar locked in her safe."

DJ caught Max's countenance softening slightly, and her eyes darted from DJ to Craig. "What photos?"

DJ laid one hand on his forehead, covering his eyes. "I can hear you."

"I didn't see them," Craig responded softly. "I'll let DJ fill you in, but if you can, please give him a break tonight."

She threw back a curt nod. "Fine. But he needs to sleep in the guest room. He reeks of tobacco."

DJ looked up in time to see Max point to the side of the house where another unoccupied guest room awaited. She wrapped her arms around her body. "I have no interest in cozying up to a dirty ashtray."

DJ smirked and shook his head. "I guess the honeymoon's over, eh?"

"You think?" she deadpanned back.

"It's okay, Max," said Craig, sounding somber. "I'll take care of him."

Craig slung DJ's arm around his neck and lifted him in one finite move. Together, they hobbled to the guest room while Max followed.

Craig helped DJ into bed and turned his lamp off while Max lingered in the hallway. "Be easy on him," Craig said to Max before closing the guest room door.

CHAPTER 22

The Rocket Palace was hopping by the time Skylar returned to her room. She thought about her encounter with James and tried to make sense of it. They had lunch as strangers. *What are the odds?* He told her she reminded him of someone. *Did he recognize me?* If not, she had discovered a whole new side to him. He was humble. And something told her they were similar in many ways. And, of sublime importance, they shared a music connection. She missed her Spotify playlists—missed music in general. There were a few music channels on the cable television in her room, but they were mostly easy listening or country. Crap tourists listened to.

She took a hot shower, brushed her teeth, and put on her pajamas. She cranked up the heat before huddling in bed. It was too early to go to sleep, but she was so cold from the blustery day that she just wanted to be cozy and warm. Her feet felt like two heavy popsicles under the covers. She got up, found another blanket in the closet, and threw it on the bed.

She ended up falling asleep with a book on her chest and waking to the sound of her hotel room phone ringing. She glanced at her watch and contemplated answering. She was not sure who would be calling after 9 p.m. *Who the hell even knows I'm staying here except for the front desk staff?*

She let it go to voicemail. But after several minutes, the phone light didn't flicker on. Skylar picked up her phone and dialed the front desk.

"Hello, this is Jordana Tinley in room 501."

"Yes, Ms. Tinley, what can we do for you?"

"Did someone from the front desk just call me?"

"Not that I'm aware of."

"Oh," was all she could think to say. "Maybe it was a misdial." And she hung up.

Around 15 minutes later, Skylar was back under the covers with the lights turned out. She tossed and turned, unable to sleep. A soft scratching noise came from the door of her room. She sat upright, clutching the covers, a massive shudder curdling up her spine.

Scratch. Scratch. Scratch.

There it is again! She scrambled out of bed, fumbled for her small flashlight, clicked it on, and panned the room. Her backpack was on the dresser. The scratching on the door continued. She padded over to her backpack and silently pulled out her handgun. She held the flashlight between her teeth and checked to make sure the gun was loaded. She cocked it and slowly crept forward. Her chin quivered as she neared the door, which she had double-latched.

Skylar stood with the gun poised to shoot, fingers

trembling. She half-expected whoever it was to kick the door in, so she stayed just far enough away.

In the silence, she sidled up to the door, hands shaking. She put her ear close, straining to hear. The only sound was the eerily ticking clock near her bed. She took the flashlight out of her mouth and switched it off.

Then she heard shuffling. Rustling. A white rectangle slid under her door. She waited, eyes watering.

The room was so dark, she couldn't tell what it was. She didn't dare switch on her flashlight. She froze and held her breath for several seconds, trying her best not to move or make a noise.

After several minutes, Skylar heard footsteps slowly fading and the elevator ringing, which was about 20 feet from her room.

She sighed in relief when she heard the elevator door close. She turned on the hallway light and saw the envelope at her feet.

She rushed to retrieve it, heart thudding in her chest, still clutching her handgun in one hand. Someone had printed her alias, *Jordana*, on the envelope. She set the handgun down on her bed and tore at it with shaky fingers, pulling out what looked like a photo.

She held it under the light and gasped in horror. The photo was of her—another nude shot, but this time, she was lying in a dark pool of blood, facing the corpse of her dead pimp, bloody knife by her side. The memory of that dank, musty apartment and that man's horrible breath and body odor—the stench of his blood everywhere—came back to her like it was yesterday. Skylar clasped her hand over her mouth, feeling the vomit rising. She dropped the photo and scurried to the bathroom, where she purged her guts in the toilet.

When she became aware of her surroundings, she shakily got to her feet. She stared at herself in the bathroom mirror and ran cool water before splashing it on her face. "Pull yourself together, Skylar," she admonished aloud.

Her mind swirled with rampant thoughts. *Someone is following me.* Someone knew she was using the alias, 'Jordana.' The only people she had told were the hotel front desk, Clay, and James. Clay wouldn't tell a soul. *But what about James?* Suddenly, a horrible thought caused the hairs on her neck to stand at attention. *What if James is out to get me?*

She tried to imagine James, in his smart navy peacoat, scratching at her hotel room door late at night, and it didn't make sense. He was too savvy to stalk someone in person. But he could have hired someone to do it. She was reminded of his temper. And the way his face flushed in the heat of an argument. She had seen it many times throughout their tenure. She thought back to the time they met with Brit in the Cork Wine Bar and how she ran out on him. He had called to yell at her. Shortly thereafter, she found the red roses with the taunting note about the murder.

She walked herself back through the annals of her relationship with James. *He's up for my job.* Skylar had always been in his crosshairs. He never hid his animosity toward her. If she were out of the way, he would easily slide into the CEO role when DJ retired. With Skylar there blocking his path, it might be more difficult. She thought back to the moment Brit made her entrance, first via email and then in person. Her initial fear was that James would somehow find out and use the information to take her down. *Could it be that James has been behind it the whole time?*

Skylar's head clouded with dizziness. She staggered out of the bathroom and lay down on the bed, one hand on her head, the other on her abdomen. James was brilliant. Everyone knew that. He was also wily. *He kept me just close enough to make me feel comfortable without making me suspect him.*

James had been in on every aspect of Brit's reappearance. In fact, he could have been the one who summoned her from Amsterdam. He even called Skylar the night of DJ's wedding with some lame question about the media plan. Perhaps he was checking her reaction to an email from her estranged mother.

The whole thing came together like a mind-boggling mystery, with all the lost pieces of the story fitting into place. James was the first to bring up Maud and Sal at lunch that fateful day, after they had both modeled the Marco uniforms. James claimed he hadn't met Maud, but he could have been the one who set her up with Sal in the first place.

Skylar recalled the meeting with Brit in her office that day she was having coffee with James. She remembered Brit's words, "How would you like the *fancy Irishman* to know the truth?" She hadn't considered it at the time, but how would Brit know James was Irish, or who he was at all?

Oh God, what am I thinking? I'm spinning now. James has an unmistakable Irish brogue. Anyone could hear it. But what if I'm right? What if James is stalking me?

And now Skylar had ignorantly spilled the tea with James over lunch earlier. She hated herself for being so gullible—so naïve and stupid. She chided herself for fantasizing about James—even seeing him as a form of protection from the cruelty of her predicament. Of course, there had been no chance 'meet cute'. Their lunch had been premeditated. James had been following her the whole time. He had the photos. He knew about the murder. *He's out to make me pay.*

Skylar glanced around at her things strewn all over the cheap hotel room. *There's no way I can stay here now.* She began gathering her belongings, frantically thinking about her next move. *Where can I go?* Not home. Not to Clay's.

When she had her things packed and the handgun tucked away, she gazed out the window at the thin beam of moonlight. Soon it would be dawn, and she needed to get out of the hotel before daybreak.

She had no appetite, but knew she'd need her strength for whatever the future held. She pulled a protein bar from her bag and sat, forcing down small bites. She sipped her bottled water and began pacing. Finally, she stopped and examined the photo again. She couldn't believe someone had taken the photos in the first place. *Who was there when I was being raped? Who was there when I ultimately committed murder?* She tried to remember the flophouse that was her pimp's apartment. It was filthy enough; the floor was covered with dirt and sawdust. The sink was piled high with grimy dishes, and the bathroom was rank. Skylar used his shower to rinse the blood from her body. There was no soap and nothing to dry herself. She recalled using tatty shirts hanging in the closet to dry off before tiptoeing around to retrieve her clothing—the clothing that had been torn away before the pimp tied her up. But the place had seemed empty. Deserted. It had to have been Brit there taking photos, and she somehow slipped out noiselessly. Regardless, there was evidence—actual hard proof that Skylar had committed murder.

Brit had asked DJ for $2 million. James must have set her up to do the dirty work—exposing Skylar to the world. Once Brit had the money, James would send her back to Amsterdam. The murder would soon be out in the open, and James held the key to who would see it. *Mission accomplished.*

She peered out the ragged drapes and saw the sun starting to clear the horizon. *I have to get out of here. Now.* She could try to find another hotel and check in under a new alias. Something told her James would be trailing her everywhere. She sighed. *That's not an option.*

She searched her thoughts and decided the longer she stayed at the Rocket Palace, the more vulnerable she was. She grabbed her backpack and stole out of the hotel. Then, like an unmoored sea vessel, she set out walking, with no idea where she would end up.

CHAPTER 23

Overwhelmed by a fierce headache, DJ sauntered out of the guest room the next morning, barely remembering why he was there in the first place. Then it all came back to him. The argument with Max. And Craig's intervention. He saw the kitchen light on. *She was so mad at me last night.* He couldn't recall all the things he'd said, but he knew he'd crossed a line—especially by openly smoking in their home. He let out a raspy sigh. *Time to face everything.*

He slowly crept to the kitchen, expecting to see Max waiting there with an austere, disappointed expression. Instead, he found Craig scrolling through his tablet. He looked up when DJ entered.

"Hey," Craig greeted him. "How're you feeling?"

DJ took a seat at the kitchen table and cast a doubtful look at his brother. "How bad was I?"

Craig closed his tablet. Naturally, he was all put

together and smartly dressed in a black wool pullover sweater and dark wash jeans. He crossed his long legs. "Pretty bad. Want coffee?"

DJ nodded and watched Craig pour him a cup from the shiny silver pot sitting on the table. He set it in front of DJ.

"What happened to you last night?" Craig asked. "You were crazy."

DJ shook his head and drew in a deep, wheezy breath. "I guess I lost it. It was a shitty day. You know that. The whole thing with Brit. Skylar missing and those photos … *oh God, the photos*. It fucked me up. I lost it. I'm sorry."

Craig raised his eyebrows and gave him a half-smile. "No need to apologize to me. But Max may want to hear from you."

"Do you think she'll leave me?" DJ asked, tracing his fingers along the buttons down the front of his pajamas.

Craig chuckled. "I doubt it, but you have some making up to do." He leaned forward. "How did my name come up during your fight with Max?"

DJ had a sudden memory flash of Craig's polished abs in the dim light of the evening lamp. "She made comments—comments about the way you look."

"Is that what set you off?" Craig asked, unfazed that yet another man's wife, albeit his own brother's, was attracted to him.

"It was the last thing I needed to hear, Craig. Everyone knows what you look like. She was trying to cut me where it hurt." DJ glanced at his belly, which was stretching the pajama buttons out of their holes. He had an intense craving for a cigarette. He took another long sip of coffee.

"Well, you can't blame her for wanting you to take

better care of yourself." Craig rested his head on one hand. "Look, Max loves you. I feel like you're deliberately trying to sabotage the relationship."

"What?" DJ couldn't believe what he was hearing. "What makes you think that?"

Craig looked him in the eye with those killer Keller orbs. "It's like something changed when you guys got married. I understand the psychology—I went through it with Alessandra and then again with Jane."

DJ recalled Craig's messy divorce from his first wife, and then the games he played with Jane afterward. Craig was an arrogant playboy most of his adult life. He'd had so many women before, during, and after his first wife that everyone doubted his future fidelity with Jane—especially Jane. The difference between Craig and DJ was that Craig could get away with it. "How did you change?" he asked.

"Jane stood up to me." Craig briefly lowered his eyes to his coffee cup before making eye contact again. "She refused to put up with me being my old self."

"You mean your old *asshole* self," DJ smirked. "Are you saying I'm being an asshole?"

"All I'm saying is if you're going to stay married, you have to let Max in. She's your wife. You're no longer single and making unilateral decisions."

"Have you been seeing a therapist again?" DJ knew Craig had been going to a woman psychologist for at least a year while he was seeing Jane.

Craig grinned. "Not recently. But she'd tell you the same thing. You're not getting any younger."

"What's that supposed to mean?"

"It means *this is it*." He swept his palms open toward DJ. "It's not easy to find the right partner. You want to start over?"

"And what am I supposed to do when she openly admires my own brother—while we're in bed."

Craig gave him a tight-lipped smile. "Tell her what she wants to hear. That you'll start taking better care of yourself. And, by the way, it might be beneficial if you actually kept your word."

DJ placed his hand on his forehead. Craig's lecture was actually making sense. "Fine. Okay, bro. You got me on that. I'll make a better effort with Max." Then he realized he hadn't seen her yet. She couldn't still be sleeping. "Did you talk to her this morning?"

Craig nodded. "She went to the airport to get a flight out to Scottsdale. Said to tell you she forgives you and will call later." He finished that sentence with a grin.

"Ah, yes." DJ recalled the plan for Max to meet Elena Vincenzo. "I hope she's successful."

Craig got to his feet and went to the sink to wash his coffee cup. DJ gave him the once over. *I need to get back to the gym.* The smoking and drinking were out of control. And Craig was right. Max wouldn't tolerate his behavior in the long term.

When Craig returned to the table, DJ was still lost in thought. "I was going to find a flight back to LA unless you need me for anything else," Craig said, adding, "Not sure if you saw the news, but the wildfires are getting close to Malibu and Jane's anxious."

DJ was so engrossed in his drama that he hadn't watched the news in days. "Oh man, that doesn't sound good. You'd better get home. I'll figure out this mess on my own from here."

Craig shifted uncomfortably in his chair. "DJ, about your daughter … don't you think it's time to get the police involved?"

DJ shook his head. "You kidding? That would cause a major scandal. If we involve the police, I'll have to turn over the contents of Skylar's safe. Those photos are potential evidence. I'd also have to drag Brit and Sal into it. And you know I can't do that. Hell, Sal doesn't even know we were ever married."

Craig's eyes widened. "Are you going to share the photos with Max?"

DJ shook his head, vaguely recalling Craig mentioning it to Max last night. "Listen, Craig. Don't say anything more about the photos. To anyone—Max, Jane, whomever. Okay? I need to keep the whole thing under wraps to protect Skylar."

Craig twisted his lips to one side and nodded. "Okay. Then we need to move forward with our plans to get rid of Brit the minute Sal's out of the picture. After that, things will work themselves out."

CHAPTER 24

Fremont Street was still relatively vacant when Skylar stole out of the hotel. Biting, frigid wind whipped her hair around, and she flipped the hood of her sweatshirt up, fastening the laces tightly at her throat. She knew someone could be watching, so she needed to hide. *But where?*

She reached a corner, and the wind kicked up so violently, she retreated into a small alcove near a bank ATM. That's when she realized she would need more money. Regardless of whether it was, in fact, James who was blackmailing her, she would need payoff money. Even if he got a share of the $2 million Brit was demanding from DJ. Skylar wondered how much James would want. She knew his salary, including benefits, was in the $2.5 million range. Skylar still had the remainder of the cash she took from her safe the night she left; however, she'd need more. A lot more. She couldn't withdraw money from the bank or use credit cards without leaving a paper trail.

She bit her lower lip and burrowed further into the bank alcove, thinking through her options. There were several offshore bank accounts she could access. But that would require getting into her cell phone, where she stored all the information. And getting her phone would require a visit to her home.

She thought about her car sitting parked in the Rocket Palace garage. No one would bother it there, but if she took it out, someone could trail her. She pulled out her phone and dialed Clay.

He answered right away. "You okay?"

She heard slot machines trilling and loud voices.

"Not exactly," she replied. "Can you talk?"

"I'm in the casino. Give me 10 minutes."

Skylar stayed huddled by the bank as people began milling around downtown. The day had begun, and businesses would start opening. She inhaled a deep breath and lowered the heavy backpack as she waited for Clay's call.

A voice came from behind her. "Excuse me, ma'am."

She jumped, startled. An older man was staring her down.

"I'd like to use the ATM."

"Oh, of course. I'm sorry." Skylar hoisted her backpack and trudged down the street, seeking another place to have a private conversation as she fended off the relentless wind.

Her phone rang. "Clay?"

"Sorry it took so long. There are major events in the casino this week. I just had to brief Evan so I could slip away for a few minutes. What's going on with you?"

Skylar spotted a bench where she could plant herself.

"Someone's following me," she said, breathless. "I had to leave the hotel, and now I have nowhere to go."

"How do you know you're being followed?"

"Someone called my room last night, then was at my door, scratching on it. It was so creepy. But whoever it is, knows who I am. They slid a photo under the door, and it's …" her voice trailed off while she caught her breath. "It's very incriminating."

He was silent for a moment. "Jesus, Skylar, what are you going to do?"

"Listen, Clay. I need your help. I need you to pick me up and take me to my house. My car's in the Rocket Palace garage. I'm afraid to drive it because I might be tailed. I promise, it'll be quick. I just need to get into my safe. My cell phone's in there."

There was a long pause.

"I know I'm asking a lot."

"Sweetie, you know I love you, but I just don't know if I should get more involved than I already am. Your dad's onto me. If we're caught together at your house, who knows what might happen?"

"I know, but there's information on my phone that I need right away." Desperation was gnawing at her gut. "I can't take an Uber, and you know how the taxis are— they won't do a trip to suburbia because they can't get return rides."

"What if this person follows us?" His voice had become fraught. "What if your dad has your house under surveillance?"

Skylar could feel his anxiety. Clay had a naturally calm demeanor and didn't worry about insignificant things. But this situation had to have pushed him so far out of his comfort zone that he was beginning to panic.

"Clay, I wouldn't ask unless it was absolutely necessary. It'll be easier in broad daylight when everyone in my neighborhood is at work. And I seriously doubt my dad has my house under surveillance. When can you get away?"

There was a long pause. "I suppose I could have Evan run things for a couple of hours. He's been my right hand with all these events. Where are you?"

Skylar looked around and walked to where she could see the street signs. "Near the state bank on South 4th street."

"I'll be there in 20 minutes."

⸺

Skylar's hands and feet froze into icy slabs as she waited for Clay, shivering in the gusty wind. *Vegas is unseasonably cold this year.* Finally, she saw his black SUV pull up and beelined to him, waving him down.

She opened his backseat door and offloaded her backpack, then climbed into the front seat.

Clay leaned over to hug and kiss her. "Hi, sweetie. I've missed you."

Skylar took one look at his loving expression and blinked back tears. *He's the closest thing to home I have left.* She rubbed her hands together in front of the heater vents, feeling her fingers slowly defrost. "Thank you for doing this, Clay." She pulled her hood down off her head, leaning her face toward the warm air.

Clay did a double take. "What the hell did you do to your hair?"

Skylar's hand flew to her dark wig, and she flipped down the mirror to have a look. In the sunlight, it appeared even darker and redder than it did in her dim hotel bathroom. She fluffed it with her hand. "Don't worry. It's just a wig. Glad I fooled you, though."

"That's the most hideous shade I've seen—looks like cherry Kool-Aid. Where did you even find it?"

"Serge's," she replied, studying Clay's face as he drove. "And I needed something totally different. How's my baby?"

"Sesame's doing fine. I think she's desperate right now because she actually slept in my bed last night." He tore his eyes from the road and glanced at Skylar. "I'm a poor substitute for you."

She grinned and hugged her arms around her body. "I'm sure that's not true—especially with this hair." She felt the tension in her shoulders unwind for the first time that day. The warmth of Clay's car was heavenly.

"Do you have any idea who's following you?" he asked.

"Well. There's someone …" She wasn't sure how much she should share with Clay about James—her suspicion of him. Then she remembered Clay was the only one she could trust. *I have no choice.* "I think …" She paused and looked up at Clay. "I have a strong feeling it's James."

Clay's face registered the information, and then his mouth gaped open. "As in the Monarch?" He gave Skylar a look before returning his attention to the road. "Why would you even go there?"

Skylar sighed. "Clay, I ran into him yesterday."

"What? Where?"

"I was having lunch at a restaurant downtown. I called you from there. After we hung up, James magically appeared and asked to share my table." She watched Clay's face for a reaction as he tapped the turn signal.

"Did he recognize you?"

"If he did, he hid it well. I introduced myself as Jordana and told him I was a tourist staying with friends. I pretended to have laryngitis so he wouldn't recognize my voice."

He let out a smirk. "That's pretty sneaky, Skylar. Are you sure you haven't done this before? What did you guys talk about?"

"Not much. He was flirting." Skylar thought back to their meeting and James's invitation to see live music with him.

"Flirting?" Clay turned to look Skylar in the eye. "You should have gone home with him. At least you'd have somewhere to stay."

"Clay, that's not the point. He's flirting with me to bring down my guard. All the evidence points to him. He wants me out of the way so he can take my dad's job."

Skylar looked out the window and realized they were turning into her neighborhood. She felt a wrenching sadness that she had to sneak into her own home—her sanctuary, violated.

"Where do you want me to park?" he asked.

Skylar looked around. The street was empty enough. "Drop me here, and park somewhere but not in front of my house. I'll let you in from the back patio door."

He nodded as she climbed out of the car and walked briskly to her home. She put her key in the front door, opened it, and heard her security alarm beeping. She tapped in the code and looked around her living room.

The whole house smelled like a new home with no one living in it.

She saw Clay's shadow pass by a side window, and she hurried to the patio door to let him in.

"Did anyone see you?" she asked.

"I don't think so."

"I'll only be a minute. You stay down here—I just need to run upstairs for a few minutes."

Clay nodded, fidgeting with his car keys, as Skylar skittered up the stairwell.

When she got to her closet, she gasped. Her hanging clothes had been swept to one side, and the shelf where she kept the safe was empty. "Oh my god!" she yelled. She looked wildly around the closet. *Maybe I moved the safe.* She tried to recall those final moments when she evacuated from her home.

She heard Clay bustling up the stairs at warp speed. "Skylar, are you okay? What happened?" He burst inside— eyes wide open.

"I'm okay, I'm okay. Someone stole my safe!" She put her hand over her mouth and just shook her head in disbelief.

"Are you sure you didn't put it somewhere else?" Clay asked.

"No. Someone was here." She looked around and noticed that her drawers were all unevenly open. *Someone broke in and went through my personal things.*

"Does the Monarch have a key or your security code?"

Skylar thought about it. The only people who had her key were DJ and Axel. Axel was the only one with her security code. James had neither. But that didn't mean

James couldn't find a way into her house—he was used to dealing with hustlers and criminals—absolute casino scum. He could have hired someone to break and enter. She finally shook her head. "No. But that doesn't mean he's not involved."

Her head was dizzy again. She shakily made her way out of the closet and into her bedroom while Clay followed. She collapsed onto her bed and lay her head down. "I don't feel well."

Clay looked around uncomfortably. "We probably shouldn't stay for long."

"I have nowhere to go now." She pulled a fuzzy throw over her icy body and curled underneath it.

Clay sat on the edge of the bed and rubbed Skylar's arm. "I wish you could stay with me."

Skylar dug her head into her soft, familiar pillow. "I know. I have to find a place where no one knows me." She glanced up at Clay, who was frowning, chin drawn in.

"What's wrong?" she asked.

"It's just you," he said, examining her face. "You're so beautiful—your features are unique. Even with the hideous wig. There's no way the Monarch didn't recognize you."

She rubbed her temples and tried to remember her encounter with James. He acted like he didn't recognize her. But he had to have been pretending. The meeting was so random—too random to be a coincidence.

Clay gently patted her arm. "Skylar, does *anyone* have your key and security code?"

"Axel," she answered. "But why would he break in and take my safe? It just doesn't make sense."

"What's your relationship with him?" Clay wore a suspicious frown.

"He's … my cousin." She thought about the night of DJ's wedding, and how Axel used his key to get into her house—how she thought he was an intruder and pulled her gun on him. "He's always been sort of mercurial," Skylar added. "But he wouldn't do this. There's no reason."

"Are you absolutely sure?"

"No. Not absolutely." Her thoughts were again spiraling. Axel was the one who had busted her to DJ. He had also been reluctant to help with the contract to keep Sal at bay. Something odd was going on, and Skylar was having a tough time reigning in her suspicion of everyone in her life. *That's called paranoia.*

"Maybe it was your dad—I told you how he was interrogating me," Clay said. "He's got to be really worried by now."

She shook her head. "There's no way. He's only been to my house, like, twice since I moved in. He wouldn't just come in and search for my safe. He's too busy to do something like that."

"Yes, but he could have hired someone to do it." Clay nervously surveyed the room. "Don't you think we should head out soon?"

Skylar sat up on her bed and nodded. "I have to find somewhere to go."

Just then, Clay's face lit up. "This is weird, but what about the Las Vegas Rescue Mission? We do that program—*Full Plate*—you know, where we send the uneaten food from catered events at the end of each day."

Skylar nodded. "Right. My dad's on the board of directors. Do you think I could hide out there for a while without being recognized?"

"I don't see why not," Clay said. "They have clean beds and showers. You'd have to really go undercover, though. Given your dad's on the board, there's a chance someone might see you and recognize you, even with that God-awful hair—and especially if the Monarch already knows."

Skylar considered it. She was out of options. *Yes, someone might recognize me, but it's worth the risk if I can pull it off.* "You go to the car. I'll grab a few things and meet you outside after I've locked up here."

He nodded, and Skylar tore off toward her guest bedroom, where she kept her coats. She pulled out a long black wool trench and threw it around her shoulders. Then she realized she would stand out wearing the expensive cashmere piece, so she grabbed an old down jacket she used for skiing. She ran downstairs, punched in her security code, locked the door from the outside, and hurried down the street to meet Clay.

Chapter 25

"Come in," DJ barked toward his closed office door. He had been anxiously awaiting Max's call to let him know how things went with Elena Vincenzo in Scottsdale. They had a quick phone chat while DJ drove to work. She still seemed wounded at DJ's behavior the previous night, but they agreed to iron it out later.

James opened the door and popped his head inside. "Sonia's not here—do you have a minute?"

"Sure," DJ responded, getting to his feet, and gesturing toward his couch in the 'living room.' His eyes moved toward the pack of cigarettes sitting on his desk, but he resisted the urge to smoke. He had gone more than four hours without lighting up, and he was going to try to make it until the end of the day. James was a welcome diversion to the nicotine withdrawal and random ugliness of his current situation.

DJ took a good look at James, wondering why he never saw him with a woman—not once. James might have been gay. But somehow, DJ didn't think so. There was a quiet, masculine air about him that belied that theory. He was extremely private—DJ noticed it as soon as he started working at Donovan. In fact, they had never had a conversation that wasn't centered on work. He thought about James's complex relationship with Skylar. His mind went back to that day in his office when James brought up Skylar's relationship with Craig and what he described as an awkward conversation. Come to think of it, that was the first dialogue he'd had with James that *was* personal. *What was James trying to tell me about Craig anyway?* And what was *his own* role in the drama surrounding the new Marco uniforms? DJ realized then that he didn't know James very well, and that if he was choosing James as his successor, he needed more information—a better grasp of what made James tick.

James lowered himself onto the couch and crossed his legs while DJ took the easy chair.

"I just got a report that Sal lost $2 million last night playing blackjack," James said matter-of-factly.

DJ felt his eyebrows shoot upward. "That's the most he's ever lost at one time. Any color to the story?"

James gave him a wry smile. "You mean who he was with? Mila said the entire posse, including Maud, was by his side all evening."

DJ pictured Sal losing that sum of cash, and he shook his head. "He couldn't have been in too good a mood after that. Did Mila throw some comps at him?"

James nodded. "Of course. She said he wasn't interested in anything but getting back to his suite."

"I'm sure his gang of seven cheered him up later," DJ

answered. He thought about the timing. If Max succeeded in rousing Sal's need to get home to his 'ailing' wife, they could get him out the door before he tried to win any of his money back. That would be an ideal scenario. DJ could oust Brit with the $2 million Sal had lost. So, Sal would be the one paying Brit to go away. He couldn't help but chuckle at the thought.

James cleared his throat. "Glad you still have a sense of humor."

"It's a necessity in this job," DJ quipped. "What else?"

"That's it. Any news about Skylar?"

"Not yet. Why? Do you know something?"

James shook his head. "You put a trace on her phone, yeah?"

DJ tried to remember what he had shared with James. The last conversation they had was before he put a trace on Skylar's phone and later discovered it was in her safe—along with the disturbing photos. He didn't want to lie about the phone, considering it was company property and James, in his role, would be privy to its whereabouts. "She left it behind."

James's eyes widened, and he uncrossed his legs. "Why do you think she did that?"

DJ shrugged, observing James's reaction. He seemed genuinely concerned. "We're working on it." He decided to change the subject. "James, there are a couple of meetings I'd like you to attend this week—charity boards and one with the Las Vegas Convention and Visitors Authority. Skylar would normally attend that meeting, but in her absence, I'd like you to be there. Sonia has the list."

James straightened up on the couch. "Right. Of course."

DJ got to his feet and sauntered over to his office window, desperately craving a cigarette. Naturally, James would be happy to take on Skylar's responsibilities. DJ was well aware of James's unbridled ambition. It was why Skylar never liked him. He decided to probe James a bit about his personal life. They were in the 'living room,' where his work family had honest discussions. "You know, James." He turned to face him. "I'm beginning to think more about retirement."

James fidgeted, a curious look on his face. Clearly, he wasn't expecting the comment.

"Let me give you a little daylight," DJ added, again studying James's expression. "I'm not getting any younger— at least that's what I'm being told."

James raised his chin slightly, dark blue eyes focused on DJ. "You sound serious."

"Well, think of it this way. I just got married. Max and I want to enjoy life more—together. Don't you ever think about things like that?"

"You mean retirement?" James chuckled. "For fuck's sake, I'm only 32 years old."

"No. I meant marriage." DJ sauntered to his easy chair and plopped down into it.

James stared at him with a perplexed expression, like no one had ever asked him about that. "Sure, I think about, you know, finding the right person—someday."

"But …" DJ prodded.

James hesitated. "But that person hasn't come along yet."

DJ studied James. He was a good-looking guy, as far as DJ could tell. He was in good shape. He had to be in high demand—especially with the accent. "Aren't you looking?"

He grinned. "This is getting deep. Let's put it this way: I went through a bad breakup last year. We lived together for a while. She hated my work schedule and ended up cheating with another bloke in my own bloody bed. Tried to lie about it. Needless to say, we split, and she moved out." James looked DJ in the eye. "And that's the last time I've thought about a relationship."

Now I know he's straight. "Sorry, dude. Cheating's bad. Lying's the worst. You did the right thing." He shifted in his chair and put his feet on the ottoman. "But you can't give up. Don't you ever want to see a home-cooked meal on the table?"

James let out a bitter laugh. "The next best thing to a home-cooked meal can be delivered in five minutes with an app. Relationships do nothing but bog you down."

"Okay, okay. Enough," DJ said, chuckling. "But I've been seriously thinking about retirement." He wasn't lying. He had been considering retirement for several months, especially after marrying Max. And the sobering conversation with Craig that morning hit him hard. *The question is: who can I trust to take over my business?* He had always thought James was the right candidate. But he would need to test James's loyalty. It sounded as though James was wholly focused on his job, at least at the moment. DJ's eyes darted to the open pack of cigarettes on his desk. "James, I'm looking for my successor. It's just a matter of when. How do you feel about that?"

James drew in his chin, and he ran his fingers through his tousled hair. "Um … are you asking *me* to be your successor?" His accent sounded more pronounced.

"I'm thinking you're the top candidate for now."

James bit his lip and briefly lowered his gaze to his lap before looking DJ in the eye. "Well, I'd be lying if I said I didn't want to be considered."

"I thought that might be the case," DJ replied. "Right now, you're the *only* candidate I have in mind."

James's face brightened, and he nodded. "Brilliant." He paused, and his look became subdued. "I don't know if it's appropriate to ask, but does Skylar know of your succession plans?"

DJ squeezed his eyes shut and then opened them. "If you have to ask if it's appropriate, the answer is probably no."

James looked uncomfortable. "I know … she just … well, you know she's always wanted your job."

DJ sighed. "Skylar's got bigger issues than taking my job." He strode to his office door and opened it for James. "Let me know when Sal's back in the casino."

James approached the open door but paused to shake DJ's hand. "Thank you. Regardless of who takes your role, I'll do everything in my power to build on what you've accomplished."

DJ swallowed hard, locking eyes with James. "It goes without saying this is confidential. Any moves I make would require board approval."

After James left, DJ stood and stared out his office window, thinking about what it would be like to retire—to give up his position—his identity as CEO. He pondered his career—it was a blur of meetings, events, customers, and employees. The more he envisioned his life after Donovan, the more he felt like he needed it to be sooner rather than later. He did a small promenade around his office and stopped at his desk. He picked up the photo he kept of himself and Max at their engagement party. He studied his face and saw the stress signs—heavy lines in his forehead and crow's feet. But the look in his eyes told a deeper story. He looked preoccupied—not at all present—as his bride-to-be stood proudly next to him, a broad smile on her face. Max, unlike DJ, appeared to be right there in the moment, relishing the idea of being his wife—embracing her future as Mrs. Keller. This past week had made him feel as though he'd failed everyone.

He grabbed his houndstooth jacket and slid it over his shoulders. He snatched up the envelope with the photos and stashed it in his messenger bag. Then he marched out of his office, onto the casino floor, and to the parking garage where his Jaguar awaited. He would beat Max home that evening.

Chapter 26

The line to get into the Las Vegas Rescue Mission stretched all the way down D Street from the entry gate. The Mission only took in the homeless twice daily, and Clay dropped Skylar off just in time for the 3 p.m. intake process. She wrapped her down jacket tighter around her body and shuddered in the madly blowing wind. Her backpack had slid down the sides of her arms, so she hoisted it up, thinking about her handgun and wondering how thoroughly they would search her belongings. She had hidden it in a large box of tampons, hoping whoever was working the intake line would be too embarrassed to look inside. Clay informed her that there weren't any metal detectors, but her anxiety escalated as the line slowly nudged forward.

When she reached the front, a pleasant-looking woman with short brown hair greeted her. "Good afternoon, ma'am, may I have your name, please?"

Skylar hesitated. She could no longer use Jordana Tinley. Her stalker already knew that name. "Rumi," she answered, conjuring the image of the anime hero from the fictional girl group, 'K-Pop.' "Rumi Hunter."

"Nice to meet you, Rumi. I'm Grace, and I'll need some basic information to register you, and then I'll send you for the eligibility screening." She pulled out her tablet and began tapping her fingers on the screen.

Skylar nodded, thinking she was going to have to think fast in bluffing her way through the screening process.

"What is your contact number?" she asked.

Skylar rattled off a fake phone number, feeling a tinge of nervousness. Clay was the only one with her burner cell number. But she had to give something. Hopefully, there would be no need for them to call the number.

She managed to squeak by the eligibility screening, having made up a sob story about how her boyfriend was abusive, threw her out on the street, and there was no family to assist. When asked about her employment status, she tearfully confessed that she had no education and no job. She said she didn't have a current driver's license, and all her forms of ID had been burned by her boyfriend.

Skylar took a top bunk in a 68-bed open berthing area for women. It looked like a massive warehouse with a sea of bunk beds, and she was given a small locker near her bunk to stow her personal items. She stashed a few of her things there, knowing she would have to leave the next morning with all her belongings, only to check back in that evening. It was a strange experience, but it was her only hope of avoiding her stalker.

Dinner was served in another part of the shelter, where everyone carried their own trays and stood in the buffet line while kind-hearted volunteers scooped out portions of chicken, potatoes, and green beans, plus dessert, which looked like a small fudge brownie. She took a folding metal chair at an empty picnic-style table. There was no use in chatting up the locals—she didn't want to elaborate further on her phony story nor arouse anyone's suspicion. She had noticed immediately that most of the other occupants looked lost and troubled—exactly the way she felt. She put her head down and picked at the meal, which tasted like seasoned cardboard. She considered buying her own dinner and bringing it back with her the next day, but that would also attract unwanted attention.

After dinner, she retreated to her bunk and climbed atop, lugging her backpack. She rummaged through it and pulled out her cell phone. Clay had texted to check if she was okay. She typed him a message and put the phone away.

Skylar had a tough time falling asleep, especially knowing that breakfast was at 6:30 a.m. and that she must leave the premises by 7:30 with all her belongings. She had removed the wig to make sleeping easier, but that didn't help.

Time had become an elastic, monotonous haze while her former life overwhelmed her thoughts: Clay and Sesame, her career, her clothes, and even her appearance. Just being in her house for a brief few minutes that day made her long to return to her real life. She missed her comfortable bed and her privacy—her routine of showering, dressing, and applying makeup for work. She missed weekends when she could sleep late and relax at home—her hot baths. And, as warped as it sounded, she longed for her dreaded high heels. Those torture traps lining her closet were a part of her normal identity. She dreamed of returning to simple pleasures like sitting at her kitchen table on a Saturday morning with a cup of coffee or browsing the pages of a fashion magazine. She thought about what she was doing now: hiding and running scared. What first felt like freedom to wander the streets of downtown without being recognized now felt like a hellish prison. The thought that she had to wipe out all traces of Skylar Van Ness frightened her. And pure loneliness hung on her shoulders like a weighted vest. The worst part was that she was in limbo, without a clue about when she could go back—if ever. *What if I have to run for the rest of my life?* She hugged the flimsy covers around her body, and her thoughts returned to Sesame—soft, sweet Sesame, who was always at her side. She choked out a loud, long sob.

Someone from another bunk yelled, "Shut up! Some of us are trying to sleep."

She turned over in bed and muffled her crying into the pillow.

***

The next morning, Skylar exited the shelter at 6:30 sharp. She skipped the Mission's breakfast to buy her own meal and began hiking up and down the streets again. Her only advantage over the other unhoused people was that she had money. She had cash and could buy whatever she wanted. She spotted other homeless women—women she'd already seen at the shelter—digging through garbage dumpsters for discarded items. *At least they're being fed regularly.* She imagined they were looking for household items and clothing. She longed to give them money but stopped herself. If she did, everyone would know she'd lied her way in. She sighed and wandered along to find a coffeehouse to sit in. On the way, she dialed Clay.

"Hi sweetie," he answered. "How was it?"

"Not terrible," she said, thinking back to her sad, sleepless night. "It's a place to go, at least."

"That's right—just temporary until we can find you another place."

"Anything going on at work I should know about?" Scraps of intel from the office kept her mind occupied and gave her a false sense that she would one day return.

"Other than you're sorely missed? Not really. I saw your dad leave sort of early yesterday. Looked like he was in a hurry."

"Really?" she asked, picturing DJ marching out in his determined way, with that unmistakable swagger.

"Yeah, after I saw the Monarch come out of his office lobby. You know, I can't even look that guy in the eye right now after what you told me. What a damned snake!"

"Clay, you have to keep that to yourself for now," she warned.

"I know. I know. Don't worry. I'm sending Evan down to the Mission kitchen later with shrimp scampi. We made it for an event and have a ton left over. Make sure you get some for dinner tonight."

"I will. That sounds a lot better than what I've had so far," she answered, thinking about the greasy chicken.

"Do you need anything else while you're over there?"

Skylar shivered. "No, just keep an eye on what's going on at work—especially where James is concerned."

"Right, of course." And Clay hung up.

At 2:30 p.m., Skylar once again stood in line for intake at the Las Vegas Rescue Mission and, like the day before, she could only stay until the next morning.

She wandered down to the food hall and picked up a tray, remembering Clay's leftover shrimp scampi. She immediately spotted it and helped herself to a generous portion. They must have originally planned another meal because the sides didn't go with the scampi—buttered cornbread and vanilla pudding for dessert. She sat down at an empty table but wasn't alone for long. A woman about her age plopped down across from her.

She wore a black racerback tank top, and her arms were liberally peppered with tattoos. She smiled shyly at Skylar, revealing a jagged row of lower teeth. "Mind if I join you?"

Skylar looked around. "No, not at all." She picked up her knife and fork and began cutting a large shrimp into bite-sized pieces, spearing a piece with her fork, and then putting it in her mouth. The garlic from the scampi tasted pungent.

"How'd *you* get here?" the stranger asked congenially. Her eyes were so big, they reminded Skylar of a cartoon fawn. She wore long, dangly blue and red earrings that sparkled like a neon fish when she moved her head.

Skylar was not sure how to answer. She stared down at her plate.

"Oh, you don't want to talk about it?" The woman slathered butter on her cornbread and took a huge bite— so huge that crumbs fell out of her mouth. Once she had chewed and swallowed her food, she examined Skylar. "My name's Anji." She pronounced the name, 'awn-jee.'

Skylar gave her a tight-lipped smile and continued cutting her shrimp.

"You really are a quiet one," said Anji, before taking another bite of her cornbread. "I came here from Alabama with my man and two kids. But we got the gambling bug and lost all our money."

Skylar nodded. The story, unfortunately, was not uncommon. "I'm sorry to hear that." She paused and thought about stopping there. Then she added, "What happened to your kids?"

"They're in foster care," she answered with a sad look on her face. "I'm trying to make enough money to get them back. That deadbeat cut out of town, and I have no money, so I had no choice but to give them up. I miss them, you know." Her eyes watered.

"I can imagine," Skylar said. She realized that every person in the shelter had a different story and was trying to recover their lives in some manner. *I'm no different.*

"What's your name?" Anji asked.

Skylar hesitated. "Rumi. And I don't plan on being here long. It's just temporary until I can sort some things out." *That part is the truth.*

Anji nodded empathetically. "I know the feeling."

Skylar had no desire to stay longer. She felt sorry for Anji, but her own paranoia gnawed at her stomach, growing with each agonizing moment she spent sitting there. She felt her heart rate accelerating and her breathing becoming shallow. *Am I having a panic attack?* She put her napkin on her plate and began to gather her things.

"You finished already?" Anji asked, examining her almost-full plate. "You didn't eat nothing."

"I really need to go take a shower," she said, hoisting her backpack and grabbing the food tray. "I'll see you later." She hauled the tray to the assembly line, set it down, then hurried to find a bunk in the sea of beds.

Chapter 27

When Max got home, DJ was already in their bedroom. He had opened a bottle of Max's favorite champagne and pulled out cheese and crackers. He even lit the candles that flanked their bed, turned down the covers, and changed into his softest pajamas—the ones Max had bought for him one Valentine's Day—dark blue paisley silk.

He felt inept at this whole romance thing. He had always been terrible at it. That's why most of his girlfriends didn't last. But he'd never been with anyone like Max. He thought back to when they first met. He was masquerading as Hendrik Van Ness, and Max was working for him. She was beautiful, but that wasn't all. She had class and brains. He fell in love with her quickly, never imagining someone like her would date him, let alone say yes to a marriage proposal. *I never thought I'd be so lucky.* And here he was, sabotaging the best thing that had ever happened to him, exactly as Craig had pointed out.

He gazed into the mirror. "You're a fool," he said to his reflection. "And you don't deserve her." He tousled his long blond mane with his fingers and checked his teeth. He didn't look half-bad. *Craig might even approve.*

"DJ," Max called as she entered their bedroom. "Are you here?"

He watched her expression soften when she spied the setup.

He sauntered over to where she stood. "I thought you'd never get here."

"You've been up to no good, I see," she said, a playful smile curling the edges of her mouth. "I didn't know you could light anything other than cigarettes."

His stomach roiled in embarrassment. "Hey, Max," he said, taking her hands and pulling her toward him. "I'm sorry for all that—for smoking in our house. I'll never do it again. If I do, you can leave me."

She looked up into his eyes. "Honey, I'd never leave you." Then she let out a sigh. "I just worry about you."

"I know, but I'm trying to stop. I promise." He gazed up at the large wooden clock on their wall. "I haven't had a cigarette since this morning."

Max smiled. "I'm sorry for what I said about Craig. It was inappropriate. I just said it to get your attention."

DJ chuckled softly. "You got my attention all right. I couldn't stop thinking about you falling for my brother like every other woman. It made me crazy." He shook his head.

"I'd never do that to you," she responded, dark eyes sparkling. She put her arms around his neck, and he felt the warmth of her body as she settled against him.

He pulled her closer, expecting a flood of arousal, but

there was none. He couldn't seem to rein in his rampant thoughts—Brit's threats—Skylar missing—the pressure of Sal's whims and even James with his covetous stare, eager to take over Donovan the minute DJ stepped out of the picture. *Stop the madness and focus on your wife! She's beautiful, and you love her.*

Max lifted her lips to his mouth, and he moved in for a kiss. He had brushed his teeth several times to rid his mouth of cigarettes, but he was self-conscious. He withdrew in anguish.

"What's wrong?" she asked. "You don't even want to kiss me?"

DJ rested his chin on her shoulder. "I'm sorry, Max. Of course, I want to kiss you. I want everything with you, but my life is fucked up."

Max took his hand and led him to the bed. She sat on the edge and pulled him next to her. "Is all this about last night? I told you I was sorry."

"Not entirely," he answered. "Yes, I'm insecure about my brother, but not where you're concerned. It's just this fucking situation, Max. My ex-wife is wreaking chaos, I have no idea where my daughter is, and … well, I just feel fucking old." *And I want a fucking cigarette so bad, I'm ready to crawl out of my own skin.*

Max squeezed his hand. "I have an idea," she said, standing. "Let's just lie together. No pressure." She pulled her cream-colored sweater over her head and unzipped her black skirt, letting it fall to the floor. She tugged down her black tights and tossed them aside.

DJ watched her strip off her bra and then her underwear. He studied her, naked, from head to toe, willing himself to devour her as any normal, red-blooded male would do. But the nicotine cravings were so intense, they won out. He melted down onto the bed and let his head hit the pillow in despair.

A full hour and one bottle of champagne later, DJ and Max still lay under the covers. Although they had not yet made love, they were at least nuzzled together. DJ inhaled her citrusy scent and realized getting healthy for Max was going to be a major challenge, especially with everything else going on in their lives. *I don't know if I'm up to it.*

Max raised herself onto her elbows and picked up her glass of champagne. "Feeling any better?" she asked before taking a sip and setting the glass on her nightstand.

"Oh, yeah." DJ reached for a piece of cheese and a cracker and popped them into his mouth. "How about you?" he asked while crunching away. DJ observed her mouth. It was what had initially drawn him to her—the pretty, heart-shaped lips. She usually wore red lipstick, but it was late in the day, and most of it had bled off, creating a faded reddish stain.

She smiled and rolled over to face him. "Much better. In fact, I'm feeling no pain." She lowered the covers to her waist and gave him a provocative look. Her hand slithered down the waist of his pajama bottoms.

DJ knew Max was a lightweight when it came to alcohol. The half-bottle of champagne she drank must have given her a buzz. *I wish I could still feel that way from a little bit of champagne.* His thoughts went back to their fight and how she had spent the day in Scottsdale. "You haven't told me what happened with Elena Vincenzo."

Max sank back against her pillow, lips cracking into a grin. "You sure know how to spoil the mood." She pulled her hand away and drew the covers back over her breasts. "I did see Elena, and we had a nice talk. I don't think she suspected that I went there expressly to see her."

"So, what's next?" DJ asked, picturing Elena sitting in the bar at Mariposa, flanked by shopping bags with an eternal cocktail attached to her hand. He tried to remember what Elena drank. For some reason, a Cosmopolitan came to mind. *Something pink for sure.*

"I called Sal and left him a voicemail." She glanced at her watch. "He'll probably call back soon, so you'll have to pretend you're not here."

DJ nodded, thinking about the messy game they were playing. "Max, don't you ever get tired of this shit?"

She looked up in surprise. "What shit?"

"*This* shit," DJ responded, reaching for his champagne glass and taking a swig. "Think about it. We work our asses off day and night, worrying about trivial crap like what Sal Vincenzo's wife thinks." He sighed and shook his head.

"I get what you're saying," Max responded, sitting up in bed and facing DJ. "But this isn't exactly small stuff here. Your ex-wife is on a rampage and is on the verge of taking the biggest business we have away. We can't afford to lose him."

"Yeah, I know, but you're the one who's always saying life would be simpler if I just retired." He studied her face for a reaction.

Her expression softened. "I do want you to retire—if just to get healthier and spend more time with me. But remember, once you do, you'll still be a shareholder and chairman of the board. That means you're going to be worrying about Sal well into the future."

He considered her words, then nodded. "Jesus … that sounds dismal."

Max's cell phone rang, and she grabbed it off her nightstand. "Speak of the devil," she said, sitting up straight and pulling the covers tightly around her body. "Good evening, Sal. How are you?"

DJ rose and found his pajama top crumpled on the floor beside the bed. He quickly put it back on and sat next to Max, awaiting her next words.

"I see. Well, then maybe you'll end up breaking even," she said, giving DJ an eyeroll. "Listen, Sal, I don't mean to take you away from your game, but I wanted to run something by you." She paused. "You see, I was in Scottsdale today for a meeting, and I happened to run into Elena at Neiman Marcus—she was having a cocktail."

DJ heard Sal's muffled Jersey-tinged voice utter, "Now that's a surprise."

"Yes, I know," Max said with a little laugh. "But there was something I noticed and … well, it's probably nothing, but she just didn't look well."

Again, Sal's muffled response. DJ rose to his feet and paced, anxiety mounting with every step, nicotine withdrawal at an all-time high. He considered getting some gum or patches. *I need something.*

"I know, but I just have a feeling," Max said. "It might not be a bad idea for you to check on her, you know?"

Silence. Then more muffled Jersey talk.

"It wasn't anything specific, you know, she just seemed … well, pale and fragile. You guys are like family to us, and to be honest, I'm worried about her."

DJ smirked and put a fake gun to his head with his fingers. *Max could grin-fuck like no one's business.*

"Your sister? Oh, I didn't know you had a sister in Scottsdale. She's in Glendale? Well, then I guess you're covered. Again, sorry to pry, it's just … we're always looking out for you."

Pause. "Okay, well, good luck tonight. Thank you. I will. Good-bye." She put the phone down and sank into her pillow.

"I take it that's not good news," DJ said, stretching out on the bed next to her.

She shook her head. "You heard. There's a sister close by. He's not going anywhere for now."

DJ leaned over and kissed her forehead. "You gave it one hell of an effort, Max. We'll have to think of something else."

The truth was that DJ was out of ideas. His daughter was still missing. His ex-wife was still squatting in his hotel. *And I'm no longer allowed to smoke.*

Chapter 23

After dinner, Skylar tugged her backpack to the women's bathroom, where she found toilet stalls and one large shower area with multiple faucets. She had been showering without the wig, so she could wash her natural hair, and then sleep without it. But here, she had no privacy. Some individual shower stalls with curtains existed; however, they were usually full. Skylar decided the private stalls were worth waiting for, so she stood until a pregnant woman finally came out of one stall.

"Oh, sorry I took so long," the woman said, hugging her towel around her mid-section and draping another towel over her hair. She fastened it snugly and stood aside to make way for Skylar.

"You're fine," Skylar responded, studying her. She could hide her natural hair for the night by covering it with a towel, the way this woman had. Once she was up in the bunk, she could take off the towel and sleep wig-less. She smiled at the woman. "Thank you."

When she finished her shower, she toddled around the bathroom area with one towel wrapped around her body and the other around her hair. She rolled up the wig and hid it in her backpack. Once she found a bathroom stall, she dressed herself in her street clothes, lifted her backpack, and started for her bunk.

On the way, she noticed a group of suited executives standing in a walkway that led to the food hall. At least 10 people looked as though they were on a tour of the facility. That's when Skylar spotted him. *James fucking Monarch!*

What the hell is he doing here? Skylar almost didn't believe her eyes. She froze, wondering if the universe was playing a sick joke on her. Then, she remembered that DJ was on the board of directors. They must be having a meeting, and DJ sent James in his place.

The pack of suits was heading toward her, and there was no way she could avoid them. She needed to get around the group to reach the women's dormitory. *Stay cool, Skylar.* She made her way toward them and, as she scooted around the group, the towel on her head slipped off onto the floor. She felt her damp platinum locks tumble down past her shoulders. She swooped down to grab the towel when she heard a man's voice. *Of course, it was James.*

"Let me get that for you," he said in his charming accent, crouching down and grabbing the towel before she got to it.

She looked up, and they locked eyes for a long moment. Prickles of fear ran through her.

They both rose to their feet. He handed her the towel, a dumbfounded expression on his face. "Skylar?" he said, eyeing her with curiosity. "Is that you?"

She felt her eyes water, but she didn't avoid his glare. "I don't know who you're talking about," she said in her natural voice.

His mouth dropped open, and he took a step toward her. He examined her from head to toe. "Holy shit, it *is* you. What in God's name are you doing *here*?"

She backed away from him slowly at first, then turned and tore down the hallway, burst through the women's dormitory entrance, and let the door slam behind her. He couldn't follow her. Men weren't allowed in the area. But her cover was blown, and she had to get out of the Las Vegas Rescue Mission without him seeing her leave.

Her eyes darted madly around the open berthing area, stopping on the emergency exit. She hopscotched toward it and bumped right into Anji, who fell backward onto the floor.

"I'm so sorry," Skylar said, breathless. "Are you okay?"

Anji stared up at her. "What the … you really a blonde?"

Skylar's hands trembled as she rummaged through her backpack. She found the envelope of cash and grabbed a few hundred-dollar bills. She thrust them toward Anji. "Here."

Anji sat up, gawking at the bills, mouth jutted open. "Are you for real?"

"Yes," she answered, eyes returning to the emergency exit door. "Buy your kids something. But in exchange, I want you to forget we met. Forget we talked. And forget what I'm about to do. Got it?"

Anji nodded and grabbed the money. "Forget what? Lady, I never saw you in my life, including now."

Skylar didn't stay around to hear more. She charged

through the emergency exit and, as the alarm sounded loudly, scurried down D street toward the gate through which she had entered. She ran as fast as her sneakers would allow, the heavy backpack weighing her down, her cold, wet hair clinging to her head, until she found a deserted alley and stopped to catch her breath.

Still heaving from the long run, she heard a car motor and then spotted headlights flashing as the car rounded the street corner and slowed to a low rumble in the alley. She turned and ran until she found a dumpster. She ducked behind it and waited for the car to pass. The vehicle slowed to a stop right where she was crouching. She held her breath as she heard the engine turn off and the driver's door open and close. Footsteps crept closer.

"Skylar," James's voice broke the silence. "I saw you. Just come out. I'm not here to bust you."

She took a deep breath, unzipped the top of her backpack, reached in, and pulled her handgun from the tampon box.

"Skylar, I know you can hear me. I know you're in trouble. We'll go somewhere—a place where we can talk. Privately. I promise. I won't tell anyone."

Skylar collected herself, straightened to her full height, and confidently stepped out from behind the dumpster. "You won't tell anyone, because you won't live to," she said in the throaty rasp of someone who'd just run 20 blocks. She stared into James's eyes, which widened into what looked like huge dark round ink spots when he saw her gun.

He put his hands out in front of him. "For fuck's sake, Skylar. Put the gun away. I'm your friend."

Skylar cocked the pistol and leveled it toward his

head. "You're my friend? *Really?* You've been stalking me for weeks—pretending to be my friend while you taunted the hell out of me with shit from my past."

James took a step back, eyes on Skylar's gun. "I don't know anything about your past. All I know is everyone's looking for you. Your father's gutted. Now I find you, and you pull a bloody gun on me?"

"Oh, I'm sure everyone's *gutted*. Especially you. I'm sure it's just killing you that you're attending all my dad's meetings. You've cleared the way to take his job," she growled.

James drew in his chin. "What?"

"You wanted me out of the way—that's what you've always wanted. That's why you summoned my mother here—that's why you forced me out of my house and into hiding." She waved her gun around wildly. James's eyes followed it. "You forced me to be homeless—here, in this cesspool. You ruined my life so you could trample over my corpse and take over."

His face twisted in disbelief. "Skylar, that's delusional. I would never do anything to hurt you. All I want to do is help. Now, will you *please* put the gun away?"

Skylar kept the gun pointed at James, intensity crackling between them. "No. Get back in your car and move along."

"And where will you go?"

"Any place where you *aren't!*" She stared right into his eyes. "And don't you dare try to follow me. I've got nothing to lose at this point. You made sure of that."

He returned her stare, open-mouthed, then nodded. "Fine. I'll leave you here." He backed away toward what

Skylar thought to be a black Range Rover. He opened the door and paused, turning to look back at her. "A lot of people care about you, Skylar … and I … I happen to be one of them." His voice broke as he said that last part. Then he slid into his car, shut the door, and turned on the engine. She slowly lowered her gun as she watched him drive away.

Skylar drifted along the downtown streets like a wild animal, not sure where she was headed. She didn't know her way around this part of Las Vegas and felt like she was walking in circles. She kept turning to scan her surroundings—behind her—sideways—forward—everywhere. She was still convinced James was following her—that he wouldn't stop until he had her in his car. *God knows what he would have done if I'd gone with him.*

She went over their dialogue repeatedly in her mind, trying to make sense of his reaction to her accusations. He had seemed surprised to see her at the Las Vegas Rescue Mission—that moment when their eyes met, and he recognized her. *He's a good actor.* And he had a knack for lying. *He has that Irish charm.*

Her thoughts returned to what James had said at the end—the part about caring for her. His voice had even cracked. She caught her breath. *He should win an Oscar for that performance.*

Rain began to sprinkle down, and Skylar still had no idea where she was. She needed to find some kind of shelter, but there was nothing. She rounded a corner into a dark alley, then changed her mind and turned in the opposite direction, almost running right into a bearded man who appeared out of nowhere.

"Watch where you're fucking going!" he screamed into Skylar's face, then spit at her.

She bolted away from him, scurrying down the dark alley she had initially tried to avoid.

After muddling her way through more sketchy, caliginous streets, she found herself on Main Street again. At least she knew her way around there. She stopped to look up and down the pathway, glancing at her watch—almost 9 p.m. She had been walking for a couple of hours. She suddenly felt exhausted and needed to find a place to safely stop and rest.

Skylar stumbled upon the Velveteen Rabbit, a bar that was open and serving cocktails. She slogged in, found a plush booth, and sank into it. Her feet were frozen and sore, and her legs were tired from so much running—even in her comfortable sneakers. She felt blisters forming and longed to take off her shoes. She scanned the bar menu, dying for a cocktail. At first, she resisted. *I need my wits about me.* A cocktail server passed with a tray of martinis. *Still, just one wouldn't hurt, would it?* She ordered a non-alcoholic beer when the server asked.

She pulled out her cell phone and dialed Clay.

"Where are you?" he said with angst. "I've been calling for hours."

"It's a long story," she said, looking around. Groups of young women in bright, sparkly outfits were tittering with laughter. She caught herself wondering if she were ever that carefree—in her entire life.

"Did you get any of the shrimp scampi I sent?"

"Yes. But my meal got cut short. My stay got cut short. I had no choice but to bolt because James was there having a meeting in place of my dad."

"Oh shit—what happened?"

"Clay, he's the one who's been following me. I'm sure of it now."

"Did he see you at the Mission?"

"Yes. We … he caught me out of disguise, and there was a full-on confrontation. I escaped through the emergency exit. But he followed me in his car and tracked me down. I unloaded on his ass like you wouldn't believe." She paused to catch her breath. "I pulled my gun on him."

There was a long silence on the other end.

"Are you still there?"

"You have a *gun?*" His voice was incredulous. "Since when? And you threatened the Monarch with it? Are you Thelma or Louise?"

"Come on, Clay—I had to do something. The man's following me."

"Skylar, that guy's second in command to your dad. He's connected in a zillion ways to everyone in this town."

Skylar felt her heart sink. Her best friend was questioning her behavior. "I know. But he's harassing me—blackmailing me. Why don't you believe me?"

"Because I don't know what to believe anymore," he blurted, voice wrought with tension. "Where are you now?" His radio erupted in the background, with a fuzzy voice and static. "Wait a minute—don't go anywhere."

"I won't."

"Give me a few minutes to finish my call," Clay instructed whoever was on the two-way radio. Then the requisite background static from the radio cutting out. "Are you still there, Skylar?" he asked.

"Yes. Listen, I'm at the Velveteen Rabbit. I had to stop walking. I'm totally exhausted, and I need to find a place to stay."

She heard Clay exhale into the phone. "Okay, tell you what, sweetie. Just stay there. I have an idea."

"What idea?" she asked, voice shrouded in hope. "You mean a place to stay?"

"Maybe. But don't leave the Velveteen Rabbit for now. Do you understand?"

"Yes," she said. The phone went dead.

CHAPTER 23

There was no other place for DJ to blow off steam but at the casino. He'd left Max sleeping soundly in their bed, likely dreaming of the husband she wished she had, while he showered and dressed for the office. *My priority is to keep an eye on Sal's wins and losses. That and Brit's machinations.* He hated to admit it, but he also longed to inhale the secondhand smoke in the casino to try to get a grip on his nicotine withdrawal. *Just until I crawl over the dreadful hump of going cold turkey.*

His fingers trembled as he buttoned up his crisp white shirt and tucked it into his black trousers. He grabbed the matching suit jacket, threw it on, and took a quick look in his full-length mirror. He ruffled his blond mane before turning to leave his home.

DJ entered the bustling casino as clouds of smoke hovering above the blackjack tables drifted into his nostrils. It filled him with an intense jolt of satisfaction. He sauntered through the chaos of pit bosses, customers, and card games as he weaved in and out of the tables, saying hello here and there to his employees and stopping to shake customers' hands. He didn't see Sal. Not yet.

He meandered through a labyrinth of slot machines, glowing with animated graphics, as players sat mesmerized, feverishly hitting buttons, cheering out loud when the right combination of images lined up. The casino noise was something DJ was able to tune out—he was so used to the environment—the relentless din of bells clanging, the spinning of roulette wheels, card shuffling machines, and the stacking of chips on tables. This was his kingdom, and he ate it up. He enjoyed presiding over his masterpiece—the thrilling world he and his family had created at Donovan.

From a distance, he spied Clay on his two-way radio, standing between two rows of video poker machines. DJ caught up, noting the look of consternation on his face.

"Everything okay?" DJ asked as soon as he was close enough to be heard.

Clay jumped at the sight of DJ and put his radio down. "Yes, fine. Just managing my events. How are you this evening, Mr. Keller?"

"Well enough, under the circumstances. Have you heard anything from my daughter?"

His eyes widened, and he clumsily dropped his radio. He knelt to pick it up, then faced DJ. "N-no, sir."

"You know," DJ said, taking a step toward him. "If you have intel on her whereabouts, you're obligated from both a moral and ethical standpoint to inform me. Do you understand?"

DJ caught a visible shudder. Clay seemed even more jumpy than the last time DJ had spoken to him.

"Yes, Sir. I understand."

Before DJ could say anything else, Clay peered over his shoulder at someone.

DJ turned quickly and saw James approaching.

"There's something I need to urgently discuss with you," James said to DJ. He shot Clay a look and added, "In your office."

DJ noticed James's pale complexion under the warm glow of the overhead chandeliers. He appeared spooked about something. "Okay."

The two walked side by side through the casino and into the elevator. DJ unlocked his office door and ushered James inside, at once spotting the half-empty pack of Marlboros sitting on his desk. The craving was so intense, he almost beelined for it.

James cocked an eyebrow, glancing at the pack. "You may want to have one."

DJ looked up at him in surprise. "Oh?"

"Yes," James answered, subtly smoothing the collar of his sky-blue button-down so that it sat perfectly underneath his dark navy suit jacket. "This is about Skylar."

DJ stared into James's eyes, trying to read what he was about to lay on him. "What about her?"

His fingers grazed his forehead. "I saw her. She's downtown."

"What? Is she okay?" DJ had imagined Skylar in a million places, but downtown Las Vegas was not one of them.

James paused. "DJ, she's completely lost it. I found her at the Rescue Mission."

DJ felt his mouth fall open. "What was she doing there?" Again, he glanced at the cigarette pack on his desk.

"*Living.* She's living there. I saw her in the hallway that leads to the women's dorm. Her hair was wet, so she had obviously just showered. When I said her name, she panicked and ran off. I drove all over downtown and found her hiding behind a dumpster. When I called her name, she turned a bloody gun on me."

DJ drew his head back quickly. "Are you certain it was her?" Then he remembered going through her nightstand and Axel telling him she kept a handgun there. "Never mind. Of course, it was her. Why do you think she pulled the gun on *you*?"

"She thinks I'm after her—thinks I'm stalking her because I want *your* job. She said I'm holding something from her past over her head. I told her I don't know anything about her past. DJ, she even accused me of bringing her mother here to cause trouble."

DJ gave him an incredulous stare. "You're right. She's totally lost it. Why do you think she's doing this? I mean, why the hell is she living at the Las Vegas Rescue Mission? She's got to be the richest homeless person on the planet."

James lowered his chin and made solid eye contact with DJ. "I don't know. But she's in real trouble."

DJ paced his office, pausing near his desk and gazing at the cigarette pack.

"Now's not the time to be quitting," James noted. "For fuck's sake, I'm ready to take it up again myself."

DJ ran his fingers through his hair, swaying a bit. He looked up at James. "Where did you see her last?"

"She was in an alley about two miles from the Mission. I tried to get her to come with me. That's when she got out the gun. I had no choice but to leave her there."

DJ grabbed his keys. "Let's go look for her. We'll take my car.

Ten minutes later, DJ and James were headed downtown. They first stopped at the Las Vegas Rescue Mission. The two men announced themselves at the D Street entrance. Once they had been admitted, the manager on duty, Grace, greeted them at the front door.

"We're looking for my daughter," DJ said, anxiety creeping up his neck. "She was staying here until a couple of hours ago—name's Skylar Van Ness."

"I'm sorry, sir. I don't recognize that name. Would you like me to look through our logs to see if I can find her?"

"Yes. I have a photo of her." He got out his cell phone, scrolled until he found Skylar's photo, then thrust his phone toward Grace.

She leaned forward and studied DJ's phone. "Hmm. She doesn't look familiar. We have photo identification on all our intakes, so if she was here, her photo's on file with us."

"Great," DJ responded while Grace sat at her computer and opened a file.

"You said her last name is Van Ness?" she asked. Both

DJ and James nodded. She frowned and looked puzzled as she sifted through the photos of people who had come in that evening. "We don't have anyone by that name. Is there a chance she used another name? Lots of women here use aliases."

The two men exchanged glances.

"I'm not sure," DJ said, leaning in. "But we can go through the photos ourselves."

She looked briefly up at him. "I can't let you go through the photos, because we have to protect the privacy of our residents. But I can go through them for you."

"I understand," DJ said. "That's fine. She's very tall—almost six feet—blonde, and incredibly pretty. You'd remember her."

Grace squinted her eyes and pursed her lips. "Gosh, I don't know of anyone who fits that description." She continued scrolling on her computer, a perplexed expression on her face. "I'm sorry," she said to DJ.

"Are you sure you can't allow us to look for her?" James asked, stiffening his posture. "We're one step away from involving the police."

DJ heard the word and frowned at James. "We are?"

"Wait," Grace said as though she'd just had an epiphany. "There's one woman who's very tall and thin—too thin. She's been in here the past few days. But she's dark-haired, not blonde."

"What name did she use?" DJ asked, holding still in anticipation.

"I don't recall, but she has a tattoo—big one on her left wrist—goes halfway up her arm. She doesn't say much—just eats here—very little—and sleeps—keeps to herself."

DJ's head sank. "That's not her. Skylar doesn't have tattoos."

"It looked pretty fresh—still a little swollen," Grace added.

"Wait," said James. "What is the tattoo of?"

Grace rolled her eyes upward as though trying to remember. "Hmmm … I think it was flowers—yes, that's it. Flowers and something else … some kind of musical note?"

James's face lit up. "Was it a treble clef?"

She shrugged. "I don't know what that is. What's it look like?"

James pulled out his cell phone and scrolled through before handing it to Grace. "Did it look like this?"

Her eyes brightened. "That's it."

James turned to DJ, gently biting his lip. "I met that woman. She was at a café downtown a few days ago. Said she was staying with friends."

DJ's patience was waning. The lack of nicotine wasn't helping. "James, that's great. But we're looking for Skylar, not some woman you're trying to hook up with."

"Yeah, but there was something about this girl. She …" his voice trailed off, and he turned to Grace, shifting his weight back and forth. "Did she register under the name of Jordana? If you have her photo, I can identify her."

"I don't have a Jordana. But I can show you the photo of the woman with the dark hair and tattoo if you'll wait for me to find her."

"That's great," James blurted before DJ could interject.

DJ pulled James roughly aside by the sleeve of his suit jacket. "Look, I don't want to get in the way of your sexual conquests. But whoever you were chatting up at a café has nothing to do with my daughter. For all we know now, she could be in real trouble. Especially armed with a handgun."

"I know you want to find Skylar. I do, too," he said, eyes wide and shining. "But there was something about this girl. She was strangely familiar, and I couldn't put my finger on it. Her expressions—her mannerisms—they all reminded me of Skylar. I shrugged it off. But what if it *was* her, with dyed hair, just not wanting to be found?"

"Here," Grace said triumphantly. "I found her."

DJ scooted around the desk and examined the photo. "That's her!" He exclaimed, looking up at James. "That's my daughter. And she *did* dye her hair."

James moved quickly around the desk so he could look. "That's the woman. That's Jordana from the café. And yes, she does look like Skylar." He moved his face closer to the screen to read her information. "Says her name is Rumi Hunter." He glanced at DJ, puzzled.

"She's registered to a bunk. Would you like me to see if I can wake her?" Grace asked.

"Yes," the men answered in unison.

"We'll wait right here," DJ added.

When Grace left, DJ turned to James. "You fucking had *lunch* with Skylar, and you didn't even recognize her? The fuck, James!"

James blushed and lowered his eyes to the floor. "I'm sorry, DJ. She looked totally different, and it was out of context. You're right, I should have recognized her."

DJ stomped around the room, wondering whether he might take a swing at James for being such a dumbass. He decided against it because he needed him to help find

Skylar. "That's poor fucking form, dude. How long have you known my daughter?"

He shook his head. "I know, mate. She bloody fooled me."

DJ loosened his collar and glanced at his watch. "Where the fuck do you think that woman went, anyway? I mean, Skylar's either sleeping here or she's not."

James leaned in. "There's a strong possibility she's not here. Because remember, she took off when I saw her."

"But that was hours ago. She's got to sleep somewhere, right?"

James nodded as Grace reappeared. "Guys, I'm afraid she's gone. The report from earlier this evening says someone tripped the emergency alarm and went out the back door. It must have been her because her bunk's empty. I'm sorry."

"That means she's out there somewhere." DJ handed his business card to Grace. "If you see or hear from her, please call me." He turned to James. "Let's go."

James tried to retrace the path he took hours earlier as DJ piloted his Jaguar through the edges of downtown Las Vegas. There was no sign of Skylar.

Finally, DJ turned around and headed back toward the Strip. "This is like finding a needle in a fucking haystack. It's not going to happen tonight."

Chapter 30

kylar was on her second non-alcoholic beer when Clay called. "I've been waiting for you to call back. What's going on?"

"Sky, you wouldn't believe who I just ran into."

She glanced around nervously. The Velveteen Rabbit was rumbling with raucous activity.

"Your dad … and the Monarch!" He was breathless as he uttered the last two words.

"What did they say?" Skylar asked, zipping up her jacket and hugging it tighter. Her hair stuck to her head because she hadn't dried it properly. She shivered.

"Your dad was questioning me about you. No, it was more like a threat. He said if I knew anything about you and didn't tell him, I'd be in big trouble."

"Calm down," she said, legs fidgeting. "What did James say?"

"Nothing, to me. He walked up and told your dad they needed to talk in his office. Then they left."

Skylar shuddered. Her worst fears were materializing. James must have filled DJ in about their interactions. "Damn him!" A few women sitting near her stared. She lowered her voice. "Where are they now?"

"I don't know, but I'm sure they're on the hunt to find you. Evan said he saw them leave the casino together."

Skylar pictured them circling the streets she'd trudged up and down for hours. Her dad in the same car with her stalker—the guy who put her in this position in the first place. *That bastard!* "You said earlier that you had an idea of somewhere I could go."

"I do." He hesitated. "Look, sweetie, you don't know Evan well, but he's a good guy, and he's my right hand at work. I've not shared what's going on with him, but I trust him to take good care of you. No questions asked."

She recalled the freckly nerd who originally wanted to date her. She pulled her jacket down, so it felt more like a blanket. "What are you suggesting?"

"He's got an apartment downtown, and he lives by himself. I'm sure if I asked him to put you up for a couple of days while this whole thing blows over, he'd be happy to do it."

Skylar fell silent, considering this option. She didn't know Evan, but Clay seemed to rely on him for everything. He was under the radar enough that neither DJ nor James would suspect she had anything to do with him. Her only problem was that Evan was a stranger—a stranger who had a crush on her. She let out a deep, weighted sigh. "I don't know, Clay."

"Sky, you don't have an alternative. I mean, you could find another hotel or leave town, but DJ and James are onto you."

"But I don't know him. He's a stranger," she protested.

"Then where are you going to sleep? In your car?"

Skylar sighed again into the phone, thinking her original plan to hide in plain sight was failing miserably. "My dad thinks James is the good guy. How am I going to get him to see the truth?" She sneezed loudly and worried she might be getting sick. She thought she had detected the start of a sore throat earlier in the night but had chalked it up to running for so long. She wiped her nose with the sleeve of her jacket.

"Are you okay?" Clay asked.

"Yeah," she answered. "Just need to figure this out." Then she had an idea. "Listen, Clay. I'll stay with Evan if you promise you'll go directly to my dad and tell him what's going on—about James and all the harassment."

He fell silent.

"Come on, Clay—please? You can tell him you know where I am, and you'll lead him to me. But he can't involve James."

He let out a nervous cough. "And tell him I've been lying since the day you went off the grid? That I'm taking care of your cat? Are you serious? The man will fire me … right after he kills me."

"But he's all talk. He screams and yells, and then he listens. He'll listen to you."

"Of course, he does with you. *You're his daughter.*"

"Then I'll tell him you were only protecting me … and he'll listen to me about what to do about you." Her voice rang with desperation.

There was a long pause, but she could hear Clay's heavy breathing.

"Okay. What should I tell Evan?"

"Tell him to pick me up at the Velveteen Rabbit."

Evan didn't say anything to Skylar when he met her in the bar. He simply nodded, smiled, and led the way to his vehicle. He drove an old, scratched, and dented white flatbed pickup truck with a loud, grumbling engine. He made her put her backpack behind the seat for the ride, which worried her because both her cell phone and her gun were tucked into it. She wondered what Clay had said—how much of the sordid tale he had revealed about Skylar's demise. She decided to let him do the talking.

He turned on the ignition, and his two-way radio piped up. Clay's voice came through with a scratchy edge. "Evan, is everything okay?"

Evan picked up his radio, which sat in the console, and hit the button. "Yes, Sir. All good." He twisted a switch on his radio, set it back in the console, then put his truck into drive.

Skylar tried to pay attention to where he was driving, but at some point, she got turned around. She rubbed her hand down her pant leg. "Where abouts do you live downtown?" she asked, studying his profile. His nose was a sharp, unattractive hook. With his longish, shaggy brown hair, he reminded Skylar of a ferret.

"Just around the corner," he replied without taking his eyes off the road.

She eyed the street signs. "No, I mean what area of downtown—I don't know my way around here much."

"You'll see in a few minutes," he answered, again without turning his head.

His voice was low and silky. She had never noticed because she never paid attention to him before now. She sure hoped Clay knew what he was doing.

He finally pulled up to a shabby-looking building adjacent to a strip mall. Skylar saw a green sign flashing a logo 'Thai One On Massage,' and her stomach churned. Those kinds of massage parlors usually offered *happy endings*, as Skylar had mistakenly gone into one for a foot massage years earlier. A woman did her foot massage and then asked her what else she wanted. She pumped more cream into her hands, rubbed them together, and worked her way up Skylar's long legs. Skylar allowed the woman to continue, thinking a leg massage would be lovely. It wasn't until the woman slid her warm, moist fingers underneath Skylar's robe, between her legs, that Skylar let out a loud scream, jumped off the bed, and ran out.

Evan pulled into a dark garage underneath the building and parked his truck. He grabbed his radio and swung out, running around to Skylar's side to open the door. He held his hand out to help her down.

"I'm good," she said, shaking out her hands. The dingy, musty-smelling parking garage didn't promise much in terms of what his apartment was going to be like.

She picked her fingernails and watched as he hauled her backpack out from behind the seat. "Here, I can carry that," she offered.

He shook his head. "This is heavy. I'll carry it for you."

The elevator was out of order, so they took the stairs up to his apartment on the third floor. Skylar's sore throat was getting worse, and she was grateful for only a few sets of stairs to climb.

Evan corralled her to his unit, which she noted was number 332. He unlocked and opened the door, and Skylar cringed at the interior. It had to have been the ugliest, most spare apartment she'd seen in years, only lit by what appeared to be battery-operated lanterns. The furniture looked like it had been there for a century—worn and faded, a color she couldn't identify—it was either slate blue or gray. A mildewed odor that had been masked by some type of men's cologne penetrated her nostrils. She pictured Evan spraying it around before he left each day, in case he hooked up with a woman and took her home. She swallowed hard and pinched her lips shut.

"Here it is," Evan said with a sarcastic grin. "Home sweet home."

"How long have you lived here?" she asked, watching him set her backpack on one of the hideous easy chairs.

"Not long." He glanced around the apartment. "I know it's not what you're used to, but it's cheap, and it's a place to sleep." He turned to look her in the eye. "There's only one bedroom."

Skylar's stomach lurched. "That's okay. I'll sleep on the …" she looked around, trying to assess which was less disgusting, the floor or the couch.

"You can have the bed," he said. "I'll sleep on the couch." He turned and stepped into his kitchen, which was right off the front door. He switched on a lantern. "Would you like a drink?"

She shuddered. *Does this guy think he's on a date?* She couldn't believe Clay had set this up. If he were here right now, he'd regret it for sure. But there was nothing Skylar could do at this point. Everywhere she went, James would be on her tail. She could only imagine the lies he was telling her dad to get him on his side. Maybe he even shared the photos—*those fucking photos!* The thought of James and her dad browsing through them and seeing her like that—naked and tied up, in the most frightening, unconscionable moments of her life—made her feel dizzy and faint. She let out a low, raspy cough. "I'd like some water, please."

"Oh, sure," he called. "I'll get you some."

"And, um, where's the bathroom?" She was now afraid she might vomit right there on his dirty gray rug. She also needed to pee.

"In my bedroom."

Did I imagine it, or did he sound lascivious? She felt her skin tightening, thinking she just needed to get through one night before she could leave in the morning. She slowly approached a closed door and twisted the doorknob. She pushed open the door and poked her head into the darkness, feeling along the wall for a light switch. She found one and tried to flick it on. Nothing happened. She turned back and almost ran into Evan, who was right behind her, holding one of the free-standing lanterns.

"Don't you have electricity?" she asked.

He shrugged. "The power's been out for the last few days."

He handed her the lantern, and she proceeded into the bedroom. A small twin bed was slung against the far-right corner. A black bedspread covered it. There were no books, no personal items, no art on the walls, no nothing. *Why would he live here? Why would anyone live here?* She knew what managers made at Donovan, and the salary would afford a much nicer arrangement than this.

She found the bathroom and closed the door behind her. She held the lantern up and peered into the mirror. She couldn't believe how scared and tired she looked. She felt her forehead. Definitely coming down with something. *This is temporary, Skylar. You have no other choice.* She unzipped her jeans and tugged them down her thighs. She thought about squatting over the toilet rather than sitting on it, but she had no more strength in her legs from all the running. She pulled down her underwear, sat on the ice-cold toilet seat, and urinated. When finished, she realized there was no toilet paper. She looked around the tiny bathroom and leaned over to open an adjacent cabinet. There was nothing inside. She looked for a hand towel, but there were none. *This guy doesn't even have towels.* She would have to wait a few seconds.

Just as she rose from the toilet to pull up her underwear, Evan burst through the door and thrust a roll of toilet paper at her.

Skylar gasped. "Oh my God, what do you think you're doing?" She grabbed the roll. "Get out and close the door!"

He hesitated for a moment, lowering his eyes.

"I said get out!" she shouted, throwing her hand up to back him off.

He retreated from the bathroom and closed the door.

She quickly finished and rinsed her hands—there was no soap—then shook them dry in the sink. She left the lantern on the counter.

Evan sat on the threadbare couch, holding a plastic cup in one hand and a dark green bottle in the other. He set the cup on a deep brown, badly chipped wood coffee table. He smiled and patted the place beside him. "Come over here. You said you wanted water." He gestured toward the plastic cup.

"I can't believe you just walked in on me," she scolded. "You don't do that to *anyone*. It's gross."

He shrugged and smirked a bit. "Don't worry, I didn't see anything I haven't seen before." He patted the seat next to him again. "Come here."

Skylar marched to the opposite end of the couch from where he was. When she sat, the couch springs sank so low, she thought she might fall through the cushion. "You could sure use some new furniture."

"Yeah, well, this place came furnished. You think I'd actually *buy* this crap?" He released a loud guffaw that didn't at all fit the situation. Then he picked up the green bottle and examined the label. He looked up at Skylar. "You ever had real Dutch gin?"

Skylar recoiled, then her thoughts returned to her first encounter with Evan. He had mentioned Dutch gin then. She tried to remember why … something about Brit and Sal.

Evan stood, moved to where she was sitting, and handed her the bottle.

She pressed her knees together while scrutinizing the label, which read, "Old Duff Genever" with a drawing of some kind of animal face with horns. She guessed it was a ram. Underneath the logo was "Real Dutch Genever," and "Holland" printed at the bottom. She recognized the bottle. The pimp who raped her had that same bottle. He kept forcing her to guzzle shots of that biting stuff. She could still feel the burn of the alcohol in her throat. She handed the bottle back to Evan. "I don't drink."

His freckly face broke into a giant, goofy grin. "Oh, come on, Sky. You don't mind if I call you Sky, right? Let's just have one. You'll feel more comfortable." He walked to a bookshelf where two shot glasses sat. She noticed his ass was completely flat in tan cargo pants. He picked up the shot glasses, blew dust out of them, and then returned to sit next to Skylar. He uncorked the bottle and poured two full shots.

He pushed one shot toward Skylar and picked up his own. "Skoll," he said before gulping it down. "Your turn."

Skylar got to her feet, thinking she needed to get out of there. Fast. *This guy is creeping me out.* He walked in on her when she was on the toilet, and now he was trying to get her to do shots. *Does he think I'm desperate enough to have sex with him?* The mere thought made her stomach cartwheel. She coughed loudly. "You know, I should probably call Clay and tell him I'm okay."

His face became serious, and his eyebrows furrowed. "I already radioed him. You heard me. He's the one who asked me to pick you up, remember?" He gave her a sickly smile and patted the front pocket of his cargo pants. "I carry the radio everywhere, so don't worry."

She eyed her backpack, which remained sitting on one of the easy chairs. "Still, I'd feel more comfortable if I told him myself." She advanced to the chair and bent forward to unzip her backpack. She rummaged through but could not find her cell phone. She thought back to where she could have left it. No, she clearly remembered leaving the Velveteen Rabbit with it. Out of instinct, she checked for her handgun. She couldn't find that either.

Her hands trembled, and her body tensed as she drew

herself to her full height, turning to face Evan. "What the fuck have you done with my cell phone and gun?"

Evan gave her a blank look. "I didn't take them."

"Don't fucking lie to me, you little nerd! Give me my cell phone and gun right now, or I'll beat the shit out of you." She took two steps toward him.

He rose from the couch. "You know, Skylar. You're not being a very nice house guest." He disappeared in his kitchen again, this time emerging with something behind his back. "I've got a little surprise for you." He approached her, again with that perverted smile.

She retreated a step. "Do not come closer."

He edged forward until he had backed her against a wall and then pulled both her cell phone and her gun from his back. "How much do you want these?" he teased, pointing the gun at her while stashing her cell phone in the back pocket of his cargo pants.

"You're going to give me my things, and I'm going to leave." She glared at the gun as he moved it so close, the nose dug into the bodice of her hoodie.

"You're not going anywhere until I get what I want," he said, now with a vengeful gleam in his eye.

"What do you want?" she asked, eyes on the gun—her gun, which she knew was fully loaded.

"What do you think?" he retorted with sarcasm.

"I… I don't know." The nape of her neck tingled.

"You've come a long way," he said, tapping the gun against her chest with each syllable.

"I don't know what you mean," she said, eyes glued to his. She was close enough to see tiny pimples covering his forehead.

"Yes, you do ...." He paused before letting out a strangled laugh and then lifting the gun to point it at her throat. "Yes, you do ... *Slipper Girl*."

Skylar's mind wildly careened, and a deep shiver cleaved through her. *How does he know that name? How would he know anything that personal about me? DJ never knew about that. Brit never even knew. Only someone who went to the same school as me in Amsterdam would know.*

His eyes glowed a demonic red as he moved the nose of the gun to her temple. "You don't remember me?"

Skylar swallowed hard, feeling the pain of her sore throat. She shuddered. "Are you from Amsterdam?" she asked, thinking she needed to stall him. "If you are, I think I may remember you."

"I was a grade ahead of you in school," he explained, not moving the gun from Skylar's temple. "I remember when I first saw you. You were the most beautiful girl I'd ever seen. So tall, you looked like a princess. I got to school early every day just to watch you walk to class." His eyes widened slightly. "Then that one day you wore your bed slippers, and everyone made fun of you."

"I ... um ... I remember. Th-that was one of the worst days of my life," Skylar said, shifting her weight to stop her legs from shaking.

"But not *the* worst." His mouth tightened into a seam, and his eyes squinted.

A chill skittered up Skylar's spine as she tried to think of a response. But she had none. She had crammed her body tightly against the wall. But it was either that or allow the gun to penetrate her temple further.

"I followed you everywhere like a sad little dog. You

never noticed me." His voice choked up like he might cry. "I followed you everywhere, Slipper Girl. *Everywhere*."

She thought back on those confused days of living at her mother's apartment and turning tricks for spare change. *I had no idea someone was following me.* "Look, Evan," she stammered. "I had a drug problem. I was also an alcoholic. If I didn't notice you, it's because I didn't notice anyone or anything."

She observed a slight softening in his expression in the murky glimmer of light from the lanterns. *He might take to flattery. That's my only hope of getting out alive.*

"I brought a camera to school, so I'd have pictures of you—pictures just for me," he continued, gun still poised for action. "Then I followed you after school to that man's house. I hid behind his couch and watched him rip off your clothes and beat you." He paused to take a long shivering breath. "Then he tied you up and raped you. I saw it all. I saw every depraved act he forced you to do. I took pictures of the whole thing." His mouth pinched shut as his eyes landed directly on hers.

Skylar felt like someone punched her in the gut. *I'm looking right into the eyes of my stalker. Someone who's been stalking me my whole life. Someone who's stalking me now.* He had been in her house, bedroom, everywhere. He had the pictures. Her stalker was neither Brit nor James. It was the guy in front of her. *And he has my gun!*

Skylar swallowed hard, eyes watering, but she didn't respond.

"I wasn't expecting what happened that day." He bit his lower lip. "I wasn't expecting …" his voice faltered as though he were remembering something awful.

"What weren't you expecting?" Skylar heard her own voice quaver. She knew what he was about to say, but she wanted to draw it out of him. She wanted to face the ugly truth head-on.

"I watched that guy tear out your hair and punch you down … and I couldn't take it. You blacked out on the floor, so I jumped on him. He was so surprised, he dropped his knife, and I got hold of it."

Skylar held her breath, awaiting his next words.

"I stabbed him. Over and over in the chest. He bled all over the place, and once I was sure he was dead, I left the knife there."

"Wait," Skylar blurted, lips quivering. "Are you saying *you* were the one who murdered that man?"

He nodded, a vacant look in his eyes. "I had to kill him, Skylar. *I had to.*" He turned his eyes to her. "You never should have gone with him. If only you'd noticed me—been with me. None of this would have ever happened."

"But when I woke up, the knife was in my hand, and no one else was there." She was now breathless.

"I put the knife in your hand because *you're* the one who should have murdered him. I wanted you to wake up knowing you defended your honor and killed him yourself."

Another wave of nausea pelted Skylar's stomach. "If you killed him, how did you get out of his apartment without getting blood all over everything?"

Tears were now streaming down his face. "I cleaned myself up in his bathroom—used all the towels, then burned them out in the field." His hands shook the nose of the gun, which was still touching her temple.

Skylar couldn't believe what she was hearing. *I've*

spent the past 15 years agonizing over a murder I didn't commit. And she had no idea Evan was there until this very moment. Evan had killed the pimp and disposed of the bloody towels. *That's why there were none left when I went to clean myself.*

"I'm not a murderer. I swear, Skylar. I'm not." Evan's demeanor was becoming more unstable as he stood there, pleading with Skylar, his face tear-stained, and the gun still pressed against her head. "It's not murder if it's justified. And it was. That man deserved to die after what he did to you. You would have killed him yourself, and you know it."

"Evan, I know you're not a murderer," Skylar muttered, struggling to find the right words, heart jackhammering. "Y-you killed him to defend my honor—when I didn't believe I had any. You …" she paused to take a breath. "You must have really liked me."

He stopped and stared at her. "*Liked you?* I loved you. I love you now. I want to be with you. That's all I've ever wanted. That's why I tracked down your mother." He lowered his gun, so it was pointing at her chest again.

"My mother?" Skylar's thoughts jumbled together as she fought to think of a way to lead this conversation, which was getting crazier with every passing second.

Evan's lower lip trembled. "When I saw a picture of you in the paper with your father, you know, announcing his wedding, I couldn't stop thinking about you. You looked just as beautiful as the first day I saw you. I did some research and found out you never married."

He paused for a few seconds, blinking rapidly. "Why did you never marry?"

Skylar swallowed. Her hands were now trembling

violently. "I don't know. Um … maybe I never found the right man. Tell me how you found my mother."

"It wasn't easy. She changed her name to Maud Jansen. But I found her, and I sent a copy of the photos to her work address." He stopped to glance around his beater apartment. "I've never had money. And I thought if I could get my hands on a couple of million dollars, I could approach you as a real man—offer you something better."

Skylar released a deep shuddery breath but didn't respond.

"Your mother called me, and I told her I'd turn her daughter in for murder if she didn't get me the money. She told me she'd seen news of the murder, but she never knew that guy had been with you. She seemed distraught. But she swore she'd get her hands on the money, and she begged me not to turn you in." He dug the gun deeper into Skylar's chest, twisting it a little.

The whole nightmare was starting to make sense. Brit had come to Las Vegas to get the money to pay off Evan. She had approached Skylar and then DJ. Skylar couldn't believe she'd gotten it all wrong. Brit was not her enemy. Brit was trying to protect her child from going to jail for murder.

"How did you get the job working for Clay?" Skylar asked, fidgeting against the nose of his gun.

"It was easy. I applied for the banquet manager job. He was so desperate to fill the position, I got it on the spot." He pressed his lips together and glared at her. "I saw you with him so often. At first, I was jealous—until I found out he wasn't into women. Getting that job was my ticket to watch you all over again—watch your every move."

"Wait, you were in Amsterdam the whole time? How did you get into the country with all the red tape?" She was dumbfounded by how quickly this could have happened, and without her knowledge.

"I have dual citizenship—the Netherlands and the U.S. My Aunt has a house in Connecticut. I spent summers there most of my life." He smiled. "That's how I perfected my American accent."

He paused as though he lost his place and couldn't remember the rest.

"Right," she said, voice shaky and faded. "Did you ever come to Las Vegas? I mean, before now?"

He nodded. "Once. It was when I turned 21. I looked you up and saw … something I didn't want to see." He stared into her eyes, nostrils flaring. "I spied on you for a few days and then followed you to a bar." His voice broke a little as he recalled the scene. "You were with a guy."

Her whole body broke into a cold sweat. *If he were 21, I had to have been 20.* She tried to recall who she was with. "He must have been my boyfriend."

"I watched him kiss and touch you." He scowled and drove the nose of the gun a little deeper into her chest. "You were out of it. I couldn't stand to watch." He clenched his teeth. "I wanted to kill that guy, too. But I didn't. I went home to Amsterdam the next day."

She lowered her eyes to her chest, where the gun was buried. *I need to change the subject.* "Clay said you … Clay said you had a crush on me."

Evan's face softened into a smile. He momentarily lowered the gun to his side.

Skylar saw an opportunity. "Evan, I'm really thirsty. I need water. Will you get me some?"

His gaze became clouded, and he rubbed his face with

his free hand. Then, he slowly backed away from Skylar, gun in hand. "Okay. But don't try anything funny."

She licked her lips and forced a smile. "There's a cup on the coffee table. Okay if I get it?"

"I guess," he answered.

She slowly moved to his couch, picked up the water he'd left, and took several sips, struggling to keep her shaking hands steady and not spill the water. She set the cup back down and forced another smile at Evan. "Why don't we talk more over here?" She needed to find a way to get her cell phone and gun, but she would have to be careful. This guy was dangerous and obsessed with her—insanely fixated—she had to tread delicately. *My life depends on it.*

He hesitated, then plodded over to where she was sitting.

Again, Skylar made her best attempt to smile encouragingly, as sweat soaked her back.

He lowered himself onto the threadbare fabric, springs creaking under his weight. He rested the gun in his lap, facing her.

"Evan, this can all be straightened out," Skylar said, shifting her body toward him. Their knees touched, and Evan jolted, moving a few inches from her. He had a frightened look on his face.

This is my only chance. Skylar scooted closer until their knees were again touching.

"What are you trying to do?" His voice splintered.

"Get to know you." She leaned over until her face was about an inch from Evan's. She smelled the acrid stench of his body odor commingled with the musty fumes of the threadbare couch. "Get to know the man who literally killed for me."

Chapter 31

*C*lay was waiting for DJ when he returned to his office. "Mr. Keller," he said. "I'm sorry to show up unannounced, but I need to talk to you."

DJ was in no mood to see anyone, especially after his fruitless expedition through downtown Las Vegas with James. "Yeah, spit it out," he growled. He realized at that moment he hadn't eaten anything since the cheese and crackers he'd had with Max. That seemed like an eternity ago. He was also still in nicotine withdrawal hell.

"It's personal. Can we talk in your office?"

DJ drew in a breath, puffed up his cheeks, then blew out the air. "Why not?" He motioned for Clay to enter. DJ went behind his desk and sat. Clay scanned his office, then took one of the seats opposite him.

"Look, Mr. Keller, I know where Skylar is."

"Really." DJ felt his eyes widen, and he leaned forward. "Where is she?"

"She's staying with someone who works for me."

"And how do you know that?" He felt his heart speed up.

"I sent him to pick her up. He has a place downtown. She asked me to talk to you because … well, James Monarch is threatening her."

"The fuck?" DJ jerked his hands through his hair and sprang to his feet. "James Monarch is a senior executive who's eventually going to be CEO. So, you'd better fucking be right if you're going to accuse him of anything."

Clay's hands shook. "Oh, I would never accuse him. It's what Skylar said. But she needs your help. She asked me to talk to you."

"I see. How long have you and Skylar been in contact?" DJ asked, his ire growing. *I knew this guy was lying— withholding information.* He cracked his knuckles.

"Um, well, she …" he stopped. "I'm sorry, sir. She's not been herself."

"Well, go ahead and state the fucking obvious, why don't you? She was living at the Las Vegas Rescue Mission, for fuck's sake." He crossed his arms over his chest. "Now you're on slippery ice, here, buddy. So, as Skylar always says, you'd better *drop some tea.*"

Clay's whole body appeared to shudder at DJ's blunt anger. "Sh-she told me someone was following her. The person broke into her house several times and left threats. Skylar was beside herself. She said something …" he hesitated.

"She said what?" DJ dropped his arms to his side and stepped around his desk. He stopped right in front of Clay, crossed his arms over his chest again, and leaned against the desk. *I want him to be scared shitless.*

"She said she'd committed a crime—a long time ago, but she could still be in a lot of trouble. She didn't say what the crime was." He hesitated before continuing. His eyes had become damp and overly bright. "Then one night, she dropped off her cat with me and went to stay at the Rocket Palace downtown. But James—er—whoever's following her, found out she was there, and she fled to the Las Vegas Rescue Mission. James saw her there, and she had nowhere else to go. So, I sent my employee to pick her up."

DJ felt his mouth drop open. "You mean to tell me you were lying to me the entire time? Even after I asked you repeatedly?" He slammed his fist on the desk and shook his head. "I don't know whether to kill you or fire your fucking ass!" He eyed the pack of cigarettes on his desk, then turned his glare on Clay. "Consider yourself fired. But you're going to tell me where Skylar is first."

"I'm sorry I lied, Sir," he said with glistening eyes. "But Skylar was afraid for her life. She was afraid to drag you into this—that's why she swore me to secrecy."

DJ shook his head. "I asked you where she is, and you're going to tell me. Now."

"Let me radio Evan. Evan Meyer. He's my banquet manager, and we're in constant contact about events. I'm sure everything's fine, Mr. Keller. Skylar's like a sister to me. I'd never put her in harm's way."

"Whatever," DJ growled. "Get this guy on the phone."

Clay pressed the button on his radio, fingers trembling. "Evan, are you there?" He released the button and waited while DJ stood scowling at him. "Evan, if you can hear me, I need to talk to you right away. Please call me."

A full minute went by, and Clay's face turned pale. He

looked like he might pass out. "I'm sorry, sir. He must be busy or out of range."

"This guy's a manager, and you didn't issue him a company cell phone?" DJ clenched his fists and paced the room, then collapsed in his chair. *How stupid is this guy?*

"He refused to use one—said he prefers two-way radios. I figured radios are what the police and military use, so maybe he had a good point. He's never let me down yet … not sure what's going on. I'll get his address from the employment file."

"You think I'm dumb enough to let you out of my sight?" DJ snarled through clenched teeth. "I'll go with you to get the fucking employment file."

Still fuming, DJ followed Clay to his office, which was clear across the casino. Something wasn't right with this guy's story—his demeanor. He had willingly and successfully pulled one over on him—on everyone. *I'm going to flatten him.* He deserved to be fired and discredited throughout the industry. At least he was loyal. Loyal to Skylar in her apparent mental crisis. That's what it had to be. She had a nervous breakdown as soon as her illustrious mother barged into her life. *That bitch!*

As they traversed the casino, DJ's anger mounted toward his ex-wife. *Why the hell am I such a pussy? I should have forced her out, even if it meant losing Sal.* Right then, he spied Brit traipsing through the casino carrying a giant half-full margarita. They had been running a promotion at one of the bars—margaritas the size of one's head—at a low price. The secret? Cheap tequila.

"Hold on a second," he said to halt Clay. "Don't you move from this spot, understand?"

Clay nodded, his eyes wide and his face ashen.

DJ diverted his path so he would run right into the hated one. When he got close, she stopped and stared at him. Her eyes were glazed over from crying. Her mascara bled down her face as she nursed the oversized chalice filled with what was left of her mammoth margarita.

"Where's Sal?" DJ demanded, giving her the once over and almost wincing at today's hideous montage of garments: a red leather miniskirt with white go-go boots. Her black bra peeked out from under a red, see-through blouse. He shook his head. *What a spectacle!*

She wiped her eyes with the back of her hand and sucked on the straw of her margarita. "He threw me out." She blinked and scowled at DJ, as though it were his fault. "You know I was really starting to like him."

"Spare me," DJ grated, his jaw clamping shut. "Although I'm glad old Sal finally wised up."

She adjusted her blouse and took another sip of her drink before setting it on an empty blackjack table. "You don't understand how a woman feels," she said, sniffling. "You never did."

"Look, Brit," DJ growled, gripping her elbow. "Now that there's absolutely no reason for you to be here, I'll have Sonia book your flight back to Amsterdam in the morning."

She wrenched her elbow from his grip. "What about the $2 million?" she cried, a desperate glower darkening her face. "You promised me if I left, you'd give me the money."

DJ released a caustic roar. "Are you kidding me?" He glanced at his watch. "That offer just expired. You get nothing. Except for your flight home. You're lucky it's illegal for me to send you home by air freight. Now move along."

He tried to side-step her, but she blocked him and grabbed his arm.

"You don't understand … I need the money *for Skylar*."

Now what in the hell is this idiot talking about? "Skylar has all the money she'll ever need. You want to know what she doesn't need? You. Now MOVE ALONG!"

"Damn it! She's in trouble. Real trouble." She blew her nose into a cocktail napkin. "You'd know if you paid more attention to your own daughter—instead of running off to Bali with that wax figurine."

He dispatched a nasty chuckle. "I went to Bali with Max, not Craig."

"How can you joke at a time like this? Your daughter …" she paused to look around, then yanked DJ by his jacket lapel, propelling him toward her.

He grasped her by the wrists and pushed her away. "Don't touch me, sleaze queen."

"*Our* daughter committed *murder*," she blurted.

He felt his mouth drop open, quickly looking around to see if anyone had heard. "What the fuck are you babbling about now?"

"She killed her pimp," Brit whispered. "Back when she was 12. I didn't know she was seeing him—didn't know any of it. But I have pictures—pictures of her with that man—the one she killed." She picked up her margarita and slurped from the straw.

DJ was suddenly sobered. "Let's have this conversation in my office."

Before she could say anything, he grabbed her by the wrist and corralled her in the direction of his office. Brit allowed herself to be pulled along, but she kept a tight hold on the margarita, which was in danger of spilling all over her.

DJ made sure their path to the office intersected with Clay, who was still standing at attention, waiting for DJ.

"You—get the employee's address and bring it to my office. Now."

Clay stared at Brit with curiosity. "Yes, sir."

In DJ's office with the door closed and the drapes shut, DJ took a good look at Brit. She was nervous and scared, but he didn't trust anything she said.

Brit looked around for a place to sit, but DJ was not about to let her get comfortable. "You said something about a murder. And pictures. Want to tell me what the fuck you meant?"

Brit took a long sip of her margarita and moved closer to DJ. "Pictures of Skylar having sex with that man. There was also one of her after she stabbed him to death."

DJ felt his pulse doubling. "I have those pictures. Only I don't have the one you're describing. Who took them?" He was having a tough time picturing Skylar with a knife in her hand, murdering the guy she slept with. But as he recalled the sickening photos, it didn't look like she was enjoying it at all. *If the man in the pictures was assaulting her, she had a damned good reason to kill him. That's a justifiable homicide.*

Brit's chin sank, and she closed her eyes. "I don't know. She was turning tricks. It's all my fault for being the worst mother on earth." Her hand flew to her throat, and she started ugly crying, mascara-laden face distorted like a wrung-out sponge. "Someone sent those photos to the department store where I work in Amsterdam. He left a number, and I called to try to reason with him. He swore he'd turn Skylar in for this man's murder if I didn't get him $2 million. I'm sorry. I played you." She broke down and sobbed, free hand gripping into a fist, tears creating large droplet stains on her red blouse.

"How do I know you're telling the truth? I mean, let's face it, Brit. You're not exactly an honest woman." He studied her eyes for some indication that she was being truthful. And somehow, the crocodile tears didn't convince him. "What if you're *playing* me now?"

"You have to believe I'm not." She turned and bent slightly to set the margarita on his desk, and her red leather miniskirt tipped up.

DJ got a brief glimpse underneath the skirt and her round, tanned ass in a black lace thong. He was almost shocked at how smooth and shapely she was at her age. But Brit had always been tall and slender. He felt a twinge of arousal. The fact that she could turn him on at this moment confused him. *What the hell am I thinking?*

He cleared his throat and drew himself to his full height. "Did the man who sent the photos give you a name?"

She shook her head. "Not really. He only identified himself as 'E.' And he threatened to track me down wherever I went." She wrung her hands and began to cry again.

"Hey, Brit," DJ said gently. "Take it easy. If you're telling the truth, we'll work this out." He struggled against the urge to console her. *She's so broken.*

"I'm a failure at everything but especially as a mother," she sobbed.

He realized then he had misjudged her. *She still is, and always will be, a hot mess. But she cares about Skylar.* And she understood what a horrible parent she'd been. *We both were. And we both failed our daughter.* He touched Brit's shoulder and drew his fingers softly down the sleeve of her blouse. "It's okay, Brit. We were both awful. We have to live with that."

She watched his fingers on her sleeve, tears streaming down her cheeks. "But I loved you." She lifted her gaze to him. "I *really* loved you. And it broke my heart when you put me out."

DJ noticed how glittery Brit's pale blue eyes were with the cleansing rush of tears. She was still beautiful, even with the scourge of hard living. "I didn't know that. I thought you wanted to be free. That's why I let you go."

She shook her head. "I never wanted to leave. I wanted to stay with you and raise Skylar, but your father hated me, remember? He wanted me out of your life."

DJ nodded slowly. "I remember. There wasn't a lot I could do at that point."

"You could have fought for me!" she cried. "But you threw me away. I was never good enough." She shook her head in frustration.

It hit DJ with sudden ferocity that Brit felt about him the way he felt about Max. *There's always one person in every relationship who has the upper hand.* "Brit, I'm sorry. I'm sorry for all of it. I was young. I had a whole other identity you never knew about."

She sucked in a deep breath, then nodded. "I found out when I saw your wedding announcement." She glanced up at him. "*Donovan James Keller.* You looked so positively handsome in the newspaper. All the feelings I had for you long ago came back. I couldn't sleep because all I could think of was everything I'd lost."

She thinks I'm what? DJ snickered. "I'm sorry, Brit, but you need glasses. Your eyesight is obviously failing."

She took a step back to observe him from head to toe. "You're gorgeous. Your hair and those big brown eyes. You think your brother's the one with the looks, but he's nothing compared to you. *You're* the star."

DJ felt his cheeks flush. "Now I know you're lying."

She let out a small giggle and shook her head. "I'm not."

She moved closer and leaned in, so her mouth was near his left ear, and whispered, "You're even more attractive now."

He felt her warm breath tickling his earlobe. She moved her mouth, so it was about a half inch away from his, and he whiffed her tequila fumes—something he found profoundly sexy, in a dark sort of way.

He smiled. *Brit's always been a bad girl. It's why I had the hots for her in the first place.*

She closed her eyes. "I've been thinking about how much I still want you ever since that night playing darts."

"Is that right?" He had a sudden image of their early days as a young couple—they couldn't get enough of each other, and the sex was out of control, which is why she got pregnant so quickly with Skylar. "A game of darts turns you on?"

She shook her head. "Not the darts—YOU."

He leaned even closer, and their lips met. He opened his mouth to her, feeling an intense erection. He put his arms around her waist and pulled her closer.

She tangled her fingers in his long hair while they

kissed, then lowered one hand to the crotch of his pants and felt his hardness.

As the kissing intensified, he could no longer control his lust and no longer cared about the consequences. He gathered her up in his arms and carried her to his leather couch, where he lowered her onto her back. He scrambled on top of her, one hand wandering underneath her leather skirt, and the other unbuttoning her see-through blouse. She had successfully unzipped his pants and crawled her fingers under his boxers to grip his erection.

"Jesus, Brit," he said breathlessly between kisses. "I can't stop."

"Please don't," she pleaded, tearing at the waistband of his boxers to remove them, and then wrapping her long legs around his body.

He yanked her skirt up to her waist, tore the black panties off, then thrust himself into her, feeling the tingly sensation—the intensity of wanting someone who desperately wanted him. The idea of him being hotter than Craig—of a woman craving his body instead of picking him apart—made him feel like he might explode. His wedding vows flew out the window, along with any thoughts about Max. All he could think of was how intense his orgasm would be with Brit.

DJ and Brit lay on his couch, side by side, in varying stages of undress.

"You okay?" he asked.

She smiled. "What just happened?"

DJ got up, found his boxers, and pulled them on. He

retrieved the pack of cigarettes from his desk along with his gold lighter. He returned to the couch, took two cigarettes from the pack, and offered one to Brit. "Whatever it was, I think it deserves a cigarette."

She accepted it, and they puffed away until DJ's phone interrupted them.

Sonia called to let him know that Clay was waiting outside.

"Tell him to give me a few minutes," DJ said before hanging up. He glanced at Brit. "Better get dressed." They dashed their cigarettes in the ashtray and hobbled around picking up their clothes that had been tossed everywhere. Once they had repaired their clothing, DJ opened the door and invited Clay inside.

He gingerly walked in and did a double take at Brit, who was smoothing her hair and adjusting her miniskirt. 'Oh, hello, Maud."

She gave him a sheepish half-smile. "Hello, Clay."

"Did you find the address?" DJ asked impatiently.

Clay shook his head in defeat. "No. All he put on his application was a post office box."

DJ ground his teeth together. "Are you telling me you accepted a fucking PO box instead of a physical address from an employee?"

"He was new in town and didn't have a permanent address yet when I hired him," Clay answered with a shiver. "He was looking for a place downtown but hadn't settled on one."

He began pacing the office, marching back and forth. He shook his long blond hair, face heating up. "You have to be the most incompetent fuck I've ever employed."

"Don't yell at him!" Brit scolded. "He's her friend. And we need his help."

DJ clapped his hand to his forehead in frustration.

"Mr. Keller," Clay said. "I've been trying to radio Evan, and he's not responding. But I do have a number for Skylar. It's a burner phone she got when she left her house. She hasn't been answering my calls or texts, but she might pick up if you call." He handed DJ a piece of paper.

DJ grabbed the paper, turned his back on Clay, and dialed the numbers.

CHAPTER 32

"Don't do that," Evan warned as Skylar reached around his neck and ruffled his stringy shag of brown hair, pulling him closer.

"Why not?" she asked, knitting her brows in mock innocent confusion. Her nausea was so intense, she wanted to vomit. But she kept a tense smile on her face. She was channeling her old promiscuous self to quell her intense fear that Evan was about to murder her. She'd had a blind confidence back then. And most men, she found, weakened in the face of her pure sexual power.

"It's … well, I want you to feel the same way I do," he said, voice sounding fraught. "I've seen you with other guys—how they look at you. They only want one thing. Especially that Irish guy."

Skylar's thoughts went to James—the man she had accused of stalking her. Guilt stabbed her in the gut. *How in the hell could I have suspected James of any of this?* James, with his charming accent and sincere, crooked grin. She had felt something for him long ago, and her feelings sat simmering while she disguised her deep attraction for him as contempt. She knew that now. She chided herself for not accepting his help when he offered it. *"A lot of people care about you, Skylar, and I happen to be one of them."* Those words almost choked her up. If only she'd said yes, she would be with him now, safe, instead of holed up in this disgusting apartment, at gunpoint with a sick, perverted madman. James had been trying to protect her. *And what did I do? I pulled a gun on him—just as Evan is doing to me now.* "His name is James," she said softly without looking up. "The Irish guy's name is James."

"Are you in love with him?" he asked, giving her a sullen glare.

Yes, you imbecile! I'm totally in love with him, but it's too late now because I turned him away. She shook her head. "We just work together."

"I *hate* that guy," he snarled, baring his lower teeth. "I'll kill him."

"Stop it," Skylar scolded. "He's not a threat to you. I don't even *like* him." She needed to convince Evan that he was the only one she wanted. A thought that made her physically ill.

"What about me?" he asked.

"You … well…" She hesitated, again channeling her younger self—the one who once threw herself at her own uncle. "You're cute," she lied, forcing a flirtatious smile and looking him in the eye. "I bet you'd be even cuter if you put my gun down."

"Are you saying you'd marry me?"

Skylar curbed the urge to laugh in his pathetic face. "I said you were cute. I didn't say anything about marriage."

His face twisted into a scowl, and he pointed the gun at her again. "I knew it."

Oh shit, why didn't I just agree? "But Evan, we don't know each other," she said, trying to keep the panic out of her voice. "We will, though. That's what I want—to get to know you. Clay told me I should date you." Her mind went to her best friend, who had been bamboozled into hiring this clown and helping him get a date with the object of his obsession. Clay had trusted Evan with Skylar's life. He would be beside himself if he knew what was going on now.

Skylar's cell phone began ringing from Evan's back pocket. They both froze.

"Um, would you mind seeing who's calling?" Her voice was saccharine.

He frowned. "Why would I do that?"

She froze, feeling her legs stiffen. "Because it could be Clay. If he gets no answer, he'll worry."

"He can radio me anytime he wants." He pointed to his front pants pocket. Skylar remembered the small red radio. Clay and Evan were constantly in contact via a two-way system. She hadn't heard a peep since the drive to the apartment. She tried to recall whether Evan turned the volume down or switched it off while they were in his truck.

Skylar bit her lower lip as the phone continued to rattle. *I've got to get him to answer it.*

He removed it from his back pocket and studied the screen, then held it up for Skylar to see. "Whose number is that?"

Skylar tilted her head to the side and squinted to see the screen. She recognized the number instantly, and her heart skipped a beat. *Dad!* The only way he could have had her burner phone number was if Clay had spoken to him. *He knows I'm in trouble.* She thought about what she could say to allay Evan's paranoia long enough to allow her to answer her phone while it was still ringing. "That's my dad," she said, with forced control. "He's probably just worried about me."

Evan's face tightened. "You can't answer it. That man's scary. He yelled at me once. There's no way you're going to answer it."

"But what if I just tell him I'm fine? Because if I don't answer, Clay will tell him where I am, and he might come here. And you definitely don't want that."

"Clay doesn't have this address. No one has this address," he said with an evil sneer.

Skylar's stomach roiled in exasperation. "You know how scary my dad is, right?" she blurted. "He'll find it somehow. He's *connected*, you know." *If he only knew.*

"Clay has a post office box. That's it. It's not my fault he never checked my employment application." He chuckled at Clay's apparent stupidity.

"You have a truck, don't you? And a driver's license? We all know you can't get those with just a PO box." She eyed the phone in Evan's hand as it continued to ring, and she rapidly blinked her eyes. She couldn't believe Clay would be so sloppy, but that was just his way. He occasionally made heedless mistakes—especially if he liked someone. In Skylar's opinion, it was why he topped out at a director level instead of moving up into a vice president role. "Listen,

Evan. I'll stay on for one minute." She swept a shaky hand across her forehead to get rid of the sweat. "Just let me tell him I'm doing fine. Otherwise, he may call the police."

That got his attention. He hesitated and then handed the phone to Skylar, pointing the gun right at her forehead. "Keep it short."

She closed her eyes and answered. "Hello."

"Skylar?"

"Yes, Daddy," she said, forcing her voice to an even tenor. "How are you?"

"Um … I'm okay." He cleared his throat. "Where are you?"

"I'm great, Daddy. Just enjoying some much-needed rest."

"Ah, I see … are you with a guy named Evan?"

"Yeah, just relaxing for a few days." She dipped an encouraging smile at Evan, who frowned.

"Downtown, right? Do you have his address?"

"Oh, Daddy, that's not necessary." She feigned laughter, out of the corner of her eye, watching Evan's facial expression. The gun was still touching her temple.

"Got it. You don't have the address. Is there anything you noticed on the way there? A landmark so we can find you? Assuming you weren't blindfolded or locked in a trunk."

She rifled through her memory of earlier in the evening and recalled a green-lit sign. *What did it say?* The massage parlor, along with the bad memory it triggered, popped into her mind.

"No worries at all, Daddy. Just getting ready to *Thai One On*." She gave Evan a seductive look and leaned back. She unzipped her hoodie and shrugged it halfway down her shoulders, the way the old Skylar would have. She pretended Evan was someone else. She blurred her eyes and imagined he was really Craig—she had finally managed to seduce him—to take him away from Jane.

Evan's lips parted, and his eyes lowered to her breasts in a snug white T-shirt. She wished she hadn't worn a bra.

"Tie one on?" DJ repeated. "Does that mean you're planning to drink a lot?" He then sighed into the receiver. "Oh shit. Did this guy tie you up? Is he touching you inappropriately?"

"Hmmm … yes, I believe so. But things are going great, and I can't wait to see you when I get back." She smiled and drew her hair behind her ear with her free hand.

"Hang up," Evan mouthed, a surly expression on his face.

"Okay, Daddy, I need to go now. I love you."

"Wait—don't go yet. I need a little more information."

Evan edged even closer, still pointing the gun at her forehead.

"Yes, I'm in a bit of a hurry." She threw another sexy look Evan's way. "Bye-bye, Daddy."

She ended the call and handed the phone to Evan. Then she boldly put her hand over the nose of the gun and guided it down to the crotch of Evan's cargo pants, again, picturing Craig. "Want to have some fun?"

"No!" he screamed, yanking the gun back so fast it flew out of his hand and slid along the floor to the other side of the room. He jumped up from the couch to retrieve it, but Skylar was faster.

She kicked Evan in the groin, and he doubled over on his side, curled up in pain. She lunged toward the gun and grasped it. She squatted, pointing it directly at Evan. "Make one move, asshole, and you're dead."

Chapter 33

DJ put his phone in his jacket pocket and turned to face Brit and Clay. "That was weird. And telling."

"What did she say?" Clay asked, gnawing his thumbnail.

"Not much. I know she's in trouble," he responded. "She called me 'Daddy,' and she's never called me that in her life."

"Did she give you any idea of where she is?" Brit asked, pale blue eyes wide.

"Not really. She's with that man, Evan. But she said something odd—something about tying one on." He turned to Clay. "How well did you know this guy before you told him to pick up my daughter and take her to his house?"

Clay's face reddened. "I'm sorry, sir. I thought he was a decent guy."

"You thought … you *thought*," DJ scorned, shaking

his head. He pulled out his phone and dialed James, who answered right away. "I need some intel on an employee by the name of Evan Meyer. Banquet Manager."

"What do you need to know?" James asked.

"Everything. "He's …" DJ hesitated. "He's got Skylar. Somewhere downtown. We need to find his address and anything else we can get on him. He's got to have a Sheriff's Card to work here."

"Right. Let me make some calls."

"Meet me in my office as soon as you have something—anything."

He turned to Brit. "I'll put you in a hotel room until all this is resolved. But I want you to stay there in case I need to call you. Understood?"

She nodded, eyes rolling heavenward. "Will you let me know if you find her?"

"Of course. You can pick up your room key at the front desk. I'll call them now."

There was a brief, awkward moment between her and DJ. They locked eyes. He felt his lips unconsciously part. *What is this I'm feeling?* She had once told him she loved him. He didn't want to say it to her, but he had loved her, too. Nothing could erase what they'd just done. It was all surreal. If nothing else, they had broken down barriers.

"Thank you," Brit finally said, raking her fingers through her hair. She exited his office.

DJ turned to Clay. "It goes without saying, but if you hear anything—*anything*—from this guy, you call me. *Capisci?*"

"Yes, sir," he said. "I'll keep trying him on the radio."

"Good," DJ responded, then dismissed him with a wave of the hand.

Alone in his office, DJ got a surprise video call from Max. When he tapped the answer button, she filled the screen. Only she was naked, in the bathtub, body obscured by bubbles. She was holding the phone above her head so DJ would have a full view.

"Woah!" he exclaimed, thinking about the steamy session he'd just had with Brit and feeling a twinge of real guilt. "What's going on there?"

She cleared the bubbles away so he could see her breasts. "Everything," she murmured in a sexy tone.

"Why do I always have such shit timing?" DJ put his free hand to his forehead in mock distress.

"Go to your car, and get here, now," she ordered, sloshing water on the camera lens of her phone, and standing so DJ could see the rest of her.

How am I supposed to tell her I'm spent from screwing my ex-wife? "I can't go anywhere right now," he said.

She panned the camera down her body and closed in on the area between her legs. "I don't care. I want you … now!"

Just then, James burst into the office with a grim look on his face. "Oh, sorry, I didn't know you were on the phone."

"I want to do *everything* with you," Max purred.

"Hold on, Max—James is here." DJ slid down in his chair. "We're trying to find Skylar. I'll call you later." DJ didn't wait for Max to respond before he disconnected the lustful call. *What's gotten into her anyway?*

A flush crept across James's cheeks. "Look, I didn't

mean to interrupt a private call. Do you want me to come back?"

DJ shook his head and got to his feet. "Just tell me what you found out."

James cleared his throat and swallowed. "Evan Meyer has all the work cards, including a TAM and Health Card, because he handles food. But his residential address is in Connecticut, not Nevada."

DJ began pacing. "Fucking Connecticut? How?"

He shrugged. "Happens all the time. You don't have to live in Nevada to get the cards. How does Skylar know him?"

"Through her buddy the *Conference Director*," DJ answered, fresh scorn in his voice. "Guy I'm putting on an ice floe as soon as Skylar returns."

"Do you want to get Metro involved?" James asked, pulling at his collar to straighten his shirt.

DJ knew that would be James's next suggestion. But getting Las Vegas Metro Police involved was the last thing DJ wanted. If it were true that Skylar had committed murder, that would not only cause a scandal, but she might be extradited back to Amsterdam for a trial. He just couldn't do that to her—especially in light of how he and Brit had neglected her for most of her life.

He sighed. "No, James. I know it sounds crazy. But we can't. There are some things I just found out—things that could impact our business if Metro gets involved."

"Then, what's our next move?" James was staring at something on DJ's floor near the couch.

"There's got to be a way to find out where they are," DJ said, squishing his eyebrows together. "I asked Skylar if there was anything near where she was—a business—

something. She said she was going to 'tie one on,'"whatever that's supposed to mean."

James ran his hands through his hair, then pulled out his cell phone. "Tie one on," he repeated absentmindedly as he began typing. After a few minutes, he looked up at DJ. "I just searched *tie one on downtown* and here's what I got." He handed his phone over.

DJ examined it. There was a business called "Thai One On Massage" within a strip mall somewhere in a seedy area of downtown. It had to be one of those 24-hour joints that offered more than just a massage. He rubbed the back of his neck. "Holy shit!" DJ exclaimed. "That must have been what she was trying to tell me. She's got to be somewhere near there."

James nodded, now cocking his head toward the floor near the couch.

"What the hell are you looking at?" DJ finally asked.

James took a few steps toward DJ's couch, swooped down, and retrieved something from the floor. He eyed it, then immediately dropped it like it was flaming hot. His face flushed.

"What—what the hell is it?" DJ advanced to where James stood and stooped to examine the small piece of black fabric. It struck DJ that James had found Brit's lace thong—the one he'd torn off her just moments before.

"I'm sorry, man," James said, cheeks even redder. "I shouldn't have, um."

"Never mind." DJ shook his head, stooping to pick up the microscopic piece of lacy fabric. "Max has been on some kind of kick lately. She's insatiable." He stashed the thong in his pocket.

"You're a lucky man," James commented, clearing his throat. "Want to take my car this time? It's a little less conspicuous than the Jag."

DJ nodded. "Let's go."

James and DJ rode toward downtown in silence with the GPS set to lead them to Thai One On Massage, which was just north of Commercial Center, a downtrodden strip mall replete with swinger bars, wig shops, shabby restaurants, and customers donning biker gear.

"You don't still carry, do you?" James asked.

DJ thought back to his days working for Luuk before he became CEO. He carried a concealed pistol in his jacket—and was never without it. Max had persuaded DJ that it was a bad idea to carry a gun in a crowded casino, especially with his new title and life with her. He shook his head. "No gun. Not anymore." He turned to study James's profile as he drove. "What about you?"

"I have one at home. I don't carry." He tore his eyes from the road to look straight at DJ. "You know, since we can't call Metro, and neither of us is armed, don't you think we should have backup?"

"Backup?" DJ repeated. "I said no cops."

"I'm not talking about cops. I'm talking about … you know, friends who can handle this type of thing."

DJ shook his head. "I don't consort with those types of *friends* anymore. It's part of having a gaming license."

James stole a sideways glance at DJ. "I'm talking about *my* friends, not yours."

DJ laughed. "Nah—we don't need any of your Trinity frat boys."

"I'm not talking about frat boys. I'm talking about the Irish mob from my neighborhood in Belfast."

DJ did a double take. He had James all wrong. "I thought you were born in Dublin, with a silver spoon in your mouth."

"Sometimes looks are deceiving," James said, eyes focused on the road.

DJ shrugged. "Fine. Just make sure they don't break the law without cause."

James dialed someone's number, then turned off Bluetooth. "Lorcan, it's James. You got anything going on right now?"

There was silence.

"This is confidential. I'm with my boss, and we're trying to find his daughter. She's been kidnapped by a guy who's holding her hostage somewhere near the Commercial Center. I have an address if you'd care to meet us."

CHAPTER 34

Skylar approached Evan slowly and deliberately. Pain flooded her jaw from clenching her teeth. He was still lying on his side, clutching his groin in agony. "Hand me my phone," she ordered in a throaty snarl when she got close enough.

His watery eyes rolled upward. "You're not going to get away," he said in a husky voice. "I'm tied to you forever … *Slipper Girl*."

She kicked him in the side, adrenaline rushing through her body. "Stop calling me that, or I'll pull the trigger now. And no one will give a shit that you're dead." She stared down into his eyes.

"You won't do it," he muttered. "After all I did for you. I killed the man who raped you. And you owe your life to me. You could go to jail if those pictures get to the police."

"I said, *give me my fucking phone!*" she shouted, kicking him in the side again for emphasis. She backed a few steps away, continuing to point the gun at him. "Slide it over to me. Don't make me shoot you."

He slowly reached into his back pocket, retrieved the phone, then sent it skidding towards her.

She grabbed it with her free hand, then backed away further. Her breath came in gasps as she thrust the phone in her hoodie pocket and made a run for the door. She unhooked the chain and twisted the doorknob, but the door wouldn't open. She found the switch on the doorknob and frantically flicked it, but the door remained locked. "Damn it!" she screamed aloud, looking back toward where she had left Evan. *He's no longer on the floor!*

She jiggled the lock again, but the door still wouldn't open. She pulled out the phone and began dialing 9-1-1, her fingers trembling.

"You really want the cops, Slipper Girl?" Evan's voice echoed from the kitchen area. "Those pictures are here, you know. They'll find 'em."

Heart racing and sweat dripping down her face, she feverishly searched the apartment for another way out. Her eyes stopped on a window overlooking the parking lot. *Will I be able to climb out?* She tried to recall the floor they were on. *What apartment is it?* Her fear had overtaken logic, and she couldn't remember. She recalled it was a lower-level floor. She scurried to the window, unlocked it, and began pushing it upward. It wouldn't budge.

Oh my God, please open! She could only shunt it open a crack. *I'll have to use the gun barrel to break the window.* Before she could act, a huge butcher knife came out of nowhere and chopped at the window latch with a piercing, metallic clank.

"Need some help?" a shrill, out-of-control voice came from behind her.

Skylar froze, eyes watering. She spun around and leveled the gun at him.

His hair wildly framed his face with bloodshot, crazed eyes. He held the knife with both hands like the hilt of a sword. Before she could pull the trigger, he lunged at her with a swift and sudden movement, slicing into the flesh of her right hand. The gun fell to the floor with a sharp thwack as a bright crimson arc oozed from her palm.

"Oh my God!" she screamed. She held up her hand, and blood trickled down her forearm. "Look what you've done!" She clutched her palm with her left hand to apply direct pressure. The mere sight of blood nauseated Skylar, and this was no ordinary cut.

Evan stooped to retrieve the gun, pocketed it, then inched his way toward her, still gripping the bloody knife. "You didn't think I'd do it. But I did. And I'm not finished yet."

Skylar's heart thudded in her chest as he closed in on her. *This is it. I'm going to die, and no one will be able to find me.* She remained as still as possible, left hand clamped over her injured right, veins throbbing a visible pulse beneath her skin. She held it so close that she could feel the hot blood seep into the fabric of her hoodie. She gulped hard. *I'm going to throw up.* She wasn't even sure how deep he'd cut. *Am I going to bleed to death?*

He edged his way forward, a diabolical glow in his eyes. "You ruined everything, Slipper Girl. You ruined it! We could have been together. We could have had everything." His words were strangely clipped and uneven. "But no one's going to have you now. I'll make sure of it!"

Skylar's heart pounded in a sick rhythm with her throbbing hand. Her vision turned fuzzy, and nausea attacked her gut. She knew she was only a brief moment away from fainting. "Evan, please. You really hurt my hand—I need a doctor."

"A doctor?" He let out a huge guffaw, discharging a load of fetid saliva into Skylar's face. "You ruined your chances of getting any help, Slipper Girl." He laughed again, this time pointing the tip of his knife at her breastbone. "I'm going to carve you up just like I did to that guy who raped you. You won't need a doctor—you'll need a coroner."

Skylar searched her mind for one more tactic. She'd tried to seduce him. That didn't work. But she had rebuffed his marriage idea. "Evan, we can still have everything. You and me! We'll get married." She blinked rapidly and forced a smile. "My dad will love you—once he gets to know you. But if you kill me, we'll never get the chance."

Sweat drenched her body as she glanced wildly around the room. "You don't have to stay in this place. You can come live with me. I have a pool, you know." Her voice reeked of despair.

"I've seen your house a million times. I've been *in* it. I know what your bed smells like. I know *everything* about you, Slipper Girl." He pressed the tip of the knife to her chest, and she winced at the sharp point of the blade.

She was now shaking uncontrollably, gulping for breath. "Then you know how wonderful your life can be. But you have to let me live. Come on, Evan, let's have a great life together. Please?"

CHAPTER 35

When DJ and James entered Thai One On Massage, no one was at the poorly lit front desk. A pink paisley curtain hung over the doorway.

DJ saw a note with a bell next to it. "Ring for service." He rang the bell loudly until a man appeared from behind the curtained doorway.

"You want massage?" the man asked DJ. He was in his mid-forties, balding, and wearing glasses.

DJ tapped eyes with James. "We're looking for someone—a woman. Tall, very slim, and blonde." DJ took his phone out to find a picture of Skylar. He vaguely noted several missed calls from Clay. He found the photo and thrust his phone toward the man, who crinkled his eyes as he examined it.

"We have no woman like that here. You like Thai woman?" he asked.

"No, we're not here for a massage," James reiterated.

"We're here to find this woman." He gestured to DJ's phone. "Have you seen her around here?"

But the man wasn't listening. He parted the pink paisley curtain and yelled something in what DJ assumed was Thai vernacular.

"Hey, we said we're not looking for a massage," DJ erupted. *Time is running out.*

The man held the curtain open, and a petite, attractive young woman with long black hair appeared, wearing a short green kimono. She split her heavily shellacked, full red lips, unveiling straight, pearly white teeth. "You together?" she asked, appraising the two men with one glance.

DJ shot James an exasperated look. "No, we're not. We're looking for a woman." He held up his phone to show Skylar's photo.

She examined the photo and shrugged. "I wear blonde wig if you like. You like big finish?"

The man grinned, revealing a shiny gold canine. "Big finish cost more money."

"Let's get out of here," DJ barked. And the two exited to the parking lot.

A white Cadillac had pulled in and parked next to James's Range Rover. The driver rolled his window down.

"Lorcan," James greeted him. "Glad you could get here."

The man opened the car door and got out. DJ did a double take at his full-length black fur coat.

DJ shot James a look. "Am I in a Guy fucking Ritchie movie?"

James gave DJ a half-smile. "Lorcan, this is DJ."

The two men shook hands. The guy had obviously seen too much of the desert sun. Or maybe he spent all his spare time in a tanning bed because his face looked like a burnt tomato. His closely cropped white-blond hair gave the appearance of deep pile velvet.

"We're looking for my daughter," DJ said, holding his phone out so Lorcan could view the photo of Skylar.

He studied it and then scanned the parking lot. "You think she's here somewhere?"

DJ noted his accent was much more pronounced than James's.

"We're not sure," James answered. "We had a lead to this place." He pointed at the Thai One On Massage sign. "But we're pretty sure she's not in there."

Lorcan turned and walked around to survey the parking lot. His fur coat twirled as he moved in a circle. "No other businesses are open. What about that old apartment building?" He pointed to the other side of the lot.

DJ turned his eyes to the dingy, grey building. "That dump?"

"You said on the phone some guy had her," said Lorcan. "Is it possible she's there?"

Again, DJ and James exchanged glances. "I guess anything's possible," DJ said.

When the three men reached the building's entrance, DJ stared up at the windows. They were all blacked out except for one on the third floor.

"God, what a shithole," DJ commented without thinking.

"It was recently condemned," Lorcan said.

"How do you know?" DJ asked, now alarmed that Skylar might be in there.

Lorcan turned to look him in the eye. "I've heard it's a *meeting place*, if you know what I mean."

DJ turned to James. "If she's here, how do we even go about finding her?"

"We'll have to go door to door," James responded.

"I'll watch the parking lot," Lorcan said, pulling his fur coat aside to show his gun in its holster.

"Be careful with that," DJ warned.

DJ and James went ahead through the entrance into a dark, dust-laden lobby. They found an old, abandoned security desk with a framed glass-covered list of apartment numbers affixed to the wall behind it. An old-school push-button phone with a stretched-out curly cord hung next to it.

DJ tried to find a list of names, but there were none. "This place looks totally deserted."

"Call her number again—see if she answers," said James.

DJ took his phone out and tapped Skylar's number. His gaze darted around as the phone rang at least 10 times. No one answered.

James picked up the old phone and pushed some buttons. "Totally dead." He turned to DJ. "I know this is tedious, but we'll have to knock on each door," James suggested. "If the guy knows we're looking for her, he might freak out and let her go."

"Or he'll freak out and act on impulse. I don't know, James." Although it was risky, DJ knew they had no other options.

"We have to try. Let's split up but keep your phone on. We'll start at the first level and work our way up."

Chapter 36

Evan's face softened, but Skylar wasn't sure she'd been convincing enough to stop him from stabbing her to death. She could still feel the sharp tip of his knife pressing against her sternum.

He finally lowered the knife to his side. "You're beautiful when you beg, you know that? It's almost a shame to kill such a beautiful girl." He put his mouth up to Skylar's, so close she smelled sickening gin vapors. "Kiss me," he demanded. "I want a kiss before you die."

She felt his mouth suction onto hers, and his disgusting tongue slither between her lips and under her teeth. She couldn't stop herself. She bit down hard on his tongue.

He shrieked and dropped the knife. Skylar stooped to grab it and scampered past him into the bedroom. She locked herself in the bathroom, threw the bloody knife in the sink, then put her ear to the door, but all she could hear was her own heavy breathing. Nausea engulfed her, and she gagged at the taste of Evan's blood. She bent over the sink, turned on the faucet, and rinsed her mouth. Then, she stepped back and examined her blood-soaked right hand. *He cut me deep.* She was getting more lightheaded with every passing second. She knew the cabinets were empty, so she removed her hoodie and tied one arm sleeve around her hand, stretching the material tightly into a makeshift tourniquet. She caught a glimpse of herself in the mirror and almost gasped aloud. Her face was splattered with blood. It had even dried in her hair.

A loud knock jolted her whole body. She grasped the edge of the sink to steady herself. The knocking continued, but it was slightly muffled. *Is it coming from the front door?*

"Hello," a voice boomed from somewhere outside. And it was unmistakably familiar.

The knocking became louder and more persistent. "Hello, I'm looking for Skylar Van Ness."

She flung open the bathroom door and rushed to the front entrance. "James, I'm here!" she screamed.

"Skylar!" he shouted. "Are you okay?"

"No!" she cried. "Hurry—he's got my gun."

Boom! Boom! Boom!

"Open the door!" James shouted.

A loud moan came from behind her. She spun to face Evan.

His mouth gaped open, and blood seeped down his chin, soaking into his shirt. He held the gun in one hand and cocked it at her. He made a garbled noise that sounded like a wounded animal, and another pool of blood dribbled out of his mouth. "Moo oon uth!" he howled.

Skylar barely made out what he was saying: *"You ruined*

us." She snapped her head back at the front door, then ducked into the kitchen, frantically searching for another knife. *There's got to be one here!*

Another moan came from the kitchen doorway as Evan moved toward her, gun still in hand.

She faced him. "Evan, it's over now. My dad's here. Any minute, he's going to come through that door." She pointed behind him. "Do you want to go to jail for murder? Is that what you really want?"

DJ knocked on door after door until he heard James.

"She's locked in 332, and the guy's got a gun!" James yelled.

"Be right there!" DJ bolted around the corner to where James was.

"I just called Lorcan—told him to fire a shot up at the window to scare the shit out of this guy."

"You and I both know you killed that man when I was 12," Skylar said, backing out of the kitchen into the living room while Evan slowly followed, eyes glazed.

"But I won't say anything," she added. "No one needs to know. It's a cold case. The Dutch police don't care anymore, if they ever did, considering who that man was. You'll be in the clear to live your life. We both will." *I have to sound believable. But with this lunatic, who knows?*

Evan used both hands to steady the gun in her direction. Just then, a gunshot blew from outside, and a bullet crashed through the window, shattering it and casting flinders of glass in every direction. Evan yowled, and both he and Skylar dropped to the floor amidst the broken glass.

Boom! Boom! Boom! Skylar turned her eyes to the door, then again at Evan. Her heart rate doubled in her chest. She quickly got to her feet as the banging got louder. The door flew open, and in rushed DJ and James.

She felt Evan's hot hands grab her neck and pull her into an arm-locked choke hold.

"Dad!" she screamed. "He has my gun!"

DJ and James froze.

"Easy," DJ said. "I'm not going to fuck with you. I just want my daughter. Alive. Release her from your grip. There's no need for this."

Evan tightened his clutch around Skylar's neck and leveled the gun at DJ.

Skylar's heart pounded, and her breath diminished to shallow panting.

"Theeth nuttin butha ho!"

"What did you just bloody say?" James demanded through gritted teeth. Skylar saw the recognizable flush spreading over his cheekbones.

Evan mumbled the same phrase, hampered by his chewed, bloody tongue. Louder this time.

Skylar easily translated his tongueless gibberish, eyes locked on her father. "He said, … 'I'm nothing but a whore!'"

Before she could get those last words out, James charged forward and grabbed Evan by the collar. The move was so sudden, Evan lost his grip on Skylar, and she landed on the floor, flat on her back. James planted a blow to the left side of Evan's jaw, just as a deafening gunshot rang out.

Skylar saw blood spatter everywhere and heard a body thud onto the floor close to where she lay. She looked up and saw Evan's thick frame there, rolling from side to side, hand over his mouth. The gun lay on the floor near him.

DJ dove to retrieve it while Evan scrambled up and hurried toward the open front door.

"Stop or I'll shoot!" DJ yelled as Evan rounded the corner out to the building stairs.

"Wait!" James shouted, clutching his bloody left shoulder. "Lorcan's outside. That little wanker's not going anywhere."

Skylar hoisted herself to her elbows.

Another gunshot sounded outside. James started for the door, but DJ stopped him. "My turn."

"No," James protested. "You stay with Skylar while I finish this guy off."

DJ handed him the gun.

As soon as James was out the door, DJ knelt on the floor next to his daughter. "You okay?"

She sat up and swallowed hard. She opened her mouth, but no words came.

DJ put his arms around her. She felt the warmth of his body holding her close, and she couldn't stop the tears. She cried hard—deep, long sobs that shook her whole body.

"Hey, Sky. It's going to be okay," he said, rubbing her back. "Do you hear me? Everything's going to be just fine."

She buried her head in his shirt and inhaled her father's familiar scent. "I'm sorry, Dad. I'm sorry for who I am." Another deep sob wracked her chest. "I never wanted to … disappoint you—I never wanted this."

"Shhh, stop it." DJ felt a lump in his throat that

threatened to choke him up. Then he could no longer break from his own emotions. He held her tighter. "I almost lost you," he breathed, kissing her head. "I almost lost you."

Skylar cast her eyes down and felt a surge of relief. The terrible, painful nightmare was now over. She let him hold her in his strong arms, tenderly rocking her as though she were a young child—protecting her from further harm. She dug her face deeper into his chest. They stayed, father and daughter, sheltered together until DJ finally withdrew.

He wiped the tears from her face and then brushed the hair out of her eyes. "Listen to me, Skylar. Don't you ever apologize for who you are. Not now. Not *ever*. Do you understand?"

She looked up into his earnest honey-brown eyes, and she sniffled. "But, Dad, you don't know everything … about my past."

He squeezed his eyes shut and then looked her in the eye. "I know more than you think, Sky. And I still love you. Do you understand?"

She looked up at him. "No. I don't."

"Honey, your mother told me you were running because of a *murder* you committed."

She shook her head. "But I …"

"Shhh. Listen to me." He gripped her shoulders. "Whatever you've done, I'll do everything in my power to protect you. I have the pictures. I know what that man did to you."

Skylar's heart sank in sick humiliation. "Oh my God, Dad, you *saw* those pictures?"

He breathed deeply, knowing how hard this must be for her. He loosened his grip on her shoulders and softly caressed them. "Yes. They were in your safe."

"You have the safe?" she exclaimed. It all made sense to her now. DJ had taken her safe, cracked it open, and gone through everything. He had her cell phone. He had been trying to find her as soon as she went missing. *He loved her.* There was no question in her heart now. And he was willing to defend her for the unthinkable. She let out a deep, shuddery sigh. "Dad, Evan sent me those photos. He's the one who took them in the first place."

DJ nodded, seeing the utter distress in his daughter's eyes. "Sky, I know what happened. I know what you did was in self-defense. I'll protect you from any repercussions."

"But that's just it, Dad. I didn't do it! *Evan* did. He confessed to me right here in this apartment. *He* was the murderer. I passed out, and he stabbed the guy to death. It wasn't me after all!"

DJ felt his whole body expire with one relinquishing breath. "Thank God for that." Then he perked up. "That guy needs to live. We'll need his testimony in court."

Skylar hadn't gone down that road yet. She pictured an ugly courtroom battle in which her name would be smeared all over the media as a teenage Dutch sex worker accused of murder. She could take down her father's business. She touched her hand to her forehead.

"I know what you're thinking, and I won't let that happen," DJ said calmly, rising to his feet. "Believe me, we'll have the best lawyers." Then he stood back so he could look at her, his eyes drawn to her right hand, which was still wrapped tightly in her hoodie sleeve. "What happened there?"

She held it up. "Knife injury."

"Jesus, Sky. We need to get you to a doctor."

He helped her up, put his arm around her, and led her out of Evan's apartment.

Before they emerged from the building, a gunshot sounded from outside. "Wait," DJ cautioned Skylar, guarding her with one arm. He peeked out the entrance and then motioned for her to follow him. Outside, James stood a few feet away from Evan, who was on the pavement, curled in the fetal position and not moving.

Lorcan stood beside Evan, gun pointed downward. He looked up when he saw DJ and Skylar. "Got him right in the balls," he announced in his thick accent.

"You shot him where?" DJ asked.

Lorcan let out a chuckle. "Well, now. We don't want this fucker to breed, do we?"

"Is he dead?" DJ asked, staring at the inert body on the pavement.

Lorcan shook his head. "Nah, but he's going to wish he was when he comes to." He opened his fur coat on one side and returned his gun to its holster. "Need anything else, lad?" he asked James.

James shook his head. "Thanks, man."

They all watched Lorcan drag Evan's motionless body to his white Cadillac and load him into the trunk. He gave a little salute before shutting the trunk, getting into his car, and roaring off.

DJ turned to James. "Where do you think he's going?"

"He'll drop him at the hospital entrance and then disappear."

"Wait, whoa, James," DJ protested. "What's going to happen to your friend? His bullets are all around here somewhere." He glanced around the now-empty parking lot. "Or buried in that guy's nuts. Someone's bound to catch him."

"Don't worry about Lorcan," James replied, handing Skylar's gun to DJ. "He flies under the radar—hasn't been caught yet."

DJ still had a hard time believing James consorted with a man like Lorcan. *It's impressive.* DJ drew a deep breath and slowly let it out, giving James the once-over. That's when he noticed the blood all over James's left shoulder. "That looks like it hurts."

James examined his shoulder. "Yeah, that guy got me right before I clocked him in the jaw. It's not bad."

DJ moved his gaze to Skylar, who stood still, clutching her right hand. "Let's get you guys fixed up."

James nodded. "I'll start the car."

CHAPTER 37

"You can go in," Sonia told Skylar. "Your father will be here in a few minutes. He's just over in Axel's office.

Skylar nodded. It was her first day back at work since she had taken a voluntary leap into the void of Fremont Street, the Rocket Palace, and the Las Vegas Rescue Mission. It all seemed a surreal nightmare now—the running—the hiding—the melting into downtown Las Vegas, seeking safety in the shadows.

She entered DJ's office and went to sit in one of the chairs opposite his desk. Then, she changed her mind and took a seat on the couch in the 'living room.'

Her hand had only been peripherally sliced, and although it was a deep cut, the damage was not as bad as she had expected. She toyed with the bandage and thought back to her return home. Her dad took the guest room for a whole week to make sure Skylar felt comfortable there again. He made her a full breakfast every morning and took her to fancy restaurants for dinner every evening. He was on a mission to 'fatten' her up. They talked about everything, and for the first time, Skylar felt like she had a real father. Clay returned Sesame to her on day one. She smiled at the thought of cuddling Sesame in her arms for the first time since they'd separated. She buried her face deep in the cat's fur to catch her sweet smell and hear her soft purring, then snuggled up in bed with her.

Her thoughts were interrupted by the office door opening.

Her father entered with Axel in tow.

"Hey, Dad. Hey, Ax," she called.

"There's my girl," DJ said, dropping files on his desk. He walked toward her, leaned down, and gave her a kiss on the cheek. "How've you been holding up on day one?"

She grinned. "It's good to be back."

Axel moved to where Skylar sat and knelt to hug her. "It's great to see you, Cuz."

DJ plopped into the easy chair opposite her. "I just went over everything with Axel, and we have some good news."

"Oh?" she asked. "What's that?"

Axel stole a glance at DJ. "I'll let you two discuss it alone." He turned to Skylar. "Let's get dinner soon."

She smiled up at him and watched as he exited DJ's office.

DJ set his elbows on the chair armrests and interlaced his fingers. "Looks like those tapes your friend Clay gave us are admissible in court."

She straightened up on the couch. "What tapes?" She

wondered what Clay possessed that would exonerate her from the murder as depicted in Evan's incriminating photos.

"He tried to call me several times the night we found you. I thought he was pestering me about getting his job back, which is why I never returned his call," he rasped, propping his feet on the ottoman. "But he left voicemails explaining how Evan mistakenly clicked his two-way radio button, and it stuck—in the one-way position. Clay heard the whole thing … Evan confessing to you. When Clay realized what was going on, he hit the voice record on his cell phone. It's a little scratchy, but you can still make out the murder confession."

Skylar stared up in disbelief. "Clay didn't tell me. He brought Sesame, and we talked about the whole ordeal— he apologized a thousand times for trusting Evan, but he never said he had a recorded confession."

"That's because I told him to keep his mouth shut until I ran them by legal." DJ paused to snicker. "I had him scared shitless about his job."

Skylar shook her head at DJ's dismissive manner toward her best friend. "So, what happens now? We take Evan to court?" She pictured his horrible ferret-like face on the stand while she relived the frightening trauma all over again.

"Not hardly," DJ said with a smirk. "When I found out Clay had the recordings, I paid a little visit to our friend in his hospital bed. Sick bastard looked pretty miserable. But you should have seen the look on his face after I played the recording for him." DJ stopped talking to chuckle.

"Oh my God, Dad, what did he say?" Skylar pictured Evan's wretched countenance in a hospital bed and cringed.

"Well, the dude can't speak—mouth looks like the opening of a fucking drainage pipe. But that was a good thing because all he could do was listen." DJ paused and looked around his office, then continued in a lower tone. "I told him he was going back to Amsterdam and that if he breathes a word about any of this, I'll have him tracked down and killed."

"You did what?"

"All I had to do was threaten another visit from Lorcan, and I swear I saw his soul leave his body." He dispatched another loud chuckle.

The image of Evan on a flight back to Amsterdam, mouth and genitals still oozing, came to mind. He had been silenced on all counts. Skylar shuddered at the image, and her thoughts returned to Brit—how she had tried to fend off Evan while attempting to extract payoff money. "Dad, what's going to happen to Brit?"

He let out a deep, wheezy sigh and leaned back. DJ and Brit had developed a surprising bond since their fling in his office—an event he would never share with Skylar—or with anyone, for that matter. But he could no longer force her to go back to Amsterdam. She had redeemed herself in his eyes, and he wanted to make sure she was taken care of—at least financially. "You know, I have to hand it to her—if she hadn't come clean with me when she did, we might not have gotten to you in time. Plus, we found out how resourceful she is at keeping VIP guests happy."

"Speaking of Sal," Skylar said, recalling it was their relationship that had forced Skylar's disappearance. "Are they still together?"

DJ shook his head. "According to your mom, Sal

dumped her, and they were never together anyway. Not in the way we thought. She told me he kept her around because of the girls, but he was never going to leave his wife for her." DJ had a flashback to sharing a post-coital cigarette with Brit on his couch—the very couch Skylar sat on now. Brit told him Sal had been verbally abusive toward her, always bringing up her age in a disparaging manner. Secretly, DJ was pleased that nothing had ever gone on between them—Sal was such a scum ball.

"Dad, why did she take up with him in the first place when she could have paid off Evan's $2 million with your money?"

DJ placed his hand on his forehead and gave her a wry smile. "In her pursuit to get the $2 million for Evan, she decided to skim a little extra for herself—can't fault her for that. That's just Brit being Brit."

Skylar nodded. It struck her that Brit brought the girls there to keep Sal happy, and the peep show idea was the only way she could keep them there with Sal while she stalled to get the money to pay off Evan.

DJ stood and sauntered to his office window, peering out before turning back to face Skylar. "I hope this won't upset you, but I'd like to give Brit a job in Player Development. She'll be the one poaching customers from other casinos, so we don't have to rely so heavily on Sal and his cronies."

Skylar noted a change in her dad's voice lately when he mentioned Brit. He actually sounded positive. That was new and she wasn't quite used to it. During the week he had stayed with Skylar, he explained how his relationship had improved with Brit—not that he endorsed what she'd done to Skylar in the past—but that he'd forgiven her so they could all move forward.

"She'd be off-property most of the time, so you wouldn't have to see her that often," he added, knowing that might sit better with Skylar.

Skylar hesitated, trying to picture the scenario.

"Well?" DJ pressed. "Are you okay with all that?"

She felt the corners of her mouth tug into a smile. "Yes, Dad." She rose from the couch. "I'd better get back to my office. There's a lot of work piled up."

"I'll bet," he said with a smile. "Before you go, there's one other thing I want to share with you."

"I almost made it out," she joked. "Is this also good news?"

He rolled his eyes to one side, then shrugged. "That all depends."

"Well?" Skylar examined his face and noticed her dad had a peculiar look—a little sheepish.

"Max and I have decided to separate," he said, watching for her reaction.

Skylar felt her eyebrows raise. "Oh my god—Dad, it's not because of me, is it?"

He closed his eyes and shook his head. "Hell no. We just have differences." He thought back to his sobering conversation with Max. Unfortunately, when DJ got home that night, Max discovered Brit's lace panties in his pocket. He refused to tell Max who they belonged to, and she had a tantrum so violent, she threw a crystal bowl at him, narrowly missing his head. Once she calmed, they discussed going their separate ways.

"But I thought you two were made for each other,"

Skylar said. Max had been the rock DJ needed in his life—the lion tamer, so to speak. *Dad needs her stabilizing influence.* Skylar recalled the daily chaos he lived in before Max—and before Craig, for that matter. "What happened?"

He sighed. "She wants things I'm not ready to give. She wants me to retire. Hell, I'm just getting started."

She gave him an ironic smile.

"I mean, not really. But you know me. I want to be the one making that decision. I want to be in the driver's seat."

She crossed her arms over her chest and stared at the lap of her navy pantsuit. "That's a bummer. I love Max." She looked up at DJ. "But I want you to be happy. Do you think there's a chance of reconciliation?"

DJ felt a pang of sadness. He didn't want to leave Max, and he missed her terribly already, but their differences outweighed all of the warm and fuzzy parts of being with her, and he just couldn't go back. *Not now.* "The separation's temporary, so who knows? We'll always be friends," he finally said. "At least for right now."

Skylar nodded, sadly. "I'm glad you're on good terms."

"Speaking of being *on good terms*, can we talk about James for a minute?" DJ asked. "Have you two finally buried the axe?"

Her thoughts went back to James, whom she hadn't seen since that momentous day at Evan's apartment, and she felt a wave of sadness. She lifted her gaze to meet her dad's and nodded. "I owe him my life. I owe both of you."

Those were the exact words DJ wanted to hear. He hoped she would have changed her feelings for James. The whole ordeal of searching for and finding Skylar proved to DJ that James was not only trustworthy but also a blood brother worthy of taking over the business as CEO. "Good, because there will come a day when I do retire, and I may just tap him to be my replacement." He pulled a cigarette from his packet and set it between his lips.

Skylar closed her eyes, slumping in her chair. She had always known James would be the logical next CEO. She had just never heard her dad say it out loud. And with all her impulsive stunts over the past several weeks, she had shown DJ that she was nowhere near ready for such a position.

"How do you feel about that?" DJ asked, lighting his cigarette.

She opened her eyes and nodded slowly. "I'm sure James *is* the right candidate. I mean, look at him—he's got an impressive resume and track record."

He tilted his head back and paused. "Come on, Sky, cut the bullshit. I know you're disappointed."

"Of course, I am. But I have too much baggage for that job." She wrapped her arms around her body.

"Well, while we're on the topic of baggage, James isn't all high tea and Trinity College." DJ laughed and leaned toward her, his leonine mane falling forward. "Did you get a good look at Lorcan?"

She looked up at him, confused. *Who the hell is Lorcan?*

"Tall guy. Fur coat. Shot your buddy Evan in the balls," DJ said, widening his eyes. "That's James's *friend* from Northern Ireland." DJ took a long drag, blew out a cloud of smoke, and set his cigarette in the ashtray to smolder.

"I was wondering who that guy was." She pictured James hanging out with the fur-clad thug she'd glimpsed briefly, hauling Evan off and stuffing him in the trunk of a white Cadillac. "But there's no way they're friends."

"You'd be surprised." He chuckled. "Anyway, don't be too disappointed. I've got a few things in mind for you, too." He gave her a sly wink. "You'll see." Skylar didn't know it yet, but she was slated to be the new Chief Commercial Officer. That position would be right underneath James, and they would work side by side. He wanted to save that news for a different time and place.

Skylar smiled inwardly. She knew her dad would take care of her, but now, more than ever, she wanted to show him she was worthy of a promotion. "Well, then I'll have to just keep dazzling you."

DJ frowned and lifted his chin. He stood and moved to where Skylar was standing. "Something's different," he said. "You seem … shorter."

Skylar lifted a leg of her suit slightly to reveal her lower-heeled wedges. "I am. At least three inches. Will you still look up to me?"

They both laughed, and Skylar walked out of his office. For the first time ever, her heart felt light. There was nothing more to worry about—nothing to be frightened of—nothing to hide. There was no murder. No problem with Brit. Nothing looming to force her into the shadows. But most importantly, she had a father—an honest, loving father. She was a part of his life. They had finally let each other in. She smiled. *And this is only the beginning.*

***

Her office was much like she had left it. She spent the day going through emails and catching up with Sebrina, who believed the phony story that Skylar had been on a leave of absence. She had no idea what had really transpired, and Skylar wanted to make sure of it. She told everyone at work that the injury to her right hand had been a hiking accident. The only ones who knew the truth were DJ, James, and Clay. And they wouldn't breathe a word.

Emails from James filled her inbox. She opened each one with the faint hope that there was something personal. But there was nothing. Not even a *welcome back* message. He was all business. She wanted badly to call him when she returned home—just to apologize for the encounter in the alley when she was running from the world. But mainly to express gratitude for his courage in confronting Evan.

She picked up her cell phone, scrolled to his name, and then lost her nerve to call. There was something she really wanted to say to him, but that would require going out on a limb. *I like him. A lot. And I'm deeply attracted to him.* But the concern he didn't feel the same way filled her head like a persistent migraine. She put the phone down and took a deep breath. A side of her prayed he would call—just to check on her. But that call never came.

Skylar worked straight through until 6 p.m. and began gathering her things to leave for the day. She made her way through the casino toward the parking garage. She stopped as soon as she hit the garage because she had forgotten where she parked. She looked around, bewildered, then realized her Mercedes convertible was hiding behind a large black Range Rover. It suddenly occurred to her that it belonged to James. *He must still be working.* She felt a wistful twinge as she circled his vehicle, imagining him driving it to find her that night after they ran into each other at the Las Vegas Rescue Mission.

As soon as she passed the rear of his vehicle, she

gasped out loud. James stood by the driver's side of his car, buttoning his shirt, which was open halfway to his belly button.

He jumped at the sight of her. "Oh, it's you." He glanced down at his bare chest.

Skylar couldn't help but admire his lean, muscular upper body, peeking out from underneath the shirt. "Um, what are you doing out here?"

"I know this looks a bit odd, but I'm changing my shirt." He fastened another button.

"Why didn't you just change in the office?" Skylar asked with a grin. It was hard for her to tear her eyes away from his chest.

"Because I didn't want my team to catch me leaving early in my going-out clothes. They're all working late—getting ready for a VIP junket."

She nodded and watched as he finished buttoning up the shirt, recalling his left shoulder injury from Evan's shot. "How's your shoulder?"

"It's better." He peered into his car window to check his reflection. Then he turned to Skylar. "How do I look?"

"Fantastic. Is it date night?" *Oh, why did I just ask that?* Skylar felt her face flush at how desperate she must look—wanting to know what he was doing and, more importantly, who he was doing it with.

He chuckled. "Nah. Just seeing a band downtown with the lads." He paused to adjust his shirt collar. "Band from Ireland's playing." He looked her in the eye. "I'd invite you, but my lads are a bit sketchy."

She recalled DJ's comments in his office about James's connections. "Are they friends of Lorcan?"

He gave her a wry grin. "You have to forget you saw him. I only call in Lorcan when I have a *major* problem."

She nodded. "He gave Evan a pretty nasty wound."

He ran his fingers through his disheveled hair. "You didn't do so bad yourself. Tell me, Skylar, what did you do to that guy's mouth?" There was a slight curl of amusement on his lips.

She thought back to the moment Evan demanded a kiss and shuddered with disgust. "He … forced me to kiss him, so I bit his tongue. Hard."

James grimaced. "Kiss of death. Good to know."

"Honestly, James, I'm not a violent person," she insisted. "Not under normal circumstances."

He smirked. "I don't know, Annie Oakley. You seem pretty comfortable with a pistol."

He must think I'm a lunatic. She didn't know how to explain the mental state she was in the night she threatened him with a gun. "But I never would have pulled the trigger!"

"How would I have known that?" He eyed her purse. "In fact, how do I know you're not going to pull that thing out right here in the parking lot?"

She grinned. "*You're* the one I found hiding behind your car *half-naked*." She lowered her gaze to his torso again, and she caught her breath, recalling the impact of getting a glimpse of his flesh—of seeing anything more than his hands and face exposed.

"This is true, but *I* had an excuse," he reminded her.

She let out an exasperated sigh. "I … James, I don't know what to say … I didn't mean any of that—I was just really freaked out."

"*You* were freaked out," he remarked with sarcasm. "I

mean, I knew you hated me, but I didn't think you hated me enough to kill me." His tone was playful.

She shook her head. "James, I was wrong—so totally wrong about you. I was wrong for years about a lot of things."

His face softened. "Skylar," he said, shaking his head. "I'm just taking the piss, yeah? This isn't necessary."

"No, but it is," she insisted, staring up at his face. "For whatever it's worth, I'm sorry. I hope you can forgive me."

He gave her his most sincere crooked smile. "I forgive you." He paused. "Tell Jordana I forgive her, too."

She let out a giggle. "Oh my god. *Jordana.* I … you must think I'm crazy."

"I've always known you're bloody mad," he quipped, looking around. "But I wouldn't have it any other way."

She tilted her head to one side. "Okay, tell me the truth. Did you know all along that Jordana was really me?"

He shot her a sideways glance. "Well, that's not the story I gave your dad, so I'd appreciate it if you'd go along with the lie. Unless, of course, you'd like to see me out on my arse for good."

"Why didn't you just bust me *then?*" Skylar had a tough time believing James would not tell her dad immediately.

"I should have. Might have saved us all a bit of hardship, yeah?"

"But you had no reason to cover for me." She focused her gaze on his eyes. They were midnight blue and strikingly clear.

He shrugged. "I don't know, Skylar. I figured if you were willing to go to such lengths to hide, you deserved privacy. It wasn't my place to blow your cover."

She edged a little closer, longing to touch him.

"Plus," he added, "Jordana seemed a lot more fun than Skylar, so I owed it to myself to get to know her a wee bit." A smile curled the corners of his lips.

She beamed. "Well, the James Jordana met was a lot more fun, too."

"In that case, you think Jordana might be free tonight? I know she fancies live music."

"Hmmm. I think Jordana may have gone away. But Skylar's free." She lowered her voice slightly. "She might be a lot more fun than you ever imagined."

"Is that right?" he took a few slow steps toward her until she was close enough to smell his woodsy scent. "Let's see, shall we?" He touched her chin and lifted it slightly, staring straight into her eyes.

His look was both familiar and heart-wrenching.

"What are you doing?" she whispered, breathless.

"Giving you a chance to push me away," he said, tilting his head down.

When their lips touched, she felt a fluttery sensation in her stomach. She opened her mouth to him and let his tongue gently explore, inhaling and tasting his essence. She felt the warmth of his hands caressing the back of her neck, lingering there, then softly combing through her hair. He lowered his hands to her waist, his fingers softly grazing her behind. He pulled her closer until their bodies were pressed tightly together. Her pulse quickened, and twinges of pleasure flooded through her. She let out a soft moan.

He suddenly withdrew, panting. "We should stop here."

Her mouth was still open, her lips and tongue still tingling. "What? Why?"

His eyes rolled toward the ceiling behind her. "There's a camera right there."

"Oh my God," she whispered. "Surveillance just watched us."

"I'll make sure they destroy the video." He drew her closer. "Want to get out of here?"

All she could do was nod.

He led her by her good hand around the car and opened the door for her. She climbed in and fastened her seatbelt as James got in on the driver's side.

He turned to look at her. She studied his face, thinking she was in the middle of a fantastical dream. Or a fairytale. They exchanged some unspoken dialogue.

He hit the ignition and adjusted his rearview mirror, taking a closer look at his reflection. He wiped the corners of his mouth with his thumb and forefinger.

"What's wrong now?" she asked.

"Nothing—just a wee bit of your lipstick."

"Sorry about that." She felt her face flush.

"Oh, I'm not complaining. It's not blood, and I can still talk. Both good signs."

She let out a nervous giggle.

As James propelled them toward downtown Las Vegas, they stayed silent until James's cell phone rang on Bluetooth. Someone named *Seamus McCormick* was calling.

Skylar turned to look at James, who eyed the Bluetooth screen for a couple of seconds as though reluctant to answer.

On the fourth ring, he finally did. "Seamus."

"Don't come," Seamus said in a thick Irish brogue— much stronger than James ever sounded. "Stickies in the house."

James shot Skylar an anxious look and quickly took the call off Bluetooth. "Right. Okay, thanks mate."

She watched him in silence while he drove, a look of consternation on his handsome face. "Did he say *Stickies?*"

James gave her a bleak look. "Long story."

"You can tell me." She had the feeling some awful news had just been delivered.

He took a deep breath and glanced in his rearview mirror like he was being followed. He tore his eyes from the road to glance at her. "Skylar. There are a lot of things you don't know about me. And they're not all good." He examined the rearview mirror again.

"James, no matter what you say, you're not going to shock me," she said, thinking there were a lot of things he didn't know about her. *But that's the beauty of intimacy.* The details were meant to be revealed over time.

He nodded, and she observed his profile. He was rugged and masculine, but also refined. And learning he had secrets—something that might surprise her made him even more attractive—like a kindred soul she was about to discover.

"You like pizza?" he suddenly asked.

"Love it."

"Good. When we get home, I'll order out, and we can have a long chat about all of it." He gave her his uneven smile.

She laughed. *"Home?"*

"I just said that didn't I? And I didn't even ask you." He snapped his fingers with a mock look of regret. "Fuck's sake, Skylar." He looked over at her. "Would you like to go to my place?"

"Yes," she said straight away, imagining his house, which she was about to see—where this gorgeous man actually lived—his kitchen, his furniture, his *bed*. A joyous shiver worked its way up her back. It was so strong, it got James's attention.

"If you're cold, I've got a wood-burning fireplace and some blankets that'll warm you up."

She smiled. "I don't think either of us needs to be warmed up."

He stole a quick glance at her and grinned. "Right."

Skylar couldn't put her finger on the feeling, but it was profound. A deep, longing within her—a tender aching from childhood that had never been soothed—was about to melt away. All she could feel now was the exhilarating glow of her future. And he was right there. Right next to her. Driving to their next destination.

THE END.

Dear Readers,

I want to thank you for choosing to read *Slipper Girl*. If you enjoyed it and would like to keep up with my latest releases, please consider subscribing at the following link. Rest assured, your email address will remain confidential, and you can unsubscribe whenever you wish.

adeleroyce.com

If you really loved the book, I would greatly appreciate if you could take a moment to write a review. I'd love to hear your thoughts, and your feedback can really help new readers find my books for the first time.

If you'd like to share your thoughts directly, please connect with me through any of the links below. I'm grateful for you!

Warmly,
Adele

www.amazon.com/author/adeleroyceauthor

Goodreads.com/author/show/20623059.Adele_Royce

@adele_royce_author

@AdeleRoyceAuthor

Acknowledgements

Thank you to so many friends, family, and colleagues who made *Slipper Girl* possible.

I appreciate my critique partners, especially Author Don Daniels, for his careful contribution to the final version of this work. Thank you for digging deep into the dimensions of the story and its characters.

A special thank you to my incredible beta reading team: Gail Chobotov, Emerson Fersch, Marty Goldman, Dana Gross, Beverly Melasi-Haag, and Amanda Totaro. I appreciate all your comments, encouragement, and enthusiasm. I truly value each and every one of you.

I'm beyond grateful for the magical photography of Merrell Virgen. Thank you for all the beautiful images, and, most importantly, for your friendship over so many years.

Thank you also to Alexa Nazzaro and her team at the Aaxel Author Group for being exceptional partners in the publishing of this book.

And finally, thank you to my husband, who has supported every crazy idea and, in many cases, added a few. I love you madly.

--Adele Royce

1. **Skylar's Journey**: How has Skylar evolved from her childhood in Amsterdam to her role as Vice President of Marketing? What key experiences do you think have shaped her into the fighter she is?

2. **Mother-Daughter Dynamics**: Discuss the re-emergence of Skylar's mother, Brit. How does her arrival impact Skylar's character and decisions? What does this relationship say about family ties?

3. **Father-Daughter Dynamics**: How does Skylar's perception of how her father feels about her differ from his actual feelings? How does her perception change over the course of the novel?

4. **Moral Ambiguity**: Are there characters in the novel who you believe cannot be completely categorized as good or evil? How does this complexity affect your empathy for them?

5. **Deception and Trust**: Trust is described as a luxury that Skylar can't afford. How does the theme of deception play out through the novel, and what does it reveal about human relationships?

6. **Resilience and Redemption**: In what ways does the theme of resilience manifest in Skylar's actions? What does redemption mean to her, and does she achieve it by the end of the story?

7. **Identity**: How do past experiences shape one's identity in "Slipper Girl"? How do Skylar's past secrets inform her present choices?

8. **Twists and Turns**: What were your reactions to the major plot twists in the story? Did any surprises stand out to you, and how did they influence the overall narrative?

9. **Setting and Atmosphere****: How does the setting of Donovan Resort and Casino contribute to the feeling of suspense throughout the novel? What role does the environment play in shaping the tension between characters?

10. **Pacing and Tension**: How did the pacing of the novel affect your reading experience? Were there specific scenes that felt particularly tense or drawn out?

11. **Comic Relief:** How did the author's use of humor and irony contribute to the story? Which characters and scenes made you laugh?

12. **Realism in Fiction**: Do you think the challenges Skylar faces are realistic? How do her struggles resonate with real-life issues people face today?

13. **Your Own Resilience**: Skylar's story is one of perseverance. Can you relate to her journey in any way? How do you handle challenges in your own life?

14. What are your thoughts on the resolution of the story? Did it satisfy you as a reader, or were there aspects you wished were explored further?

Playlist

"Sounds of Blue" | Morcheeba

"Deadcrush" | alt-J

"Someone Somewhere (In Summertime)" | Simple Minds

"Lost in the Ocean" | Glass Animals

"Cat People" (Putting out Fire) | David Bowie

"Burn" | David Kushner

"Lazuli" | Beach House

"Where is my Mind?" | The Pixies

"Naive" | The Kooks

"Routines in the Night" | twenty one pilots

"Bleed" | Malcolm Todd & Omar

"Supersonic" | Oasis

"Blue Sky & The Painter" | Bastille

"Undressed" | Sombr

Find *Slipper Girl* on Spotify at AdeleRoyceAuthor

Photo: Merrell Virgen

Adele Royce holds a BA in English from Arizona State University, where she graduated magna cum laude. Her published novels include *Camera Ready*, *Princess Smile*, and *For Position Only*, which was a BookLife by Publishers Weekly Editor's Pick, and *Summer's Blood*, which received the coveted Kirkus starred review. An advertising and PR executive, Adele spent most of her career on the Las Vegas Strip, an experience that gave color to her latest novel, *Slipper Girl*.

She is currently working on the sequel to *Slipper Girl* as well as *Deadly Sins*, a collection of short stories.

Adele owns a marketing consulting firm in San Diego, California, where she resides with her husband and two cats.

Learn more at www.adeleroyce.com